Another Day in Paradise

EDDIE LITTLE

Another

VIKING

Day in
PARADISE

VIKING
Published by the Penguin Group
Penguin Putnam Inc., 375 Hudson Street,
New York, New York 10014, U.S.A.
Penguin Books Ltd, 27 Wrights Lane, London W8 5TZ, England
Penguin Books Australia Ltd, Ringwood, Victoria, Australia
Penguin Books Canada Ltd, 10 Alcorn Avenue,
Toronto, Ontario, Canada M4V 3B2
Penguin Books (N.Z.) Ltd, 182–190 Wairau Road,
Auckland 10, New Zealand

Penguin Books Ltd, Registered Offices:
Harmondsworth, Middlesex, England

First American edition
Published in 1998 by Viking Penguin,
a member of Penguin Putnam Inc.

1 2 3 4 5 6 7 8 9 10

Publisher's Note
This is a work of fiction. Names, characters, places, and
incidents either are the product of the author's imagination or
are used fictitiously, and any resemblance to actual persons,
living or dead, events, or locales is entirely coincidental.

LIBRARY OF CONGRESS CATALOGING-IN-PUBLICATION DATA
Little, Eddie.
Another day in paradise / by Eddie Little.
p. cm.
ISBN 0-670-87217-2 (alk. paper)
I. Title.
PS3562.I78279A82   1998
813'.64—dc21   97-24283

This book is printed on acid-free paper.
∞

Printed in the United States of America
Set in ITC Century Book

To the Ritas

Acknowledgments

Patty Felker, who believed I could do it.

Jerry Stahl, who's to writing what Mel was to crime.

Trevor Miller, who was there when I was all the way down and out.

Al Silverman and Jariya Wanapun at Viking, who went far beyond the call of duty to help me finish this.

The Fabra Clan and my homeboy Carman.

Thomas Pitbull.

Vanilla Gorilla and Mama Malone.

Don and Mom.

David Vigliano—Ace Agent.

Johny Angel.

Chucky Weiss, Jimmy Woods, Spider Middleman, Mindy Jay.

Frank Clayman Cook, Texas Terry, and the Hollywood Crew.

Big George L.

Dave Kelting—Computer King.

Stephanie Ann: H.E.A.

Bill Gotti—literally a lifesaver and the maker of the best spaghetti and meatballs in California.

Frank and Susan Stephenson.

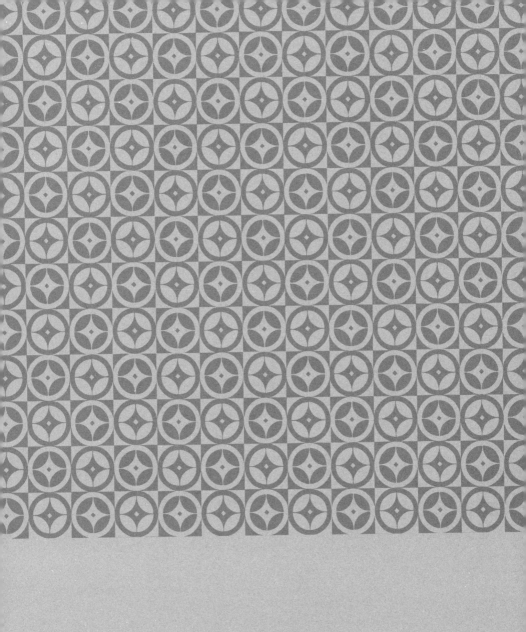

Book I

*M*ost people think you open a safe with high-tech instruments and incredible skill. I once thought the same thing. That was a long time ago. I was still young and pretty. . . .

Mel was huge, a human wrecking-machine. Even at fourteen I knew that refrigerators with feet came a dime a dozen. What I liked was that this huge, dangerous person liked *me*. But more important—what was *crucial*—Mel *knew* things. Not what they taught in school—practical things: how to crack a safe, the best way to set up bogus checking accounts, when to force a door with a pry bar and when you could use a celluloid to slip the lock, the fine art of cutting through walls and ceilings, how you could slip into the crawl space beneath a building and tear through the floor to gain entry. . . .

Just as important was his advice on day-to-day life. Like never, ever buy your drugs from niggers. Always call cops "Sir." When you can't avoid a fight, use a weapon, first choice being a gun. If you're not packed, grab whatever is handy, and if there's nothing to pick up, no bottles to break, no bricks or rocks to use, stick your index finger in their eye. Ram it right through, turn the eye into pulp, shove your finger all the way into their brain. Guaranteed they'll leave ya alone.

. . . .

The world according to Mel wasn't exactly a Boy Scout manual, but it was absolutely the guidance I needed. Before Mel, I was shooting speed, eating pills, occasionally slamming stuff . . . surviving by robbing vending machines, petty burglaries, stealing stereos out of cars, and boosting.

This generated a couple, three hundred bucks a day—well over a

ONE

grand a week. But wanting more was part of me, just like the whiteness of my skin, something I was born with and couldn't change even if I wanted to. The American Dream in person. Hustling, stealing to steal. Blowing the cash as fast as I could get it. Shooting speed till my nose bled, till my eyes crossed; ether fumes rolling out of my lungs like clouds of toxic waste. Staying awake for days on end. Amphetamine psychosis in full bloom.

Giving money away, giving drugs away, and always stealing so I'd have more for me and more for the borderline crazies, bust-out junkies, psychotic scooter trash, ex-convicts, Vietnam vets—kill 'em all, let God sort 'em out—fools and dope fiends I ran with, looked up to, and loved like a normal person supposedly loves his brothers.

A riotous fourteen-year-old dope-fiend Robin Hood. That was how I saw myself.

Being that young, one of the best things was the girls—older women—all sixteen, seventeen, some even in their twenties, each and every one of 'em fascinating, astounding, sweet as candy and vicious as vipers—walking, talking, silk-wrapped razor blades. They were tracked-up, shot-out female children who were my surrogate sisters and mothers, crime partners and lovers.

One huge sad family. Leaning on each other like rotting fence posts.

Each of us desperate to make it. If anyone had cared enough to ask me what "making it" meant, I wouldn't have had any more idea than going out in a blaze of glory. James Cagney blowing up in *White Heat*— Top of the world, Ma!

. . . .

When I met Mel, I was a very fucked-up kid, a statistic waiting to happen. What he taught me was a way to survive in the world that I lived in. Better than survive—how to actually thrive, prosper . . . kinda like Jesuit training for thieves.

Rosie was the closest thing I had to a girlfriend. She was seventeen—three years older than me—Puerto Rican, and Irish. She had the saddest, loneliest brown eyes anyone has ever seen, highlighted by a crazy, lopsided, *fuck you* smile. Her skin looked like caramel and felt softer and smoother than the best heroin rush.

The first time I fucked her it was a religious experience, her broken pieces and my broken pieces fitting together. A jigsaw puzzle with only a couple of things missing.

The way her skin felt, and those sad, lost eyes looking up at me as she took my cock into her mouth, her head going back and forth, up and down so fucking slow it felt like I was dying, and finally stopping and pulling me inside her, whispering, "Give it to me, mijo." And I did, screaming and moaning like coming was ripping my heart out through my throat.

The other girls had been crime partners and lovers, great to scam with and fun to get loaded with. Rosie was the first one that made me want to protect her, have diamonds dripping off her fingers, never ever let anything or anybody hurt her, make sure she had nice things, could always stay loaded, stoned, blitzed. Happy. Happy. Happy.

. . . .

We are lying on a single mattress, the mattress sticking to the floor, soaked with sweat and come, covered with old bloodstains and mystery spots. The floor's covered with bent spoons, burnt bottle caps, old wine bottles, and trashed syringes. Nothing on the walls except a bloodstain that looks like my idea of modern art—splashes and drips, the blood left by the loser in an argument over a bottle of a hundred Desoxyn.

I know nothing about atmosphere or ambiance, that possibly our surroundings leave something to be desired. What I feel is contentment. My veins are full of good drugs, the pocket of my jeans full of cash. We have three brand-new syringes and enough speed to kill both of us twice.

Best of all, this beautiful girl is curled next to me, gently stroking my skin, looking at me like I'm something special. I feel more than content—I feel invincible. Not scared of death. Knowing it's close, the idea of living to twenty absurd.

I ask her how she'd learned to do the things she did, how she knew how to make me so crazy, where this miraculous talent had come from. I'm in awe of this girl with the saddest eyes in the world. The saddest eyes, the hottest body, the most talented lips.

She stops stroking my side and rolls onto hers, ignoring me now. So I nudge her and ask again, trying to make a joke.

"Didja go to school or what?"

When she answers, I'm hooked like a laboratory monkey, would commit murder for her in a heartbeat, whatever it takes to make this little hooker dope-fiend girl happy—fistfight King Kong, if that's required.

She rolls back onto her other side and, looking down at the mattress, starts picking at one of the old bloodstains that spot it. Red fingernails, against brown blood, against light blue mattress. Shiny black hair hanging down, framing her hand.

From beneath the hair she starts whispering, voice getting stronger with each word.

"School, mijo? Nah, I learned at home. My father taught me how to do that, how to lick it, and suck it so slow like a Popsicle—he usta tell me it was a special treat." She laughs as she finishes this statement, swings her hair out of those eyes and turns 'em on me full power.

"So now what, mijo?" Smiling her lopsided smile. "They taught me good, don't ya think?"

Not knowing how to respond. Wanting to be cool. I'm overwhelmed by my own rage, the hate that's fueled my life since I was a baby, remembering the bruises on top of bruises, the black eyes, the broken bones, the daily humiliation until the state stepped in with their kiddy pens and foster homes.

Instead of a cool, unflustered reaction, what tears its way out of my throat is a shriek.

"Where was your motherfucking mother, baby? How come no one stopped him?"

She laughs again and starts kissing my neck, licking and working her way down my body, running her tongue over my armpits and down my sides. The rage is still flowing through me like 220 current, fueling my response to her. I grab her hair and pull her head back, my voice a hoarse rasp.

"Tell me. Now."

Looking down at her, those eyes turned golden, lips puffed up from friction. Feeling the tension going down my arm, through my hand as it pulls her hair, making her look at me. She laughs again.

"I like that. Pull harder, baby, and I'll tell you. Tell you about how the only thing I do better than suck cock is eat pussy—tell you all about moms. Tell you how she tasted, and why nobody did nothing—tell you about all of it."

And now she's crying and I'm holding her and rubbing her and mumbling about how everything is gonna be OK.

Like I have some idea what that means. Feeling like a sun going nova. Being consumed by pure strong hate, burning with it, but doing my fourteen-year-old best to be strong and loving, trying to give this born-to-lose girl what I think she needs. The same things I need but haven't gotten.

. . . .

I leave Rosie at the pad. We've shot all the drugs that were left, spent the cash on booze and downs so we could crash—even killed off the last of my peanut butter and jelly.

Knowing that panic time has arrived. No dope, no money, dragging my ass down the stairs, trying to get it together, feeling the ever-present fear starting to build, needing drugs and wanting to be a hero, to wake Rosie up with a syringe full of good shit. I hit the street.

Walking because I don't know how to drive. I can steal a car in minutes—I learned that when I was twelve—but actually getting a car from point to point is beyond me. The times I tried ended in wrecks and, once, with a GTA beef. I'd rather walk—till I learn how to drive without guaranteed problems.

There's a sharpened screwdriver stuck down my pants, a sixteen-inch Craftsman. A great burglary tool—as much leverage as a pry bar, point filed down so it's sharp as a razor, complete with a lifetime guarantee, good at any Sears.

I walk for hours, prowling public buildings, in and out, checking for vending machines. Dollar changers are best, cigarette machines second, laundry rooms absolutely a last resort.

Desperation is coming on fast. Trudging nonstop, running up and down stairs . . . Every time something looks promising, someone comes by, or people are too close. Tearing steel machines open makes a lot of noise, and one thing I don't want is problems, or getting interrupted by John Q. Citizen.

The sun is starting to go down. I'm completely worn out, beat, starving, so hungry that it hurts, and feeling the hangover from the pills and booze. Needing some more speed bad. Worried about Rosie, wanting to take care of her and realizing it's taking too long, knowing she'll end up tricking or boosting if I don't make a score soon.

Dragging on to a college campus. Entering the first building I come to. Hearing the quiet. Feeling the empty. All the students and staff gone, smoking pot, drinking beer, eating dinner. Whatever regular people do.

I go down the stairs into the basement and there it is. Heaven. A room full of machines—not one or two—all the machines you could want. A dollar changer that'll have a few hundred in dollar bills; cigarettes; candy; sandwiches; soft drinks—even coffee. Six of 'em, all mine and all bursting with change.

No one's around and I'm starting to rush. A minute before, I was dying, miserable; now I'm in hyperspace, with no drugs and no rocket ship. It's like magic once the adrenaline kicks in. Everything is painfully intense: the fear raging in my stomach, the nerves from my eyes and ears connected directly to my arms and legs. No thought processes to slow reaction time. Nothing but getting the job done. The Zen of crime, although then I'd never heard of Zen.

It's always like a combination of Halloween and Christmas. Trick or treat, and all the fucking presents are mine—payback for the holidays I never had.

Check all the hallways. No one's around. Listen to the sounds of the building, trying to detect the movement of anyone that might interrupt the festivities. Hear nothing except myself. No footsteps, no doors opening or closing, no conversation, no breathing except mine. Just me. My heart trying to claw its way out of my chest, my blood pumping so hard it has a noise of its own, a faraway roar. It's time to go to work.

There's an empty cardboard box lying in the vending-machine room, left by a lazy vendor. It once held candy. Now I hope to fill it with money.

The adrenaline's running so hard my entire body is shaking. I place the box under the dollar changer. The lock mechanism on these things is pretty simple to break. Hard steel and brute force will do it.

What I lack in size and strength is more than compensated for by desperation and need. With every one of my 130 pounds, I force the screwdriver into the upper-right-hand corner, where the top lock is.

Leveraging, both hands on the handle, and the metal is starting to bend and rip; swinging up, planting both feet on the wall, using my legs, arms, everything, feeling like my head is gonna explode, and the door rips off that first machine. Opening the presents. Oh, boy.

I finish the last machine. Stumbling out, pockets stuffed with hundreds of one-dollar bills, box filled with coins . . . over a thousand bucks, easy. Later on, a grand would be pocket change. But now it's a fortune.

As I'm leaving, I look back to admire my handiwork. A room full of scrap: nuts, bolts, shattered glass, broken locks, ripped sheet metal, candy, sandwiches, cigarettes all over the floor . . . and I am rich.

Feeling a moment of peace. No more shaking. Adrenaline spent. Knowing that soon my stomach will be full, I'll have scored, and be back in bed with Rosie. Happy. Happy. Happy.

That's when the security guard grabs me.

I have the box under my left arm and have no intention of letting it go. He's taking in the wreckage, mouth hanging open and holding my arm. Starting to twist and it hurts and I'm not gonna let go of my box of money. I'm trying to pull away, and now he's yelling and trying to tear my arm off.

The guard's a very big guy, fat and strong. I can hear the breath whistling in and out of him as he's trying to break my arm. And then he punches me. I can hear my nose break. The blood gushes out and I taste it as it pours down my throat.

Compared to me, this guy is a giant, way over two hundred pounds, and he's hurting me bad. Everything is in slow motion, him yelling, "I'm gonna kill ya, ya fuckin' little punk." Grating noises are coming from my right shoulder as he's beating my head into the floor that's already covered with my blood.

I release the box which is now stuck under me like I'm stuck under shithead, who's enthusiastically pounding my kidneys into Jell-O. Grabbing the screwdriver, shoving it into his leg, the only thing I can get at. Now he's off me and starting to shriek, sounding like a homicidal parrot.

I can't use my right hand at all and this prick charges me. I'm screaming as I slam my left into his belly, doubling him up over the screwdriver, burying it all the way to the handle, dropping him to the floor. He's still making noise and I'm kicking him in the head, till he finally shuts up.

It looks like a bomb went off on top of the wreckage already there. Blood covers the floor and walls. My nose and mouth are still bleeding and old superhero crimebuster has got the screwdriver stuck in him and is bleeding from the leg, nose, mouth, stomach, and where one of my kicks had sent his jawbone through the skin.

It looks like hell with fluorescent lighting.

Grabbing the box, I start to run out the door. Get about ten feet and stop. Walk back and pull the screwdriver out of superhero's guts.

I'm not scared or panicked; it's like Novocain's been shot into my brain. There are no citizens around; either the basement walls have stopped the noise or whoever heard the mayhem had the good sense to stay far away.

Hobbling up the stairs to the men's room. Take off what's left of my shirt, throw it into the trash. Wash off the blood that covers me, get as cleaned up as possible. Looking in the mirror, eyes starting to swell and bruise, but not too bad yet. All that looks really scary is my nose. It is way off center, and blowing up like a balloon.

Shoving the screwdriver into my boot, limping out the front door and down the sidewalk, head throbbing in harmony with the coins in the box.

This is my last amateur theft.

. . . .

As I walk away from the mayhem, reality starts to break through the adrenaline high that's kept me going the last twenty minutes.

The farther I get, the more the pain grows—shooting, throbbing pain from my eyes and nose (which is now under my left eye), my face feeling like it's gonna burst, kidneys so damaged that every step sends bolts of agony from my lower back up to my head, where it dances with the trauma there.

The closer I get to safety, the more wildly the ground spins beneath my feet, the more reality fades in and out—and the heavier that fucking box gets.

I don't know about concussions and have no idea what internal bleeding is. All that matters is I'm hurt real bad, not giving up, holding on to that box and making it back to what I think of as home.

Staggering more by the second, I finally make it to the stairs leading to safety, pulling myself up the banister, holding on as tightly as possible because the entire world has become a swirling vortex pulling me down.

Finally getting to the top and falling through the unlocked door. Hitting one knee and slamming the door shut, dropping the box and watching quarters fly out of it. Everything whirling like a hurricane on acid. Falling onto my side, starting to puke, not able to move at all 'cause I'm in the hurricane.

I'm lying on my side, face pressed into the floor, gagging and smelling the vomit. Everything is blurred and jumbled, my eyes feeding my brain fragmented images, the puke smell making me sicker—and everything hurts so bad.

Doing my best to call out for Rosie, gagging between words, trying again, realizing that I'm not talking, only making noises. I fade out, come to for a minute, knowing there's no one there. Only me. Feeling so lonely and scared it slices through the pain like it isn't there. Able to deal with being hurt, but so fucking lonely it's like being in hell.

Starting to gag again, trying to get to my knees, falling back to the floor—this time on my back—knowing I'm passing out again, and happy about it.

. . . .

The next days are a blur: me crawling here and there through the dried puke and congealed blood, thinking I'm dying, fading in and out of consciousness.

Then, I don't know how many days or how many hours later, feeling someone shaking me and hearing a voice echoing through my head; being dragged to my mattress and how soft it feels. The voice getting louder and more scared, cutting through the insulation in my head. It belongs to Dan Slacker, a hillbilly kid from Tennessee who comes over to get loaded and hang out when life at home gets too bad.

Finally responding to the fear in his voice, forcing my right eye to open through the swelling to see what's wrong. Him looking like he's gonna cry, panicking, saying, "Y'all ain't gonna die, no way boy, please don't die man."

His face is all blurred. He's kneeling on the floor, ropy muscles popping out of his arms as he's shaking me and yelling at me.

"Talk to me, motherfucker! Talk to me, you son of a bitch!"

The best I can do is moan.

"Y'all gonna live, just keep breathing in and out. I'm gonna go get my uncle Mel. He was a medic till they throwed him out of the navy. He got guys through combat and shit. You just breathe in and out till I get back with him."

This time I managed a garbled "Thanks" and a groan.

Passing out again, but this time feeling like everything might be OK.

. . . .

Coming to, shivering, freezing cold and staring up into a face as big as a plate on top of a huge neck that goes down into monstrous shoulders. The face's framed by blond hair shot with gray, blue eyes, and a two- or three-day growth of beard.

The swelling's gone down because my head's packed in ice and I'm lying on ice packs for my kidneys, feeling like I'm gonna freeze to death.

This monster is looking at me like a bug under a magnifying glass, completely deadpan, no expression whatsoever, the chilliest look I've ever seen on another human being.

Suddenly the gorilla smiles, growls, "You're gonna be OK, kid. I'm Mel. Just kick back. I don't got no morphine."

As he's talking, he's emptying a cap of powder into a spoon and starting to cook it.

"But this is the best smack around—if this don't kill the pain, nothing will."

Remembering that he's supposed to be a doctor or medic or something like that, I find my voice. "So you're a sawbones, huh?"

He stops drawing up the heroin, laughs, and looks at me out of the side of his eyes.

"You got a lot to learn kid. I'm a junkie and a real good thief—they kinda go together. That's it pal. Beginning of story, end of story."

Mel finishes drawing up the smack, hands it to me, eyedropper one-quarter full of clear liquid, needle stuck to the end of the outfit, made tight with a strip of a dollar bill.

"Thanks," and I'm looking for a vein.

He starts talking just as I get the register, blood rushing up into the eyedropper. "Kinda like you ace, just older and not quite as dumb."

That's how I met Mel, and the beginning of what I still think of as my apprenticeship.

*T*he next few days are a real drag. I haven't developed a full-blown love affair with opiates yet—that will come later. Speed is my thing, and I am shut off.

Mel has talked Danny's folks into letting him watch a sick friend for a few days; what the story was I don't know, but I'm sure it wasn't that he was gonna baby-sit some kid who had his brains scrambled during a robbery.

Sitting on the floor, he starts talking. His voice is friendly, almost paternal.

"Here's the deal, pal. You look like shit. The cops are looking all over for ya, you're hotter than a freshly fucked fox in a forest fire. Danny boy here pulled me out of a nice, deep nod to drive all the way cross town to be an accessory after the fact to robbery, burglary, and attempted murder." I look at Danny and shrug. He just sits there, mute.

Mel pauses, and I notice he's not breathing—not only is he not breathing, but his eyes are starting to protrude from his head and his face has become so pale it's almost translucent. I'm thinking the poor old guy's having a heart attack, when he suddenly starts talking again, voice now completely flat and emotionless. Enunciating one word at a time.

"I iced your nasty little ass down, stopped most of your internal bleeding, put ice packs on your little teeny head so maybe your brain damage won't be too fuckin' bad, gave you plenty of *my* good heroin and have now spent *two fucking days* in a shithole I wouldn't send my worst enemy to, watching over you to make sure ya don't go into a coma."

Mel finally runs out of breath. He sits there staring at me, looking like his head is gonna explode, but not making a sound.

TWO

Standing up, seeming to fill the whole room, he starts talking again, dragging each word out, almost whispering, so that you really have to listen to make sure ya don't miss what this terrifyingly serious monster is saying.

"If ya leave here, they'll bust ya. If you shoot any more speed for the next month, your brain'll pop like a fucking balloon. Danny boy here is gonna baby-sit you, make sure ya eat and rest. I'm gonna leave you enough skag to keep both of ya right for a couple days and I'll stop back by your beautiful residence in a few days to see how you're doin'.

"If you leave here or do *any* meth, I'll break every bone in your body. All of 'em, one at a time, from your fingers to your spine. Then I'll kill you. After I've ripped *your* heart out, I'll beat the shit out of Danny for letting ya do it."

We're both straining to catch every word, me and Dan shooting each other looks because there's no doubt he means every fucking word. Ray Charles could see the violence radiating from good ole Uncle Mel.

He starts talking again, each word coming out like ripping sheet metal.

"Check it out, Bobbie: the Orientals say if you save a guy's life, you owe him for the rest of yours, ya dig? Like, if you're stupid enough to interfere with someone's number being up, fuck up the status quo, make someone alive who should be dead, then you are responsible for them."

Mel pauses. Having all this directed at me and needing to show that I have some say in what I do, hating the idea of not doing speed and staying locked-down, and not knowing what happened to Rosie, I get out, "Hey man, uh . . ."

Expanding like the hood of a pit viper, somehow getting even bigger, huge, looming, now towering over me like a psychotic sequoia, spit shooting out of his mouth, screaming.

"Pay attention asshole! I have put a lot of energy into keeping you alive, and God knows you need someone to keep you from self-destructing, and if those gooks know what they're talkin' about, I'm stuck. So that means, if you get yourself busted or die, I ain't doin' my job, so believe me when I tell ya, you ain't gonna do any speed for a while and you are not even going to *think* about going out that door."

He pauses, then says very softly, "Are you with me on this?"

Even with the incredible confidence you have at fourteen, knowing that I'm tough as nails, having been as badly beaten as a person can be by my dear old dad and still keep breathing, coming out the other side stronger than ever, knowing that no human can scare me, Mel is still beyond scary—so thoroughly intimidating that the only response I can muster is a strangled, "Yikes."

Danny does much better. Sounding like a West Point cadet, he snaps out, "Yes, sir!"

The transformation is amazing, like magic. There's a different guy there now, a big, jovial, roly-poly, happy sort of guy, beaming with good-will, a beardless Santa Claus who just happens to have Satan's baby brother hiding inside of him. The dude's fucking eyes are actually twinkling as he says, "Cool. So I guess we understand each other, right guys?"

Once more me and Dan exchange looks and, like it was rehearsed, say, in harmony, "Abso-fucking-lutely."

. . . .

The funny thing about heroin is that the more you use it, the better it is. That doesn't mean you won't build up a bone-crushing tolerance, and it certainly doesn't mean you won't come to hate it. Even knowing that it's killing you, there is no better feeling than that shit creeping through your veins when you're dope-sick, knowing that the nightmare is over for a minute or two. . . .

The first fifty or sixty times I fixed narcotics—heroin, morphine, Dilaudid—I wasn't that impressed; but, then again, I was using it to crash with, just like any other down. What happens is, something changes in you, and one day, instead of just being groggy, itchy, and nauseous, it's like coming home, and if you've never had a home, that's one hell of a sensation. This incredible feeling of well-being and confidence combines with euphoria, and, amazingly, what was once nausea and puking becomes a sexual purging, what was an unpleasant itching, like having ants all over you, becomes incredibly sensual, scratching till you're a bloody mess. The height of entertainment.

Days pass, marked only by eating Oreo cookies, candy bars, and, the mainstay of our diet, peanut-butter-and-jelly sandwiches. The second day into this, Mel drops off a TV, so we now have soap operas and Gilligan to watch between nods.

About the fourth day, Danny gets so tired of itching and puking that he quits doing the smack, just sits there and sullenly watches the tube. I want the rush of meth, that hair-raising, overwhelming chemical voyage into hyperspace—but anything is better than the ever-present fear that lives inside me, like gibbering goblins when there are no drugs to muzzle them. The idea of voluntarily not doing heroin, just because I don't like it that much, is completely alien to me. If dope is available, I'll take all I can get, thank you.

The bruises on my face fade, go from black to purple through blue. Now they're a sporty shade of yellow. I quit pissing blood, so my kidneys have started to heal, and I'm bored out of my mind. The only cheering thing is that, as time goes by, nodding and scratching are becoming very pleasant. Apparently I am developing a taste for stuff.

There's a dirty sock tied around my wrist. I'm poking around in my hand, trying to find a vein, really looking forward to the nod, tired of Danny, tired of TV, nothing to read—my one secret vice, the shame of being a closet bookworm.

I reread an old Louie L'Amour. Dan's reaction is bad. Reading means I'm ignoring him. He's not a happy kid. He's sitting on the floor, seventeen years old, a lanky hillbilly kid covered with sweat, miserable, the temperature around 110, the air wet and sticky, and he's too stupid to get loaded, forget about how much life sucks. . . . Instead, he's trying to keep the flies off his mug and trying to make conversation.

"What ya gonna do after this, Bobbie? I mean, like, the cops aren't gonna quit lookin' for ya and ya don't got no trade. . . . Maybe ya could go into the service. Uncle Mel did OK, till they booted him out. Ya can't just keep doin' the shit yer doin', ya know what I mean? Look at ya—all bruised up, peeing blood, stickin' needles in ya like some kinda fuckin' voodoo doll, scratchin' and pukin' all the time, living like a nigger—

don't even got no tube. We'd be sittin' here starin' at each other if my uncle hadn't brought us a TV. Goddamn, man! Fuckin' flies all over your face and ya don't even care, just keep digging around in your fingers with that fuckin' harpoon. *Shitfire, man!*"

Danny leaps up, whirling like a dervish, flinging his arms past my head, screaming, "Shoo, fuckin' flies! Shoo, you nasty cocksuckers! Get out of here!"

The flies that have been driving me nuts, crawling around in the sweat on my face, doing the backstroke for all I know, buzz away. I tell him, "Thanks Danny." The two words are the best I can do. I'm completely focused on getting a hit; a nuclear bomb could go off and still not distract me.

Finally, the blood gushes into the outfit. Slamming it home, feeling that slow rush that gets better every time. A mini-orgasm. The world changes. Dan suddenly makes sense and is very likeable, the pain leaks out of my body and well-being flows in. . . . Rosie is a distant concern, and I don't know how, but I know everything is gonna be all right.

. . . .

Chemical well-being encases me, sweat is running off me in torrents. Sitting on the mattress, waving the flies away, scratching my face lackadaisically, trying to convince Danny that reading is a good thing.

"See, it's like this: ya hate reading cause ya had to do it in school, and school sucked. Ya turn on the tube and boo-ya you got cartoons, or Gilligan or whatever, and ya turn into a turnip. Right? Your brain goes away, know what I mean? Shootin' drugs or whatever, my brain's workin'; if I'm readin'—even if I'm loaded—I gotta use it, figure shit out, why's this guy doing this or that. . . . It's better than the tube. Ya get into it, you ain't even in your body. Check it out," and I throw the old Louie L'Amour at him.

"Sh-eeet, man, you gotta be the weirdest motherfucker I ever met, wanta jus' sit aroun' with yer nose in a fuckin' book, if y'all ain't stealin', or shootin' them drugs and gettin' ready to steal, and fuckin' those gals, ya gotta be readin' some weird shit."

Danny wings the paperback at my head, and laughs. "Give it a break boss—we're different as dogs and cats. I love the fuckin' TV, I hate stealin'—it scares me. I don't even like gettin' high that much—shit, I'll probably go into the service or somethin', and you . . . who knows?"

Soft rapping on the door interrupts our conversation. Danny asks who's there and opens the door. Framed in the doorway is Rosie, diminutive, beautiful, the bruises on her face matching mine, bilious yellow, old and fading. I'm so glad to see her, it's almost like having fixed. I get up, moving slowly, from heroin and injuries, hobble over to her. I grab her, holding her as softly as I can, asking, "What happened, baby, who socked ya up?"

She gives me that smile, buckling my knees before she says a word. She turns her face so I can inspect the damage, touching her front tooth.

She says, "Motherfucker chipped my tooth. Son of a bitch said he'd give me twenty for head, so I say good, sounds good, let's do it. . . . You disappeared. Ya know I waited as long as I could. You know that, right Bobbie?"

Saying, "Yeah, I know, pretty. So who is this piece of shit?"

She's talking fast like an express train, trying to get it all out, stumbling over words.

"Who knows, mijo, some trick. Fat son of a bitch got me in his car, I start doing him and all of a sudden he's pullin' my hair and callin' me bad names. Callin' me whore, cunt, nasty bitch, like that. Well I just wanna get outta there, but he won't let me go. I'm tryin' to pull away, and he rips my top, starts punchin' my face in, beatin' my head on the dashboard. Goddamn pervert, wanted ta kill him."

She's smiling, tears swimming around in her eyes, doing her best to be a tough guy. . . . She's wanting not to cry, but losing the battle.

"So I tried to rip his eyes out—clawed his face up good, did my best to hurt him—but he was just too big. He made my mouth bleed and chipped my tooth. Ya shoulda seen me—I fought pretty good for being so little. But he just kept punchin' me."

She's crying now, hiccuping and gasping for breath. Tears flowing like waterfalls.

I'm holding her. Can't say a word. Don't know what else to do.

Still hiccuping, Rosie says, "The slimy piece of shit made me finish doing him, then threw me out of his car. The cops pulled up right after, so I tried to tell them. . . . I'm standing there, clothes all ripped, one of my tits hangin' out and I'm tryin' to cover it, these cops checkin' me out when they shoulda been lookin' for this cocksucker and bustin' him. But they bust *me*. I'm tracked up, and they see it—my marks—and cuff me. Couldn't make bail. Been sitting an' rottin' cause I got *my* ass beat! I just got out, got time served this morning. Took those bastards all day to release me."

Wanting to make everything good and not knowing how. Got this weird feeling in my chest, almost crying myself, want to find this fat trick and blow his brains out, but know we'll never find him in a million years. The dude's back home with his old lady and kids, invisible.

Maybe later in my life I could have expressed what I was thinking, done a better job of comforting her. But right now, stomach in knots, rage cutting through the heroin, and, unavoidably, overwhelmingly, so glad to see her, feeling so many strange emotions I say, "Shit, baby, wanna fix?" Which, all things considered, is about the only option I have.

. . . .

Twenty minutes later—have you noticed that everything happens at once?—the door comes swinging open. Me and Rosie are on the mattress, her head pillowed on my leg, playing with my hair, both between here and nod-land. Dan's stuck in front of the TV. Mel's through the door, smiling, obviously in a good mood. He does a double take, checks Rosie out, whistles, says, "Poor girl, who beat your ass? Not these guys, right?"

"Nah, these are nice guys. Matter of fact, Bobbie's my protector." She pauses. "Who the fuck are you, anyhow—Mr. Heavyweight?"

He's laughing, says, "Shit, girl, you must be the ringleader. I'm just some poor mook who comes around to nurse your boyfriend here, you know, make sure he's comfortable, got enough to eat, dope to shoot, new points to do it with. . . . Maybe I'll clean up around here, if he'll let me; maybe iron his blue jeans—that's me, honey, Harry Helpful."

Still chuckling, happy as a guy can be, he looks at me, raising one eyebrow.

Says, "Got a live one, huh kid? Listen, not to tear ya away from your sweetheart, but I want to show ya something down the street." Throwing me some shades, saying, "Come on, killer, put these on, cover your black eyes. Let's roll."

Reaching to catch the shades, feeling the pain rip down my back and through my head, I look at Rosie, shrugging, tell her, "Stay here till I get back. We got food and Danny knows where the stuff is—besides, I like havin' ya around."

We're driving a brand-new Cad, leather interior, black on black, windows up, AC on as high as it'll go, sweat drying so fast I'm getting goose bumps, from hot to cold. Rock and roll on the radio, not real loud but there, nice backbeat. Janis Joplin pouring her heart out.

Baked city floating by, the Cad's so smooth it's like flying. Mel's keeping time with the radio, beating on the steering wheel, singing along with Janis. He looks over, smiles, and does a cartoon wink.

He says, "Anyone that tells ya crime don't pay only knows guys like you." Busting himself up, laughing like a loon.

I'm still intimidated, but too pissed off not to respond.

"What's up? Why are you insulting me, motherfucker? What makes you want to do that? My old man usta always insult me. If I wanted to get fucked with, I'd call him. What are ya talkin' about anyhow? I just made thirteen, fourteen hundred bucks—what's your claim to fame? I got this stealing thing wired, I ain't gonna take shit just 'cause you look like King Kong and got this glide, man. Motherfucker. One minute you're saving my life, the next you're picking a fight—what's the story, pal?"

He's quiet, no more keepin' time on the steering wheel, no more singin'. I'm expecting mad, angry, ballistic, gettin' beat up. . . . What I get is silence, not mad silence, just quiet. AC hum, radio telling us who to buy our new appliances from, music coming back on, John Fogerty, and Mel starting to hum along, tapping time lightly, using one finger, both hands on the wheel.

Hitting the freeway, cruising, out of the city, suburbs rolling by . . . I'm waiting. Mel looks over, inspecting me, finds whatever he's looking for and returns his eyes to the road. Still hummin' he turns the radio off, saying, "Whoa, tough guy, getting all excited like that, you're liable to scare people. Before you go into your mad-dog routine, you should make sure it's warranted. You know 'warranted'? It means deserved, justified, like that. I see ya read a lot. I like to talk. I ever use a word ya don't know, tell me and I'll explain. I'm not puttin' ya down, don't go getting all upset and scaring me again. What I'm trying to establish here is communication—we exchange ideas, ya dig? That don't mean I do all the talking. You say what's on your mind. I do the same. I can teach ya some shit that'll probably extend your life. Maybe even enable you to spend more of your life on the street than you do in prison. Definitely make it more profitable. . . . Whatcha think, still wanta beat me up, killer?"

"Nah, man, I'll give ya a play this time."

We're both laughing, zooming down the freeway, chilly cool, heat waves rising off the road in front of us.

I ask, "What's this shit about prison? Who says I'm gonna do time? Whatcha got, a crystal ball?"

"Hell no, kid. Crystal balls are bullshit. I got second sight—I'm the seventh son of a seventh son, born under a full moon with a caul over my face—I see all and know all and fear nobody in the shadow of the valley of death 'cause I am the baddest motherfucker in the valley. Whatcha think of that, ace?"

Stopping to inhale, whistling, he says, "This white boy can talk shit with the best of 'em. Look, Bobbie, I don't know how old ya are but I'll bet money ya got a driver's license that says either eighteen or nineteen and I'll bet even more, shit I'll give ya ten-to-one odds that it's off by two or three years. You're already shootin' dope all day, every day, and stealing with both hands. See, you think you're a thief, but really what you are is a bust waiting to happen. Ya don't got a clue, you think a couple grand is a lotta dough, but it ain't nothin'.

"Here's the thing—there's still a few pros around, but they don't do dope. Eventually the drugs are gonna make you fuck up, cause they're your priority and boo-ya, you're in the pen. It's all part of the game. A pro only steals when everything is in his favor, when he knows he's gonna get away with it. Guys like us gotta steal, no matter what, so we end up busted. Always. The thing is to get busted as rarely as possible."

He pauses, waiting for a response, not getting one. I'm staring at the road rushing by, wanting a Cadillac of my own, wondering how hard it is to learn to drive. Mulling over this last monologue, wondering if he's right. Reaching forward, turning the radio on. Led Zeppelin. I feel no need to talk. I'm content, the smack is still working. I'm scratching and enjoying the air-conditioning. Mel's voice breaks through my seminod.

"So how old are ya?"

I look over, trying to figure him out. I decide to tell the truth and see what happens, not seeing any way it can hurt me. For the first time in two years, I tell someone my real age.

"Fourteen."

"Shit, I'd'a lost that bet. I figured sixteen or seventeen. . . . What's your ID say?"

"Nineteen."

"Never get hassled?"

"Nah, why should I? Cops don't care, long as ya got the ID—and I look eighteen or nineteen anyhow."

"When'd ya leave home?"

"Right before I turned twelve—couple, three years ago. How come ya wanta know? What difference does that shit make anyway?"

"Nosey guy, kid. I'm always trying to figure things out. Even when there's nothing to figure out. Got one of those brains that won't quit working—it's a pain in the ass, tell ya the truth. Which brings us to the reason we're having this heart-to-heart. Do you know what a contact alarm is?"

"Can't say that I do."

"If ya want, I'll teach ya. Reason being, I know this place, it's just dying to get robbed. But to do it, somebody's gotta hide inside till they're closed, then they have to circumvent the alarm and open the front door. I'll do the rest. See, the thing is, the inside guy has to be pretty fucking small—about your size, as a matter of fact. Has to have balls made out of stainless steel, 'cause he's gotta stay in this little teeny cramped space for like nine or ten hours. When this guy leaves, he'll have made a score that makes your last one look like chickenshit. How's that sound, Bobbie?"

I think about it for at least ten seconds, answer, "Good, man, sounds real good to me. So show me how to beat this alarm."

I stick my hand out.

"Shake."

We shake hands, start heading home.

Stopping in front of the pad, getting out into the hot, sticky air, Mel says, "Be ready to leave tomorrow. You're gonna be going to Chicago for a few weeks—you might not want to come back to your current palatial surroundings. Figure out what ya wanna do with your girl-friend. If you're gonna bring her, make her understand what's up—no psychotic behavior allowed. Got it? Send Danny down; I gotta get him home, it's been long enough. I'll see ya tomorrow."

I'm standing there, one hand on the door, almost in shock, thinking about what this dude just said. I have no idea what a "girlfriend" is. More than that, my whole life has been spent learning how *not* to need anyone, how *not* to care—about myself or anything else.

Mel's yell cuts through my temporary confusion.

"Shut the fuckin' door, ace. It's hot out there."

. . . .

Going up the stairs is possibly the scariest thing I'll ever undertake. This Rosie has really rocked my world. Deep down inside, where we all really live, I know that I'm the original born-to-lose kid. I feel like any-thing I want is doomed, and overwhelmingly so. No matter what I do, I feel like I'm bound to end up with the blues. Beatings, jail, fucking dying, are not nearly as terrible as getting my feelings hurt.

We're lying on the mattress, naked, sweaty, nervous. Both covered with fading bruises. I'm touching her as lightly as I can, not knowing much about women but wanting to be gentle, hoping to give her as much pleasure as she gives me. Stroking the inside of her thighs, slid-ing my fingers in and out of her, slowly, softly, running my tongue down her neck, over her entire body . . . burying my face between her legs, licking and sucking, hoping that I'm doing it right. Liking the way she tastes—salty, hot musk.

Feeling her start to respond, belly writhing up and down, making little mewling noises, getting more and more intense. She's grabbing my hair, pulling me up and I'm inside of her, moving as slowly and gen-tly as I can, and now we're tearing at each other, rocking, fulcruming against each other. . . . She's saying, "Give it all to me, mijo, give me your come. . . . I want it *now!*"

Starting to scream in harmony, coming together. Moving so slowly now, sweat pouring from us, half on, half off the mattress. I'm staring into those sad eyes and I really don't know what a girlfriend is or what ya do with one, but knowing I'm much happier when Rosie is around. This is the first time I make love. It is much more intense than fucking.

I'm doing my best to sound like I know what I'm talking about—when you're fourteen, it's very important to know everything. Otherwise you might get hurt.

We're sprawled on the mattress, facing each other, sweat starting to dry, smelling each other together. I'm looking at Rosie, thinking how fragile she looks, that the bruises look bad . . . but somehow that chipped tooth makes her more elfin, hotter than ever.

I tell her, "If you want to come along, I'd like that, kinda like my girl-friend. . . . Mel's a real good thief—he said he'd show me some good moves, how to really make a lot of dough. . . . You wouldn't have to trick anymore—we'd have a lot of fun, I mean, if you like me, too. Whatcha think?"

She looks at me, staring into my eyes like if she stares hard enough she can see my soul. She finally shrugs her shoulders, asks, "You mean it, mijo? You really like me that much? 'Cause if you do . . . it's you and me till the wheels fall off."

"Yeah, I'm happy when I'm with ya. Come with me, Rosie, we'll give it our best shot."

I pause for a second, trying to remember what they say in fairy tales.

"We might even live happily ever after."

. . . .

Sitting on the curb, too excited to stay inside, got my new shades on, think I'm looking pretty cool. . . . Rosie's standing, doing a little dance from nerves. All we know is we're getting out of town. Don't know where we're going and don't give a fuck. Everything we own is stuffed in two paper bags—jeans, T-shirts, tank tops, matching wardrobes, just different sizes.

It's not killing-hot yet, the sun only now really starting to go to work, air getting wetter, more cloying, waves of heat just starting to come off the blacktop as it softens, horseflies out on their missions, teeny pieces of flying malevolence.

Air-conditioning is the height of luxury. Having only experienced it in stores, knowing Mel's short has got AC is very exciting. The Cad comes gliding in, gleaming, glossy black, chrome shining in the sun, windows up.

Riding shotgun is this broad, at least thirty, maybe even older, long, bleached-blond hair, pretty, but with a real-hard look, bright red lipstick, staring at us through the side window. She opens the door, leaning forward so we can get in. We throw our bags in back and climb aboard. She's checking us out, and starts to smile.

Turning back to the front seat as Mel puts the Cad in gear, she makes a clucking noise, says, "Oy vey, Melvin, Melvin, Melvin. . . . What am I gonna do widja?" East Coast accent so heavy it's almost like a different language. Turning back to us, she asks, "So you two are Bonnie and Clyde, huh? I love desperados. I'm sure we'll have a real good time. I'm Sydney, with a Y—call me Syd, OK? My dim-witted friend Melvin sometimes has what they call poor impulse control."

She pauses to point to the paper bags.

"Your luggage. Tell me if I'm wrong, but it looks like there's nothin' in there but jeans and shit, which means that to have ongoing success eluding the forces of law and order, you're gonna both need new wardrobes. Melvin, *poor dear*, forgot to mention that you kids were this hard up, being the absentminded-professor type that he is. I'm sure he didn't notice that you both look like you're starving to death. You look like escapees from fucking Dachau, if I may be so bold as to mention the apparent state of your health."

Syd turns back to the front seat, punches Mel hard enough to cripple anybody else, and states in one of the shrillest voices I've ever heard, "Schmuck! Let's get these kids some calories before we got two dead bodies back there. Look at 'em!"

Mel looks back, winks at me, nodding his head vigorously, and starts talking like W. C. Fields.

"Bobbie, Rosie, my most heartfelt apologies. We will stop forthwith and acquire sustenance—bacon, eggs, pancakes, and the like. And for you, my little yenta, perhaps some lox and cream cheese. However, I must tell ya, one more Melvin out of your mouth and I'll snap your neck like a rubber band." As he's doing this routine, he leans across the front seat and kisses Syd on the forehead.

Rosie looks at me, raises one eyebrow, touches the side of her head, and whispers, "Locos, mijo."

I'm a happy guy. These people are as entertaining as any I've ever met. Rosie's sitting beside me, and the AC is on.

Wiring and electrical contacts are all over the table. Diagrams are spread out, marked with red Magic Marker. The ashtrays are overflowing.

Mel is surrounded by empty beer bottles and, for what seems like the hundredth time, I'm stripping the insulation off the wires that lead into contacts, applying alligator clips to one section, running wire from the stripped section to the next, then clipping it. This gorilla is actually making me do it with my eyes closed, feeling the contact, tracing the wire out of it, stripping the plastic covering, applying the clip, running the wire from the clip to the next contact, strip it, clip it, all by feel. . . . Stripping small wires of their insulation with your eyes closed is hard. Try it.

He's talking the whole time I'm working.

"There's no room for error kid. Ya fuck up, the alarm goes off. Woohoowoohoo. Cops are all over the place. You're surrounded. Boo-ya—it's all over but the crying and this is all a waste of time. If we can get ya bailed out we will, but if they run your prints, find out ya got warrants, then that's it; time for Rosie to get a new boyfriend.

"Concentrate. You got to be perfect. Ya need a nice light touch on shit like this. If the current gets broken, even for like one tenth of a fucking second, it's all over. That's why they call 'em 'contact' alarms: the wire is live. Ya got contact points on all the doors and windows. This is about the simplest type of alarm, a great one to cut your teeth on—but you cannot fuck up. That's the deal. Let's do it again."

I'm feeling like this is the only chance I'm ever gonna get. Loving living in a hotel—clean sheets, air-conditioning, fucking room service . . .

THREE

suddenly life is grand, and I'm not gonna blow it. I don't say a word, keep my eyes closed, and start on the next wire system.

. . . .

My fingers finally start to rebel, cramping up, refusing to work right; nerves are shot, got a headache the size of Texas; my back feels like a pretzel from being hunched over, tracing goddamn wires. Wanting to kick back, drink beer, anything but mess with alarm wires. Been working nonstop for hours, Mel lecturing the whole time.

Seems like he intends to keep this up forever and I'm determined not to quit. Do it perfectly every time for the last ten times, and finally he says, "Good enough for now, killer. Let's take a break. I'm getting worn-out watchin' ya. Have a beer, slam, whatever. What's the story man, can ya beat one of these now?"

Grabbing a beer, popping the top, watching the suds come bubbling up out of it, thinking that I don't even like beer, then downing half of it anyway. Lighting a cigarette, slumping back in the chair, asking, "So what do ya think, am I doin' OK? I ain't never worked this hard at anything in my life. Quit school in fuckin' seventh grade—well kinda, didn't really quit, just stopped goin'. Didn't see any sense in it, you know what I mean? I can make more dough in a half hour than my old man made in a week. Shit, I get these alarms and whatnot down, I'll really be rolling, have my own badass Cadillac. Get me and Rosie a nice pad, the whole deal. So what's up man, whatcha think?"

Mel smiles, takes a hit off his beer, belches, says, "Yeah man, rollin', makin' so much money ya can't spend it all."

Feeling the sarcastic edge, knowing that Melvin here has got it made, living a life that I'd never dreamt existed; looking around the hotel room—color TV; huge, comfortable king-size bed; deep-pile carpeting—all sparkling clean—fresh towels hanging in the bathroom, for Christ's sake. Wanting to make conversation, trying to find out what made this weird cat act the way he did, asking, "How'd you get into the game? You're big enough to play football or somethin', ya talk good, like you've been to school . . . you ain't like the rest of the dopers I've run with. What's your story Melvin?"

He laughs, puts the beer bottle down. He walks over to the dresser, looks in the mirror, stands staring at himself for a minute. Shaking his head, he reaches into his suitcase and comes out with his kit.

He starts putting his rig together, tearing a strip off a dollar bill and wrapping the end of an eyedropper with it, to make it seal. He twists a 26-gauge Yale needle onto the end. I'm watching, waiting for a response. Mel lumbers back over to the table, laying down the outfit— a spoon, water, and five caps of stuff. Rolls one cap across the table and throws me a disposable syringe.

Saying, "You're about the rudest little motherfucker ever to walk on two legs, aren'tcha?"

Starting to empty his four caps into the spoon, talking as he's doing it. "The trouble with booze, all that fucking beer I just downed, is it plays with your emotions. It doesn't kill 'em like good drugs do. Alcohol is the most dangerous drug around, makes ya feel all kinds of shit, act crazy as a shithouse rat, crying one minute, killing people the next."

He pauses to cook the stuff, drawing it up, holding the rig up, tapping the air bubbles out of it, pointing it at me and saying, "This shit is just sneakier. For a while it gives you control, then it starts nibbling away at ya. . . . See, it's all about control—guys that use this shit get to the top of the heap all the time. It gives you nerves of steel, doesn't seem to slow your brain down, makes you feel like God's on your side."

He pauses, wrapping his arm with a necktie, slamming all four buttons at once. . . . Sighing, starting to scratch, seems to have forgotten I'm in the room.

Cooking my own button of scag. Draw it up, looking for a vein. Ask him, "What else, ace—ya got God on your side, got nerves of steel . . . what else does a guy need? Shit, Melvin, ya got it going on, what else could ya want?"

Scratching, voice all gravelly from the heroin, Mel replies, "I can't figure out if you got balls like a Christmas tree, or if you're just kinda slow-witted.

"A: never call me Melvin again—*ever*—dig it? B: never ask a guy where he's from or where he's going—in these circles, it's a terrible faux pas—bad etiquette—in poor taste, even. C: what I was getting around to is that, while I've known plenty dudes who've gotten to the top of whatever heap we may be talking about, I don't know any that stayed there that were using.

"When I started fucking with this shit, I really did have it going on, as you just put it. Halfway through med school, I joined the service— not just any branch, mind you—navy, motherfuckin' SEALs. Went to Nam, Cambodia, Laos, picked up beaucoup fuckin' medals, also picked up one hell of a habit. Being a medic, you watch a lot of guys—nice guys—die, come out crippled, faces blown off, balls blown off, worse than dead. . . . Being SpecialOps, your people have to be able to count on ya, and, kid, no matter how much you want to be solid as a rock, no matter how fucking tough as nails you are, no matter what a bona fide certified killing machine you are, no matter how much you care about your guys, if you're a junkie, that comes first, and no one can count on ya. . . . So they booted me, dishonorable discharge, and I don't fuckin' blame 'em—I let a guy bleed to death while I nodded.

"So, anyhow, here I am, 'into the game,' like you called it, doing my best to stay in control. . . . Told ya that booze will make ya crazy as a shithouse rat—I'm babbling like a certified looney tune."

I'm staring, forget about my own slam for a little while, feel my mouth hanging open, snap it closed and respond, trying to understand.

"Jesus, you've really been through some shit, why don't ya just quit or cut down or something, go back to med school—ya can tell you're smart enough . . . how come ya want to take all these risks if you don't got to?"

"Kid, nobody just quits. Next few days, we're gonna hit the biggest speed doctor in Chicago, probably in the whole Midwest. I'll turn that speed into forty, fifty, maybe sixty thousand in cash, even after you get your end. I'll be able to live the way I want to, do whatever I want, whenever I want, buy whatever I want, and, most important, get as high as I want. If you think I can give that up, then you are as crazy as that shithouse rat I was talking about.

"See, some day Syd and I will retire, get a couple hundred grand together and buy our own little pharmacy, maybe go somewhere that doesn't have all the fucked-up laws we got here. One thing for sure, we can't do it on forty, fifty grand; and I'm not quitting till I can do it in style."

I've got the syringe shoved into the crook of my elbow, at that time still my best vein. Sending the stuff home, feeling the overwhelming quinine rush, vision doubling, itching so intense that scratching feels like coming, smack so powerful I feel myself buckling, face headed toward the table, dropping temporarily into the dreamland that real china white provides, Technicolor illusions of grandeur.... Coming back around, still scratching.

Mel says, "Lovely fucking shit, ain't it?"

"Yeah man," is the only response I feel is necessary. I'm very involved in scratching, how good this feels; no fear at all, the feeling of terror that I seem to have been born with erased like it was never there, the hole in my gut filled with opiate-induced comfort.

Mel rolls a pink-and-white cap across the table. Catching it, picking it up, looking at it, wondering what it is and then eating it, taking a hit off my now-flat beer I ask, "What was that?"

"Benadryl. You've ripped half the skin offa your face; you wanta be successful at this shit, ya can't be running around looking like you've got leprosy. Benadryl does two things: stops itching, and it's a narcotic potentiator. So you don't rip your fuckin' skin off *and* ya get a little bit higher—good deal, huh?"

Now I'm thinking about the sixty thousand in cash so I ask him, "What's my end on this score? What kinda doctor has that much meth and shit just laying around? 'Cause I've gotta tell ya, Mel, I've hit doctors' offices before, just busted in ya know, fast in-and-out, and the best I ever did was petty cash, like two, three hundred tops, and a small bag of samples. Ups, downs, a few chickenshit painkillers. Shit like that. I'm sitting here in Chicago, and I dig it and everything, and I'm down for whatever I gotta do, but what are we talking about here, pal? I haven't ever heard of a sawbones having that kinda stash."

He responds, "This guy is so big, he's got his own pharmacy right in the office. He's got three clinics in Illinois, a couple in Indiana, and his own monster operation here in Chi Town. Every fat housewife, every closet speed freak, every executive that uses the shit to make 'em function better, they all go to this schmuck. He orders right from the manufacturers, doesn't even fuck with pharmaceutical supply houses. He *is* one. All his clinics order from him, so the first of the month he's got truckloads of ups being delivered—everything from bennies and dexies to liquid meth—plus he supplies a shitload of dealers black market—college kids, truck drivers—it's one sweet operation, and we're gonna take it all.

"You mentioned petty cash—this goniff has an old Mosler safe for cash receipts. A fuckin' cracker box. It'll have a few grand in it. He does a bank drop every morning, but he's open Saturday. So we hit him Saturday night, get two days' worth of receipts. The first is Thursday. We nail him Saturday. We'll probably want to keep some of the Desoxyns and liquid meth, dump the rest of the crap wholesale, count all the cash. Your end is a third. Two thirds for me and Sydney. This is a business, like any other—there's expenses. They come off the top. I had to pay one of his receptionists for the schedules and so on, we bought a van to do it in, Syd rented a garage for storage till we unload. . . . That's it. If I missed anything, let me know."

I'm going over everything Mel had said, studying it, and find what I see is a major flaw. Instantly paranoid, I wonder if he's trying to run some kind of game. Getting my nerve up to confront this three-hundred-pound, pistol-packing fool, puffing my chest out as far as it'll go, narrowing my eyes, doing my absolute best to look like a bona fide killer, I find myself saying, "Bought a fucking van? Who are ya bullshittin'—we can steal one anywhere, any fucking time. Shit man, as long as you'll drive, I can have the ignition pulled and we'll be out of Dodge in under three minutes. . . . You're confusing me here, Mr. Big Time. Why would we want to spend good cash on something that's so easy to steal? Name the kind and year ya want, I'll go to any fuckin' parts store, buy the goddamn ignition for that model, hunt one down, and it's ours. All you gotta do is drive it away. Fair enough?"

Mel takes a deep breath, blowing it out and letting his lips flutter like a horse. Says, "Bobbie, Bobbie, Bobbie, what did I tell ya? We have *conversations*, exchange *ideas*. . . . There ya go, gettin' all puffed like a homicidal rooster and scaring me again.

"Let me go over a few things widja. One: the only guys that use a hot car on a heist are amateurs and fucking idiots. Two: the only reason to steal something is if you're gonna sell it or keep it. Three: we aren't fuckin' car thieves—you might be—but not if you're working with me.

Four: reading between the lines, it sounds like you're not too sure about your ability to drive the thing once ya steal it. Five: a broad is less likely to get stopped than a guy. Syd's driving once the van's got its own plates back, and I like her a lot more than I like the money it cost to buy this motherfucking piece of equipment.

"If you will bear with me for just one more minute I'll explain. Picture this: we've done the score, got all this cash, all these good drugs. We're miles away from the scene of the crime and for some reason— bad taillight, failure to signal, whatever—we get pulled over. No registration, maybe the van's already on a hot sheet—who knows?—but one thing for sure: we're busted.

"Ain't gonna happen if the thing isn't hot. Just clip bogus plates on four, five blocks away, pull 'em off after we're done. Syd drives the van to the garage, we follow in the Cad. If the Man hits the van, it ain't hot. They write a ticket—that's it. Shit hits the fan, and we're there to use the Cad as a crash car, if we gotta go that far. You and me'll get busted for reckless driving and fleeing the scene of an accident. Sydney'll just drive away, stash the van, and bail us out.

"So, like I said, the van is an expense. Right?"

Feeling like an idiot, ashamed because no one had taught me fundamental things like this, I'm blushing so hard my face is burning, wanting to apologize, but having no idea how to do it.

"Yeah, makes sense, right on man," is the best I can manage.

Mel grins, shrugs his shoulders, says, "We all gotta learn sometime, kid. We're done for tonight, go on back to your room. Tell Syd it's bedtime, get her ass back here to keep me company. Tomorrow, you're gonna do the alarm routine wearing gloves, and with your eyes closed. It's tougher with gloves on. Tomorrow night we go out on the town. We'll have some fun pal—a guy's gotta take his girl out on Friday night. Say hi to Rosie. Good night kid."

Nodding all the way out, mouth hanging open, snoring lightly within seconds of finishing the word "kid," Melvin's gone to the world. I just sit there for a few minutes, digesting all this new information, trying to get a feel for where this is all going, not really having any idea what my options are. I'm feeling the excitement come, and for the first time in my life, I'm really applying my mind to learning something. Liking the experience.

I say, "Night Melvin" to the snoring giant, and saunter back to my room, and Rosie.

. . . .

I shave close, not sure what this face is all about, sleepy blue-gray eyes, nose a little bit crooked and, even back then, scars over the eyebrows. Pulling my hair back into a ponytail, putting slacks on, button shirt, jacket over the shirt, dress boots. Rosie's wearing a dress, stockings, pumps, just a taste of makeup. Sydney's done her makeup and put her hair up onto one side. They're giggling and whispering the whole time.

Rosie looks hotter than molten steel. A knockout. And when she smiles, that chipped tooth multiplies it by ten.

I feel weird, off balance. Slacks hitching up where jeans just hung, shirt tucked in, but trying to pull itself out, and feeling tight around the neck like it's gonna choke me. Jacket not acting right, makes it hard to move, stiff and awkward. Boots feeling way too light and not broken in. These clothes hate me. I'm fucking miserable. All I want in life is to get back into clothes that feel right.

Rosie is ecstatic, posing, so fucking excited about going out that she's glowing. Sydney, blond hair, wide mouth, pale pale skin, is suddenly like a little girl, all the hard edges melted away like bad dreams from yesterday. Mel's bouncing from room to room, all the way upbeat, changing clothes, getting Syd's opinion on each costume, snapping his fingers and making bad jokes, acting like a three-hundred-pound game-show host.

Me, I hate these clothes as much as they hate me. Don't wanna go anywhere that requires such foolishness. Thinking that they're all very silly but not wanting to spoil their fun. Not wanting to look like a square. Just want to kick back. Fix. Maybe get a pizza.

Sydney and Rosie stop conspiring in the mirror and both focus on me. Rosie says, "Pobrecito, what's up, mijo? Don't feel good?"

"Yeah, mija, just these clothes feel kinda weird." I'm thinking how pretty she is and tell her, "I know I look like a lame, but you are so fuckin' gorgeous, looking at ya makes my knees buckle, so if I gotta put on this monkey suit to get into these joints, it's OK with me."

"Shit, mijo, you look so fine I'll be knockin' bitches out all night to keep 'em offa you. . . . Nice clothes, all clean-shaved, got those bedroom-blue eyes . . . you're happening, Bobbie."

She starts giggling like she's about three years old and says, "And you're *my* happening fucking guy, so don't be gettin' confused when all these bimbos start makin' eyes at you tonight, got it baby?"

"Yeah, I'm your guy, but I still look like a lame."

I'm still feeling bad, but their good mood is contagious, so I cheer up whether I want to or not.

Sydney jumps in with machine-gun delivery, "Check it out, ace, all your life ya been a schmeckel. Now it's time to be a schlong, put on fine clothes, go to nice places, do nice things. . . . Ya can't spend your life shootin' dope, not bathing, and eating at Burger King. We all like wearing jeans and T-shirts, but not twenty-four seven. This little girl looks at ya like you're a pork chop and she's starving. Ya know what I mean? She's nuts about you. To take care of her, you gotta take care of you. To take care of you, you gotta improve your act. Dig it?

"We're gonna have a ball tonight, eat steak and lobster and listen to old niggers play the blues—they're the guys that invented it, they make those fucking guitars cry. Smile baby."

Mel's leaning on the wall, hands stuffed into his pockets. Says, "Bobbie, ya know the difference between a schmeckel and a schlong?"

Not having heard of either of these things before, I've got no choice but to admit my ignorance, say, "Nah, don't know what they are."

"Well, pal, a schmeckel is about this long," holding his fingers about an inch apart. "A schlong goes way down to here," grabbing his leg right above his knee. "So let's get ya up to schlong status. Just like your pal Mel," and starts laughing so hard it infects the whole room.

Syd says, "Whatever you say baby—you lie and I'll swear to it."

By the time we hit the steak house, I'm into it. Maybe these clothes don't feel right, but I'm thinking that possibly I look OK; probably not happening but OK. It's party time. I got the most beautiful girl in the world, driving around in a black Cad with people who really like me, gonna eat the best steak money can buy, and tomorrow we're going to be rolling some serious numbers.

If I'd have dreamt about nice places, the restaurant would have fit. Since I've never allowed myself to focus on anything more than getting through the day, I'm stuck. Not only is this a new experience, it's a complete surprise.

Against the far wall is a fireplace you can park a car in. Logs, actual fucking *logs*—not sticks, not kindling, *logs*—burning in it, an ornate grate covering the opening. Not far from the inferno, a grand piano, not that I know the difference between a grand and a stand-up player, but that's what it is. A gaunt man with white hair, wearing a tuxedo, is playing; the noise swelling out of it and across the room completely different than rock and roll, soothing, fucking majestic. The whole place dark, firelight dancing off the walls, linen on the table so white that it glares like a spotlight on your retina, set off by gleaming, heavy silverware. The people there not only clean—spotless. Not talking, *conversing*. Not eating, *dining*. Not downing their drinks, *sipping*. It scares the shit out of me.

Mel and I have huge sirloin steaks, baked potatoes with cheddar cheese sauce, and fresh green beans. We drink Wild Turkey old-fashioneds all through dinner. I have no idea what to order, so I memorize what he says and say exactly the same thing: "Sirloin, black and blue—burnt outside, raw inside—baked potato, lots of hot cheddar cheese sauce, green beans, plenty of butter. Double old-fashioned—use Wild Turkey—blue cheese on the salad. Got it?"

Rosie and Syd have lobster and say it's delicious, but that heart attack on a plate is the most wonderful meal I'd ever had.

Leaving for the blues club, half drunk, so full I'm moving in slow motion, driving down streets that are steadily getting smaller, dirtier, and more fucked-up, going into the South Side.

Mel says, "Listen kid, we're probably gonna be the only white people there. We should have a lot of fun, but it's not unlikely that you'll run into some asshole before the night is over. Don't let your three-hundred-pound mouth overload your hundred-and-thirty-pound ass—there's racist assholes down here that make those clowns in the Klan seem like nice guys. If something goes down, let me handle it.

"See, the thing is to have a good time, but never let yourself get caught flat-footed; if someone wants to start shit because we're white, we do the best we can to just slide on out of Dodge, not prove what dangerous motherfuckers we are. OK?"

Seeing myself walking into a hostile environment, not able to understand why anyone in their right mind would go into a situation where they might get shot because their skin was the wrong color. What I want to say is, "Fuck this, I haven't been listening to the blues and have gotten along just fine, what makes ya think I gotta start listening to 'em now? What are ya nuts?"

What I say is, "Sure man, I'm down."

The club is so smoky it looks like fog, the floor covered with sawdust and cigarette butts. The bar curves around the room, a cracked mirror taking up the entire wall behind it. All the stools are full—one open table—all the booths full . . . black people all staring at us, not so much hostile as wondering what the hell we're doing on the South Side, in their club, and not lost, panicked tourists looking for a way out, but sitting down. Mel going to the bar, coming back with four beers and four shots of bar whiskey, talking quietly and waiting for the band.

An old black guy and a big fat black guy are fronting, both with guitars. The rest of their guys get up on the stand, and Sydney was right: I've never heard anyone play guitar like that. The motherfucker makes it cry like a baby and howl like a cat in heat, singing songs about the kinda pain I've felt all my short life. The rock I've grown up on sometimes has the anger I feel in it, but this shit is about the pain that preceded the anger. . . . It hits something inside me that I've done my best to keep buried. Anger is so much easier to live with than pain.

Eventually I forget to be paranoid, get completely lost in the sounds, downing shots and beers. We stay till closing, the owner telling us thanks for coming down and meaning it, telling us to be careful getting out of the South Side and meaning that also.

Staggering out, arm around Rosie's waist. No assholes tonight. Stumbling into the Cad, falling into the backseat. Rosie's got her head on my shoulder, snuggling as close as we can get, cross-eyed drunk and having the best night I've had in a long time. Ready for tomorrow and announcing in a voice that sounds slurred even to my ears: "This doctor's office is gonna be a piece of cake. What're we gonna do next?"

Mel and Syd both looking back and laughing. Mel saying, "It ain't *ever* a piece of cake, kid. Before, during, or after, ya never know when shit is gonna go wrong, but it always does. It ain't ever easy, but it's always a rush."

Syd saying, "Get some sleep tonight. You two should fall out as soon as we get back—don't keep each other up doing calisthenics all night. Tomorrow is gonna be heavy and you gotta be on top of your game. A score like this is always a pain in the ass. We're all gonna be workin' for the next week or so twenty-four seven, turning all this crap into cash. Let me tell ya, that's its own fucking nightmare, dealing with the scum of the fucking earth, staying on top of every deal. . . . You two will see, it's a drag."

. . . .

All the skin ripped from my body; eyes pulled out of my head, rolled in broken glass, and hammered back into the sockets; muscles pulled off the bone, stretched, shredded, tied in knots. . . . Like that feeling of fear has been taking massive doses of steroids, like the gibbering goblins have become the size of Godzilla, buffed to the hubs and starving, feeding on what small amount of courage I have. The knowledge that things will not go right, that everything will fail in the worst way possible is as obvious as the fact that somehow my once soft, clean sheets have been replaced with sandpaper, my pillow with a bag of concrete.

Opening my eyes makes it worse. The fucking room is spinning like a top, the pain is so intense that my hair hurts, and I'm terrified. My liver, kidneys, spleen, and intestines have decided they want to see what the world outside of me is like—and they want to do it *now!*

Levitating into the bathroom, hitting my knees like a true penitent, praying between each heave. Oh God, motherfucker, God, oh man, motherfuggin' son of a . . . Oh God, shit, fug, shit.

Not a prayer recognized in any church, but one I've used countless times, before and since. Looking into the mirror, wiping my mouth, seeing maraschino cherries with blue centers looking back at me, out of a face as haggard as the grim reaper's.

Lurching out of the bathroom, staggering toward the bed as Rosie flies past me, into the head. Holding my face together with my hands, emitting a low moan as Rosie says the same prayers in the same penitent position.

I watch her shaking her way to the bed, looking like a very small Madonna with St. Vitus' dance. I stroke her forehead when she collapses next to me, feeling my mug contort into what I hope looks like a smile as she says, "Ohhh—holy fucking Christ, I'm dying, my brain feels like it's gonna explode . . . kill me, put me out of my misery . . . oh motherfucker, mijo, why did we get drunk? Ohhh, Mary mother of God, this sucks."

Face stuck in the rictus that's supposed to be a grin and now won't come off, I mumble, "I know pretty, I feel like I'm gonna die too. My old man usta get like this every morning, until he had a few more drinks. Then he'd be all right. You gonna be OK, just hang on."

I'm mouthing platitudes like a Hallmark card, stroking her head and, having no control over the God of hangovers, feeling completely fucking useless. Compounding the Milky Way–size cloud of nameless dread and anxiety that was becoming the core of my universe. Not feeling good at all.

The phone rings, making Rosie groan and sending concertina wire ripping through my head. Shit, I answer, "Uh, what?"

It's Syd.

"Good morning, bubeleh, are you and your baby up and about, overjoyed to greet a new day, happy to be alive, and all that good shit?"

My response is less than enthusiastic. "Fuck, Sydney, I think we're both gonna die."

That voice tears its way through the wires. "Bobbie, wad's wid ja, wash ya faces, rise and fucking shine! You're too young to be sniveling like that. I'm ordering room service for yaz—pull on some clothes, me and Melvin'll be there in a minute."

Hanging up, I say to Rosie, "Pull on some clothes, the Jewish kamikazes are on their way. Shit baby, they're fucking old—they're in their thirties for Christ's sake—and still got fifty times the energy I do. Syd sounds like she just got a solid night's sleep. Up and at 'em, dingy fuckin' bitch is ordering room service. I *think* about eggs, I'll start pukin' again."

Rosie's pulling on her jeans, saying, "Bobbie, they're crazy. Bobbie, they gotta be dying too. She doesn't really want to eat, does she?"

Saying, "I don't know, mija, sounded like she meant it to me. She takes this eating thing real serious, wants to fatten us up. Says we got malnutrition. Think about it—I know I've eaten more in the last week than I usually do in a month."

Rosie's standing there, hands on hips, looking at herself. Jeans only half buttoned, pubic hair peeking out where they're still unbuttoned; hips jutting out, blending into a tiny stomach, going up into peach-size tits; collarbones showing, hair cascading down over her shoulders. Shaking her head, rubbing her stomach, that *fuck you* smile in place, she asks, "So what are you saying, Bobbie? Huh? That I'm getting fat? You gonna love me anyhow! I'll be your little gordita, your little fat girl—there will just be more of me to love."

She's pushing her stomach out and filling her cheeks with air, waddling like she's the size of a truck, then says, *"My* baby gonna love me no matter how fat I get. We'll make five—no *ten*—niños, we'll eat rice and beans. . . . I'll get as big as Mel, only shorter, and you can rob the world and we'll live happily ever after. Right, mijo?"

I'm laughing, but it makes my head hurt even worse. I say, "Sure you're right, but ten ain't enough. We gotta have at least fifteen kids— and steak and lobster instead of rice and beans, and for you I'll rob the world twice. Whatcha think?" Laughing and wincing at the same time.

Syd's at the door, pounding like she wants to break it down, and yelling, "Rise and shine. Open fucking sesame seed."

Rosie's pulling her shirt on, and I hobble over to the door, feeling like I'm a hundred years old, thinking there's no way I can get my nerve back and quit shaking before we do the score. I open the door, saying, "Hi Syd. So I guess ya feel pretty good today. How is that possible?"

She pushes past me, looking around, bouncing over to the mirror, fluffing her hair. Sitting on the dresser, she says, "Clean living honey. Can't you tell? Then again, maybe it's just years of practice. I ordered you kids breakfast—gotta keep ya healthy. You're looking better by the day—both of ya, by the way."

She's digging in her shirt pocket, pulls out two caps of stuff and tosses one to each of us.

"Here ya go: breakfast of champions. Slam these. Room service will be here soon, so ya gotta hurry. Let's get a move on—we got a gang of shit to do today: gotta check the van, get the bogus plates, pack you a lunch. . . ."

Pointing at me as I'm doing what I would later know as my wake-up: my hands are shaking from the hangover and I'm trying to pay attention to Syd and get a register at the same time. I'm mumbling, "Uh-huh, right."

Syd continues, "Ya gotta have nourishment. Can't sit up in a crawl space for eleven hours without eating. We'll hit a deli, get ya great stuff to nosh on while you're up there."

I interrupt, "Eleven hours? Up where? Nosh, what's nosh?"

Syd's machine-gunning, "Oy vey, what's nosh? Nosh is to nibble, to eat, to consume food—ya can't be going that long without no food. . . . To be a thief ya gotta be healthy, brain's gotta work, body's gotta work, so ya gotta eat. Dope fiends don't eat, so they fall apart, fuck up, get busted. Mel's takin' ya under his wing, and I'm growing real fond of yez, so you gotta do this shit right. Being healthy is part of it.

"There's a trapdoor. It's in the men's room, over the commode. Lets ya into the attic. You go in there, Mel follows ya, picks you up, shoves you through the trapdoor. All you do is sit there. You got a clock—it's got numbers that glow in the dark. Ya got a flashlight, you got your tools, wire, all that shit. . . . You got food and ya got some dope—ya even got an empty jar to piss in. Can't have urine leaking through the ceiling, right?

"You go up there at four in the P.M. Ya come down at three in the A.M. Eleven hours. Should take fifteen minutes tops to rewire the alarm; we give ya an extra fifteen. You open the back door at exactly three-thirty. You and Mel pile everything by the back door, all boxed up nice and neat.

"I pull up in the van at four-fifty. The cops have shift change at five— they're at the station house from quarter to five to five-fifteen. We have the van loaded by five after five, I take you and my baby to the Cad. We pull the plates, takes fifteen minutes to get to the garage. So, as long as you do your end right—the alarm—our total exposure is the last five minutes to the garage. Sounds pretty good, huh? Nothing's ever perfect, but this is about as close as ya can get."

I'm dumbfounded, want to ask her to *please go through all that one more time*, but too embarrassed, thinking a real pro would have got it all with no problem, possibly offered a couple of improvements. Definitely not be confused and bewildered by this barrage of information. So I focus all my attention on getting a vein in my foot, find it, hit it, and the relief is astounding, the only thing better than fixing is fixing when you're kicking or in pain. The terror disappears, the Godzilla-size goblins shrink down to anorexic mice, the pain runs for the hills, and healthy well-being takes its place. The ultimate hangover cure, removing a headache by selling your soul.

There's a knock at the door. A voice calls out, "Room service," and a guy—looks like a college kid, hair semilong, wanting to look cool but having a hard time doing it in his little red uniform—appears pushing a cart full of food that comes clanking into the room.

Mel comes strolling in behind him, leaning on the door. We all watch silently as the bellhop uncovers the feast—a six-pack of beer, two carafes of coffee, scrambled eggs, fried eggs, potatoes, sausage, bacon, biscuits, pancakes . . . it looks like enough food for a small army.

Mel says, "Here kid," holding out cash. The bellhop does a double take, obviously can't figure out who we are, aside from a very strange group of people. He says, "Thanks," looks at the dough again, and repeats, "Thanks. Wow, you don't want any change, huh? Thank you very much sir, you need anything let me know."

Closing the door, Mel says, "If ya like gettin' your ass kissed and getting great service, always overtip. I personally like both of those things. Life can never be too good, ya know what I mean?"

. . . .

The day has been hectic. Putting everything together, Mel pounding away at the details. Syd agrees to bring Rosie along to steal the switch plates that evening. Getting the hot tags is the last thing to do before we clean the place out. They're gonna steal 'em in a residential neighborhood, while me and Mel are inside, so that even though the bogus plates will only be on the van for minutes, they won't be reported till the next morning.

We're sitting at the table. Sydney and Rosie are out shopping. Mel's got everything spread out, going over the details again and again. "You go in first, walk directly to the men's room, count your steps; there's gonna be some light from the street, but if something goes wrong—streetlights go out, flashlight don't work, whatever—ya gotta know how to get in and out of your target, even if it's pitch-black. Ya hit the head, wash your hands, comb your hair, pretend you're takin' a shit, you gotta kill three, four minutes. I'll come in, we lock the door, I lift ya up to the trapdoor, all you gotta do is push it out of the way and pull yourself up there."

He points at the briefcase he's got lying on the table next to him.

"I carry this in with me—all the shit is inside, in a canvas bag. I hand the bag up to you. The first thing you do is take the gloves out and put 'em on. They *stay* on ya till we leave with all the swag. Do *not* take them off—eat with 'em on, fix with 'em on, whatever—they *don't* come off your hands till we're out of there. If ya gotta pee, ya do it in the jar, cap the jar, and leave it, 'cause as long as ya got your gloves on, it won't have no prints. Ya with me so far?"

I'm completely focused, going over every word, visualizing the steps as he lays them out. The fear and excitement are mounting, knowing I have to do this perfectly, have to handle the dread I know is going to mount through the day; knowing that, if I can pull it off, get all the way through without fucking up, I will have officially entered the Big Time.

I reply, "So far man, I got it all."

Mel says, "OK, your tools are gonna be in one bag, mine in another, so you won't have to dig around. All your bag's got in it is clippers, wire, alligator clips, and a flashlight. Mine's a lot bigger, so there's no confusion. Everything goes inside the one big sack that I hand up to ya. Simple. Right?"

I respond, "Right."

Mel's studying me, got his eyes squinted.

Rubbing his face, he says, "What's up, Bobbie? Something is bothering you besides handling this lick. You gotta let me know when something is wrong—we're working together here. You're not scared of the dark, are ya?"

I'm hesitant. Any emotions except fear and hate are so deeply buried that they feel alien.

Getting my nerve up, I say, "This thing with Rosie—I don't want her stealing plates or nothin'. How come Syd said she could go with her? I can do whatever I gotta, but I don't want *her* in any fucking jackpots. She's had enough grief already, don't ya think, Mel?"

He's silent, staring at his hands; then he lights a cigarette and says, "Shit kid, we've all had enough grief to last a normal person through five, six lifetimes. . . . Here's the thing: Rosie wants to help, she don't want you to be a trick and just take care of her; she wants to contribute and, I gotta tell ya, that's a rare thing. Most people, men or women, want a free ride; no one wants to pay any fucking dues. Your average dope fiend—shit, humanity in general—is too lazy to work and too scared to steal . . . fucking scumbags, bloodsucking shitheads, useless fucking parasites.

"Not to put too fine a point on it, but that little girl is a thorough-bred—you can't make her just kick back and do nothing and have her feel good about it. Sydney's the same way, except Syd loves being the shot-caller, so I go along. When ya really like somebody, ya got to make fucking compromises. Things work better that way. Trust me on this, OK?"

I'm thinking about what he said and I want to argue, get him to agree with me, but the thing is, even though I hate the idea of Rosie taking any risks, I know that the fucking gorilla is right. I just nod, say, "OK."

Mel pulls on a pair of gloves and starts loading the individual bags full of tools, wrapping everything so it won't clank around. He moves slowly, handling everything meticulously, finally loading it into the sack.

Pulling off the gloves, putting them into his back pocket, he says, "Never touch anything you're bringing on a score with your bare hands. *Never.* Ya drop something, lose something, as long as there's no prints, you should be all right.

"The last thing we load is your picnic; Syd'll get it wrapped at the deli, just to be on the safe side. Ya dig?"

I'm terrified, but can't wait to start rolling, knowing that once we're actually doing it, the fear will vanish and I'll be flying on pure adrenaline. Running through everything over and over, repeating the process I'm going to go through. . . . It's like a mantra singing inside my head.

I say, "Yeah man, I'm up and in, gloves are on, alarm's a piece of cake, you're in, and we're shitting in tall cotton!"

Mel hands me a watch—a Rolex stainless Submariner, which, at the time, means as much to me as a Timex. I'd never heard of Rolex.

He says, "Here, Bobbie, I've had this kicking around for a while and don't like the stainless. It's yours, just in case your alarm clock breaks. I don't wanna be standing outside with my dick in my hand, waiting till daylight. This thing keeps perfect time, just like this one."

Lifting his shirt sleeve, he shows me the same watch, but made out of gold. Then he says, "They're synchronized, so this should go perfect—and, if ya notice the time on your new watch, it's almost time to go to work. Are you ready?"

The pterodactyls have gone insane, the adrenaline isn't kicking in yet, all I got is fear. I'm scared that my voice is going to shake and betray the fact that I'm terrified. Before, if I got busted there was nothing to lose. If I fuck up tonight I lose Rosie, let Mel and Syd down—maybe get them busted—and have to give up clean sheets, air-conditioning, and room service. I'm scared to death.

What I say is, "I've never been readier pal. As soon as Syd and Rosie get back, we're rolling, gonna take this motherfucker *down!*"

. . . .

The streets of Chicago float past the windows of the Cad. Sydney has Willie Dixon on the eight-track and Mel is singing along, doing pantomime, "I'm a king beeee, buzzin' around your hive." They seem to feel no tension whatsoever; they're both as loose as kids on the way to the circus.

I am wired for sound, my mantra flying through my head: shove the door open using the back of my hands, pull up, gloves on, do the alarm, open the door. . . . Feeling my body going through the motions without moving an inch. Rosie is curled next to me on the backseat, softly rubbing my shoulders; she knows I'm nervous and is whispering, "Oye, mijo, everything is gonna be all right. We don't gotta do this—ya want baby, I can make enough dough trickin' to take care of us. I'm scared, Bobbie. I really like being with ya. What if you get busted?"

Her eyes are fucking pools of despair, little gangsterline who has more fear in her than I do—something I've always thought is impossible, that someone could be more scared by life than me. A revelation. The one thing I've mastered is shoving my emotions down so deep that they'll never see sunlight. That's what happens to the fear that's tying my guts in knots. What takes its place is indescribable and certainly unnameable. It feels like something is trying to tear its way out of my chest.

I want to squeeze Rosie so tight she'll become part of me. Take all the fear and pain out of her and absorb it myself. There are a lot of things I want to tell her. What I say is, "This is gonna be a piece of cake, baby. By the time the sun comes up, we're gonna be on our way to living happily ever after. . . . Everything is gonna be all right, you'll see. You ain't never gonna have to trick again. I swear to God."

We pull into the parking lot, surrounded by shrubbery and flower beds, flowers in full bloom, all the colors of the rainbow. An old Asian guy working on the vegetation—it's really pretty, something I wouldn't normally notice. But I'm starting to get jacked up, all my senses are on overdrive. I'm ready.

Parking, surrounded on all sides by nice cars—no particular type— Chevy station wagons, Mercedes, everything in between, all clean, all respectable, middle America represented vehicularly. The office itself is two story, brick and glass, very modern, all straight lines, glass tinted dark, encased in shiny steel. I lean over to kiss Rosie and she grabs my face and says, "Te quiero, mijo. Te quiero mucho, Bobbie."

I'm already inside emotionally, mentally, just got to get there in person. But this stops me. No one except my mother had ever said they loved me and I don't know how to respond. I'm frozen looking at her and hear myself say, "Yeah, I'll see ya in the morning, mija."

I'm out of the car, walking as sedately as possible down the path leading to the front doors; push through them and see the same boring variety of people in the waiting room as the cars in the lot. Middle America, lining up to get their legal speed. I feel the rush coming on, hoping they're all paying cash 'cause checks won't do us any good, knowing that if everything works right I'll be leaving with enough ups and dough for me and Rosie to live in style for a couple of months.

I'm past the reception desk, through the waiting room, down the hall, into the men's room. There's some skinny geek at the urinal, I walk past him, go into the toilet, close the door, drop my pants, sit there waiting. This fucking asshole is taking forever. About a week later the urinal flushes; a month later, he finishes washing his hands. I've been sitting in the head for what seems like a year, and finally he finishes drying his hands and leaves. I'm up and in the mirror, combing my hair, washing my hands, combing my hair again.

Mel comes through the door. Locks it behind him, smiles, winks, says, "We're gonna have to stop meeting like this. . . . Let's do it, kid."

He steps under the trapdoor and cradles his fingers together. I put my foot into his hands and am propelled to the ceiling; I shove the door out of the way, grabbing the wooden casing, pulling myself up and swinging my legs up and through the opening. I'm perched in the crawl space.

I look down and watch him open the briefcase, throwing me the bag full of tools and stuff. I catch it, pull it in with me, and he says, "Well, ace, so far so good. See ya at three-thirty. Don't wear yourself out up there."

Two-by-fours are cutting into my knees. I look around before sliding the door back into place, see only dust whirling crazily in the light, shooting up through the doorway. Spiderwebs and cobwebs not only blanketing the crawlway but covering my face and arms, stuck in my hair and eyebrows; there's already a spider doing recon on my arm. I crush it and, looking down, tell Mel, "This is gonna suck man."

"Shit kid, if it was easy, everybody'd be doing it. Put your gloves on and slide the trap closed."

I pull it shut, getting as comfortable as possible, the adrenaline rush dying off. . . . Got eleven hours to go and I'm already bored. Getting everything together, pull the clock out of the bag, setting it on one of the two-by-fours, numbers glowing green. I'm gonna try to wait till eleven to eat and fix—that's seven hours away. Right now, that seems like forever.

It's impossible to stand up or lie down completely, so I'm sprawled against the wall, legs kicked up on a crossbeam, unable to move around 'cause that will make noise. I'm doing my best to be as silent as the spiders crawling on me. The dust is going up my nose, and the place smells of mildew and rat shit.

"Welcome to the Big Time," I whisper, and settle in for the night.

. . . .

Listening to the place slow down. The cleaning crew finishes at eight, and there's nothing left to distract me. My brain, spiders, and dust. At five after eleven, I break for lunch.

I put the flashlight under my shirt to diffuse the light. Slamming immediately. Unwrapping the food, each time the paper crinkling so loud it sounds like thunder. . . . Finally getting everything unwrapped: roast beef sandwich on rye, huge fucking pickles, chocolate chip cookies, and a quart of warm root beer. Taking the first bite of the sandwich, opening the bottle of root beer, the fizzing sounding like a geyser. . . .

Chewing and looking up at the crossbeam running past my face, staring into the eyes of the biggest rodent in the universe. This guy has to weigh twenty pounds—Super-Rat in person. His head is waving back and forth, nose and whiskers vibrating, little brown eyes darting from the sandwich to me and back. Standing on his hind legs, Super-Rat starts washing his face, watching me and not scared at all. Not knowing what the proper protocol is when busted trespassing by the king of all vermin, definitely not wanting to antagonize this motherfucker, I very slowly reach down, pick up one of the cookies, and slide it onto the crossbeam in front of him.

He pauses in his hygienic efforts, sniffs at the cookie, and grabs it. Sitting on his hind legs, he starts eating, very neatly consuming the whole cookie. I give him another, finish my sandwich and root beer, and watch him until he gets bored and scampers into the darkness.

It's 11:35. Three hours and fifty-five minutes to go. I turn the flashlight off and try to get comfortable.

The last ten minutes drag like sandpaper—time passes faster when you're getting teeth extracted.

Exactly 3:01, and I'm sliding out of the crawl space, bag of tools in my teeth. I let go with one hand, grab the bag, release my grip with the other hand, and gravity does the rest. Feet stinging from the impact, dancing around to get my body working right, grabbing paper towels and wiping all the dirt and crap offa my face and arms.

Opening the door an inch at a time, listening for any unexpected noises and hearing none. So far so good. Get through the door and hit my hands and knees, crawling, so if anyone's still here, doctor working late, cleaning crew guy passed out in the office, I'll make no noise. No matter how quietly you walk, even if you fucking tiptoe, it makes some noise. Crawling, while not very cool, is completely silent, and puts ya below the line of sight: most people look ahead, not down.

I make it to the end of the hallway, lie flat, and poke my head out an inch at a time. I study the waiting room and reception area, listening with my whole body, holding absolutely still, not even breathing. It's empty.

Getting on my hands and knees, I crawl through the reception area and into the back office. I look at the back door—the drug storage area is to the right of it, the safe against the far wall, no windows, light reflecting from the glass in the reception booth.

Standing up and stretching, heart running like a racehorse, but feeling real confident, I saunter over to the door and hit the alarm with the flash for a second, just to make sure it's what is expected. I feel laughter bubbling around in my chest and whisper to myself, "Yeah man, piece of fuckin' cake."

When the second hand of that Rolex hits 3:30, I swing the door open, contacts linked by wires, alarm circumvented.

Mel's leaning on the doorjamb, smiling. He stands ramrod straight, salutes, and says, "Congratulations, Captain. Couldn't have done better myself. Let's get it done, boss."

I hand him his bag of tools, feel like I just got the congressional Medal of Honor. I ask, "What now, man?"

"First we close the door, then we crack this fuckin' Mosler. Close the door, kid."

Realizing he's already inside and I'm still holding the door and grinning like an idiot, I pull it closed.

Mel says, "Check this out, ace."

Pulling a stethoscope out of his bag, he walks over to the safe, puts the earpieces in, and blows on his fingers. He bends over and has the safe open in under ten seconds.

I'm awestruck, and say, "Jesus fuckin' Christ man, how didja do that so fast? I've never even heard of anybody opening a box that fast."

"Well, pal, after years of study and practice, having good ears and incredibly sensitive fingers, ya put all that together and it ain't too hard. Plus, when I bought the delivery schedules from that receptionist, she also gave me the combination to the safe."

He's laughing and trying to hold it in and says between chuckles and snorts, "I saw a guy do that in a movie and wanted to see what it felt like. Plus the look on your face was worth every bit of it. Ha ha ha!"

I make a face, grinning and saying, "If everybody thought you're as funny as you do, you'd be a fuckin' comedian. But they don't, shithead. Let's get to work—at least till ya get your act completed."

I walk over to help empty the safe. Bundles of cash, banded by denomination. Mainly twenties, followed by tens, a few fifties and hundreds—a sackful of cash, more than I've ever seen at one time.

Mel says, "Come on, let's get the drugs. You won't see this in any movies, but it's the fastest way to open a good door lock." Taking the bag of cash, Mel lumbers over to the door leading into the drug room and taps on the door. Getting a metallic ring, he says, "Check it out—door's made out of steel; steel jamb's set into brick; Schlage dead bolt made out of case-hardened steel. Can't loid it. Might be able to force it if we had all night and didn't have to worry about noise. How are we gonna open it?"

"Pick the motherfucker? I don't know man."

"That's James Bond shit, like opening a safe with a stethoscope. Sounds good, might even work if ya got enough time and were a certified locksmith. . . . Schlages are a fuckin' nightmare and we're in a hurry. Right?"

"Yeah, man."

Reaching into his bag, Mel pulls out what looks like a dent puller.

He says, "What we got here is a modified slap hammer, kinda like auto body guys use. Instead of a hardened sheet-metal screw, this one has a specially forged titanium screw, covered in little teeny industrial-grade diamonds."

As he's saying this, he's screwing it into the keyhole. When he finishes, he pulls out of his bag what looks like a dumbbell with a ball-bearing slide running through the middle, extending about two feet. He begins attaching it to the screw mechanism.

"Instead of an eight-ounce weight, the slapper on this one weighs fifteen pounds. Slides smooth as silk."

Taking a deep breath, he rips the slapper down the slide. One loud crack, and the door is open.

"Needless to say, shit like this is custom-made."

It's 3:43. There are boxes of speed filling the shelving on two walls; inside each box, pharmaceutical bottles yielding one hundred tabs per bottle on the Desoxyns and up to a thousand per bottle on the shittier stuff. I'm not scared. I'm in shock.

Mel says, "Let's get it stacked, I want to be out of here six minutes ahead of schedule, so we gotta hustle."

We're sweating like hogs, working frantically, reboxing, making everything as compact as possible. We stack the boxes by the back door. We get done fifteen minutes early. Now the pterodactyls are back. Waiting is not my strong point. Mel's sitting crosslegged on the floor. He lights a smoke and throws one to me, raising one eyebrow and saying, "So far so good. You know the joke, right, Bobbie?"

"No brother, can't say that I do. What is it?"

"This dude jumps off the Empire State Building. The whole way down, people see this cat's lips moving. Anyhow, he hits the ground and boo-ya, splatters all over the place like a fucking broken egg. So there's this broad on the tenth floor, and she's a lip-reader, right?"

"Yeah?"

"Everybody is asking, 'What was he saying on the way down, what was he saying?'"

"Uh-huh?"

"So the chick says, 'I'm a lip-reader. He was saying, "So far, so gooooooood."'" Mel starts laughing like a hyena.

I say, "You really bust yourself up, huh pal?"

"Somebody's got to, right?"

"So are you saying we're gonna hit the pavement?"

"Eventually, kid. Hopefully not any time soon."

At exactly 4:50, Syd pulls up with the van, Rosie riding shotgun. I feel like going psychotic, not wanting Rosie around this shit at all, but choke it down, thinking about what Mel said earlier and keeping my mouth shut.

Syd's talking very quietly—not whispering, but in a very low voice: "We'll assembly-line it. Mel, throw the boxes to Bobbie. I stand by the back of the van, he throws 'em to me. I hand 'em to Rosie in the van and she stacks 'em."

She looks at Mel and raises her eyebrows.

Mel responds, "You're a genius, baby." He raises his hands and, chuckling, looks at me, saying, "Let's do it."

We have it done in under nine minutes, and are on our way out of the driveway before 5 A.M.

Syd is driving at exactly the speed limit, Rosie riding shotgun. Me and Mel are stashed in the back, the theory being that two women are less likely to get pulled over. We turn the corner, drive about three more blocks, and Mel is already opening the door in the side of the van, saying, "Pull the front plate, Bobbie, let's go," as the van comes to a stop.

We're already out of the van, not running but moving real fast. I grab the front tag and rip it free of the clips holding it in place over the real plate. I spin around, walking past the van, and jump into the Cad. Syd and Rosie are already a half block away. The Cad's running, but we wait till they turn the corner before we start following them; Mel maintains two blocks between the vehicles. I ask, "What if the cops stop them? You got your gun?"

Mel looks at me like I'm crazy, says, "Why would I take a gun on a burglary? I'm not gonna shoot some poor schmuck who interrupts us. If I can't run, or knock the guy out, I'll take the bust."

"What about cops, man? I don't want Rosie gettin' busted. What if the crash car thing don't work?"

"Bobbie, check it out: we're thieves, not fucking animals. A cop is a guy doing a job—a miserable job on top of it—got a wife, kids, parents . . . a real human being, not the fucking enemy. If we don't do *our* job right—stealing—then they gotta do their job, and bust us. Those guys are way overworked. To make their lives easier, we have to be real good at what we do so they don't have to take us down. Right?"

"I don't know man, I gotta think about this one, Mel, ya know what I mean? I'm confused here—if they're not the fuckin' enemy, who is?"

"Assholes, kid. Assholes are the enemy. People who threaten your life, people who make stupid laws and don't have to enforce them themselves . . . the idiots that made narcotics illegal . . . some of the scumbags we have to deal with are the enemy. Human beings that act like jackals, niggers that hate all white people, rednecks that hate all black people . . . fuckin' cowboys that hate all Indians. Assholes. Know what I mean?"

The strange thing is that as soon as he gets done talking, I do know what he means, and know that he is right. I think about it, run it through my mind. I say, "So the crash car thing will work, huh?"

"Always has so far. I hate to disappoint ya, but I'm not gonna be able to demonstrate it this evening, or, should I say, morning? 'cause they're pullin' into the garage as we speak."

Mel parks and hands me a cigarette.

I analyze this last monologue as I watch Syd and Rosie walking to the car, realizing I'm still angry with Syd for letting Rosie get involved, still mad at Rosie for taking risks I didn't want her to take. I get out and hold the door open so Rosie can get into the back, and climb in after her. She looks really tired, frazzled, but smiling ear to ear. I'm very glad to see her, and say, "See baby, told ya, fuckin' piece of cake." After all, if you really like somebody, you have to be willing to compromise.

We come out with $9,900 and change. The van and garage come to a grand, two thousand for the bent receptionist—my end of the cash is $2,300. I'm ecstatic.

Rosie and I are in our room, having shot enough speed to put us both past Pluto. I'm on the bed, got that slow-motion thing going on that comes when you do exactly the right amount of meth—almost enough to kill you, just a whisker away from falling off the edge, plunging into the void, but not quite. Aware that if you move too fast your heart will explode—that's when it's real good. Speed makes most people babble. I never talk a lot under any circumstances. Meth makes me even more reticent.

Rosie's saying, "You my baby, Bobbie. *My* blue-eyed gringo devil. No one's ever took care of me before. I told you I'd trick for us and you said no. I never tricked for anybody, just me. I was so scared you'd say yes, but whatever it took, I'd do. You make me want to take care of ya, but you take care of me."

My immediate reaction is to tell her to cut the shit, run that drag to someone who's never heard bullshit before.

She's pacing from the bed to the dresser and back, saying, "All my life I've been lonely, felt like I wanted to go home, but didn't know where home was—there was no such place, only in my head. . . . It sure wasn't with my parents. Since we been hanging, mijo, sometimes I feel like I'm home, like I belong somewhere."

"Don't count on nothin', mija. I've never seen nobody stay together and it be any good. It took my mom years to leave my old man, even though he beat her up all the time and sent me to the hospital every time he got bored."

FOUR

"It don't have to be like that, Bobbie. I know it don't. You're good to me. I'll be good to you. We'll be happening."

"Yeah, I hope so."

"Mijo, my whole life has been a nightmare. This is the best I ever felt. We can rob everything that ain't nailed down, put some shit together, maybe really have those kids."

It hits me that she's serious. The concept that someone could really feel so strongly about me that they'd want to make plans is as alien as trust, as bizarre as caring, as crazy as love. I want these things, but never admitted it, especially to myself; feel these things, but don't believe in them. All I've ever seen are heartache and pain, people cru- cifying each other in the name of love.

I say, "Can't argue with the part where I rob everything that ain't nailed down. . . . The rest of it, who knows? It sounds good. Let's see what happens."

"Baby, when I offered to trick for ya, I meant it. I've really been through some fucked-up shit—the only person I'd do anything for was me. After what my folks did, I've always felt like it was my fault, like somehow I made them fuck me. Crazy, huh?"

. . . .

It comes back to me, all of it. I'm five years old, trapped under the kitchen table, screaming, crying hysterically. The smell of bacon and eggs lying heavy in the air, my mother crumpled in the corner, one shoe knocked off, skirt hiked up around her hips, blood gushing out of her mouth and nose, and my father picks the table up and throws it across the room, onto her legs. My dad is six feet two and weighs 250. I'm a small kid, maybe 50 pounds. He's kicking me around the kitchen, send- ing all 50 pounds of me flying into the air with each kick, breaking ribs, smashing them into my lungs. . . . Finally, tiring of kicking me, he picks up one of the red-Naugahyde-and-tubular-chrome chairs and beats me with it until the seat goes flying like a Frisbee and the chrome breaks apart, and he says, "Little blue-eyed bastard, this is all your fault, you piece of shit, your whore mother fucked the postman and you got his eyes. Get big enough, you gonna wanna fuck her too? Everybody else does, little fucking bastard!"

My dad is a very sick guy. Lying in the hospital, I know it's my fault. Not that he beat us up, but that I didn't try to stop him. I feel like the ultimate piece of shit because I'd hidden under the table instead of attacking him when he started beating my mom, knowing deep down that I was a coward and that he was right. I deserved to die. I determined to do my best to try and take him with me next time around. That's a heavy load for a five-year-old kid. Sadly, it's many years later, and every time I look in the mirror I see a shorter, blue-eyed version of him. Pops has strong genetics. The postman is much better looking.

. . . .

I say to Rosie, "I know, baby. It's fuckin' nuts. None of that shit was your fault, don't none of us ask to be victims."

"I don't know, Bobbie, I always feel like somehow I make all the bad shit happen, or maybe like God hates me or something."

"Why would God hate a beautiful little Latina like you, when he's so busy hating me? Huh, mija? Tell ya the truth, I don't think he hates us, he just forgot about us for a while."

"I don't know, mijo. I told ya I'd never trick for nobody, right?"

"Except me, pimp-daddy-Bobbie. Shit honey, I be slapping ho's and slammin' Cadillac do's."

"It ain't funny, Bobbie. Check this out, this is for real. I been doing this shit since I was thirteen. Couple times the chongos, you know, the niggers, tried to turn me out."

She stops pacing, has a look on her face like someone getting ready to dive into eternity. Running her tongue over her chipped tooth, she says, "This one, Stanley—Stan the Man—told me he was gonna be my pimp. Looked just like Harry Belafonte, real light skin, had that straightened hair, always talked real softly, seemed really nice, said he'd get my drugs, set up all my tricks, like that. I told him no, told him to fuck off."

Rosie pauses, sits on the bed, eyes looking inward, as sad as I've ever seen them. Voice starting to crack, she continues, "He beat my ass, knocked me down and kicked me so hard in the stomach I couldn't breathe. I was laying on his dirty floor, gasping like a fish out of water. Bobbie, he kept me tied up for two days. He had all his friends come up and fuck me, sold me to all these toads for ten, twenty bucks a shot."

"Shit, mija. Poor baby. Ain't nobody gonna ever hurt you again." Starting to feel mad, but this story isn't all that unusual; growing up on the streets, shit like this is part of the cost of doing business.

"The nasty motherfucker had me tied to the bed. They just kept coming, fucking me, using my asshole, fucking my mouth. They stank, there was come all over me, running down my legs and my face. He took pictures, said he'd show 'em to everybody, said I was his whore and he'd kill me if I didn't work for him, said he'd cut my tits off and pull my eyes out, said he'd fill my pussy with gasoline and light my tongue like a torch."

Voice raising in pitch till it sounded like the words were being ripped out of her soul; face contorting, like the muscles were trying to tear away from the bone and fly through her skin; staring at me but not seeing anything except the images that had been burnt into her memory.

"Where is this cocksucker, baby? He's gotta die—slowly."

I'm going into full-on rage, feeling Rosie's pain. Stories like this are almost always delivered deadpan; letting other people see your pain is dangerous—it gives them an advantage. Her tears make me responsible. Force me to share her anguish. Let me react.

Voice dropping, putting her face into her hands, she says, "He finally untied me, told me to go make some dough and bring it back to him. He didn't even let me shower—I could still smell those fucking niggers all over me. I ran home and told my pipa and mima, my mom and dad. They said it was my fault, said that's what I got for hanging around with negritos. Said if I was gonna be a whore, I'd better take care of them.

"I wanted my daddy to do something, go kill them or something, call the cops or whatever. He laughed, said the cops wouldn't care about a Puerto Rican whore, and he wasn't gonna start any shit with Stanley and his boys."

Sitting up, giving her all my attention, rubbing her back, feeling the tremors running through her like she was hooked up to a live electric wire. I light two cigarettes and hand her one; she takes a hit off it, inhaling so hard you can hear the cigarette burning.

She blows out a huge cloud of smoke and says, "That's when I left home. I'll never go back to Gary, Indiana, again, and I hope my mom and dad rot in hell with Stan the motherfucking Man and all his bros, while Satan fucks 'em all in the ass."

"If ya want, we'll go to Gary as soon as we're done here and I'll kill this pimp motherfucker." My ears have the sound of a jet engine roaring in them, my field of vision is narrowing down as my breathing intensifies, but there's not a thing I can do. Except stay here with her, do my best to make life better.

She's got tears swimming around in her dilated eyes. Her mouth hangs open; she breathes through it, touching her chipped tooth with her tongue, focusing on my eyes, watching to see what my reaction is, as intent as a moth circling a flame, waiting to be thrown away, hoping for something else. She says, "Why would God let these things happen? I was only fourteen. I swear it wasn't my fault. Do you still like me, mijo? Do you want me to go away now? I had to tell you that shit. What's going on behind those blue eyes?"

I pull her onto the bed beside me, kiss her on the forehead, and say, "Poor girl, I wish I could change all that shit. You make me happy. I don't want ya to go away—I'd like to be with ya forever."

Feeling the meth coursing through me, an overwhelming series of strange emotions slicing into it like a razor through flesh. Everything in slow motion. Stroking her skin; how velvety it is. Knowing I am gonna do whatever I have to so that Rosie never has to go through that kind of shit again.

"You mean that, mijo?"

"Yeah."

"You don't think I'm bad?"

"Bad to the fucking bone. Bad, good—I don't know the fucking difference. I know I like ya a lot."

She's saying, "Te quiero, Bobbie. Let me show you. I'll do whatever you want."

Rosie stands up, begins slowly undressing.

I can't change gears this fast, one minute it's true confessions, tears and shit, the next . . .

She's got her hands on her hips. Naked. Nipples soft, dark brown, running her hands down her body, purring deep down in her throat, saying, "Do you like this? It's yours."

The meth has me immobilized. My dick feels like it's ready to crawl back inside me, shrunk, compacted down to peanut size. Useless.

Now she's playing with her nipples, squeezing and twisting them. Making them harden. They're standing up like pencil erasers, and now Rosie's running her hands down her body, rubbing her snatch, sliding one finger inside her. In and out. Rubbing her pussy in a circular motion, putting her finger back inside her and then licking it. Falling to her knees in front of me and starting to unbutton my jeans.

I'm starting to panic. It doesn't feel like I can function; all I want to do is talk and hold her. I know that's all I'm capable of right now.

I say, "Don't, mija, I don't think I can do anything. I did too much speed. Stop, baby."

She's got my pants down by my ankles, hesitates. Staring into my eyes, runs her hand up my leg and over my balls to my chest and back down. Says, "Shhh, Bobbie," and starts running her tongue from the bottom of my testicles up and around my cock. She puts it into her mouth, and she starts to suck and lick it, all the while purring like a cat and looking up at me. She takes my cock out of her mouth and rubs it all over her face. She starts to suck again and I'm responding, getting hard and feeling the excitement spread through my body.

Stopping, smiling up at me, she says, "Wrap your hand in my hair, pull it, shove your cock down my throat. Make me do it."

I'm bewildered, wanting to *make love* to her, to be gentle. . . . Soothe her, not abuse her.

I ask, "Say that again—what do you want me to do?"

"Pull my fuckin' hair, make me yours, spank my ass, then fuck it. Make me scream. Hurt me, Bobbie, put your mark on me. Do it."

"But baby, I don't want to hurt you. Ever."

"Punk, you fuck like a bitch. I want you to use me and bruise me. If I wanted soft kisses, I'd be eatin' pussy right now instead of sucking your dick."

Eyes on fire, breathing like she's just got done running a marathon, cheeks flushed, pupils like saucers. Burning fucking hot. Reaching up, grabbing my hair, pulling so hard that my head snaps to the side, licking the underside of my penis, she says, "Like that. If you can't do it, I will."

Yanking my hair so hard, I can feel the roots tearing out of my scalp, pulling so hard that my face snaps into my other shoulder. I feel my lip split from the impact and now I'm reacting. Blood fills my mouth, tasting like thickened soy sauce, and my body kicks into overdrive.

Ever since I could remember, as soon as someone hurts me, my grasp of reality changes. A roar like an approaching train fills my ears, vision narrows like looking through a tunnel, seeing only whoever's causing me pain, fear so powerful that paralysis sets in for about a half second; then rage sweeping through me like a flash flood, driving everything before it like a matchstick hit by hundreds of tons of rushing water, leaving only bloodlust in its wake.

Madness comes on with the force of gravity and I can feel my body slam into action. Methedrine, passion, and rage. Adrenaline and desire drop-kicking any inhibitions into the next dimension.

Grabbing her hand and ripping it out of my hair, my left hand flying through the air like a fucking meteor, slapping her so hard that her eyes cross. Twisting my hand into her hair like I'm trying to tear her head off, asking, "Is this what you want?" Pulling her head back with so much force that her neck is stretched like a rubber band; looking into her eyes, kissing her. Painting her teeth and lips with my blood.

"Yeah baby, mark me. Show me that you own me."

Biting into her nipples, grinding my teeth and tasting her blood mixing with mine. Forcing her body to bend backward like an archer's bow, slamming the first two fingers on my left hand in and out of her, biting, pulling her hair and pistoning my fingers in and out of her. She feels burning hot. I tell her, "I own you, don't I baby? How much of you is mine?"

"All of me. Spank me, stick your cock everywhere I've got a hole—it's all yours, mijo, take it."

I do, rolling her onto her stomach, starting to spank her lightly. Each slap gets harder, Rosie groaning and grinding her pelvis into the mattress. Yelling at me, "Harder, baby, bruise me, make me come, do it harder."

Then I'm hitting her as hard as I can; each time my open palm whistles through the air, the impact sounds like an axe cutting into a tree; I'm wondering why anyone would like getting hurt, but loving the adrenaline rush it produces. Palm stinging, feeling like electricity is running through it, Rosie's ass glowing red, my fingers outlined on her flesh, taking my fingers out of her vagina and working them slowly into her ass, stretching it open; and when they slide easily in and out of her, positioning my prick over her rear, feeling the resistance as I push slowly inside of her, fucking her slowly, building up to as hard and as fast as I can, grinding into her. And her screaming, "Yes, yes it's all yours, come in me, your dick is mine, give me your come! Now, Bobbie, *now!*"

Pulling my cock out of her and telling her, "No, mija, you want it, first ya gotta suck it. Then ya gotta beg."

Rosie had taught me a new game, one that plugged into my adrenaline habit and one that, even then, I knew had the potential to consume me. A game that left me feeling elated and disgusted, saddened by my own enjoyment. It was an educational evening.

. . . .

The phone rings at noon. It's Mel. He's got that faraway sound in his voice, barely in this dimension, functioning only to survive. Reality is far away but unignorable, a monster waiting to consume us all, demanding constant small sacrifices to stall its inevitable consumption of my soul.

"Bobbie?"

"Yeah, man?"

"You guys wanna come over?"

"Now?"

"It's business."

"It'll take a couple minutes, gotta get dressed."

"Cool."

Rosie is tied to the bed, spread-eagled. We've been pushing her pain threshold as far as I'm willing to go, stopping just short of broken bones. I found that by bringing her to the brink of climax and then starting my baby Marquis de Sade routine, the results are wonderful.

As impressive as a major earthquake, as breathtaking as a hurricane. Bringing another human being from mind-rending agony to convulsive ecstasy *creates the illusion* of incredible power.

Leaning over her, stroking her face, I look at her and think we really are a perfect pair, know instinctively that we are two sides of the same coin. The abuse I'd gotten as a child made me punish the world. Rosie's made her demand that she be punished. I kiss her, not saying a word, and untie the torn sheets she is bound in. I ask, "Didja like that? Do you feel like you're my girl now?"

"Almost, baby. You worked on me for hours. As much as I like what you do to me, what's better is that you paid attention to me that long, you didn't just get your rocks off and leave me—you worked as hard to make me feel good as I worked on you, harder maybe. It's nice that you still kiss me. I told you things that I never tell anybody, and when I'm with you I feel safe; so, yeah, I liked that, I liked it a lot. I want to feel like I'm your girl, but I'm so scared of getting my feelings hurt. . . . Do you know what I mean, Bobbie?"

I know that knee-buckling, eye-popping, bone-crushing fear better than I know how to breathe; people like us seem to need love so desperately, but at the same time, we find it as terrifying as brain cancer. I watch the faraway lightning flicker behind her eyes, pulsing fire behind golden brown glass. More than knowing . . . understanding, from my toes to my nose. I say, "Yeah, baby. I think I know what ya mean. Let's try not to hurt each other. Get dressed, gorgeous."

"OK, blue eyes. They're not gonna try to make us eat, are they?"

"Shit, mija, I hope not. I'm sure they're wired too, though."

The hotel room's a shambles, but as far as I'm concerned I've entered paradise. Done a big score by anybody's standards, living in the Lynch House—one of the nicest hotels in Chi Town—going to get better at my chosen profession, and, after last night, feeling incredibly studly.

I say, "So do ya still think that I fuck like a broad?" I feel the smirk hit my face, as proud of myself as a young rooster; if I had wings they'd be flapping, as I crow my pride and virtuoso performance at the sky.

Rosie's got her maniac smile in place, standing hipshot, looking like an evil elf—trouble personified—the happiest I've ever seen her. She says, "Wellll, ya can't hit very hard, but you're willing to try. You're definitely off 'broad' status. . . . Who knows, baby? With a little more practice, ya got the potential to be pretty good."

So much for male ego. I say, "I'll work at it. Let's go see the senior citizens."

. . . .

The room smells of cigarette smoke, sex, and sweat. The TV is on, with the noise turned off. Mel's seated on the couch; on the other end is a guy that's so thin his bones are cutting through the skin on his face—almost an albino, hair and skin fish-belly white, eyes a reddish brown, looking like flawed rubies in a field of cancerous snow. Spread on the table are a variety of guns—revolvers, automatics, shotguns . . . all with a nicely evil shine.

Mel says, "Have a seat, Bobbie. This is Reverend James Cook. Reverend, this is young Bob, who we need to outfit. What would you suggest?"

The reverend looks me up and down like he's inspecting a horse. He says, "Whatcha weigh boy—one thirty, thirty-five? That's tops, am I right?"

He's got some kind of Southern accent, nothing soft or lilting about it. His voice is nasal and very hard. He spits his words out like malformed bullets, his lips barely moving. The Reverend Cook feels like bad news waiting to be delivered.

"Yeah, why?"

He sticks his hand out, saying, "Grab it boy—let's see what kinda grip y'all got."

I look at Mel to see if this dude strikes him as wrong as he strikes me, and realize Mel's doing a new routine, kinda like a solemn bear. I decide to go along and see what develops.

I say, "Sure, Reverend," grabbing his hand to shake it.

"No boy, I don't *shake* hands. Don'tchoo know that you must trust only in *the man upstairs?* Shaking hands implies trust, and since all men are sinners and snakes, shaking hands is bullshit. I don't lie.

"*Grab* it—I wanna see what kind grip ya got, not *shake* your fucking hand."

This guy's more than wrong—he's got venom coursing through him instead of blood.

I say, "OK," and put my best grip on his hand, feeling hinky about touching this dude, like maybe whatever he's got might be contagious.

He holds my mitt up to his face like a reverse fortune-teller and examines it. His hand feels like a piece of stone. Calluses run across the back of his knuckles, between his thumb and index finger. I start to pull my hand away and with no apparent effort, he squeezes so hard it feels like the bones in my hand are gonna be crushed into dust. Then he releases me.

"Mel here is a good man . . . for a sinning snake. One of the most honorable I've ever met, as far as man can be good—if'n he's schoolin' y'all, you're a lucky boy. For a man to survive in this world, he's gotta do what he's gotta do. If that means transacting business at gunpoint, so be it, 'cause the good Lord knows he's good at it."

He leans forward, his eyes seeming to light from within, madness flickering inside of muddy rubies, cheeks flushing. He starts to rock back and forth, his speech taking on a rhythm from somewhere that never saw city lights.

"Someday I hope that he'll accept the Lord Jesus as his savior, assure his entrance into heaven; but he's still a better man than many that have been baptized in the blood of the lamb. It's an awful world we live in, boy. Full of deceit and treachery. We must always be prepared for Judgment Day."

I look at Mel for some kind of guidance on how to deal with this guy. Fuckin' scary-looking, Billy-Graham-on-bad-acid-sounding, red-eyed, motherfucking, Bible-toting, gun-selling nut. Mel's still doing the solemn bear routine, fingers steepled under his chin, a look indicating deep thought on his face, his Rolex and diamond pinkie ring shining on his left wrist and hand.

Mel says, "I'm going to take the two Charter Arms pugs and the 12-gauge pump; I'll need shoulder holsters for the .44s and the gauge cut down—ammo for all of 'em."

Dragging his fingers through his hair, then shaking his head back and forth, he says, "Excuse me Sydney. What do you want?"

Syd and Rosie are in front of the TV, smoking cigarettes and whispering. Syd gets up and saunters over. She's barefoot, wearing a floral dress, and stands hip-sprung, looking down at the hardware all over the coffee cable.

She says, "I really like this sawed-off over and under 16-gauge." She picks up a double-barrel shotgun with the barrels cut down to about a foot and the grip modified into a pistol handle.

"What else would you recommend, Reverend Cook? Aside from saving my soul."

He bends forward, picks a small revolver off the table, and says, "Thirty-eight Smith & Wesson Chiefs Special—compact, plenty of stopping power, get the hammer filed down, sight it in, use dumdums or hollow points . . . only drawback is, it's like the pugs—it only holds five rounds. But once it's modified, it'll be combat ready and accurate up to about fifty feet. That over and under will clear a room—hit both barrels and it's like a shaped-charge bomb, no accuracy, but everything in front of you is gonna get shredded."

"For the boy, I'd say go with this," picking up a small automatic, "Colt Mustang 380: six in the clip, one in the chamber. Gives ya seven shots." Hands it to me and says, "See how it feels—you got small hands and not a whole lot of muscle; it's a small piece, not much recoil. Get it machined, ported, and combat sighted, and you got a good accurate pistol—use dumdums and you got plenty of stopping power. John Dillinger favored the same gun. It's a nice piece boy. Mel and Syd know how to shoot, sure as shit they're gonna teach ya. The gun should be like an extension of your hand; a little bit of practice, you shouldn't have to aim: point your hand at what you want to hit and it'll have holes in it. How's it feel boy?"

Having grown up state-raised, where, if you don't demand respect you don't get it, scared of this obvious madman but more terrified of allowing anyone to belittle me, I respond, "It feels great Rev, fits right into my hand. You call me 'boy' one more time, you and I are gonna have real problems, know what I mean, pal?"

"Son, I'll keep that in mind. I gotta tell ya, it's always a good idea to know what you're dealing with. You fuck with me it's like swimmin' in the Mississippi with bricks in yore pockets—it could get plumb tiring, don'tcha know. But you—Mel's schoolin' ya, so what I'm gonna do is pray for ya, ask the good Lord to give ya more common sense than the rest of the younguns I generally meet. Matter fact son, I'm sincerely sorry if I hurt your feelins and I won't 'boy' ya ever again. Promise."

One side of this freak's face is all squished up. Head vibrating. Neck starting to swell. Lips moving but not saying a word. I'm thinking that if I have to, I can kick him in the face before he can get to his feet. Mumbling to himself and suddenly looking like a little kid that got slapped, Reverend Cook says, "Sheeit son, look at y'all. Got so much pride you ready to climb right up the old reverend's chest."

Starting to rock again, voice rising in pitch, got that weird singsong rhythm going, and says, "Now pride's a sin I know about myownself—ya might think about talkin' to me about salvation 'stead of gettin' in an uproar. Scared and hostile, taking umbrage over mere words. . . . I'm sincerely sorry if I hurt your feelings. Have you met the Lord Jeeeeeesus? He can set you free. Take all that hate right out of you."

Saying all this so sincerely it makes me feel like I've abused him—and maybe I have. Overreacting is something I still struggle with. I mumble, "That's OK, man. Thanks for being concerned. So what's a dumdum?"

He smiles without showing any teeth, says, "Dumdums became popular during the First World War; then they were found to be too effective, and banned in most so-called civilized countries. You carve an X into the end of your bullet, the initial explosion causes it to mushroom out into a flying cross. When it hits its target, it explodes like a small bomb. Blows a hole in a man big enough to throw a cat through. Let me ask you, son, how the fuck do you shoot someone in a civilized manner?"

"Somehow Rev, I don't think that's possible."

"It's not son, it's not. If you shoot them, you want them to die as quickly as possible; there's nothing worse than putting a couple into some slimeball and have him still shooting back at ya. A dumdum in the chest and that's it. Conversation is over. The recipient is on their way to meet their Maker."

Eyes starting to bulge, here comes the singsong voice. The word "schizophrenia" pops into my head, not sure what it is, but knowing that James Cook seems to have it.

"Go to ongoing bliss with God, or burn in the fiery lakes of hell. That's why I want y'all to get saved. In your line of work, people will want to shoot you on occasion, and I'd rest better knowing I'd done something more than give ya some firepower."

Mel drops his hands from under his chin and stretches, his bones cracking audibly. He says, "Reverend Cook, you know we respect your beliefs and appreciate your concern, but you ain't gonna save any souls today. However, we do want the hardware. What will it cost? Guns, modifications, ammo, everything."

Feeling like I'd earned some respect, confident enough to make a request, I say, "How about Rosie? I want her to have a piece, be able to protect herself. Ya know, there's a lot of assholes around."

Sydney is nodding in agreement and says, "Ain't that the truth. A girl can't go out on the street without getting fucked with."

The reverend says, "Exactly. Animals everywhere. Armageddon is coming. If all womenfolk carried guns, these sexual degenerates wouldn't even think about rape. Men would be much more polite, not make lewd comments. Treat the gentler sex with the respect that the good Lord intended.

"Two thousand five hundred for the package, and I'll throw in a pearl handle .32 for this young lady. Fair enough, Mel, my unsaved friend?"

"One day for the modifications?"

"Three to do 'em right. Two if you want them less than perfect."

"Yes sir, Reverend Cook, may as well make 'em right. Thanks boss. What's Bobbie's end for the 380 and .32?"

"Three-eighty machined, milled, and ported, with combat sights, two fifty-round boxes of ammo, and a holster. Thirty-two revolver balanced, hammer filed, sighted in, with ammo, figure six hundred, and I'll dumdum the bullets for free.

"You're getting two Charter Arms, pug .44 caliber five-shot revolvers, combat ready with opposing breakaway shoulder holsters; one .38 S&W Chiefs Special, five-shot; filed, sighted, etcetera; Remington 12-gauge sawed-off, pistol grips on the handle and the pump; and the over under sawed-off 16 that's ready now. Ammo for all of it. Your end is nineteen hundred twenty-five total . . . I prefer hundred-dollar bills. See ya in three days. God bless you all."

Mel closes the door behind him and comes back to the couch, sitting down and rubbing his face so hard, it looks like he's trying to make his brains pop out of his ears. He says, "He gave us a good deal. For the same shit, normal black market would be about four g's. He's one of the best gunsmiths alive.

"You gotta learn to watch your mouth, Bobbie; telling that dude that he and you are gonna have serious problems was about the stupidest thing I've ever heard. The reverend is a bona fide killer. He looks like a skinny freak, right? He's packed twenty-four seven—goes to sleep with a gun in his hand. Wakes up and shoves it in a custom holster he wears at the middle of his back. Can make it appear in his hand like magic, and, if it comes out, someone's gonna die."

"Yikes. Shit man, what was I supposed to do? Motherfucker was callin' me 'boy' at the end of every sentence."

"You coulda been more diplomatic, ace; and then callin him 'Rev' was disrespecting him. He takes that shit real serious, but he let ya slide. Handling that cat's like playing with nitroglycerine—he's a heavy guy. Didja notice his hands?"

"Yeah, they were all fucked up, had calluses all over his knuckles and shit. What's wrong with 'em?"

"What's wrong with them is he uses a sack of concrete as a heavy bag. Breaks bricks with 'em up close. They're just like gettin' hit with an axe. I saw him beat two big old motherfuckers to death—we're talkin' *heavyweights* here. Drunken, inbred, homicidal, crazy, redneck, cockstrong motherfuckers—two-fifty, two-sixty each.

"Me, the reverend, a couple other guys are at this truck stop down in the Carolinas, waiting on a semi full of military ordnance that just got off-loaded at one of those little ports they got there.

"These two drunks are taking turns slappin' and kicking some little chick—couldn't've weighed more'n one-twenty, little redheaded girl. Butt-ugly little thing.

"Don't none of us want to bust a grape, 'cause we got a couple tons of automatic weapons being delivered. Anyhow, after about a minute of watchin' this shit, the rev says, 'That's it. God, thy will, not mine, be done,' and jumps into the mix. He's trying to talk to these two, but they keep getting louder and louder. His face gets all scrunched up, like it did just now. He starts shaking like he shot too much coke, praying like a motherfucker.

"One of these assholes tries to throw a punch past the rev's head, to hit this little broad, and he grabs the dude's hand out of the air, don't even miss a word in the talkin'-in-tongues prayin' shit he's doing, and this cat's partner blindsides him.

"Shit, Bobbie, that was all she wrote. When I say he beat 'em to death, that's what I mean. Crushed their fucking skulls. It looked like they got sledgehammered—eyes knocked out, brains all over the cement.

"What I'm saying to ya Bobbie is that most of the people I deal with come with a serious pedigree. I'm willing to take ya under my wing, but ya gotta cool out."

"Yeah, man. I'm learning. Just let me know what time it is, and I'll act accordingly."

"If you're selling drugs, you need firepower, 'cause most of your customers are scumbags. With pieces of shit off the street, your tough-guy routine might work; with people I introduce ya to, serious guys like the reverend, ya gotta show some respect and they'll do the same. OK?"

Mel starts laughing. Tears coming to his eyes, he asks, "Bobbie, when he started mumbling, face puffin' up like a blowfish, wadja think he was doin'?"

"Don't know man, pretty fuckin' weird, though."

"He was praying not to kill your little ass. He did the same thing with those two big old boys he beat to death, except that one tried to sucker punch him in midprayer. . . . Guess ya could call that an error in judgment, huh?

"Syd's gonna start settin' up the customers. We gotta get a second base of operations to have the score in. We went through the inventory—we should end up clearing at least sixty grand, a lot more if we don't have to cut our prices. A long way from vending machines, huh, kid?"

*T*he sign reads ABE'S INN. The place is a series of pink-and-turquoise bungalows.

We get two adjoining rooms at the back of the court; they're cockroach farms, furnished in Early Desperation. We store the dope in one, dope the store out of the other.

I'd expected shooting lessons when the guns were dropped off. Mel had solemnly assured Reverend Cook that he'd teach me to shoot, go over single-hand versus two-hand combat stance. This was great, real John Wayne shit, something that excited me as much as learning how to crack a safe.

What I get is a three-day crash course in small business administration, basic sales techniques, an explanation of Murphy's Law, a thorough ass beating, and a haircut.

. . . .

The maître d' seats us. He has a French accent, carnation in his buttonhole, and does an excellent job of ass kissing. I like him immensely.

I sip at my coffee, watching my eggs Benedict congeal. The Rolex feels heavy, sliding around on my wrist (Rosie'd explained what a Rolex was). Wearing a watch feels weird—wearing one that's worth a few grand makes me feel like a pit bull wearing a cashmere sweater and booties—very bizarre.

The pistol stuck in my back pocket feels awkward, dragging my jeans down on one side. Got my wallet over the piece so the outline won't show through the pocket; feels like one side of my ass is riding two inches higher off the seat than the other. Eventually, I'll come to feel naked without a gun's weight somewhere on me, but my first few

FIVE

✦✦✦✦✦✦✦✦✦✦✦✦✦✦✦✦✦✦✦✦✦✦✦✦✦✦✦✦✦✦

days packed, it feels really cumbersome. I try to consume some food and have trouble getting it down past the speed.

Mel is wearing slacks and a beige sport coat, white shirt open at the collar. Syd is in all white—white dress, white shoes, and a little white cap, hair brushed over to one side. Rosie is wearing a tiny black dress and the catch-me-fuck-me pumps we got her the other day. I'm in a T-shirt, jeans, and combat boots. Hair down past my shoulders feels thick and heavy and I like it, looking like I don't belong where I am at all, but still getting the VIP treatment. Life is grand.

Rosie is rubbing my leg under the table, hair swept back, staring at her eggs Benedict like it is a plate full of shit covered with puke instead of eggs covered with hollandaise; she looks at me, raises one side of her lip in a sneer, bugs her eyes out, and says, "Mmm-mmm good. Crank and chicken embryos, breakfast of champions."

Mel takes a hit off his orange juice, holds the glass up, raises one eyebrow, and says, "Cheers big ears." He looks around the table and continues, "Top of the morning, ladies and gentlemen."

Syd adjusts her cap and says, "Hey, baby, mazel tov. Morning kids."

Rosie and I look at each other and both say, "Uh-huh, morning."

Mel looks at Syd and says, "Remember when I took those guys from New York down for all that coke?"

"Yeah, the time you got completely psychotic, thought ya had bugs under your skin, thought Martians were beaming ya messages, hid in the closet for two days with enough hardware to start World War Three. Is that the time ya mean, bubeleh?"

"Yeah, that's the time."

Mel's on his second large OJ, slowly but surely consuming all his eggs Benedict. He points at me with his fork, yellow yolk drippin' off the tines, finishes chewing the mouthful he's working on, picks his napkin out of his lap, wipes his mouth, and says, "Pay attention, guys—there's a moral to this story. What else happened on that little run, Syd?"

"Not much, except for the part where ya came down with hep, turned so yellow ya looked like a big fat walkin' banana—or the part where ya lost sixty pounds in two weeks, got down to a svelte two-fifty, almost died."

Syd's smiling, pretty blue eyes got a question floating around behind them; she's watching Mel to see where he's going with this. She pauses, takes a bite of her eggs, and continues, "Or, possibly the part where ya decided the FBI, CIA, and the mob had you surrounded, and flushed eight kilos of grade-A cola down the toilet—or could it be my personal favorite, where the transmissions being beamed into your thick skull told ya that all the dough we'd worked so hard to clip along with the coke was marked and ya had to burn it? Ya got egg on your nose baby."

"Yep, those are the very things to which I was referring. Every one of them caused by sleep deprivation and malnutrition, possibly cocaine poisoning.

"You two might be wondering why I bring this up? Because if we're gonna make this work, A: you gotta sleep every fucking night or you're gonna start losing it and cause us all problems—so, starting tonight, when we wrap up for the day, it don't matter how good ya feel, how fuckin' wired you guys are, you take enough downs to knock ya out—amphetamine psychosis is not attractive. B: same thing with calories—force food down. We're gonna eat three times a day, take vitamins and all that shit, stay as healthy as we can. . . . It's like that joke: 'so far so gooood.' We ain't in any hurry to hit the pavement."

I hear what he's saying. The thing I want most in life is to be a pro, not that my ambitions are based on reality. Through whatever set of conditions that attracts most kids to sports or math or history, what I want is to be a thief.

Not a lowball thief, but a real class act, something that is based on my dreams and illusions, based on the concept that there are such things as real stand-up guys that beat the odds and never have to compromise, that maybe life could have a happy ending.

The amount of energy I put into learning my craft would have gotten me through med and law schools; the work I put into my body over the years would have produced a world-class athlete under different circumstances.

Mel is my mentor. Not only a serious outlaw, but a dope fiend who seems to have it under control. It appears to be the best of all possible worlds. The idea of trying to live drug free is as attractive as ramming a red-hot poker into my eye; whatever's required to succeed at this field of endeavor is acceptable.

The one thing I'm aware of is how ignorant I am, how much I have to learn. I cut a chunk off my eggs Benedict, smelling the rich aroma of the hollandaise. I say, "I guess I need to gain some weight, anyhow," and start chewing.

. . . .

Mel and I are sitting in the living room of the cockroach palace. The rug's got grooves cut in it from thousands of shuffling feet making the same journey: couch to barely functioning TV and back, couch to fold-out bed, couch to toilet.

A gilt mirror, speckled with dead flies, and an oil painting of the two ugliest children in the world complete the room's furnishings. There are cobwebs in the corners, extending from the overhead sixty-watt bulb to the urine-colored ceiling; the kitchen is so greasy that walking on the cracked linoleum feels like ice-skating.

Syd and Rosie are next door. As customers show up, me and Mel ascertain if they have the cash, and Syd or Rosie brings the drugs over. All the sales for the day are scheduled the night before. A one-day supply is brought from the garage each morning. This is what Syd called "risk management."

The television is crackling, voices badly distorted. I'm perched on the edge of the couch; to lean back is to have broken springs stab you. Mel's folded into the couch, immune to small stab wounds. We've both just slammed some heroin.

We're smoking cigarettes, and I ask Mel, "When are ya gonna teach me how to shoot?"

"Right now, ace." Mel stops to scratch and then continues, voice gravelly from the smack, blue eyes so pinned and glassy that they looked like marbles. "Grab 'em with your left hand, shove the piece into the guy's chest with your right, pull the trigger till it's empty. Guaranteed they'll leave ya alone."

"Cut the shit big-time. For real, I wanna learn how to shoot."

"I'll teach ya how to aim and all that shit, but most gunfights take place with the shooters within feet of each other."

"So what about what the rev said?"

"What about it? All that stuff is good to know, but what matters is who fills their hand first, and makin' sure ya hit who you're shooting at. Stick the piece into 'em and ya don't got to worry. Like the rev says, 'End of conversation.'"

Barry and Phil, our first clients, show up, little skinny guys with pointy shoulders, matching hair—very long and not quite groomed—overly hip college guys with glaring tudes. Getting everything paid for by mommy and daddy, think this shit is cool, a great story to tell back on campus. They want five thousand Biphetamine capsules at sixty cents each. Phil starts weaseling immediately.

"How's fifty cents each?"

Mel laughs and says, "No way, pal—sixty or we don't do business. Black beauties are selling two, three bucks each."

Phil sneers, saying, "Don't be a weenie—twenty-five hundred, cash money, right now."

"I been called a lot of things, but never a fuckin' 'weenie.' Sixty cents or get the fuck out of here."

Mel leans forward and pulls both .44 pugs at once. He has a pistol in each hand, looking like he'd like nothing better than to blow chunks out of the college kids. He says, "Give my partner the dough to count. If ya got it all, you get the black beauties and you're out of here. If you came short, we're just gonna take it."

I count the cash—thirty one-hundred-dollar bills—and say, "Yep, three g's." I pick up the black rotary phone to call next door and say, "Five thousand Biphetamines."

Syd drops 'em off, ten bottles of five hundred each, inside a brown paper bag. Mel sets 'em on the coffee table that's all dinged and scarred up. The college guys look the bottles over. Syd's leaning on the wall, waiting for them to leave; Mel's practicing his fast draw and is pretty fucking impressive. As soon as they're out the door, Syd's turning red, saying, "Melvin, you fuckin' putz, schmuck, motherfuckin' moron . . . what's with the Fast-Draw McGraw bullshit—scared those kids to fuckin' death."

"Shit darlin', he called me a 'weenie'—guy's gotta defend his honor. Ask Bobbie, he'll tell ya—fuckin' Phil had me scared to death. Huh, Bobbie?" Mel's got his aw-shucks grin on, starting to blush. Imagine King Kong blushing and ya got what Mel looked like at that minute.

I don't know that he was fucking around till now; I think that pulling your gun is a normal part of negotiations: someone tries to chisel you on price, just stick your piece in their face, get their head right. I finally figure it out and say, "Absolutely, Syd. Motherfucker called Mel a 'weenie,' he had to throw down on him."

Syd's shaking her head, mad at both of us, saying, "*Oy* fucking *vey*—a thirty-five-year-old who acts like he's three and a teenager who acts like a twenty-five-year-old asshole. . . . What did I do to deserve you guys? Maybe I was Adolf in my last life and youse two are here to punish me."

Mel stands up. This is a small place—he seems to fill half the room. Shuffling his feet, he says, "Come on Syd, I'll be good. I promise."

Sydney looks at her watch. She says, "Our next client is due in twenty minutes—think you two can handle it, or should me and Rosie come over to run the show?"

As the door closes behind Syd, Mel starts laughing so hard it looks like he's going into convulsions—doubling up, falling onto the piece-of-shit couch, all that weight hitting at once breaking one leg off it—tears running down his face, gasping out, "'Weenie, don't be a weenie,' didja see the look on their faces? O my God, called me a 'weenie.'"

I'm standing, staring down at Mel, who's still in hysterics, and I say, "You really do have a weird motherfucking sense of humor."

It *is* pretty funny. I start to laugh. Once you adapt to his crazy shtick, he's a funny guy.

We're still chuckling as the next buyers come in.

. . . .

The air is on high, guns lying all over the room at the Lynch House. Glad to be home, or as close to it as I have come. It's the night of the second day running a store, and piled on the bed is this monstrous stack of cash, mainly fifties and hundreds, a few grand in twenties. . . . That much cash has a smell of its own—ink and sweat and paper, one of my favorite smells in the world.

Room service has come and gone, turf and surf all around, buckets of champagne. We've counted the money, stacked it, and banded it up; the pile looked much more impressive, but it's still a healthy stack of cash. We've all been slamming meth and heroin speedballs, me and Mel having shoot-outs, seeing who can do the biggest slam without going into convulsions. A very intense way to do male bonding.

Neither of us dies, but we both hit the floor doing the tuna. Syd and Rosie finally nut up, make us stop. As we're finishing up for the night, Syd says, "We're at forty-two thousand and change; we been getting top wholesale. With current inventory, and no price reductions, we can clear about another forty to forty-five. The allowances we made so we could dump fast haven't been necessary so far—I figure we should end up close to eighty ahead, not bad for three weeks' work."

Taking a fistful of tuinols each, we say our good-nights.

. . . .

Back at cockroach central, we get some dead time between clients. Syd and Rosie have gone shopping, a skill that Rosie is developing with frightening speed.

Mel and I are drinking beers, holding down the fort, sitting at the kitchen table—beers, two syringes, and a burnt spoon as place settings, Mel's 12-gauge the centerpiece.

It's oppressively hot. The room has that dead-rodent odor. It's a funny thing—a little smack, a couple beers, and cockroach central doesn't seem that bad, the smell of rotting rat wafting through the air no big deal.

Mel says, "These next guys bother me. They call themselves Hitler's Henchmen, kinda like a bike gang that don't require bikes. . . . They're into running broads, sellin' and making speed. . . . Syd don't want to deal with 'em at all, but they want so much volume, I don't give a fuck what they call themselves, as long as they got the dough."

"How come Syd don't want to sell to 'em?"

"Sydney has relatives that got concentration camp numbers tattooed on 'em, a bunch more that ended up as soap. Guys that call themselves Hitler's Henchmen aren't real high on her list of humanity."

"Shit man, can't blame her. Did you lose some people over there too?"

"Yeah, my dad—not to a camp—U.S. Marines, died a hero, 1943, fighting in Europe. His best friend was a redneck, a hope-to-die peckerwood from Georgia, Joshua Jennings. Josh adopted me when he got back. My mom tried to fly two days after she got news of my dad's death—jumped out a window twenty stories high. She died instantly, or so they said."

"Yikes."

"So, anyhow, from the time I was three, I was the only Jew I knew till I got into college. I grew up in this little town, had nothin' but peckerwoods and niggers and they usta take turns pickin' on me."

"Shit big-time, somehow I can't see too many people picking on you."

"Oh, yeah. Till I turned twelve I was just a big fat kid, scared of my own shadow. Old Josh would be dealing with my shit at least once a week, talking to kids' parents, all that kinda crap."

"So, what happened? You're a little overweight, but I can't see nobody just coming out of nowhere and being mean to ya."

Mel pauses, scratches his head. He says, "Wellll, on my twelfth birthday, I got beat up real bad. Back then, white folks stuck together, didn't perceive themselves as victims like they do now. It was fucked up—I was fair game for everybody. These three black kids beat the shit out of me and I was so mad I was crying. The local woods weren't gonna bust a grape, 'cause I was a Jew."

"I don't get it—you're white—what difference would it make what ya believe? They shoulda backed ya up."

"Do ya wanna hear this or not? Being a Jew is like being an Aryan: there ain't no such thing, genetically speaking. My people were from eastern Europe; get technical, the Jews are the tribes of Israel, which ain't nowhere near Europe. Everybody's got cut in them. Check it out, want to hear something bizarre?"

"Sure man, bizarre is my favorite sort of shit."

"You see that movie *Butch Cassidy and the Sundance Kid*?"

"Yeah, it was great."

"Two Jewish guys."

Keep in mind that I'm real young and not too bright; I bite better than Mel could've hoped for. I feel my jaw drop, ask. "Butch and Sundance?"

"Yeah, them and Billy the kidstein." He starts laughing. "No, schmuck, the actors Newman and Redford, two nice Jewish boys who look like storm troopers. I guess it's a frame of mind. That's one of the reasons I'm so nuts about Syd—she's teaching me how to do it. Be Jewish and a redneck gangster at the same time. It's a tough combination.

"I very rarely talk about this shit, but your gee-whillikers routine is so good I feel impelled, so if ya want to hear this, just listen, if not, fuck it."

I light a cigarette, tell Mel, "I'm waiting."

"So, anyhow, old Josh sat me down, gave me a Coca-Cola, told me that my daddy was the toughest man in the U.S. Marines, told me I had to be proud of myself 'cause if I wasn't, no one else would be.

"Told me he was sorry that he couldn't do a better job of teachin' me what my background was, told me that my mom loved my dad so much that she couldn't live without him, that he and Mrs. Jennings loved me like their own, told me the reason they hadn't changed my name to Jennings was out of respect to my folks and so I'd know who I came from. I gotta tell ya, ace, that little talk changed my life."

Mel leans forward, table creaking from the sudden increase in weight; I have the feeling he's talking as much to himself as to me. He has an introspective look on his face, voice coming out real soft.

"See, it probably don't sound like much, but that shit was real important to me. I guess everybody needs an identity—till then I was kinda lost. I looked like any other white guy, but 'cause my name ended in 'stein,' they thought I was different, treated me different, till I'd beaten the shit out of everybody that even looked at me cross-eyed.

"It's a strange thing, but when people know that you don't mind fuckin' 'em up, kinda enjoy it even, they change their attitude right quick. All the good ol' boys started calling me 'wood.' 'What's up, wood?' 'How's it hanging, wood?' which with those guys is a term of affection and respect. Fucking weird.

"Anyhow, Josh took me out back and started teaching me how to fight. He got me a heavy bag, taught me how to jab and hook, showed me what a head butt was, how to hit with your palm instead of your fist, how to use your elbows and knees. . . . That Monday we went to the school and got me in wrestling class; I started lifting weights every day, got strong as a bull. . . . By my sophomore year in high school, I was the toughest kid in the whole school, kicked the shit out of everybody that had ever been mean to me.

"The Jenningses got me into college, and came down to see me graduate my freshman year. A drunk smashed into their car, killed those fine people instantly—or so they say."

Mel pauses, lights a cigarette, thinks for a minute. I'm hanging on every word, getting answers to questions I didn't even know I had. I am a weird kid, always trying to analyze people, and since Mel is my all-time hero, anything he says carries the weight of the Ten Commandments. I'm wanting to hear the rest of the story, but remember the thing about not asking questions. I just sit and wait. Mel blows out a cloud of smoke.

"Vietnam came along, and I went SpecialOps. Being a tough guy is hard work, kid: first ya gotta kill all your fear."

He stops, gets this maniac grin on, and says, "Nah, bullshit, you don't kill it ever. Most of the really dangerous guys I know are scared all the time. That's what makes 'em dangerous. What you do, you make it work for ya, channel it so that you're more scared of being scared than anything else. You have to really want it, maybe it's 'cause most tough guys are scared to death from the gate. But, yeah, in answer to your question I usta get picked on."

I think of the terror I felt as a small child, and the shame I felt for being scared, preferring to get my ass beat to acknowledging my fear. I say, "That's sort of a weird thing—that's the way I grew up. I never heard nobody talk about being scared of being scared before. . . . So Syd really hates these fuckin' bikers, huh?"

"Yeah, but they ain't bikers—they got colors and copy the look, but they ain't bikers. These guys are like neo-Nazi, lightweight hoods, fucking maroons, but their money spends. Fuck it."

"Head butts, all that shit you were talking about—martial arts— whatcha think of 'em?"

"They're good, man, but a gun's better. Check it out, Bobbie. Who's really the tough guy, a guy like me, or a guy like old Josh who went to war and did whatever he had in front of him his whole life and never bitched about nothing. Who's really the stand-up motherfucker?"

I don't have the life experience to respond. I've kept going back to that question through the years. Sometimes I think I know the answer.

· · · · · · ·

Syd and Rosie get back, Syd with an obvious tude, carrying multiple bags of stuff. Mel says, "Grudge shopping, huh?"

Syd's response has all the warmth of liquid nitrogen.

"Whatever. I don't want to have to be in the same room with these cocksuckers—not gonna say hello to 'em, don't even want to see 'em. OK?"

Rosie is on Syd's side; she's giving me mean looks like it's my fault these guys want to pay top dollar for most of the shit we got left, and says to Syd, "Let's go next door. I'll bring the shit over. Come on."

Mel starts cooking a spoonful of junk as soon as they're out of the room, shaking his head and muttering to himself. Three hundred pounds of confusion. I know how he feels. Have no idea what I've done wrong, but can tell I've been dropped into the shit on general principle. Mel's muttering a mile a minute, "Fuckin' broads, yenta, JAP, bitch, doin' the best a motherfucker can. Fuckin' bullshit. Crap."

I say, "Gotta be careful there, ace. You're sounding like the world-famous Reverend Cook, talking in tongues and shit."

Mel smiles. He looks tired and old, the aura of indestructibility slipping for a minute. He says, "Just another fucking day in paradise, kid. Another day in paradise."

· · · · · · ·

Clem and Ty are the names attached to the humans sitting at the table with us. Clem is only a little bit bigger than me. He's got that classic white-trash, lean, hillbilly build, no fat on him at all, washed-out blue eyes, with a thousand-yard stare; no one living in that head that is scared by anything, long ropy muscles knotting under his freckled skin, poorly done jailhouse tattoos on both arms, LOVE tattooed on the knuckles of one hand, HATE on the other.

Ty is at least four hundred pounds—one hundred pounds of sweaty fat on top of three hundred pounds of bone and muscle; got greasy hair down to the middle of his back, shitty shop ink all over his arms, a teardrop under one eye and a swastika on the side of his neck . . . his clothes hang on him like tents. Ty smells like he hasn't showered in a week.

Clem's looking around cockroach central. He lights a cigarette, says, "We do our own cooking, make crystal that's so good it looks like glass. Huh, Ty?"

"Yep, sho yore right, Clem. Sho yore right." Nodding in agreement, fat jiggling like Jell-O with every movement. I wonder if this guy is a Nazi, why he's talking like Superfly; think it's very strange, would love to ask him, "Excuse me but since you're this badass Nazi, how come you talk like a Negro pimp?" I may be lacking in diplomacy, but I'm not stupid—I withhold the question, having the feeling that asking him might have bad results. These two don't look like they have much sense of humor.

Mel is looking at these guys with his coldest stare; he don't give a fuck how good their meth is, and is not impressed by Clem's psychotic eyes or Ty's bulk.

Mel says, "If your crank is so good, how come ya want these chickenshit ups?"

Ty gives Mel a stone mad dog. Ty is a scary motherfucker, four hundred pounds of mean, muddy brown eyes swimming in dirty whites, teeth so rotten they look like Indian corn and his breath smells like rotting meat. If these guys are supposed to represent the master race, Tyrone represents generations of breeding for ugly. Clem might not be a genius, but he's a long way from stupid; he doesn't miss a beat, takes a hit off his smoke and says, "Dead presidents, pal, just like these," and, reaching into his Levi's jacket, brings out a stack of hundreds, flipping through them. He says, "Got two hundred and fifty of these motherfuckers—twenty-five g's. Unfortunately, not everyone likes crank. Some of 'em like pills. Once we get done selling these ups, this twenty-five will turn into a hundred. That's why, big man."

Mel picks the stack up, looks to make sure it ain't a dummy bankroll, and tells me, "Make the call. Get fifty thousand beans."

Clem's doing his impression of charming. This motherfucker thinks he's adorable, cute as a G.I. Joe doll; obviously, generations of inbreeding have had their effect: he's telling nigger jokes. I'm waiting for the explosion when he gets around to Jews. . . .

Just as he's saying, "Ya cut the rope, don't ya get it? Ya cut the fuckin' rope," Rosie hits the door, box of amphetamines held in both hands. Directly behind her is a guy that looks like Conan the Barbarian, six foot five easy, shoulder-length hair, cut off Levi's jacket, muscles on top of muscles, steroids oozing out of his skin. Flanking him is Clem's big brother, much bigger, much more beat-up, nose flattened, a mouth breather, lips hanging open, revealing nothing but gums, front teeth knocked out, probably at the same time his nose got pancaked.

Clem is incredibly fast: before anyone can move, he goes from sitting at the table, leaning back on his chair, completely relaxed, to kneeling on top of the table, grabbing Mel's hair, and shoving a little teeny automatic pistol into Mel's eye. He splits the skin wide open, starting a torrent of blood that has Mel covered in seconds.

He says, "Don't you move motherfucker, don't even breathe hard— shit if you even bleed any faster I'm gonna blow your motherfuckin' eye out the back of your head."

I'm frozen. That half second of fear-inspired paralysis fucks up my being a hero; later on, I realize that even Rambo couldn't've moved fast enough. These guys are good. I've replayed that scene over and over: if I'd pulled my 380 the second I saw the muscle freak behind Rosie, placed it in Clem's ear, taken control of the situation, made everybody lie on the ground while Mel tied 'em up, took their flash roll and then just left them there bound and broke, no one would've got hurt—and I would have ended up looking better than John fucking Wayne. But that's not what happened.

I start to move and Ty hits me so hard I feel myself doing a sideways somersault out of my chair. What he nails me with is an uppercut, four hundred pounds of inbred asshole behind it. It's a bad combination—a guy that big that knows how to hit can really hurt you.

That first shot breaks my jaw and flips me up and out of the chair. I hit the floor on my head, hear and feel my neck pop as my skull slams into the worn carpeting. Then Ty starts doing his twinkle-toes routine, trying to stomp me all the way through the foundation of Abe's Inn. I can't move. I'm knocked out, fucking paralyzed, feeling the air whoosh out of my lungs with the first stomp, skin ripped from my face by the second, distantly cataloging the crackling damage done by five, six, seven, and so on, hearing Rosie start to scream—and get choked off.

Adrenaline is flooding my body, wanting to respond to her terror and being unable to move, being consumed by rage and completely powerless. Conan saying, "Gonna have fun with this spic bitch," and then he must have applied pressure to her throat, 'cause I could hear her wheezing, gasping for breath.

Ty decides that I'm dead or dying, and stops stomping me. I can't move a muscle; my eyes are stuck staring at the floor and the pool of blood that's pouring out of my head. I feel like the biggest piece of shit that ever lived—my girl is getting choked and gonna get raped, my partner has a gun stuck in his eyeball, and all I can do is lie there and bleed. John Wayne would never have let that happen. The mouth-breather says, "The spic came from next door, Clem. Their stash must be right there, with only Fat Man's Jew bitch guarding it."

I know we're set up. If they know about Syd, someone close to us has given them information. I swear that, if I live, I'll kill whoever did it, visualizing rolling up in a wheelchair and emptying a shotgun into them, not knowing who "them" is, but knowing, if I live, they're going to die. I hear the unique sound of handcuffs slamming home, twice.

Moving my eyes and seeing Clem rip a piece of duct tape off its roll and slapping it across Rosie's mouth; feeling my hands and arms, legs and feet start to tingle and realizing that my eyes have moved, knowing that whatever happened is starting to wear off; feeling the piece in my back pocket and knowing that as soon as I can move I'm gonna be using it; starting to feel and hear the blood bubbling in my lungs, and Clem saying, "Me and Ty will stay here. You two go get the cunt and the stash."

Mel says, "Listen boss, ya got the best hand—let the chicks go. Let me get the kid to the hospital. We got fifty g's stashed, I'll give it all to ya."

My body's coming back fast, pain isn't setting in yet, just knowledge that I'm damaged. You never feel the pain for a while. Moving my head, knowing that the rest of me will work, probably not too well, but my body will now do what I tell it to. Looking up I see Conan and his partner headed next door, both holding hoglegs, the big .44 mag revolvers later made famous by Clint Eastwood.

Hearing the whine in Mel's voice, I look at him—he's all scrunched up, old and fat, handcuffed and harmless; I'm thinking that he broke, is gonna start begging and crying, but realize he's getting himself into position and sucking these guys in.

He's flat-out whining now, "Think about it, sir: fifty thousand in cash—plus the rest of our drugs—and I'll sign my Cad over to ya." I'm critiquing his performance mentally and decide that 'sir' was a little bit too much; but the guy is a talent—one of the scariest people I've ever met is making himself appear fat, old, and helpless.

Now he's not only standing, he's working his way around the table; I can't figure out what he's gonna do. He's got his hands cuffed behind him and Clem has still got his little automatic aimed at him, and Mel says, "What ya think, boss?"

Clem scratches his chin with his free hand and says, "I think about the time we've pulled all your teeth out and made ya suck Ty's dick, you'll tell us where ya got your money anyhow . . . and we got better things to do with your subhuman tramps than let em go. Say Melvin, do ya know how to get one hundred Jews into a Mercedes-Benz?"

Mel's edging closer, says, "In the ashtray, hahahoho. I guess your guys should be meeting Syd right about now."

Mel gets off a roundhouse kick that smashes into Clem's head; the impact from the kick is louder than the one shot Clem manages to get off; the shot knocks Mel back about two inches but doesn't interfere with the second kick that catches Clem in the throat, sending him flying through the air like a rag doll, face smashed in, bleeding from the mouth and nose from the first kick.

I'm struggling to get to my feet, making it to my hands and knees and buckling to the floor like my limbs are made of rubber. Ty's charging across the room like a fucking enraged rhino, right arm drawn back to deliver a killing punch, and Mel kicks him repeatedly, knocking him back, but not down. Ty starts grappling, face already bleeding, and Mel head-butts him, smashing his nose flat. He sweeps his knee around and pounds it into Ty's side. Ty's throwing roundhouse punches, each one sounding like a baseball bat thunking into a melon, when the roar of a shotgun explodes next door. Ty looks at the noise and Mel does what I would know later as a spinning roundhouse kick; it takes him up into the air, sending the side of his foot crashing into Ty's face. Droplets of blood fly everywhere.

I'm halfway to my feet when there's a pistol shot next door; about a two second pause, then four more so fast it sounds like an automatic weapon.

Clem is now standing, feet planted wide, his back to me, pistol held in two hands. My adrenaline is pumping so hard it feels like I'm having an out-of-body experience; I remember thinking that Clem must be using the two-handed combat grip the reverend was talking about and that it looks pretty cool, when he shoots Mel. The first shot hits him in the lower back, the second about three inches above it.

Clem is screaming, "How you like me now motherfucker!"

He shoots Mel again.

"How ya like me now!"

I'm on my feet, wavering back and forth, my jaw is shattered, mouth hanging open, lurching up behind Clem, placing the muzzle of my gun against the back of his head, trying to yell "freeze" like the cops are supposed to, but never do. All that comes out is a loud noise—when your jaw is broke bad, you can't form words. Mel's falling to the floor, hands cuffed behind him, knees buckling, and swearing all the way down.

Ty screams, "Behind ya Clem!"

All this in slow motion. Clem's pale blue eyes rolling to look at me, he's starting to turn, and I know I've blown it. I don't want to shoot him and it shows on my face, my fear as obvious as a neon sign, his thousand-yard stare, washed-out, don't-give-a-fuck blue eyes have spotted it. He's smiling as he starts to bring his gun around. I know that I'm a dead guy.

I pull the trigger. The first shot knocks him forward two steps, sending blood and brains flying across the room. The second shot catches him under the ear, throwing him off his feet, the dumdums vaporizing most of his face.

Ty's jumping over Mel's body, coming right at me, no fear. This motherfucker intends to finish the job he started with his bare hands.

My first shot misses. The second hits him in his enormous belly, slowing him, but he's still coming like a freight train. The next two hit him in the chest, making blood roses blossom when they hit, and he's on top of me, choking me with one hand and punching me with the other, his face contorted, rotted meat smell pouring out of his mouth.

I shove the 380 under his chin, feel the barrel and sights scrape against the whiskers under his jawline as the end of the gun makes a dimple in his double chin. I'm thinking this cocksucker is bulletproof, I'm gonna die, he's gonna rape and kill Rosie. Sure that Melvin is already dead, the profanity pouring from Mel's mouth some weird kind of death throes, and that the other two goons have already killed Syd.

I pull the trigger, feel the recoil, and his head jerks back. I pull the trigger again and have no more bullets—just a useless chunk of metal in my hand. I pivot to hit him with the gun and he collapses; I see that a chunk is missing from the top of his head, blood cascading out of the hole, running through his hair and making a gory wading pool in the center of the room. Blood drips past me. Looking up, I see what Ty was using for brains—pinkish gray matter with long brown hairs stuck in it, blown all over the roof of Abe's fucking Inn.

Syd comes through the door, .38 in hand. She runs over to Mel, who's struggling to get up, and says, "Time to go. Mel's still breathin'—help me drag him outta here."

Mel says, "Still breathin'? Shit, it ain't possible to hurt this bad and still be alive. Those lames had twenty-five g's cash—grab it, and get the dope, Bobbie. Syd, if you'll be so kind as to uncuff me, I think I can get up."

The first thing I do is pull the keys out of Clem's pockets and uncuff Rosie, gesturing and grunting for her to help with Mel. I then pull the hundreds out of Clem's Levi's pocket and grab our drugs.

Rosie isn't saying a word, just helping with Mel and staring at me like I'm from Mars; looks like she's scared of me. I can't talk, and the nausea is setting in like the last time I had a badass beating. I'm scared to death—everything happens so fast there is no time to feel much.

Now it's coming on, the way Ty charged me, not going to be slowed down, even by bullets . . . Clem's last smile replaying itself in my memory. Rosie's sad eyes, scared of me, and I can't say a fucking word. It's a bad day.

Syd says, "Let's move it. You guys need medical attention, pronto." I hobble out to the Cad and fall into the backseat.

Rosie is pushed into the corner, as far from me as she can get, not making a noise, barely breathing. I want to talk to her, ask her what was I supposed to do? Seeing it in her face—I'm a fucking animal, I didn't really have to shoot those guys. Her eyes are not just sad, they're dead, looking at me like I'm not there; she's got as much animation as a Puerto Rican Barbie. I don't know what else I could have done. I'm really starting to appreciate the blues.

Every time the car hits a bump my jaw moves around, grating and sending bolts of pain through my head. Mel and Syd are in front.

Mel says, "We gotta go out to Jimbo's. He's got a whole crew working, think they're gettin' ready for Armageddon or some fucking thing. They got medical supplies, everything we need . . . probably a born-again doctor. Those dudes are their own fuckin' universe. We can get the van later."

Syd's laughing, has a real hysterical edge in it. She's got bright red spots burning in both cheeks, her hair is all fucked-up, stuck together the way bleached hair will, not even wearing lipstick. I've never seen Syd less than perfectly groomed. It's disturbing. Mel has two bullets in his back and one in his chest—that's beyond disturbing. Rosie is ignoring me and that feels like the end of the world, and one more time I'm all fucked-up, which is nothing new.

Syd says, "Shit baby, you need a *real* doctor, so does the kid. They're gonna have to wire his jaw, maybe other shit, and I know a badass like you ain't gonna let a couple little bullets slow him down, but they gotta cut 'em out and ya need a hospital for that."

"We hit a hospital anywhere in a five-state area, we're busted. Four

SIX

fuckin' 187s. We know we didn't have any choice, but ain't nobody gonna convince a jury of that. The rev's the only chance we got."

Get a sinking feeling in my stomach hearing Mel say 187, the penal code for murder one. It really brings home what we're involved in. I'm starting to get scared. The idea of having more exchanges with Mel's friend James Cook—aka Jimbo—aka Reverend Cook—is almost as disturbing as the thought of getting busted. The blood that soaks my jeans is drying, making them stiff and crinkly; the sun beats through the window so strongly that my jeans are steaming as the blood evaporates, like my hopes for a happy ending.

Mel turns in his seat, saying, "Motherfucker, this shit hurts; if he'd had a better piece, I'd be dead. You saved my life, kid; if you hadn't popped caps into those two, we'd all be maggot food right now. The dagos call that 'making your bones'—I wish that shit hadn't happened, but I got to tell ya, you came through like a champ. I owe ya."

Rosie looks at me and smiles. I feel my posture improve and try to grin, manage a wink. Rosie slides next to me and says, "Pobrecito, you gonna be OK baby. That whole scene weirded me out." The blues evaporate along with the last of the blood soaking my jeans. The various shrinks I've talked to over the years have all said that my need for immediate gratification is outweighed only by my need for outside validation, apparently not that uncommon in us sociopaths. However, I gotta tell ya, I feel like I'm pretty well balanced; I want to feel good, and I want the people I like to like me back. Fuck everybody else.

James's place is way out in the country—cornfields, trees, little rolling brooks, houses that are huge and miles apart. . . . The roads get smaller and smaller, pavement disappearing and gravel taking its place, clouds of dust rising around the Cad and gravel pinging off of it.

Mel groans and my first thought is that he must be in terrible pain. He is, but not *physical* pain; he groans again, saying, "There goes my fucking paint job, motherfucker. Wish we could kill 'em again."

Turning off the gravel and hitting a one-lane dirt road, potholes big enough to go swimming in; driving up a huge hill and near the top a chain-link-and-razor-wire fence, a little old man smoking a corncob pipe, sitting in a kitchen chair under a beach umbrella at the gate. Syd pulls up, lowers the window, says, "Hi gramps, gotta see the reverend. Like right now. *Now*. Ya with me?"

He smiles, face wrinkling up from his chin to his forehead, one huge wrinkle, not a tooth in his head, these incredibly alive green eyes set in a mummy's face.

He says, "We been waiting for y'all. Told James a Cad was coming with four people in it twenty minutes ago. He said to make y'all welcome. Go on down to the main house." He points to a huge house, painted bright red with white trim.

About a half mile farther up, at the very top of the hill, between us and the house, there are gardens, goats, chickens, and people all over, busy working, weeding, watering, all stopping whatever they're doing to wave and smile as we drive past. I've lived in the city all my life, and it feels like I'm on Mars. Not just the happy, healthy people, but all the green shit growing, weird animals running around. . . . The place sounds strange—no traffic, chickens making noises; no city stench— the place smells green, manure and vegetables . . . not my scene at all.

James Cook comes down to meet us at the bottom of the winding wooden stairway that leads up to the flower-festooned porch at the front of the house. It's funny how, you change a guy's surroundings, the guy changes. The vicious edge is gone, the madness that boiled behind his reddish eyes replaced with serenity.

There's a big black dude with him that looks like evil incarnate—till he smiles. He's got a gold tooth in front with a star cut out of it. The smile goes all the way to his forehead as they help Mel out of the car.

The black dude says, "You folks are all right now, my brother. You gonna be OK."

The Reverend Cook himself, possessor of axelike hands, the guy who can beat two big huge motherfuckers to death before breakfast, the guy who has the trick holster and don't mind killing you as a matter of principle, the born-again, kill-'em-for-Christ fucking nut, picks me up out of the backseat. He has my 130 pounds of wanna-be-tough-guy-thoroughly-beaten ass cradled in his arms, and in the gentlest voice I'd ever heard come out of a grown man, says, "You're home now, son. Ain't nobody gonna hurt any of ya, relax."

He nods at the black dude, and says, "Our brother Ben is a doctor, you're gonna be all right." Then he smiles, and his whole face changes. His eyes wrinkle up, looking like cherries in snow instead of cancerous rubies. He says, "And the Lord is with us—whatever medical science can't do, He will."

I don't know about all that, but I believe Jimbo Cook.

. . . .

When I come to, my jaw's been wired shut. The next two weeks I eat through a straw. By the time Mel gets done with the story, me and Syd are on full fucking hero status. I think what Syd did is pretty fucking impressive, but I feel like I had been on the late show; if I'd been more on top of my game, none of us would have been hurt and maybe Clem and his guys wouldn't've needed shooting.

We're sitting on the porch, a whole group of Rev Jim's people and the four of us. Syd's telling the story and I know it's for my benefit. I'd been feeling bad and it showed. Talking is a big thing—when shit bothers ya, it makes it feel better; when life's good, it makes that better too. Lets ya share it either way.

That whole scene bothers me. I keep replaying it, trying to see how I could have done something differently, always flashing back to Clem's face as he smiled and brought his piece around. No matter how much people say I did the right thing, I still feel horrible.

I'm looking at the people around us, wearing work boots, dungaree overalls, some of the women dressed in real simple skirts. . . . They look like the salt of the earth, but they're not really squares. Everyone here has a hard edge to them. I can tell they like having us here, breaking up the routine.

I got my jaw wired, but I'm sore all over and starting to feel real antsy and nervous. I get a little notepad I can write on. Syd's talking with that dese, dem, dose accent and occasionally one of the born-again group interjects a "hallelujah" or an "amen." A very weird scene.

Syd's sitting in a rocking chair, wearing a tank top and bell-bottoms; she looks pretty good for her advanced years.

She's saying, "So these two palookas come crashin' into my room, yellin', 'This is a rip off, ya sheeny bitch!' Now I knew right then these two schmucks weren't none too bright—two gorillas come running up on ya carrying pistols as big as cannons, ya know yer gettin' ripped. They didn't have ta say a fuckin' word, but they like scarin' women, real tough guys."

Syd pauses to make a face of disgust, flips her hair over her shoulder, and continues.

"They're yellin' and screamin', making so much noise that this thing had to go bad. For a minute I think they're gonna kill me for the thrill of the thing, get their wanna-be-Aryan nuts off by blowing my kike brains out. Every other word is Jew, preceded by either whore or bitch. I notice the one with no teeth is giving me that look, you know, the look."

Every female on the porch starts laughing; obviously they'd heard the story before.

I look at Rosie and scribble, "Look???" Rosie reads the note and leers at me, lets her tongue hang out of her mouth and makes pig noises—such exaggerated lust, I want to laugh and can't. I smile with my mouth and eyes. I know the look—I think I was wearing it the first time I met Rosie. Syd continues.

"That's when I knew I had 'em. I threw a Mae West at 'em, said 'Wellll, reallll men, what-a-treeeeat!' and started unbuttoning my top. My shotgun was under the table and the .38 was stuck in my pants. The toothless wonder lowered his piece so fast it looked like it weighed a ton, and jumped in front of his friend—wanted to go first don't ya know. I fired right through the table—both barrels of that shotgun. Blew Nazi One to pieces. Nazi Two tried to get his piece back on me and I had to blow him up. But if it weren't for Bobbie, here . . ."

I like Syd's version a whole lot better than mine.

That night they have fried chicken. The doctor who'd introduced himself as Ben comes up to the room I'm staying in. They're gonna make Rosie sleep somewhere else 'cause we aren't married. Third floor, small, wood floors, one big window overlooking a cornfield, only thing on the wall's a picture of a guy wearing a dress, who I guess is Jesus, talking to some kids.

I'm kicked back, feeling really poorly, trying to read one of Robert Heinlein's sci-fi novels, something about colonizing the moon, thinking that maybe I'm on it. . . . This whole place is alien to me—cows, goats, cornfields, no traffic, no smog, no dope fiends but us. Downstairs frying fucking chicken—only fried chicken I knew about was the Colonel's—and I haven't fixed all day, not happy at all about that. There's a sharp rap on the door and in strides Dr. Ben, smiling from ear to ear, flashing the gold star on his tooth, saying, "How ya doing boy? Y'all lookin' better, that's for sure."

I grunt and shake my head. Physically, I know I'm healing, and figure this is the guy that wired me back together. These guys want to call me boy, fuck it, I'm not gonna be an ingrate. I scribble, "Yeah, thanks Doc."

"Shit boy, I ain't no doctor—I'm almost a veterinarian, though. Got one year of college left."

This big black guy with the gold tooth has a great laugh—rowdy and raucous. He's still chuckling, says, "I gotta tell ya, there ain't much difference between working on your friend Mel and working on a grizzly bear—except a bear is better natured, and don't laugh at its own jokes."

He pauses, wipes the sweat off the back of his neck, shakes his head, and continues.

"See, brother James ain't always one hundred percent truthful; telling you I was a doctor made ya feel better about it, so he figured it was OK. Truth be knowed, Mel did as much of the work on ya as I did—he did all the wiring. That big old motherfucker has good hands.

"I pulled the bullets out of him real easy. They were only .25s. A .25 ain't good for much except making people mad—a piece of buckshot does more damage. Soon as I had those out of him, we went to work on you. A broke jaw's tricky, but you come out real good—don't know if it was me and Mel, or all the prayers."

The smell of frying chicken is coming through the open door. Normally it would smell delicious, but it's making my stomach roll. I can't puke 'cause my jaws are wired. I feel like shit, not just beat-up and sore, but real sweaty and nervous.

I feel all my normal fears in full force, compounded by the new and very valid terror of having achieved paradise and not wanting to lose it. I'm glad we have a place to hide out and heal, but in that short amount of time I've really grown fond of living large, getting my ass kissed by maître d's and room service every morning. Fixing all day, every day.

The stronger the smell of the chicken gets, the worse I feel. I'm really starting to sweat; the pain in my face and ribs is intense, but the anxiety that's tearing me to pieces is so strong that it almost blocks the pain.

Ben says, "You're looking kinda pale. Mel said to give ya these." He hands me two caps of smack, and has a real weird expression on his face, his lips all scrunched up, eyes a little bit crazy.

As I'm cooking it, I notice the tremors running through my body, like miniconvulsions; I'm drenched in toxic-smelling perspiration, from the top of my head to my feet. As I'm slamming the shit home, sweat's dripping off of my forehead and splashing onto my arms.

When the smack comes on, all that changes. I didn't know it, but that was my first experience with withdrawal, and the wonder of getting well.

Looking up, starting to nod and scratch, I see Mel and James in the doorway. Mel's clean-shaven, but almost as pale as his buddy Jimbo. He's got a robe on over boxer shorts, belly wrapped in bandages; he leans on the doorjamb, looking weak and all fucked-up, eyes so pinned there're no pupils in 'em.

He says, "What's up, bodyguard? Now don't be talking our ears off," and manages a weak chuckle.

James is wearing jeans, work boots, and a cotton long-sleeved shirt, and I realize that the motherfucker is charismatic—a word I've never associated with real human beings. When he's on his turf, he radiates power; when he's out in the world, it becomes madness. Here, it's like there really is a God, and old Jimbo is tight with Him.

He's got his arms crossed, staring at me. He says, "Most of our people are hiding from one thing or another—some the law, some other sheeit. . . . One thang, though—everybody here is clean."

He stops talking, just stands there, radiating. I'm thinking this is where we get thrown out, Old Jimbo is just getting his nerve up to do it. My brain is already calling him names: chickenshit, albino, punk. . . . Fortunately, I can't flap my jaws anyway, because he continues.

"I give it a lot of thought, and I figure that the good Lord hung out with thieves, hookers, and social malcontents, and I do the same, every day of my life.

"This is more a political refuge than a church. I'm a Christian, not the kind you find in most churches, but the kind the good Lord said to be."

His eyes turn inward, and he starts rocking back and forth to a beat not audible to us ordinary mortals. When he starts talking again, his speech has got that singsong thing going on.

"Judge not lest ye be judged and all that shit . . . the thing is, junkies are just plain bad news, so it's hard not to prejudge y'all.

"I love Melvin here the way you might love your brother, whether he's shooting stuff or not. I mean to tell ya, we been through some shit together, so I guess ya pretty much saved his life. Till ya get healed up, you guys are welcome here, just like it's your home.

"Ain't none of y'all married and all of y'all shoot dope like it's goin' out of style, which ain't the way the good book says to do it. But the more I studied and prayed on it, I realized, who am I to judge? As ya kin tell, I'm a long way from blameless, as are all men born of women, and as my guy Jay-sus said, 'Before I bust yore balls about the splinter in yore eye, I better get the phone pole outin' my own.' So don't chew worry about nothin', OK, son?

"See, Satan been casting doubts in my poor addled brain; sometimes I get self-righteous and today was one of those days. Pride comes in and says they gotta do it the way *you* think they should, *you* know best James—and, being full of pride anyhow, I agree, even though deep down I know that forcing anyone to do anything is as unchristian as it gets. . . . Does any of that make sense to you, son?"

I wasn't ready for theology then—don't know if I am now—but I still think it's one of the most spiritual statements I've ever heard.

I scribble out, "Cool, that means we're stayin and ya ain't gonna bust our balls about gettin born again?" and hand it to James.

James looks at it, shakes his head, hands the note to Mel, who gives another weak chuckle and says, "Tol'ja Jimbo—the kid's as diplomatic as napalm." Looking at me, Mel says, "The correct response is 'Thanks,' know what I mean, killer?"

Smiling, really feeling it hit my eyes, actually feeling a little bit of gratitude—another alien emotion—I nod my head, brain saying right on, got to heal up, shoot dope, and sleep with Rosie. . . . This Reverend James is a trip—gonna do what this good book he's talkin' about says to do, whether he agrees or not. I print out in capitals, "THANKS."

Ben's hunched down in the corner. He stands up and says, "Sheeit boy, you don't know what the reverend went through. Been pacing back and forth, talkin' to hisself all day long, not talkin' to nobody else but hisself. Lookin' all crazy. Just to figure out if he should let y'all sleep together—let alone shoot dope under his roof. This kinda shit is dangerous boy, sets a bad precedent; but he feels like this is the right thing to do, and I guess he's right. If'n he ain't, we'll sure find out, know what I mean, boy?"

I feel the implied threat but don't have the experience to understand why it's being made, don't know that in the real, subterranean world, shooting dope is like the kiss of death, that for every functioning addict there are a hundred more who are good for nothing except stealing from their friends, betraying everyone that gets close to them, and telling as soon as they get into trouble.

It takes even longer—most of my life, actually—to realize that even that one person out of a hundred would eventually fall apart behind the addiction. A very sad situation, one that I am completely unaware of at the time.

I don't know how to respond—am I supposed to confront him, or just let it slide? My brain is going back and forth and I finally decide to say nothing, get more data, figure out where he's coming from.

Jimbo looks at Ben, turns his eyes to me, and says to Ben, "Bobbie hates being called 'boy,' feels like it's a put-down. OK?"

Ben folds his arms, looks me up and down, and says, "So you got some nigger in ya? Look like a baby peckerwood to me. What's up? Why's a white boy plexin' over being called 'boy'—it ain't no thing."

I look at Mel for help, but there's none there; he just grins with one side of his mouth and raises his eyebrows, then shrugs.

Jimbo is leaning on the wall, watching to see how I'll handle this, and Ben is standing there, black and ugly as sin, got his arms folded, staring at me. Three scary motherfuckers who I want to respect me, even more than I want 'em to like me.

Having my jaw wired, I can't just react, I have to analyze my thinking and feelings and write it down—this is some kind of test and I'm determined to pass, but I know if this had happened ten minutes ago, before I'd slammed, I'd've probably fallen apart. I write out, "I treat you with respect, I want the same."

Ben reads the note and passes it. I'm starting to get pissed off at Mel—I want some fucking backup. I didn't ask to come here. Now this fucking toad is fucking with me. I'm all busted up and can't talk, couldn't fight if I had to. Self-pity is rolling in like a thunderstorm, and I know I gotta think. I raise my hands like a guy gettin' robbed in a western movie—chill out pal, I'm harmless.

Ben says, "See, the thing is, by fixin', you're disrespecting a whole bunch of people. A lot of us are ex-junkies. Now I know you're about as able not to fix as I'm able to flap my arms and fly—Mel knows what time it is—when I saw ya fix, it looked so good it made me want to drink your fucking blood. . . . So do us all a favor and keep it on the q.t., huh, baby wood?"

Mel finally opens his mouth, says, "So answer the man's question Bobbie—ya got any nigger in ya?"

I look at him like he's crazy. One, I'm about as white as a guy can get and proud of it; two, saying nigger is way uncool. I want to be a badass, but don't want to hurt Ben's feelings. I am still very liberal back then, think that words are important, don't know that all that matters are a person's actions.

I shake my head no, shrugging my shoulders at Mel's obvious lack of tact.

I'm like the perfect straight man for these guys—they all know the same jokes and all have the same warped sense of humor. Ben starts laughing before I'm done with my face-making, shrugging aw-shucks routine, and says, "Ya sure you don't got no black in ya?"

I scribble out, "Hell no. Pure white boy here."

They're all busting up, passing the note, laughing even harder, when Ben says, "So do you want some?" Even the ever-saintly Reverend James has gone all the way back to Jimbo and is in hysterics, the oldest joke in the convict world and I'd gone for it. Live and learn. Needless to say, my sense of humor is considered kinda strange by most citizens. I flip them off, sending the finger around the room and smiling; these guys are determined to laugh all the way to the graveyard. I still get real sad when I think about them—nostalgia, I guess.

Jimbo says, "I don't know about y'all, but I'm starvin'. Let's go eat. It ain't fried chicken, but they're makin' ya about a gallon milk shake, son. Come on."

. . . .

Another milk shake for breakfast. I'm behind the wheel of a mystery car. It is so fucked-up and rusted out, you can't even tell who the maker was, let alone the style. It has four doors to match the four tires.

The three stooges are with me—Mel riding shotgun, Jimbo and Ben in the backseat. The heroin I did first thing this morning has my nerves settled, but I'm still wired. I equate driving with getting in wrecks, and I'm already hurt. If my face goes through the windshield, I figure my jaw will just come off.

Mel puts his seat belt on, slaps me on the shoulder, and says, "Shove it into D—let's roll, pal."

Let's roll shit. I know I'm gonna kill us all; jaw is throbbing, hands shaking a little bit, brain's saying fear the fear, make it work for ya, piece of cake, nothing to it, learn how to drive . . . get my own short, style all over the country with Rosie riding shotgun. I put the rust-covered gearshift into drive and we're moving. Ben yells, "Go ahead baby wood, we off to the races."

Mel asks, "You praying, Jimbo?"

The reverend replies, "My ass off. Imagine all the shit we been through, the three of us get killed teachin' a youngster how to drive?"

Looking over my shoulder, running us in and out of a drainage ditch, all three of these bona fide killers screaming, "Keep your eyes on the road!"

. . . .

A couple hours later, pulling into a roadside diner for coffees and feeling so proud of myself it felt like I would burst.

Going in, watching all three of 'em order huge breakfasts and listening to 'em describe how good it tastes, as I sip another fucking milk shake. When everyone is done, I catch the look on the waitress's face, she thinking these guys are real assholes, torturing some kid who can't eat—not just eating in front of him, but raving about how good the food he ain't eating is. I feel my eyes twinkle as I give her my new, close-lipped smile and think, huh, she don't get it, this is what guys do, this is fun.

Coming out of the diner, the wind is actually blowing, clouds rolling across the sky—it's a gorgeous fucking day. Sliding behind the wheel, feeling the car lower dramatically as the fellas climb in. Slamming it into R before anyone can tell me to, thinking, yeah, man. Continuing our tour of the back roads of rural Illinois, trying to figure out what kind of car I want.

. . . .

When we get back, Syd and Rosie are sitting on the porch waiting for us, one of Jimbo's women sitting with them, stroking Syd's arm. The sun is starting to set, a red ball sinking behind the house, and the heat is finally starting to break. There's a chill in the air, and as soon as I park the car, Syd is on her way down the steps. Mel looks over at me, stares back at Syd, and says, "Oh, shit."

Rosie and the other woman are right behind her. We group up, standing at the bottom of the stairway in the grass, wind blowing the trees and shrubs, gently shaking them. Rosie is standing beside me; I slip my arm around her waist and the reverend says, "What's wrong, Mabel?"

Mabel is a classic hippie chick, could have stepped down off a poster—slim, pretty, natural blond hair, granny glasses, and a big flowing dress with sneakers peeping out the bottom, topped by a very spacey smile. But her conversation is anything but spacey.

"Brother Fred called from the state police barracks. They got a fingerprint offa one of the shell casings at the motel. It's a perfect match to Syd. They're waiting on mug shots to get here from the East Coast. Going to make this a major manhunt—womanhunt, in this case. The feds linked Mel to Syd—the shit's hitting the fan."

She pauses, looks at Mel, and asks, "Habla español?"

Mel looks like he's going to die: pale, slumped over, and I realize that the idea of losing Syd terrifies him. The same guy that could attack a dude that's holding a gun on him is ready to fold up because he's so scared of losing his old lady. I didn't understand, then; once I did, I wished I'd never even heard the word "love."

Mel starts rubbing his face frantically and makes a growling noise, sounding like a rabid dog. He looks up, straightens his posture, and asks, "So ya want us out of here, huh Jimbo?"

James doesn't even blink. He says, "Hell no. Think I got puddin' in my pants? There ain't even no link from you to me unless the fucking feds start giving up CIA files—and the good Lord knows they won't do that, not with the shit they had us doing. And Fred's down, he'll hold his mud, he's one of us—he just works for them. Everybody just relax, after the crap we've survived, this ain't nothin'. Besides, it's nice having people around that remember Jimbo. I need a break from the most reverend James Cook once in a while. Let's get washed up. It's almost chow time."

. . . .

Syd's cutting my hair. There's a mirror propped on the kitchen table. Call me vain, but I hated losing that hair—you gotta remember, this is a long time ago, before grunge, before punk, before rock and roll became an institution run by college graduates who found this way to manipulate people that puts George Orwell's Big Brother to shame. . . . Back in prehistory, real long hair was a rarity, a real *fuck you* statement; and I saw myself as a real *fuck you* sort of kid.

I watch Syd chew on her bottom lip as she combs and cuts, keeping the hair wet. Rosie is smoking, sitting backward on one of the kitchen chairs, saying, "You gonna look good baby—and with the cops looking for us, we gotta change up."

"Ain't no thing, mija, got all these lames growing their hair now anyhow."

Looking in the mirror, the guy staring back at me shows none of the emotions that are running through me—the fear of paying the price for killing those assholes, being scared for Rosie—*terrified* for Syd and Mel—and, as petty as it sounds, really bummed out about the haircut.

. . . .

The sun is just starting to come up. Nothing to be seen but cornfields. I got the speed right at sixty-five, cruising. No one on the highway but us and truckers. Large to-go coffee in my right hand, steering with my left that's got a cigarette burning in it. Very cool, able to drive, smoke, and drink coffee at the same time. On my way to take care of business. A very happening guy.

Ben's riding shotgun, snoring like a chain saw. I'm thinking about waking him up—it's one unpleasant fucking noise. I decide to wait, hoping he'll stop; kinda like hoping the sun won't rise.

My jaw's healed, but my heroin habit's grown, and it's been established that we're gonna keep on criming till we get stopped or make enough dough to enable Mel and Syd to get out of the USA in style. The split on our future scores will be the same—one third my end, and I'll learn a trade. I have no intention of ever stopping. I love it. I have no idea that everyone changes. Even me.

The plan is for me and Ben to go back into Chicago, pick up the van, dump the drugs cheap to prearranged buyers, and trade for a couple pieces of stuff. Get back to the compound with the cash and smack, not take a break—head directly for Denver and a score there, keep rolling till we get a half million our end. . . . If we can do it fast enough, it'll give Mel and Syd a couple hundred g's to split with. Me and Rosie'll have about a hundred in pocket, and we'll spend the rest living large. It's a great plan.

Not able to take the snoring anymore, I reach over and shove Ben. He looks at me all bleary-eyed, says, "Huh, what's up?"

"John Wesley Hardin killed a guy for snoring. You so loud the truckers get scared when they go by us."

"Shit man, I don't snore. And he shot that dude while he was asleep—you gonna kill me you better do the same, crazy little peckerwood. . . . Gimme some of that coffee."

I've since learned not to discuss race, politics, etc., but back then I didn't know that, as subjects go, those are useless. Now I try to stick to sex, sports, and movies. But, being ignorant of this rule, I ask him, "What's up with this 'peckerwood' thing? I heard Mel talk about 'em, now you calling me one. . . . What exactly is a 'peckerwood'?"

Ben shakes the sleep out of his head and becomes a serious guy. See, that's the reason those are bad subjects for conversation. Ask Mickey the Mope and not only will he have opinions, but he'll lay 'em on ya, and if you don't agree, you're an asshole. Not that Ben was an asshole—over the years I've come to agree with almost everything he says.

Ben starts, "Sheeit, what's a peckerwood? What kinda question is that? *You* are. A peckerwood is a white boy who's too dumb to know that he's supposed to be scared of niggers, but usually hates 'em anyway just out of ignorance. See, the Man wants us all to hate and fear each other, right?

" 'Cause whether you poor white trash, some kinda spic, or got big lips and nappy hair like me, you stuck on the low end of life. I was a Muslim for a minute or two—that ain't really true—I was a Black Muslim, kinda like the black man's answer to the Nazis. If you ain't black, you the motherfuckin' enemy, consider white people blue-eyed devils and mean it; make that Hitler dude seem like a reasonable guy.

"Take a kid out of the ghetto, tell him that hate is the answer, tell him that everything that's wrong in his life is the fault of the white man and the Jew, and what ya get is a motherfucker that's just as ignorant as your average peckerwood. I didn't last too long. I was a little bit too outspoken, and one thing anyone can tell ya, the Muslims don't like being trifled with. They're dangerous guys—ask Malcolm X."

"I thought he was dead, got shot or something?"

"Yeah . . . you a peckerwood all right."

"Whatcha mean?"

"They blew his ass up. The brother went and became a *real* Muslim—which ain't based on race—and that's all she wrote. Some people think the feds helped. They sure didn't try to stop it.

"Here's the thing: ever since the beginning of time, all tribes have hated all other tribes, 'cause of skin, or religion, or some fucking thing. I don't think anything we do is gonna change that. There's always gonna be differences between groups of people. Niggers, we got to take care of ourselves, spics the same, white trash motherfuckers like you and Jimbo the same. . . . Your friend Mel's the craziest Jew boy I ever met, but I hear they got a whole country full of 'em: Israel. Now those are some bad motherfuckers.

"Once a people respect themselves, they start getting respect. I can't blame nothin' on the white man, and the same goes for you. If a black cat does you wrong, you can't join the Klan and decide to hate all niggers. *People* fuck each other over, not races."

"So how's the thing with Reverend James work with all this race shit?"

"The motherfucker's color-blind. He knows the feds are the enemy, and he don't take shit from anybody. Plus, he's my friend; why I got him as one, I don't know, but real friends don't come along too often. That's life for ya kid, the guy I'm closest to is an albino cracker, born-again nut. We believe in the same things, want the same things for people. I don't have his level of faith—that's why I'm gonna be a vet. I like animals better than people. Jimbo . . . someday they'll kill him. Warrior saints got short life spans."

Sorting through the statements Ben has made, I ask, "So is being a peckerwood a good thing or a bad thing? You call me peckerwood, is that like me calling you nigger?"

"Man, Mel wasn't lyin' when he said you diplomatic as napalm—and I notice that choo love them two-part questions, kinda snuck nigger in there at the end.

"For you, being a peckerwood has *gotta* be good. You stuck. Just like for me being a nigger is good. I can say I'm Irish till the day I die, ain't nobody gonna believe it. Most white people will kiss my ass when I'm around, just 'cause I'm black. They think it makes 'em cool or somethin'; shit just makes 'em look weak.

"Truth be known, most brothers can respect a guy that has the balls to say 'fuck you' to your face. Think about it, black people sold our relatives to white people who may or may not have been your ancestors, so what the fuck do you got to feel guilty about? It's on you the way you *are*—if you're a nigger-hating, racist piece of shit, you *should* feel guilty; but if you're not, a black dude starts sniveling about slavery this and the evil white man that, your response should be, *So what?* But most of y'all are too chickenshit—how can we respect people like that? In turn, we lose our self-respect because your average Caucasian is so weak that they go for it.

"The one thing you don't ever want to be is a Caucasian. See, that's a white dude that feels like he's gotta apologize for it; kinda like you guys' version of an Uncle Tom. Ain't nobody gonna give someone like that respect: whatever ya are, you have to be willing to represent it. Can ya tell I'm working into the peckerwood-nigger thing?"

It sounds funny to hear Ben talking like a professor of race-ology; he's normally one of the most kicked-back members of the crew. The dude's so serious it's making me nervous.

I start laughing and say, "Yeah, man, been waitin' with baited breath. Gonna run you for president on the peckerwood-nigger ticket, so what's up with that?"

Ben starts laughing, says, "Sheeit boy, you are a fool. Here's the deal: another black dude calls me nigger, it ain't no thing; a white dude or a spic call me nigger, it's a whole different matter. Peckerwood is the same sort of thing, you can't be letting nobody but other peckerwoods use that word on ya, me included. You gotta demand respect, just like I do."

I think about this. From the time I was old enough to reason, I knew that to get respect you had to not only give it, but demand it in return. Cool. Now I understand the whole race thing. Just one thing we gotta get straight.

I say, with the infinite wisdom I possessed back then, "Check it out—all this spic shit, ya gotta drop it—Rosie's my old lady and she's Puerto Rican puro, and if there's anyone that deserves to be treated with respect, it's her. That little girl has paid some serious dues, know what I mean, killer?"

Ben starts laughing uproariously, slapping his knees, and says, "Come on kid, smarten up. If Rosie don't talk bad about niggers I'll eat the steering wheel. Everybody talks shit about everybody, blacks about Hispanics, Hispanics about blacks, and we all talk shit about crackers, Paddies, honkies, and peckerwoods; Mel's a fucking Jew, sheeny, kike; with the crew you're running with right now, you'll be spending all your time makin' sure no one gets their feelings hurt. . . . The rule is the same everywhere: soon as an ethnic group leaves the room they're fair game. . . . I got it. Anyone ever tell ya about the Vietnamese?"

"Mel, a little bit. Some of the other dudes I've run with. I don't know much about 'em, though."

"Cool, 'cause they ain't around here at all and this early in the morning I gotta talk shit about somebody, just so I don't feel so bad about being awake, entertaining your ass. Motherfuckers eat dogs. Whatcha think of that?"

The rest of the ride into Chicago is taken up by war stories, massacres, assassinations, and old-fashioned murder; flying planeloads of heroin all over Asia and how they got it into the States and got it distributed; the incredible amounts of money that were made; Mel stories; Jimbo stories; and, of course, Ben stories.

Memory has a way of polishing things, dropping bad things, retaining good. . . . A little change here, a small change there—if only one tenth of Ben's stories were true, the shit that was sponsored by the USA was beyond incredible, as far past sleazy and slimy as the Grand Canyon is beyond a pup tent. Monuments to treachery and deceit.

Mel doesn't have the gift for storytelling. Ben does. Suddenly, a lot of things become clear—not about global politics, but about the crew I've found myself adopted by. They see themselves as the targets for a campaign of murder being carried out by the U.S. government. At the time, I believed the war stories, but discounted the rest as paranoia. With the facts available today, starting with the execution of John Dillinger as soon as the FBI was formed, the systematic framing and murder of the Black Panthers, the mass murder of the Branch Davidians, shooting white separatists' wives and children to death in Idaho like they are rabid dogs, and, of course, what ultimately happens to Jimbo, it doesn't sound paranoid at all—just business as usual.

We check into a Holiday Inn or something similar; it sure isn't the Lynch House. The room service isn't bad, the rooms are OK, but I developed a preference for luxury as soon as I found it. I seem to have spent my life getting to the point where I get the best of everything, then lose it all. Starting over gets awfully tiring after you do it enough times.

We dump most of the ups for another twenty thousand, trade the balance for two ounces of good china white. Most of the dope available now is brown, weak, nasty shit from Mexico. Two ounces ain't that much, won't keep ya healthy that long at all if you've got a real habit going; but back then, two ounces was a lot of smack, not enough, but a lot.

You can lay a ten-to-one cut on it, and make one thousand nickel caps out of an ounce. If you aren't hooked like a laboratory monkey, one cap or button will send your face into your knees, leave you a drooling, scratching, puking, dreaming-in-Technicolor mass of comatose flesh.

Of course, once the jones takes over, all that become only a memory; staying well is all that matters. But I don't know about that part yet. I've always been incurably optimistic, see no reason why life has to be changing flavors of hell, which is certainly what you get most of the time.

When we'd been getting ready to leave, Jimbo had handed me another 380, saying, "Combat ready, Bobbie. The last one seemed to work OK for ya. God bless, kid."

I look at the piece now, red combat sights glinting in the lamplight, feeling the heft of it, shoving it into the back pocket of my jeans and knowing that if I have to pull the trigger I can, and feeling good about it. I wonder if anyone will ever find the other one, lying on the bottom of Lake Michigan with the .38 Syd used. Once you use a gun you have to get rid of it *immediately*—even *I* know that.

Ben knows the guys that run the South Side, the Gangster Initiates. They are going to take the rest of the ups and furnish the heroin, get it all done at once.

James and Mel had both been real concerned about Ben being around that much stuff. Mel'd said, "If it's gonna be a problem, I can go. Bobbie looks like a clean-cut kid, and my mustache is almost grown in. One thing for sure: if this is gonna make ya want to use it, it ain't worth it."

My arrogance is exceeded only by my ignorance. I'm thinking, what's the big deal? A guy only uses if he wants to. I don't have any clue that soon I'd have cut my arm off to get clean but wouldn't be able to, would end up with no more control of my habit than I had over gravity.

. . . .

Ben's on the couch, watching TV. I'm sitting at the kitchen table, reading a book I bought in the lobby, waiting for the smack so we can get back to the compound and start our trip to Denver. Like I mentioned earlier, waiting isn't my strong point. My anxiety's getting more intense by the minute. These guys were supposed to have been here at ten—it's almost midnight.

I ask Ben, "What's up, do ya think they're gonna show?"

"Yeah, killer, these guys are businessmen. We didn't front any dough, so they can't burn us. Plus, I grew up with their boss, he's actually a friend of mine. These cats are reliable. This is just part of the deal, man, waiting. The dope man is always late."

The heroin guys arrive, and for a minute I think it's gonna be a replay of the Nazis. A relatively small guy, wearing what is obviously a very expensive pin-striped suit, shoes spit-shined to a mirror finish, wearing a tie, built like a heavy welterweight, calling the shots—that was T. Not like the hot beverage. Just the letter. T.

His sidekick is Horseman. I don't ask how he got his name. Horseman looks like one and acts like T's brother, same dull threat in his every action, talks with that same pimp intonation. Physically, he's a sloppy version of Mel, a football player gone to seed. I edge away from both of 'em. Got my hand on my piece; no one's gonna have the opportunity to do shit before I'll be busting caps. Live and learn, right?

These guys know Ben and it's obvious that they're tight. No rip is gonna go down and I'm not going to have to shoot anybody. My mood improves considerably, and I'm dying to see what two ounces of pure stuff looks like. Ben and these guys are doing the multiple handshake thing, laughing and having a good time, when T says, "What's up with the white boy? Looks like you done too much time, Ben."

I'm already reacting, adrenaline kicking in. I don't even know this motherfucker and he's questioning my manhood. I straighten up from the slouch I'd fallen into when I realized that no burn was gonna go down, ask T, "What are you saying, ace?"

Ben starts laughing, says, "Cool out killer, it's a joke. Check it out T, this choirboy-lookin' motherfucker stole all this shit and put two motherfuckers to sleep that tried to take it from him. This is a very serious young man. He ain't used to being harassed by niggers or anybody else for that matter—shit, he don't even know that racism is a natural thing. . . . The boy's a genuine liberal."

T is giving this last statement some thought and says, "That's what is going to allow us to control Chicago, and eventually the country.

Look at the Jew, or the Irish—both once-despised minorities who used crime as a springboard—into the White House, in one case.

"The Italians have been calling shots so long that they've gotten soft; our people have gotten harder and more racist, rather an interesting role reversal.

"To be truly successful, a criminal enterprise must have a core group, normally defined by racial structure. At the same time, you have to be able to interact with other groups on an effective basis."

He pauses to shoot his cuffs and check the time. I know a couple of things: one, this guy likes to talk, and gives what he says a lot of thought; two, he don't like me a bit—he's so condescending, it's hard not to react. But I keep my face neutral. These guys are friends of Ben, and I don't want to fuck up the deal. I just stare at him, and he continues.

"If you are truly an enterprising young man, and run into scores like this on a regular basis, this could turn into a mutually profitable, long-term relationship. We have the capability of buying all the product you can obtain.

"Unlike those greasy fucking wops, I can put my prejudices aside to generate business. They want to sell drugs only to us, keep us in the ghettos. We, on the other hand, want to sell to everybody. Drug addiction is an equal opportunity malady, and that is what is going to provide our true power base.

"My grandma likes that punk Martin Luther King, but I believe in Chairman Mao."

He pauses, steeples his fingers under his chin, pinning me hard. Got a good psychotic mad dog, a little more understated than Clem's and a whole lot more eloquent; and I realize that, while they might not have been spiritual brothers, they were awfully close. Clem saw only the day he was in. T has a master plan. They're negative versions of the same thing. Very fucking weird. Scary.

That's when Horseman says, "Yep shore you, right, sho yo right T."

I start laughing, can't help it, flashing back to Ty saying the same words in almost exactly the same way. Hear my brain say which one's the Nazi and which one's the nigger. Feel like I'm living in a comic strip, but know there's no way to explain it to these two any more than there was to Clem and Ty. None of these guys have the ability to laugh at themselves, but I know it's funny, can't wait to run it down to Ben, see what he thinks.

Horseman shoots me with his variation on Ty's mad dog, says, "Whatup? Why you laughing?"

I think about telling the truth for about one second: Well pal, you and your partner are the reversed image of these Nazis I met not too long ago. What I say is, "Shit, man, I can steal so much dope we'll need trucks to deliver it. The idea made me so happy, I started laughing." It wasn't great but I thought it was OK.

Horseman shakes his head, says, "About a silly motherfucker."

I just shrug my shoulders and grin without showing any teeth; yeah, that's right, I'm just a silly motherfucker. Ask your alter egos—Clem and Ty—how silly I am.

Two ounces of stuff don't look like anything special, just a bunch of white powder. I'm kinda disappointed. We weigh it on the triple beam. It's exactly right. Before they leave, we test it, Ben pulls out two teeny chunks, about a third of a match head each, and we slam. The shit is unbelievable.

I can only plead ignorance; probably trying to talk Ben out of slamming wouldn't have done any good, but the fact is, it doesn't even occur to me. They say hindsight is 20/20. There's no way I could have known that that one fix was almost the beginning of Ben's end.

After T and Horseman split, Ben finds a blues station on the radio. Hitting the couch, the first thing he says is, "Check it out, Bobbie. Ya can't say nothing to nobody about me fixing, I haven't slammed since I got back to the world . . . but we had to test the shit, right?"

I'm sitting at the table, gowed, floating just this side of heaven. I say, "Yeah, right. You lie and I'll swear to it, pal. Shit man, you been clean that long, one hit ain't gonna hurt you. I ain't no rat—you don't want me to say nothing, you got it."

We get loaded through the next day, Ben changing, a guy that walked proud starting to slump, the easygoing turning into surly. . . . He quits taking care of himself immediately, goes from being impeccably groomed to completely unkempt in twenty-four hours. By the time we leave for the farm, he looks and acts like a different person: hair is all over the place, unshaved and unbathed, wearing portions of every meal eaten in that twenty-four hours on the front of his shirt.

I try talking him into getting cleaned up before we head back. The response I get is not what you would call real reasonable. What he says is, "Sheeit man, why you fuckin with me? I look fine, get off my ass, peckerwood."

I don't understand this, but I know I should have tried to stop him from slamming, feel like I should change my name to Lenny the Lop.

The ride back is made in silence. We lose the blues station shortly after we leave Chicago. Ben's nodding and has a real bad attitude, and my feelings are hurt, which, in turn, gives me a bad attitude. I feel guilty, like I fucked up. The idea of keeping it a secret is now a joke— the change is so obvious, a blind guy would have seen it. Rural Illinois floats by, ugly fucking cornfields, stupid cows, shitty roads.

I want to get out of Dodge as soon as we hit the farm. Pack our shit and go. The first thing Ben does is tell Jimbo he got loaded. I expect yelling and screaming, one of the faithful backsliding and all that, abuse to be heaped on both of us.

Jimbo is standing in the kitchen. He doesn't look surprised; then again, one look at Ben tells the whole story. He says, "Ain't no thang boss. Satan works twenty-four seven. You and me just burnt it out— probably if I could get loaded and still have a good time, I would. I'm lucky I didn't go, I'd probably be standing there all fucked and ugly as sin—and I gotta tell ya, you looking ugly, that shit don't agree with ya anymore."

Ben's got the heroin scratch going, nodding lightly and obviously miserable. At the time, I think it's a strange combination. Give that one some thought—when's the last time you met a happy dope fiend? They're either euphoric or stuck in purgatory. But never happy.

Ben's got an ashen cast to his skin, eyes covering truckloads of misery. He says, "Let's take a walk Jimbo. This shit fucked my head all up. . . . What if I keep using?"

Reverend James smiles, and says, "You won't. We need your ugly black ass. We got a lot of shit to do before our work's done. This is just one of Satan's sneak attacks—ain't even a battle. Let's stroll, boss."

Jimbo smiles and waves as they walk out of the kitchen. That's the last time I see him alive.

. . . .

Me and Rosie are sitting on the porch, rocking, not rolling, in chairs. I'm doing my feeble best to make sense out of the whole thing with Ben.

I say, "I don't get it, mija. Soon as he fixed, he changed up, got a tude the size of this fucking farm, called me peckerwood and wasn't jokin'. . . . I didn't know whether to get in his face or just hold my mud. It's a cinch domino that if we'd started rollin' and tumblin' he would've kicked my ass—that's one badass Negro."

Rosie stops rocking, staring at me with what I got to describe as joy, her face softening, those eyes that are normally so guarded and sad losing the concertina wire that normally hides below the surface. Takes her index finger and tries to drive it through my chest, says, "Mijo, for a smart guy, you pretty fuckin' stupid sometimes. Sound like you about five years old, got your feelings hurt. So sad you look just like a little boy.

"Ben's a proud dude, his anger wasn't at you, it's at himself—he feels like he fucked up. Think about it. You guys always do that shit— when you do something bad, you get mad at everybody else before they can get mad at you."

"I still don't *capise:* he didn't do nothing wrong, just got loaded. All he had to do was get cleaned up and keep his mouth shut and nobody would've known nothing."

This time she doesn't bother with the index finger, just punches me in the arm and says, "Stupido. My baby is fucking mongolico. *He* knows, and you're his friend and *you* know, and he don't want you to think he's some weak piece of shit, 'cause even though he ain't, that's how he's feeling right now."

Mel and Syd plop down in the other rockers, and I flash on how strange this is—all four of us rocking back and forth, the sun shining through the clouds, chickens pecking at the dirt below us, urban criminals transported to a Norman Rockwell painting. The air is heavy with moisture and smells of growing plant life. I'm thinking that Rosie is getting some bad habits from Syd; this punching me shit has got to stop—for somebody that weighs under a hundred pounds, that girl hits hard.

Mel says, "Feels like it might rain—all my fucking old injuries are hurting. Rosie's right, ya know, Bobbie. Ben and Jimbo both aspire to sainthood. Guys like us never get clean; I don't know how they did it, 'cause it just don't happen. Even if ya stay clean for a while, fix one time and boo-ya, you're off and running. That's why I don't even try."

Syd laughs and says, "Shit, you just scared of getting sick, and too lazy to go work. Who you trying to kid, schmuck?"

Mel continues, "See, Ben feels like he let everybody down or some fucking thing. Real life, the only one he let down is *him*. Ben and Jimbo are road dogs—Jimbo blames it on the devil, but he understands. We all shot serious dope while we were in Nam, Ben and Jim took some acid, Osley blue cheer . . . they ain't never been the same.

"Came down talking about praise God and all that shit, makes it even worse. Ben feels like God's mad at him. The reverend says that this God they got loves 'em no matter what . . . that's what they're kickin' around right now."

Syd cuts in, "Check it out, Bobbie, whatcha weigh?"

"Probably around one-thirty-five, maybe one-forty."

"Well whatcha think Ben weighs—two-thirty, two-forty?"

"Yeah, that ballpark."

"He's a full-grown man, only way you coulda stopped him woulda been to shoot him. Then you would've had the reverend hunting you. Woulda been a mess. Maybe he'll stay clean, maybe he won't. Either way it ain't on no one but him. Right?"

I hesitate, feel confused but don't know how to express it.

I say, "Yeah, it's fucked-up, though."

Mel does his hahahoho crazy laugh and says, "Till the day you die, ace, till the day you die. . . ."

Syd gives Mel one of her eye rolls. "So dramatic, bubeleh. Anyhow, we stay here tonight. Jimbo has to drop off some hardware—he should be back by nine or ten. We got two new vehicles—matching station wagons—being delivered this evening.

"The heat is looking for me and Mel, and an unidentified couple.

Me and Rosie take one short, you and Melvin the other . . . voilà. No couples. Two dudes, two broads, we all look different. . . . This time tomorrow, I'll be a black-haired babe—and I think Rosie will make a swell redhead. Melvin has his cholo mustache, and you look like a college boy.

"Ain't gonna be heat on us in Denver. We hit this gold-plating company, keep on rolling, a riotous four-person crime wave. . . . Melvin and I will be spending next summer in Brazil."

I ask, "Why all the way to Denver?"

Syd answers, "Why not? That's where the lick is. Got it scoped, set up . . . just got to do it. We're gonna head west anyhow. End up out there in La-La land, rob Mickey fucking Rodent—maybe we'll all become film mavens, movie stars and shit.

"Besides, you like the snow? I hate the fuckin' snow. Poor old Melvin gets all screwed up, can't move when it's cold. He's getting up there, you know. Poor decrepit senior citizen, look at him—has to keep up with a gorgeous young JAP like me . . . that would wear anybody out."

Mel raises one eyebrow, says, "Gorgeous, yeah, beautimus even, JAP ab-fucking-solutely, but this age thing, last time I looked we were both getting ready to turn thirty, and that was a few years ago. Don't be fucking with my frail male ego. The alternative to aging is so distasteful. I've been doing my best to avoid it."

I ask, "What's a gold-plating company got that makes it worth going to Denver, instead of just heading for the coast?"

Syd looks at me, looks at Rosie, rolls her eyes, and says, "Oy vey, what am I dealing wit here? Whatcha think they got? They got *gold*—a fucking safe full—it's ours. You and Melvin just have to extract it. Has Mel told ya? Crackin' boxes is his favorite crime in all the world. He will probably be willing to let ya do it as he supervises. Won't ya, honey?"

"Certainly will. It's tons of fun, just like the movies. You're gonna really dig it."

*T*he madness starts at 10:27 on my watch. Rosie is sprawled next to me, making sleeping sounds, and I'm finishing the sci-fi book.

There's a rap on our door and Mel comes bursting through, out of breath, got a crazy look on his mug, saying, "The feds whacked Jimbo, set him up on an arms sale. Sniped him cold. No surrender, no assume the position, just put one through his head. We gotta roll—those motherfuckers will be on their way here to tear this place apart. Grab your shit, 'cause we're out of here."

Throwing our gear into bags, running down the stairs. In the kitchen, a cluster fuck. Crying, screaming, the whole thing. Ben taking charge of the born-agains, heartbreak on his face, but all the dignity that the smack had stolen back, stronger than ever. Tells us, "It was a fuckin' 187. Used a sniper. Blew his brains out as soon as the truck stopped. I was driving the crash car. Got away. Gonna miss the red-eyed fuck. I gotta stay clean now. Those murdering scumbags will be here any minute. You gotta go. Get down the road. See ya. God bless."

We're moving fast, as Ben's doing his best to chill the situation. Down the stairs, into our new vehicles.

The night's so clear and bright, I feel like I should be able to see Jimbo on his way to heaven, a crescent moon shining to light his path.

Following the girls. Pedal to the metal, taking the curves on two wheels. Mel and Syd should have been stunt drivers. Flying till we hit the highway.

Exactly the speed limit, driving till the sun starts to peek through the back window. Stopping. Coffee, doughnuts, cigarettes, and gas. Back on the road. Exactly the speed limit.

Mel's got country-western playing; sounds like shit, but it fills the

SEVEN

gaps. Smoking. Eating a doughnut. Drinking coffee. Driving with his knee. Says, "I bet Ben stays clean—at least till the shit's over, anyhow. It's always easier when you're in a shit storm."

"Yeah." I'm frozen, can't make conversation, got no idea where we are, except headed west. Doughnuts have no taste, coffee the same. The girls' wagon is light blue, ours is yellow. I hate both of 'em, want a Cad; if this kinda shit is gonna keep going down, it seems like we should at least have leather seats.

Watching Mel watch the speedo. Driving at the speed limit is a pain in the ass. Some people say you should go five miles over, fit in more. Not Syd and Mel—exactly the fucking limit.

Hit a McDonald's, through the to-go window. Mel's driving with his knee, shoving food in with both hands. Slows down, burps, says, "The motherfuckers have been doing it forever, know what I mean?"

This after three hours of silence. I got no clue what he's talking about. Tell him, "No—which motherfuckers—doing what?"

Real serious, sad, he responds, "The feds, who else? This is their MO since they got started in law enforcement. John Dillinger got executed, shot to pieces with no gun in his hand; they been doing it ever since."

"I don't get it. How can they just hit people? Jimbo was a nut and all, but sniping him was out of line."

"They made Jimbo. Took a kid out of Bible college, dropped him into a boiling kettle of shit, added massive drugs to season it, let him deal with the guilt. . . . Doing what your country tells ya—when you're SpecialOps—can make you feel bad inside—even an asshole like me. Jimbo was a nice kid, a patriot. They made him crazy."

"I thought you said cops aren't the enemy. Maybe I'm kinda slow, but anybody gonna blow my brains out, seems like the enemy to me. Don'tcha think, ace?"

"You're on the wrong station there, pal. Those weren't cops. Probably ATF, or FBI—alphabet guys."

My nose is starting to run. The anxiety I feel is redlining; if I knew how, I'd cry. James Cook made a serious impression on me. His death is a terrible injustice. I have no idea what I'm feeling, only that it hurts. The fact that I'm hooked doesn't bother me at all—it seems like a good trade. I know that as soon as I fix, everything will be OK—my nose will stop running, the anxiety will disappear and so will the feeling of loss, sadness for Jimbo, and the feeling that I'm gonna cry. At least till I run out of stuff.

"When we gonna fix? I've had a couple of better days in my life, and I gotta tell ya, I'm startin' to feel kinda unwell. . . . Seems like I caught a habit."

Mel chuckles. "Oy vey, is that sorta like catching a cold? Walked in a room with some junkie and breathed their air, now you're feeling ill?"

"Yeah, probably *you*, contagious motherfucker that you are; shit rolls out of ya like the motherfucking plague."

"Right. Thing is, when this shit goes into remission, it's kinda like a little piece of heaven: take your medicine and boo-ya, you're better than well."

"Sho yo right, so let's get that way, quick like a hurry-up. I'm dying here, pal."

Mel accelerates, passing Syd and Rosie. Seems like the next rest stop is an awfully long way. By the time we get there, both of us got full-on runny noses and stomach cramps starting. We run into the men's room. Syd and Rosie manage to get parked and out of their car before we do; they're actually in the women's room before we get out of the station wagon. Guess they aren't feeling too good either.

. . . .

Hitting the freeway, I'm driving, following Rosie. Station wagon feels weird, staying at the speed limit a real fucking drag. Wonder if Rosie feels as uncomfortable driving as I do.

Mel starts the conversation where we left off.

"How ya think Jimbo paid for the farm? Money he stole from those dickheads offa their heroin smuggling. When they want to bust ya, first they surveil the shit out of ya, get your whole routine wired. Then they come in with serious force. Overwhelm you. Except in firefight situations, there's no reason for them to shoot anybody; with the resources they got, there's always an alternative. . . .

"Two, three teams, whatever it takes. Grab you, your people, and the evidence all at once. They don't bust one truckload of munitions when they can get it all. That was a hit, pure and simple."

"Why whack Jimbo? Seems like a lot of work to kill a preacher who sold a few guns as a sideline."

"James worked intelligence—real spook shit. Most of us were pulled from mainline service branch—SEALS, Airborne, Rangers. Real expendable. We were throwaway people. The geniuses that were calling the shots were spooks, CIA or whatever. James was the ultimate field spook. Out of all of them, he was the scariest. When he went renegade, it was just a matter of time. He knew what the story was before he did it and, quiet as it's kept, if ya had to pick a way to check out, that's about as good as it gets. One minute you're breathin', got your life in front of ya, then boo-ya, it's over. No pain. No fear. End of story."

Rolling down Interstate 80 as the sun starts to set. Steel gray clouds are starting to boil across the horizon, the way turmoil tore through our twisted lives. The setting sun is a malevolent copper ball, adding a bloodred outline to the clouds. Lightning rips from the heavens like snakes striking their prey. Thunder booms across the plains, the bass so heavy you can feel it in your bones.

As the cornfields change to wheat, we drive into a storm that hits the car like a wall; windshield wipers don't even make a dent. Seeing through the windshield is like a bad acid trip, and it's getting dark fast. I'm trying to see by force of will, the humidity so high it's like breathing steam. Holding the steering wheel so tight my hands are starting to cramp, terrified I'm gonna drive off the road. The rain is so heavy, I can't even see Rosie's taillights. Some of my fear must have shown through the wall I tried to keep up all the time. *Never let anybody know you're scared.*

Mel says, "You want me to drive till we're through this shit?"

"Hell no, this ain't nothing."

He's quiet for a minute, then says, "Driving in crap like this would shoot anybody's nerves out. Watch the line, don't even try to see the road. Keep your left wheel on the dividing line and watch for taillights. Relax."

Doing exactly what Mel says, my world narrowed down to that strip of paint flashing in front of me, my brain kicked into overdrive. Images of Clem coming around with his .25 to kill me, the look on his face when he saw the terror on mine, the feeling that my death was inevitable . . . mingling with beatings my father had administered, the look on *his* face as he broke my arm—complete power, knowing there was nothing going to stop him and he had the perfect victim—someone that loved him and assumed responsibility for the beating being administered. How could your dad do anything wrong? Knowing that if I wasn't such a rotten kid, he wouldn't have to hurt me. Imprinted deep inside that I was deserving of whatever terrible shit life handed me.

Ty and Horseman melting together into a huge, fat, racist zebra. T and Clem becoming smaller, better-talking versions of the same, and over it all visions of Rosie and me and the most overwhelming fear I've ever experienced. Her parents and my dad merging and having to keep all this inside because I *know* that showing emotion is bad. That was one of the first things I learned, and I learned it well.

When Rosie pulls over to let Syd drive, I'm overjoyed at the excuse to give up the wheel, to let Mel confront his demons while watching the broken line. At some level, I know that his flavor of hell is worse than mine; but none of us knows there is a way out—drug rehabs, twelve-step groups . . . all the shit available today is unheard of in the early seventies. We are stuck.

The sun is coming up again. That ethereal soft time between night and day coming out of an apple orchard and seeing smog hanging on the horizon. Soon there's a real skyline, skyscrapers, neon, pollution—all the things I know and love. Driving through the outlying areas of Denver and feeling better by the minute.

Bars are doing a brisk business at 7 A.M. Gutters full of trash, human and otherwise. Hookers already out working it hard, flashing their tits, yelling at the passing cars. Bikers, cowboys, and hippies everywhere, none of 'em getting along; see two fistfights on the way into downtown. It's great.

Mel's smoking, staring at the road, got a two-day growth of beard, eyes at half-mast. He says, "You're gonna dig this place we're staying—call it the Grand Hotel. Place is so uptown, the staircases are made out of hand-carved gold; red velvet everywhere . . . it's bad to the bone. This broad built it back in the 1800s. I might be wrong, but if I remember right her name was Baby Doe Tabor. Her husband was a major shot caller when they had the gold and silver rushes here. Way I heard it, she was a hooker that wanted the baddest hotel in the West. You'll trip when ya see it: un-fucking-believable."

"Heavy chick, huh? Shit Mel, fuck the plating company, let's just steal the staircases, we can all retire."

"Check this out—the state capitol has a gold dome on it. Grab a helicopter, get Ben to fly it, hacksaw the motherfucker off, and just fly away."

"Sho you right, just fly away."

It is such a great image that we both start laughing, can't stop. We pull up at the Grand Hotel with tears rolling down our faces. Bellhops there as soon as we pull up, twenty stories of opulence, topped by its own dome. When we go inside, it gets even better.

The place smells like money. For a kid that has spent his entire life below trailer park, this is like heaven. The stairways aren't edged in gold, but the landings are. The carpets are so thick that they cushion every step, make walking a pleasure. And they have Chinese rugs all over the place. The phone booths are made out of fucking mahogany, big gilt-edge oil paintings, dark heavy furniture that you know is old and expensive.

The help is the best—yes sir, no sir, this way sir. I pay a week in advance and it costs almost two grand. When I count the dough out without blinking, I feel like the ultimate big shot. For Mel and Syd this is no big deal. I look at Rosie and know she's digging it as much as I am. I try to be cool, act like we stayed at places like this all the time, but am completely awestruck by the reality of the existence of a place like this. If someone had told me that this kind of luxury existed before I met Mel, I would have thought they were lying. Gold inlay on the landings, going up fifteen stories. *Yeah, right!*

I'm watching Rosie, how gorgeous she looks, that caramel skin sticking out, the most beautiful chick here; those eyes are all the way live, taking everything in. She's pulling on her new red hair and I know she feels like she don't fit in. But if anybody ever deserved the best of everything, it's her. I confirm that I'll do whatever I got to so she can have it.

The bellhop drops our bag and I tip him five bucks. His gratitude is a wonderful thing to see. The room is beyond great: Chinese rug on top of the deep carpeting, that heavy dark furniture, mirrors all over the place, a complete wet bar, and a basket of pastry and fruit by the bed, next to an iced bottle of champagne. Rosie starts jumping up and down, going, "Yes, yes, yes! Oh, Bobbie, this is so cool, this is wonderful!"

I'm still sad about Jimbo, but Rosie being this happy makes me feel like I'm ten feet tall. I crack the champagne, shooting the cork to the ceiling, then douse Rosie with the wine erupting from the bottle. I eat the pastries and fruit, finish the champagne and call for another bottle. Drunk before 8 A.M.

Rosie pulls me into the bathroom and fills the sunken marble tub with steaming hot water; where she got bubble bath, I have no idea— but she has it.

We climb into the tub and wash each other, slowly, sensually, her nipples standing up as I soap her breasts. We're drunk, full, taking a bubble bath in the Grand Hotel in Denver, Colorado, and, grand it is, knowing that we're going to be making love soon. When she starts washing me, I'm galvanized, excitement coursing through me like electricity, my dick so hard it feels like it's going to explode.

When she lowers herself onto me, I know I'm too excited, that, if I don't take charge, I'll come in seconds. I pull her out of the tub, covered in bubbles.

Laying her on the bed, I start by kissing and licking her all over, going real slow, making her come by giving her head, loving the way she tastes. Then I enter her, so wet and hot it feels like there's a fire inside of her. I go as slow as I can, really taking my time, building gently; it feels like she's ready to let go and I ask her, "Are you ready, baby?" Coming together and her saying, "Te quiero mijo, te quiero mucho."

I look into her eyes and see nothing but joy. She looks kinda scared, too, and I tell her, "Yeah, me too. I'm nuts about ya."

. . . .

Mel's saying, "Ya gotta order the hamburger, ya gotta check this out. Get steak later—try the fuckin' hamburger, schmuck."

He and I are in one of the restaurants inside the hotel. Got Coors beers in front of us. A class place, wouldn't expect anything less in this joint. Rosie and Syd are once again honing their shopping skills, Syd swearing she's going to turn Rosie into an honorary JAP. Seems to be succeeding.

I tell the waiter, "Yeah, yeah, yeah gimme a burger."

"Very well, sir. And how would you like it prepared?"

What I want to say is, "Cooked—how the fuck do you prepare a burger?" but I'm starting to pick up some polish; I figure, if rare is good for steaks, it must be good for burgers. "Rare, please."

He's back in minutes with two perfectly marbled slabs of beef, seasonings, onions, and a silver meat grinder. When he said "prepared" he meant it; he grinds the meat, seasons it, and forms it into patties right at the table. He presents them to us for our approval and then takes them to be cooked—rare, of course.

Mel's watching me with such obvious affection on his face it's embarrassing. I don't know how to deal with someone who actually likes me and has no hidden agenda.

He takes a hit off his beer and says, "Pretty fucking cool, huh?"

"Wow," is my only response.

Mel looks around to make sure no one can hear what he's saying, drops his voice, and says, "So here's the deal: ya crawl under the building, cut a hole in the floor, rewire the alarm system, let me in the side. It'll take about three, four hours to peel the safe. We load the gold up and we're back here before morning. Simple, huh?"

"What's peeling a safe? Why's it take so long?"

"Some guys drill 'em, some guys use cutting bars, burn into 'em; some guys 'peel,' which is what ya gotta do with this safe. It's an insurance score—the owner set it up. He really wants it to look like a burglary. Anyhow, so we're gonna tear the shit out of it. To drill it, you gotta be like a locksmith—with Jimbo gone, I don't have access to cutting bars. . . . It's easier to show ya than to try to explain."

"Run down how I cut the floor. I know it sounds stupid, but I never heard of that, either."

"Ya got a hand drill, got like a one-inch bit in it. The floor's made outta wood. You drill up into it. You got a one-inch round hole, shove a keyhole saw into it and start sawing till ya got a hole ya can crawl through. You remember how to do a perimeter, don't ya?"

"Shit, could do one of them in my sleep. Piece of cake."

"So that's it, then. Nothin' to it."

"How come I gotta do all the crawling around and shit?"

"You are a pushy little fuck, aren't ya? Look at me, then look at you: I'd get stuck in the crawl space. Plus, to cut a hole big enough for me to crawl through would take a lot of time. But most important, Bobbie, 'cause you're the new guy. The new guy always does the grunt work. Says so right in the burglar's rule book. Can't be breaking the rules, now, can we, ace?"

"Hell no. They might pull your license or something, wouldn't want that now, would we?"

The waiter shows up with our burgers. I've never had a better one, before or since.

Mel takes a bite of his burger, says with his mouth full, "We'll do a drive-by this afternoon with Jewels—that's the dude that set it up. Craziest Chicano faggot you'll ever meet. Rock-fucking solid, but queer as a three-dollar bill."

I feel my eyebrows go up, got a mouthful of burger and say around it, "Faggot?"

"Yeah, dedicated. Reason I mention it is I don't want ya getting weird. This dude's a pro, one of the best setup men in the business. A bad motherfucker from the shoulders—just happens he likes to suck dick."

"Who gives a shit, long as he can take care of biz?"

"There ya go. Some people get funny. Thought I'd mention it. His real name is Julio—his handle is Jewels cause he loves 'em, has a jewelry store on each hand. Flashy son of a bitch."

. . . .

Mel's driving. Jewels is riding shotgun, diamond rings on every finger, gold chains running down to his navel, silk shirt open to the belly to show 'em off, offsetting the tattoos on his chest; a diamond-studded watch on one wrist, a wide gold bracelet on the other. I'm in the backseat, Jewels is giving directions and rapping.

"This came to me third party. It's an insurance score. Guy buys three, four pounds. Gets hit, claims twenty or something—long as we get ours, who cares, right honey?"

Mel looks over at him says, "What's this third-party shit, baby girl? More important, if it's for insurance, what's our guarantee?"

"One of my people came to me with it. Everyone knows the only thing I like better than sucking dick is kicking ass. They ain't gonna fuck with us. There it is, now slow down."

He's all excited, a very dramatic guy, goes back and forth between cholo tough guy and demure señorita—definite gender confusion. He points at the crawl space entry on the side and says, "That's it. Young stud here can be under the building and through the floor like that."

Snapping his fingers, he continues, "The guarantee is three to five pounds in ingots. So it's on for tonight. Melvin, why don't the three of us go to mi casa, smoke some eska, and get naked?"

I'm already nervous. This guy is so flamboyant I don't know how to take him. Having not really done any time except juvie and foster homes and shit, I'm not familiar with the banter that's developed in prison society. I think he's serious.

Mel don't miss a beat, says, "I'd love to, my little passion flower, but I'm still hopelessly heterosexual. If that ever changes, you'll be the first to know, and, tough as you are, tough as I am, Sydney would kill both of us and piss on our graves."

Mel's gotta throw me in the shit.

"Now, Bobbie—*there's* a pretty motherfucker, young enough ya might be able to save him from a lifetime doomed to dealing with crazy women."

"Nah, homeboy don't do it for me. He's too macho. Reminds me of all the cholitos back in the barrio, just got a different accent. I need someone that makes me feel helpless and dainty. Bobbie, nice as he is, still has gunslinger tattooed all over him, trouble waiting to happen. You, on the other hand, are mature and sophisticated, know how to treat a lady like a queen." He starts laughing and throws a jab at Mel's head and drops right back into vato loco mode, says, "And if you don't like that, we can box. Right *ese?*"

"Shit, you about as helpless and dainty as a fucking great white shark. I ain't fuckin' ya and you're forgetting I've seen you box—I'll just shoot your ass."

Dropping Jewels at his short—a classic chopped, lowered roadster, got purple paint on it that is beyond perfect, flawless, so many coats of lacquer it glows. He says, "Ándele pues carnales." And we're gone.

. . . .

Getting ready. Syd and Rosie are all dolled up—bell-bottoms, tank tops, tons of makeup—they look really good. Mel and I are wearing jeans, work boots, T-shirts, all in dark colors—not black, dark, a couple of blue-collar sort of guys on their way to work. On the midnight-to-eight shift.

It's 7 P.M. and we're on our way to a coffee shop to see Kris Kristofferson, who came on at eight. I don't know what a coffee shop is—got a vision of Denny's, with some guy singing folk music by the cash register. Think it sounds pretty weird, but we don't go to work till ten, and Mel and Syd swear it'll be fun and kill some time.

We get there. It's the Exodus Coffee Shop, a famous local hippie hangout, definitely not related to Denny's. The place is big, like an airline hangar or something. Dark illuminated by candles and footlights; chairs, couches flung about haphazardly, tables, none of which match; black-light art on the walls, and a big stage—pretty fucking cool. The place reeks with the sleepy, sweet smell of pot, overlaid by incense.

Kris Kristofferson puts on a good show, real kicked back, has a country edge to it, but urban lyrics. We drink espresso till it feels like bad speed. Drop Syd and Rosie at the Grand, so that if things go wrong we can call 'em to post bail, and go to work.

We drive into Commerce City, where the chemical smell is so strong it makes you feel sick. Some of the factories are still open, running three shifts back-to-back. The war is still going strong and business is good.

As it's getting closer, the rush starts coming on, but not like it usta be. I know what I'm doing and how to do it. It's still exciting, just not quite as intense.

I ask Mel, "What time you gonna be at the door?"

He looks at his watch, says, "Half hour enough?"

"Gimme forty minutes, in case I run into some kind of problem."

"See ya at eleven-twenty."

I'm out of the car and moving fast. I squat down and rip the wire mesh out of the entryway and dive under the building. Gravel cuts into the palms of my hands, and the smell of mildew and rotting wood hits my nose as I'm crawling between the supports and piping under the factory. I got about a two-foot clearance between the ground and the floor.

Once again, spiderwebs all over, dragging myself on my belly like Audie Murphy between the support beams. I pick a spot, pull my gloves on, get as much leverage as I can, and start drilling. This is a hand-powered drill—apply pressure with one hand, drill with the other.

I'm soaking from sweat before I start sawing. (Now they got all this neat, battery-powered shit, makes life much more pleasant.) I'm moving as fast as possible, want to cut through the floor and get this safe done and get out; this staying inside places for hours makes me crazy.

I get in ten minutes early, have the alarm rewired in under five minutes. Have to sit and wait. I sit down and light a cigarette, waiting for Mel, watching my watch, the second hand in slow motion. I get up and walk over to the safe. The thing looks indestructible, as tall as I am. It has two dials and a big bar to open it with; it looks like a nightmare. I come to find out that this particular type of safe is one of the easiest to open, but that night it has me thoroughly intimidated.

Eleven-twenty on the button, and I open the side door. Mel swings through and I pull it closed. He's got one of those bags they use to carry baseball bats in—long canvas, with a drawstring at the top. We don't go into the factory part at all, but back into the office, and I learn how to crack a safe.

Mel empties the tools onto the floor: chisels, sledgehammers, steel wedges, wrecking bars with pipe (to add leverage), and a fucking axe. If this was one of those tests—what don't fit in this picture—what would you have picked?

"Why the axe, man? Gonna bust up the furniture? Chop down a tree or something?"

"Here we go." He picks the axe up. It looks small next to Mel. He says, "Fire axe, tungsten alloy steel. This safe—low-grade rolled steel. Peeling a safe is just what it sounds like: it's layers, not just six seven inches of steel—*layers* of steel, asbestos, concrete, like that. . . . Put these on."

He throws me a set of goggles.

"We peel 'em off, one layer at a time. Watch me on the first one so you'll know how to do it; the rest should be pretty easy—smashing through concrete and shit. Hard fucking work, but once ya get the outer wall off, it's just manual labor."

We get the safe turned so that the back is facing out and Mel picks the axe back up and says, "This is the easiest way to start it."

He smashes the axe into the upper corner of the back of the safe. He looks at his handiwork, takes a trial swing to make sure he'll hit the same place, and comes around again, full force. A small cloud of white dust shoots into the air.

"This thing really is a piece of shit—the outer casing can't be over an eighth inch, and this crap inside looks like plaster of Paris. See, Bobbie, sometimes ya get lucky."

It takes us an hour to hammer and chisel the back off, using the hole made by the axe as an entry point. The rest is pure sweat. Maybe an eighth inch isn't much, but cutting a four-foot-by-five-foot block of it out has blood running inside my gloves, blisters that break till my palms look like hamburger. I exchanged railroad work gloves for the tight leather gloves you'd usually use, but I've never worked a day in my life, didn't have callus one.

I'm completely focused—all that exists is the metal in front of me, positioning the chisel, and hitting it as hard as I can. Mel's doing the same thing, working the other way. I know he's making more progress on his side, and it's making me crazy; feel like I'm in a race and I want to win bad. The muscles in my shoulders, chest, and arms are on fire, and my clothes look like I went swimming in them and rolled around in plaster of Paris. The shit is caked in my nose and covers the lens of the goggles.

Mel still finishes before I do, and he didn't know we were in a race. I feel very discouraged, keep focused, and finally hit the bottom of my side.

Mel's barely sweating, covered in dust but not winded. Looks like he could fight twelve rounds if he had to. He laughs and says, "I won." I guess he did know it was a race.

I'm still trying to catch my breath. Mel says, "Kick back, man. Looks like you're gonna die. This is like the ultimate piece of shit, as far as safes go. No layers. Watch this."

He picks up one of the sledgehammers and attacks the plaster of Paris, sending chunks of it flying. In less than five minutes he's down to the last wall. He says, "Riveted on, cut these and we're in. Six rivets each side, four at the top."

I'm studying every move he's making, focused, rushing real good. We're almost out of there. Mel cuts the last rivet and, using a wrecking bar, peels the back wall. He grabs his flashlight, shines it all over the safe, leaning way into it. Comes out and says, "We're burnt."

I can feel insanity coming on. What the fuck is he talking about, burnt?

I ask, "Whatcha mean?"

"Burnt. Current hip vernacular, indicating robbed, generally by fraud—in this case, the owner got greedy, wanted the insurance dough *and* all the gold. *Our* end included. Not a very nice thing.

"If Jimbo was here, he could preach a sermon for us—before he shot the cocksucker. Me, I just want what's owed us—plus interest, of course. He figures he never met us. We sure can't sue him for breach of contract.

"We gotta get with Jewels, find out where to catch this guy—except here. Probably bracing him at home would be best."

I gotta see for myself. I grab the flashlight, lean into the safe. Nothing that's worth anything—definitely not any gold. I am *very* angry!

I look at Mel and say, "Let's go."

. . . .

Rosie is looking up at me, sitting on the bed, legs crossed and smoking a cigarette. She says, "I'm pregnant, Bobbie, whatcha think about that?"

I'm still so mad I feel like I'm vibrating. It takes a moment for this to sink in. I have no idea how to react. I'm not fifteen yet. The idea of fatherhood's something I've never considered. My first reaction is, how did this happen? But I know. You fuck, you make babies—that's the deal.

The whole time I was living with my parents, one of my dad's constant comments was that my ma was supposed to have had me aborted. I know that my life is fucked-up, but that it is much better than no life at all. Still, I assume that Rosie will want to get an abortion.

I ask her, "So what ya want to do?"

"I don't know. What if I want to have it? What then, Bobbie?"

"Then, I guess I gotta get really good at this burglary thing. My old man usta always bitch about how expensive kids are. Do you think this is a real good idea? It might be better to wait. I mean, is this a real good time to be making babies?"

"It's never a good time. There's always gonna be something wrong. If I have it, are you gonna hang or get out of Dodge? That's what I'm asking—not if you think it's good timing."

"Shit, mija, you know better than that. Whatever you want to do, I'm there. One thing for sure: if you want to have it, I know we can do better than our folks did. Spoil the shit out of the kid, give it everything it wants. Think about it. Whatever you want to do, I'm with ya."

She's smoking with one hand, playing with her hair with the other, searching my face for signs of deceit. The fear rolls off her like fog off the ocean.

She finds the answer she was looking for and you can see the decision in her face before she smiles that crazy chipped-tooth smile, eyes all the way live. She says, "You gonna be a daddy. Whatcha think about that, peckerwood?"

Now I'm scared. Life just got real serious. I've always assumed I'll be dead before I'm twenty—this means having to stick around, make a real commitment to someone besides me. It fucking terrifies me.

I tell her, "I'm *your* peckerwood, mija. Whatever it takes, I'm down. This kid will have everything it wants."

Meaning every word of it. I been scared all my life. Something besides myself to be scared for. Not that big of a jump. The feeling of doom that lives inside of me had already expanded to include Rosie— a baby wasn't that big of a change. When you've been terrified all your life, it takes a lot to rattle you. I ask her, "Are you sure about this? You don't want to just get an abortion?"

"Yeah baby, I'm sure. I've known for about a month now. I talked to Syd about it, been thinking about it twenty-four seven. . . . I want to have it, with you or without you. But it would be a lot better if you were around."

I think about what she just said and tell her, "The only way you gonna get rid of me is kill me."

If I could have seen the future, my reaction would have been different. Like Mel said, "Sooo far, sooo good!"

. . . .

Mel's leaning on the bar, got a shot and a beer in front of him, the air full of smoke, tobacco, and pot. Strobe lights flickering and the Stones on the PA system. We're waiting for a local band, called Lothar & the Hand People, to get done setting up. Jewels is supposed to meet us and is running late. Mel is getting cross-eyed, the drugs and alcohol starting to show more and more. He closes one eye to keep me in focus and says, "You're nuts. Ya know that, right, kid?"

"Yeah man, been hearing that all my life."

"Ain't nothing more important than making babies. Me and Syd can't do it. Her insides got all fucked-up. I always wanted to have a kid, kinda gave up the idea. What are ya, fourteen?"

I take a minute to think and realize that I turned fifteen about a week before, say, "Shit man, I'm fifteen now. My birthday was August twenty-fifth. That's old enough to make babies."

"Making 'em is one thing—takin' care of 'em is another. How the fuck ya gonna do that? You're both hypes. You're turning into a real stand-up thief, but the thing is, the vacation plan sucks. Ya get busted, who's gonna take care of Rosie and your kid? You gotta give this one some thought."

"Shit man, if Rosie hadn't already made up her mind, I'd try to talk her into getting an abortion. The thing is, I know she wants this baby. It's her carrying it. If I try to make her get rid of it, if she does, she'll hate me, if she doesn't, it would fuck everything up between us anyhow. Look at how fucked-up our parents were—we came out OK. One thing for sure: we have a kid, it won't get beat up and shit. Plus, it'll have great godparents—I hit the pen, they'll take care of it. Won't ya, Melvin?"

"Yeah kid, we sure would." Mel's slurring his speech, face all slack, one eye crossing inward. He shakes his head, trying to clear it, and says, "Where's this fucking cholo? We gotta get our dough. He's usually real responsible. I hope he don't flake, put me in a position where I gotta kill him."

The strobe lights are throwing Mel into stark relief, his face showing all the damage done by the drugs and stress. I don't know it then, but I'm looking at the beginning of the end, where the shit takes control instead of giving it. For me, that's an alien concept. Drugs are still working—I really believe they'll never turn on me and rip my throat out. Narcotics are my oldest and truest friend.

Mel's downing shots fast—three shots to one beer—getting more and more fucked-up. His face looks like it's hanging off the bones under it. I'm really worried, but don't know why. Looking back, I know he was starting to lose it; at the time I just knew something felt wrong.

Jewels makes his entrance, little entourage of faggots following him like puppy dogs, a huge, fat, short-haired, jock-looking motherfucker and three classic fairies, little petite pretty guys. They group up around us and Jewels flutters his ring-encrusted hand at the dance floor, saying, "Mingle, boys. I must talk business with my hoodlum friends. We don't need any extra ears. Go on dearies, leave papa alone."

The big one gives us what's supposed to be a scary look, and they scamper off.

Mel looks 51–50, stark raving mad. He says, "You're late, motherfucker. What, do I look like I got a dick on my forehead, hanging us up like a couple a schmucks? Where's our fucking gold? It was a guaranteed three pounds—all we got were blisters on our hands and a risked rock-and-roll felony for it. What's up?"

Jewels raises his hands, says, "Slow down there, ace. Don't be raising your voice to me—just cause I'm queer don't mean I'm a punk. You want some of my fine brown ass go ahead and jump on it."

I slip my hand into my back pocket. Don't know what's gonna go down, but I know if this vato loco tries any shit, I'm gonna blow his brains out. Mel may be fucked-up and loud, but he's my partner and this dude ran us into a bunk rip-off.

You can see Mel fighting the insanity off, drunkenness receding into the distance, eyes almost focused now. He looks at me and I nod. I'm ready.

He says, "Check. It. Out. Homeboy. You set that score up. We did it on your say-so. *You* are responsible. Period. We all know you a tough motherfucker. Pro boxer, all that shit. Don't change nothin'. You owe. Forty-eight ounces—two hundred an ounce. Nine thousand six hundred dollars. 'Cause we respect you, you're gettin' a chance to make it right. You owe us an apology, and the dough. Whatcha want to do?"

Jewels drops into a fighter's crouch, wings a shot at Mel's head and pulls it. Mel don't even blink, just keeps staring at him.

Jewels goes falsetto, says, "You *muy* macho, gringo *grande*. You know how excited I get when you go into your badass bag—makes my toes curl. I swear to God, you spend one night with me, you'll never go back to women.

"Put like that, what choice do I got? A: I'm sorry for sending you guys on a wild-goose chase. B: it's gonna take a couple of days, but I'm tracking this asshole down. We'll get everything this motherfucker owns. Not just what he owes. C: since you're in town anyhow, I got three, four scores lined up you two can knock down. D: instead of my usual twenty percent, I only want ten. E: if you don't think that's more than fair, fuck you and your triggerman here."

Nodding at me.

"We been working together for years, Mel. You know I don't take shit from nobody—personally, I think that whiskey is fucking with your head. Why don't we get together tomorrow, let your brain clear out. How's that?"

Mel raises his shot glass, says, "Cool. I'll drink to that." And downs another shot.

I spend the night baby-sitting Mel. Lothar & the Hand People put on a good tight show, basic driving rock and roll. These guys have hair down to their asses, bell-bottoms, sequined vests . . . very cool.

I keep running my hand through my short hair. To be a good thief you can't look cool or flamboyant. Me and Mel just a couple of blue-collar guys, subterranean. I want my long hair back.

Syd and Rosie show up at about midnight. I'm stressed to the hubs. Mel's been picking fights, getting sloppier and sloppier as the night progresses, finally passing out on one of the couches. Two of the guys he'd fucked with see he's passed out and aren't scared at all by my body-guard routine. These are both big, healthy motherfuckers.

I'm doing my best to intimidate these two. Mel's all the way gone, snoring and drooling. Syd takes the situation in at one glance, asks, "Where's Jewels?"

"Dancing with one of his boyfriends."

"I'll be right back, bubeleh."

These guys want a piece of Mel's ass. When he was still able to move around he'd gone into a drunken rage, chased 'em both out of the bar; now they see a perfect chance to get revenge. I'm on my feet, got a beer bottle in my hand. If they force the issue, I'm gonna break it and start cutting.

Shooting these guys is out of the question; they ain't packed and I can't do it. My thinking is, if they want to beat my ass to get to Mel, using a broken bottle is justified. Since Mel started the shit with them, shooting them would be way out of line, and we'd have to leave town behind a shooting. We'd never get our dough on that sting.

Needless to say, I'm scared, doing my best not to show it. The big-ger guy has an Elvis Presley thing going on—long sideburns and a greasy pompadour.

He says, "Y'all better get your ass out of the way. We got something for your friend; if'n you keep standing there, we got somethin' for you, too."

I wish I could think of some snappy comeback, get 'em to laugh, defuse the situation. I look over my shoulder to see if, by some miracle, Mel is regaining consciousness. He's out like a light. Smooth gone.

I say the first thing I think of: "You know what, pal? Fuck you and your sideburns. Want some? Get some."

That's when the cavalry arrives. Sydney with Jewels and the foot-ball player. Psychotic anger shining out of Jewels's eyes like spotlights, the only feminine thing about either of 'em the fact that they both must have had mothers. The football player asks, "Yo Elvis, is there some kind of problem here?"

Jewels is snapping his knuckles, looking these two assholes up and down. He says, "No problemo, right guys? Matter of fact, you're probably old friends of our friend here, gonna carry him out to the car for us, am I right? Tell me I'm correct in this assumption, otherwise all four of us will be very upset."

Rosie pushes through, standing at my side. She says, "Stupid fucking Mexican—not counting Mel, there's *five* of us. Can't you add?"

Jewels's jaw drops. He wants to know who this PR chick is, calling him stupid.

He says, "Chingao, pardon the fuck out of me, mija. I guess you must be young stud's other half."

Rosie shakes her head. I'm thoroughly confused. I'm proud of her for standing up, but scared to death 'cause I know she's got our kid inside her. I decide if these guys get stupid, I will shoot them. I'm not gonna let Rosie get hurt.

She looks at me and says, "Motherfucker can't speak Spanish either. So what's up? You two barbosos gonna help carry Mel out to the car or what?"

Elvis and his partner exchange looks and Elvis says, "Yep, that's what we're here for. Bubba there don't look too good and we wanted to know if he needed any help." He looks at me and says, "Ain't that right man?"

I feel a grin going from ear to ear, rescued by faggots and a seventeen-year-old girl calling shots. Not part of any John Wayne movie I've ever seen, but definitely a good ending for the night.

I reply, "Yeah, we were just discussing the best way to carry this big drunk fucker out of here. Probably one of 'em under each arm—what do ya think Jewels?"

"I think you need to muzzle your heina. She's too mean, homeboy. Aside from that, sounds good—these two pendejos carry Mel and let's wrap it up for the night."

Pausing and pointing at the guy that looks like a brick wall, Jewels says, "This is my friend George. He plays tackle for the Broncos."

Being a small kid, I've never paid attention to football. I don't realize that not only is this guy a world-class athlete, but a heavy-duty celebrity as well.

I say, "Cool man, this is Rosie. She's my bodyguard."

Elvis and his partner are starstruck, can't believe they're talking to a famous football player. Elvis's friend says, "Wow man, you're the best! I saw you play Saturday—sacked the quarterback twice. You're a bad motherfucker."

George just stares at them, then says, "Uh-huh."

They pick up Mel, who's groaning and drooling, and drag him out to the car.

I put my arm around Rosie. Her eyes are shining like golden beacons.

I say, "Whatcha think, is Jewels right? Do I gotta muzzle ya?"

She laughs, deep and rowdy, and says, "Only if you tie me up—and God help ya if you don't make me come."

. . . .

Mel is immune to hangovers. He starts the next day bright and early. Our phone rings around 10 A.M. Mel says, "Wake up pal: early bird catches the worm and all that happy horseshit. We're meeting Jewels at noon. Gotta start putting this shit together. If we don't do something, we're gonna be broke soon. You and Rosie come on over after ya get showered up. OK?"

"Sure enough, ace. I really need to make serious bank now."

I hang up the phone and start cooking my wake-up. Mind going a mile a minute, figuring numbers; having only gone to seventh grade, that is a fearsome endeavor. But I know I've already blown close to ten grand, and don't understand how, the money flying away like magic. I know that in order to put any away for this kid we're gonna have, I have to make a lot.

The feeling of urgency and panic that I feel all day, every day, raises to a fever pitch. Where it comes from, I have no idea, but the fact that Rosie and this child are depending on me has started this feeling that the only way I'm gonna let them down is if I'm killed.

Syd's yelling. We can hear it from down the hall. Mad at Mel for getting so fucked-up last night. Before we knock on their door, Mel's voice kicks in, not yelling but loud.

Once we get inside they chill out, just ignore each other. Me and Rosie try to be circumspect, keep a low profile.

I finally ask, "So what's the plan? Does Jewels have some more shit lined up or what? And if he does, how do we know if it's gonna be any good? One more score like that last one could put a guy out of business, know what I mean?"

Mel's rubbing his face, stalling for time. He gets up, walks into the kitchen, and comes out with a beer. He opens it, downs half, and says, "Yeah, old cholo grande has one commercial burg and two residentials waiting to be done as we speak. See, the thing is, I don't like residential work. Going into people's pads ain't too cool; I don't want to find myself in a position where a family might come walking in on us and the old man wants to be a hero or some fucking thing. Could get messy.

"The other thing is this: me and Jewels have worked together on beaucoup scores. He's a pro. His business is information. The other night was the first time I know of that he fucked up, but you can bet we're gonna get our dough on that one. He's one macho motherfucker in his own weird way—no way he's gonna just let some lame burn us. 'Cause it makes him look bad."

Syd had remained quiet up to this point, but now comes in swinging. "Look bad! Oy vey! Look like motherfucking *shit* is more like it. If he don't make this one right, he's out of business. Even if we decide to write it off, word is already going around. He's gotta get the dough and make an example out of the goniff that stung us. Otherwise, no pro will work with him ever again. In this game, knowledge really is power, and he ain't gonna want to give up any, not as hard as he's fought to get it.

"Just kick back, see what his pitch is on these other things, see how they sound. If the residential shit is shaky, we'll take a pass, just do the store or whatever it is and get our gold. See, nothing to worry about my little outlaws. Emes!"

I've discovered ambition. Not common sense, not the actual use of my mind; that comes to me later. The closest I'm able to come to rational thought now is figuring the odds. There is no moral sense at all—my only loyalty is to myself. And Rosie, and, to a lesser extent, Mel and Syd.

If there are three scores to do, I think we should do 'em all. So what if it gets messy on one of 'em? If someone walks in on us, do whatever we have to and split. And that's what I say.

"Fuck it man, we all need dough: you guys gotta get out of the U.S., Rosie's going to be having our baby. . . . I say we rob everything that ain't nailed down. If it gets messy, so fucking what—blow anybody up that gets in our way. Go for it!"

Mel stops breathing, starts swelling up, and then stops. He looks sad, beyond sad—pained to the bone. He looks over at Syd, who raises her eyebrows and mimics a fast-draw artist. Index finger extended, she blows imaginary smoke off the end and holsters it in her invisible holster.

Mel shakes his head, kills the rest of his beer, and says, "Yep. Fucking gunslinger syndrome. Check it out kid—that's what we doctors call a guy that don't think, wants to blaze his way in and out of every situation. A gunslinger. I don't like gunslingers. I like you just fine, but ya got to get your head right. One of the things about being young is, you always expect things to work out right. I got to tell ya that they rarely do. You blaze in and out of everything you do, people get hurt that shouldn't, and sooner or later you go down in flames. News at eleven. Know what I mean? When we entered into this, it was pure business.

"Danny had been telling me about ya for a while, what a great thief you were and all that bullshit. First time I met ya, I saw a key with feet, not a human being. I knew with some schooling, as small as you are, you could get into places I can't. Being this big is a disadvantage in our line of work. I turned ya onto stuff so you'd be reliable—not a paranoid, crazy speed freak. The most important thing is that you can function. As a junkie you can—shootin' speed, it's out of the question. Pretty fuckin' cold-blooded, huh?

"I also know that once ya get real good, ya ain't gonna need me. Well, that's still a long way away. I'm getting sloppy, I know that. Me and Syd were talking about it all morning. I got to slow down my using and drinking or I'll get washed. Here's the thing: we never intended to adopt you guys, but the fact is, we're pretty tight. Friends even. Am I right?"

Rosie and I look at each other; neither of us has any idea how to respond to this.

I laugh and say, "Friends even. And I gotta tell ya big-time, no matter how good I get, I'll always keep ya around to take care of my light work—stick with me, kid."

Mel and Syd both laugh. Syd takes over.

"Listen, bubeleh, Mel told me about the comment ya made about us being the baby's godparents. We'd like nothin' better, but youse gotta slow down. You have to have a code, ya can't be hurtin' innocent people. You read all the time—check out Nietzsche, stuff about Buddha, the fucking Bible even . . . get some depth to ya. Get some stuff about philosophy and morality—everything is shades of gray.

"But anything that puts a citizen at risk is not acceptable. The world is full of animals—we don't want to be like them. We're thieves, which, if you give it some thought, can be a very honorable profession. We get in, we get the goods, we get out. Nobody gets hurt. We specialize in businesses 'cause they're always insured and the chances of running into a citizen are almost nonexistent. Are you guys with us on this?"

Rosie speaks while I'm still thinking. She says, "You guys know the game. Call the shots. But, I gotta tell ya, this baby's gonna be raised Catholic, go to the best Catholic schools, everything. . . . If something happens to us, you guys can't be trying to make it Jewish. OK?"

Mel and Syd start laughing, Mel so hard his whole body's shaking. Loud, happy laughter. He starts talking between chuckles, saying, "This kid's gonna have enough problems without being Jewish—poor thing would have to be neurotic on top of everything else. Ain't nothing gonna happen to you guys anyhow."

Rosie says, "The other thing is, Bobbie just wants us all to come out of this all right. He ain't no gunslinger."

Mel says, "I gotta tell you, Rosie, Bobbie is developing definite gunslinger tendencies. You gotta help him to chill out, use his brain. Guns are absolutely a last resort."

That feeling of panic is clawing its way all through my body. I want control so bad it's killing me. The drugs, the crime, sex, adrenaline—are all ways for me to feel like I have some power in a hostile universe. All I can focus on is that I have to generate a lot of cash. I feel like I'm responsible for our story having a happy ending, and know things are getting away from me.

Mel's already starting to slur his words, Syd's got at least two murder warrants out on her, possibly more. Rosie is so happy, looking at her makes me want to cry. I feel like a rabbit caught in the headlights of a tractor trailer, frozen, watching tons of hard fucking steel tearing through life, coming to crush me, and unable to move. I'm waiting for my fate to be sealed as my bones are crushed and my insides splashed all over the asphalt of reality.

I still feel that way much of the time, but that little flash frame will always burn in my memory like lightning must as it rushes at your face. Sydney smiling, a blonde no longer, lustrous black hair showing off her blue eyes and incredibly bright red lipstick. Mel big and scary, unshaved, a fighter who had been knocked out, brain hemorrhaging bright arterial blood, dead on his feet but still putting everything he had into every punch, bobbing and weaving on instinct alone. And Rosie, red hair softly curling around her heart-shaped face, eyes like candles seen through golden brown pharmaceutical glass, fireflies fucking behind amber. . . . And I feel so so scared, stuck here, waiting for impact, and have no idea why. Life is better than I'd ever dreamed of. I'm terrified.

Mel looks at me, his eyebrows going for the top of his head. He whistles and asks, "What's up pal, you all right?"

"Never better, my brother. . . . It's just that, morals and philosophy sound great, but we can't fuck up, we all need as much cash as we can get, and we need it like yesterday. You know hard times make hard people, and all that bullshit. . . . I don't want this baby to have any hard times. I don't want Syd getting busted. I think we should do whatever we gotta do."

"You about one intense little motherfucker, ain'tcha Bobbie? We walking a tightrope here—now more than ever. Push too hard, go too fast . . . no more 'so far so good.' Once you lose control, it's all about hitting the ground. Life is about control. Don't start losing it kid.

"Whatcha want for breakfast?"

The desperation doesn't subside. As we're eating, I have the feeling that Mel is looking at a mirror when he sees me, that, at some level, he knows he's starting to lose it and is hoping to take the advice himself he was giving me.

The more scared I get, the cooler I try to act. It seems to work. I almost have myself convinced by the time Jewels arrives.

. . . .

"So you like it? Or do ya like it?"

Jewels is in good form pitching these scores. He's closing the presentation—fucking guy should have sold used cars.

"Home one: sliding glass door, lever it off the tracks, open the floor safe, ya got the combination, in and out in ten minutes. The owner is in Taos for the whole week, eating peyote and howling at the moon. Can't take diamond rings and shit like that to a hippie commune, right?

"Home two: they take their kids to the movies every Saturday night—oriental rugs, jewelry, guns, the fucking rugs are worth ten, twenty thousand, no serial numbers don'tcha know.

"The commercial one is a big camera store. They got one of those new motion detectors, can be set to detect a mouse, or set so you could drive a truck through the window and not set it off. A dial is what sets it. It's got a fail safe. You can't just turn it off. What you can do is cut a hole in the wall directly below it, reach up through the wall, grab that knob, turn it all the way counterclockwise, and the only thing that will trigger it will be a fucking herd of elephants. One, two, three. Piece of fucking cake.

"One a day. Finish up Saturday with the pad with the rugs. I should have a better location on the dickhead that we did the safe job for by then. Whatcha think?"

Mel takes a drag off his cigarette. He looks at Syd, looks at me, hesitates for a minute, and says, "Sounds pretty good except for the second one. Scratch it. They come home early, one of the kids is sick . . . too much shit can go wrong. The other two are on, as long as you got a local outlet for the cameras. I think we should do 'em both in one night, get 'em out of the way. Boo-ya."

"What's the story on your friend with the plating company?"

"He's out of town, thinks we'll forget about him or something—like I said, I'll know more by Saturday."

Mel stares at me for a minute. He asks, "What do ya think, kid?"

Feeling the rush starting, wanting the cash and the adrenaline high, wanting to punish the guy with the plating company. I say, "Let's do it."

. . . .

That afternoon I find a bookstore. It is a new experience for me—rows and rows of books—a fucking universe of books. I'd always thought that everybody got their reading material at the local drugstore or supermarket. I had no idea what to do.

Finally, I get my nerve up and sidle up to the woman at the counter. I whisper to her that I want to learn about philosophy and morality. I feel like a pervert, feel like if anyone heard me say those words they'd immediately fall to the ground laughing. 'Cause I *know* normal people have that knowledge imprinted in them at birth.

I emerge with a box full of hardback books. Looking back, if the bitch working the counter had any morality she'd have passed on the big sale and gone for a couple of introductory things. But no, she knew a sucker when she saw one and loaded me up. I had no frame of reference.

Getting back to the Grand, I pull the first book out of the box and start reading Sartre. Not a real cheerful guy. I spend every spare minute from that point on wading through that fucking box. I'm determined to develop morals, become a human being . . . my ambition knows no limits.

I'd never read a hardback book till then, found 'em to be a pain in the ass—ya can't bend the covers back like with a paperback.

I have to bombard poor Rosie with all the ideas I'm discovering. And still stealing with both hands.

. . . .

That night, me, Mel, and Jewels go to check out our targets. The house is great—a fucking mansion—wrought-iron fencing all around it, set back from the road, lights on the inside to scare off burglars, the outside completely dark. It's perfect.

The store is a different matter. It is downtown, right in the center of Denver. We cruise it, riding in one of the station wagons. The whole area is well lit, lots of foot traffic. It doesn't look that good to me and I say, "Check it out, anything goes wrong, the heat is gonna be on us quick like a hurry-up. We do the alarm, and we still gotta get inside, and even more important, we got to get out with all this shit. We're talkin' about cleaning this place out. Am I right? That's a lot of time stacking, and a lot of time of exposed loading."

Jewels laughs, flutters his hand, and says, "See, Bobbie, that's why I'm worth my weight in diamonds. For you and Mel to set this up would take forever. See the roof." And he points at the sign over the store: Kirby's Camera. "No, mijo, you don't see it 'cause it's flat and has a brick wall going up three feet past it. That's why no one is gonna see you cutting into it."

We drive into the alley running behind the store, and he asks, "See the loading dock? Once again, mijo, the answer is no. It's behind that sliding steel door." He points at a security gate in the back of the building. "That's where they park their delivery van. The only exposure is gonna be Mel cutting into the wall to reset the alarm, when you climb up onto the roof, when you open the gate there to let Mel in, and when you guys leave, driving their van—which, incidentally, has the keys left in the ignition. My guys give you cash money, you give them the van full of cameras.

"So what ya think Bobbie? How's it sound now?"

I think it sounds a whole lot better than it looks. The whole thing is too fucking sweet.

I ask him, "So, with that pad you got the combination of the safe— here ya got the whole thing wired. . . . Why ain't ya doing these yourself?"

" 'Cause shit can always go wrong. No matter how good ya plan, eventually you're gonna go down. I get twenty percent of everything I put together, and the worst thing I can ever get busted for is receiving. I got good lawyers and receiving stolen property is a misdemeanor. You guys go down doing the stealing, it's a smoking-hot felony. You tell me why I ain't doing 'em myself. Whatcha think, tough guy, why ain't I doing 'em myself?"

I get back to the Grand, wait till midnight to go to work. Start reading Sartre. The guy could have never been a thief—he's way too pessimistic. Lie around with Rosie, shoot heroin. Another day in paradise.

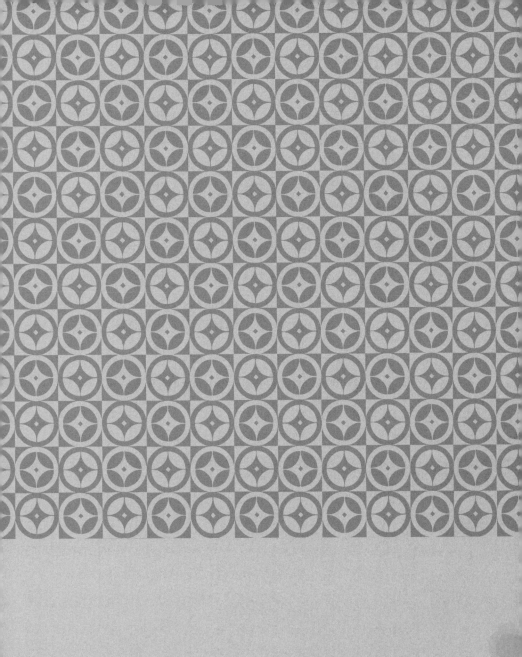

Book II

*T*ime's going by as slowly as a crippled turtle. Rosie has started reading, she's kicked back next to me wearing cutoff jeans and nothing else. I'm aware that she's gorgeous. That the room we're in is finer than fucking frog hairs. That this is as close to heaven as I'm ever gonna get but it don't fix me anymore. I don't know that you adapt to anything, good or bad, and I've gotten used to this lifestyle.

The phone rings and I lean over Rosie to grab it. Holding it to my ear knowing that something is wrong as soon as I hear Mel's salutation, Syd's voice echoing behind him carrying through the phone lines.

"Yo, Bobbie. What's up?"

"Nada fuckin' thing, partner. You called, tell me."

"Sheeit, man, Jewels says the chump with the floor safe changed the combination. That means we gotta tie off."

"How come? Just peel the motherfucker."

"Can't. It's a class-A box. Gotta punch it and pull it. Need some special hardware."

"Let me know when we're ready."

Click, buzz, and I'm listening to the dial tone. Rosie's looking at me over the top of her paperback, hair splashed across the linen-covered pillow, fingernails bright red. Forehead furrowed, she asks, "What's wrong, mijo, problems?"

"Nah, darlin', we get to kick back for a while longer than expected. Ain't no thing." She sets the book down, levers herself up to kiss me, and I can't respond—all I want to do is fix. That's what I do. Get up and start the ritual. See the pain in my girl's eyes and realize that heroin is starting to run me and there isn't a fucking thing I can do about it.

Having finished Sartre and read most of Nietzsche, trying Plato for

EIGHT

a change. Not able to shut my brain off, plotting different outcomes from our criminal endeavors.

Getting more nervous by the minute, wanting to get this shit moving, I'm as hooked on the action as I am on the narcotics, that feeling of being aware of everything.

So on top of my game I feel like I could hear a mouse fart two blocks away. The electric intensity of doing the score, whether it's peeling a safe or passing bad checks. The way ennui sets in. And the jubilation that flows through me once it's over with and we're figuring out the take.

Of course there's the flip side to that, when you're off, and you know it. Feel in your heart and soul that you're spiraling out of control, twitchy and clumsy.

Missing the signs that are always there when something's wrong, walking into a setup or maybe just have bad luck. Sirens wailing and knowing they *are* coming for you, sprinting across alleys, climbing drainpipes, running across rooftops, jumping from one to the next, and praying for mercy and grace. Screaming inside yourself, "Help, help me God, please get me through this man. *Help me!*" No bargaining, no I'll never do it again, no promises to help the sick and dying, but a plea for mercy torn from your guts and thrown up to heaven, *knowing that you deserve no mercy,* facing the reality of your own weak needs.

My aspirations to greatness, knowing that like everyone else I want what I want when I want it and when things go wrong I'm screaming for help. Not verbally, nothing you can hear, but so loud that begging for grace becomes my entire being. Not an outlaw, not a tough guy, just an ongoing cry for help.

These things define my existence. The highs that are so far beyond high that the word has no meaning.

The lows that make it clear how a wild animal feels as it chews off its leg to escape a trap.

I'm gowed, reading, and my brain *still* won't shut up. While my mind processes the information it's talking to itself.

Rosie's watching the tube. I'm doing my best to get lost in the book and ignore the compulsion to start on this crime spree immediately.

That or shoot so much dope that I'm a drooling imbecile and incapable of performing well, or not at all.

No one's around. I tried calling everyone we know in Denver and finally decided that we're just gonna have to wait for word from Mel or Jewels, hoping maybe Sydney might pop in.

Minutes drag into hours into days. My panic level keeps climbing—we're starting to run out of smack.

. . . .

There's a light drizzle wafting over downtown Denver, softening the grimy look as we speed on our way to pick up. What's waiting for us is Mexican brown, different from the white we've been shooting. Mel's driving, I'm riding shotgun. Got the 380 in my back pocket. Mel's steering with one hand, holding a quart of Jack Daniel's with the other, double-strapped .44 pugs in shoulder holsters. He's looking at the road, talking more to it than to me.

"Shouldn't have any fucking problems. Jewels set this up. Can't trust nobody else to pick up. Don't care if it's your own mother. No middlemen, that's the rules." Raising the bottle and chugging from it, offers it to me.

I don't respond, there's nothing to say, don't want any whiskey. Looking back I know that Mel was starting to fall apart. But at the time I didn't understand. I didn't want whiskey. I just felt confused. Just gonna watch the road, listen, and smoke my cigarette as the station wagon creeps through rush-hour traffic. Play with the radio, trying to find rock and roll, hit a station playing Patsy Cline and Mel snaps out of the trance state he seems to be in. Yells out, "Leave it there, pal, this bitch can make a motherfucker cry. Listen to her. The broad wails."

He's right. I wonder if this means I'm getting all the way soft. Listening to some hillbilly chick singing about being true and digging it. Hating the crawl through traffic, ask, "We do these scores, dump the wagons, get matching Cads. Whatcha think?"

Still looking at the road. Back in the fog that you can almost see all around his head. It doesn't seem like I'm gonna get a response on this one.

The drizzle and mist making life seem like it's in slow motion, matching Mel's actions and my mood. Two stoplights later Mel looks at me and laughs, keeps smiling for about three blocks and says, "Sure thing, killer. This shit goes right we'll have more than enough dough. Pick up this smack, finish here. Get some new ID, change the way we look a little bit, get the fuck on to the next deal. Gonna have to change vehicles anyhow. When ya change towns ya change everything—name, cars, and your appearance."

Patsy has given way to Johnny Cash and I still like it, decide that I've lost my mind and don't care. Ask Mel, "How come we gotta blow out of here? The hotel is beyond cool. Jewels has plenty of shit set up, now we got a connection for this brown stuff. Seems copacetic to me."

"Jewels's putting a party together for tomorrow night, a lot of people will see us. Still, we gotta hit the guy on the gold in person and what we're gonna do with this connection is *burn* him. Jewels won't give a shit, this cat's a wetback, get into the barrio and ya find out the Chicanos are killing 'em for entertainment. Jewels will just want his piece of the action. Fuck it, we're almost out of here anyhow."

I don't say a word. The rush is starting. I've never done an armed robbery before and as soon as I've processed what Mel said my hands start shaking and I can feel my heart hammering against my ribs.

I pull the 380 out of my back pocket, jack one into the chamber, and stick it into the front of my pants. Look over at Melvin and he grins, don't show no teeth, the corners of his mouth go up. Neither of us make a sound, country music and the drizzle is now pounding rain playing backup on the roof of the station wagon. For the first time in what seems like forever I'm in overdrive and it feels so fucking good.

Mel downs another big shot of the Jack and I grab the bottle, upend it. It burns all the way down. Seconds later the warmth starts seeping through my body and I can feel my aggression start to rise.

. . . .

Mel's got a gun in both hands. My 380's in my right. The pad is on the second floor of a walk-up tenement, the air is thick with the smell of refried beans, cooking onions, and the sweet smell of pot. Voices talking in Spanish echo through the dimly lit hallway. I notice the dust floating through the air, that the door in front of us has been smashed open before and poorly repaired, the blisters in the paint and the graffiti on the walls all in Spanish and then Mel's whispering, "Fuck finesse.

I'm gonna kick the door offa the fuckin' hinges, go in first and cover whoever's in there. You got one free hand, collect the drugs and cash and we're outta here."

Rushing, that roaring sound in my ears, feels like the eyes are gonna pop out of my head. "Let's do it."

Mel's foot hits the door and I'm so up I can hear the locks ripping out of the wood through the noise of the whole door crashing open, flying into the room beyond. Watching it crash to the floor in slow motion. Moving so fast we're in the front room before the door has fully settled. We're both yelling, "Freeze motherfuckers! Move—you're dead meat."

It's only two small rooms, a kitchen and a den or living room with a bathroom off of the front room, the only light coming through the windows, everything in shadow with dust from our entry so thick in the air it looks like mist.

There's one guy sprawled on the ragged sofa that takes up a full wall of the front room, but trying to get to his feet, and another coming out of the bathroom.

Mel's focused on the cat coming out of the head who's moving toward us, reaching for his pocket as Mel starts to pistol-whip him.

The one on the sofa is about halfway to his feet when the adrenaline kicks in. My combat boot crashes into his face, knocking him back into the sofa. My left hand grabs his collar and my right shoves a gun halfway up one of his nostrils. See the blood from his split face run over the barrel of the gun and hear myself scream, "Quién tiene chiva, pendejo! Pasa la chiva, pinche maricón."

The voice that comes from the guy I'm holding isn't scared, his eyes betray no fear as he says, "Un momento, jefe, un momento." He slowly reaches under the couch and pulls out a brown paper bag and hands it to me. Inside is what looks like dark brown sugar wrapped in plastic. I taste it and tell Mel, "Let's roll, we're in pocket."

Gliding across the rain-puddled pavement, rainbows forming on the oil slicks, the sun setting, a cancerous copper globe.

Coming down from the adrenaline, I wonder why we're now doing armed robberies. Liking the feeling of power, but pondering the principles laid down earlier that don't seem to be in effect anymore.

Mel's still driving smoothly, gliding through traffic, but keeps looking at me out of the side of his eye, face pale, hands so tight on the steering wheel the knuckles look like white rocks.

"What's up, pal? Ya don't look too good."

"Whiskey, man, shit makes me nuts."

"Whatcha mean?"

"You kiddin? Just did an unplanned 211. Coulda got killed, or hadda waste those wetbacks. Stupid. Feel like I got a dick on my forehead."

He looks like a kid, one that's sick. Looks the way I usta feel after one of my old man's less-serious beatings. I'm real aware that everybody fucks up, but not that when it starts it's almost impossible to stop. Self-fulfilling prophecy acts on us all, crooks and cops, virgins and vixens.

"So what's the story? We got a bagful of this brown shit, got away. Are we in the armed robbery business now . . . or do stickups only go with whiskey?"

"I don't know Bobbie, I gotta slow down. This shit's turning my brains into tapioca fucking pudding. Doing shit I don't want to do. Nuts, fuckin' crazy."

Pulling into the hotel, valets opening both doors, Mel's off balance, almost staggering. My only regret is that my mentor isn't happy. We got a bagful of brown, Rosie's waiting upstairs, and more scores are coming up. I should've been a happy kid.

. . . .

Rosie and me pull into the lot; the place is an industrial warehouse. We're early, already fixed, bored. So we're early, so what! Walk inside and I got Rosie's hand in mine, we're both in jeans and T-shirts. Rosie is getting more beautiful every day, being pregnant seems to agree with her. I feel strong and proud, even though I can't talk to her about it. . . . I'm nuts about her.

Don't feel like being around a lot of people but what the fuck, I know how to party. My first clue that this is gonna be different from any party I've been to is when I spot Jewels.

He's all the way into it wearing a perfectly tailored sharkskin suit, a wife beater under the jacket, gold chains, chokers and ropes that go down to his belly. Diamond rings on every finger and, to keep everything simple and understated, a Rolex Presidential with a diamond pavé face.

Behind him is a mariachi band, playing as they come through the door.

Making their entrance come Mel and Syd, who's so hot she's on fire. Just looking at her leaves afterimages burnt into your retinas. Touching her would surely result in spontaneous combustion. Even the confirmed   "ain't-ever-gonna-change-and-fuck-you-if-you-don't-like-it, rather-suck-dick-than-breathe" homosexuals whistle and clap.

Syd is nasty, dirty, fuck-me-quick sex on two legs. Black velvet cut so low in back you can see the top of her ass, a neckline that dips down to her belly button, the dress slit so far up the side that you know there's nothing underneath; she couldn't be wearing a Band-Aid without it showing. Mink stole that was indeed stolen and spike heels that come down to ice-pick points. One simple strand of black pearls. Hair now a lustrous black worn loose and wild, tumbling down past her shoulders.

Mel next to her beaming, happy, way in control. Not drinking. Doing exactly enough stuff to stay right. Looking good, proud of himself and proud of his ace-deuce crime partner and lover, sizzling, slinky, sensual, steaming, searing, seductive, scalding-hot Sydney.

Mel's wearing black suede bell-bottoms; a tie-dyed, long-sleeve silk shirt; a matching black suede vest; and ostrich-skin cowboy boots. It's a safe bet that Syd orchestrated his wardrobe 'cause he looks bad to the bone, too hip to slip, and way too cool for school.

Three hundred pounds of good-natured, very witty attack dog. While anyone with a pulse is checking out Syd, no one that wants to *keep* theirs makes any inappropriate comments. Singly the two are attention-getting individuals. Together they're overwhelming. Like Venus and Mars, the Goddess of Love and the God of War come to earth.

Piling in behind them is a truly bizarre crowd of burglars, boxers, bouncers, brawlers, safecrackers, stickup men, hookers and hustlers, pimps and panderers, pickpockets and purse snatchers, masters of the con game both long and short, card sharps and dice sharks, prancing fairies and psychotic leather fags, lipstick lesbos and muscle-bound, badly tattooed diesel dykes, transsexuals, and diverse degenerates.

A renegade priest wearing his collar and robes gives holy communion, hits of LSD filling in for the standard wafers that symbolize the body of Christ. Rosie and I take communion, wash the acid down with wine, and trip, wide-eyed, on the people still coming in.

Speed freaks and howler growler biscuit lovers, even some ancient jazz-playing, heroin-shooting, bank-robbing legends who've somehow survived the long hard road that being a hope-to-die dope fiend means. I see the same thing in every set of eyes present.

Time is flying by. There is no second chance.

At fifteen I'm by far the youngest dude there. A couple of the chicks might only be a year or so older. Rosie's seventeen and change. Seeing the old jazz guys, watching the way they move. One of 'em catches my eye and growls, "Happy whatever, youngster."

Looking into his eyes I know that he don't feel a day over twenty. There we are, two kids pretending to be grown-ups, the wrinkles and arthritis concealing the youth that's somehow gotten away from one of us.

His eyes continue to burn into mine. "Happy fuckin' whatever, son. Live every day like it's gonna be your last. The worst thing ya can do is get old and regret the things ya never did and wonder where the time went. Why ya don't get another chance to kiss the girls ya never kissed, take the risks ya never took, and tell all the people you've hurt how sorry ya are; for what ya did do and sometimes worse for what ya didn't do." A girl he knew slinks up to him, he winks at me, takes her by the arm, and strolls away.

Syd grabs Rosie and they disappear into the bathroom. When they come back the jeans and T-shirt are gone, replaced by leopard-skin pants and vest, nothing under the vest, pants painted on, spike heels that accentuate her legs, and makeup that brings out her lips and eyes. Rosie is a star going nova, finer than the finest diamond, every bit as hot as Syd but she's my girl and she's radiant.

Seeing her this happy is an immediate fix. I'm immediately up and as close to gregarious as I get.

This hippie pushes his way through to us and gives us each a handful of peyote buttons. He's all the way on a different planet, saying, "Eat these, kids, allow yourselves to be reborn, chew 'em up and swallow 'em, trip the light fantastic."

Some of the writers I'd been reading said that the ancient Greeks and Romans really knew how to get down. I gotta tell ya, if they had any kicks that night's party missed, they aren't worth having.

Full wet bar. Grass and hash circulating nonstop to the beat of rock and mariachi music. Day-Glo paint on the walls. Black lights and strobe lights. Naked chicks and fistfights. A pig—I'm talking a monster here, the biggest pig in Denver and possibly the whole wide world—roasting on a spit.

. . . .

When the hippie offered Rosie and me the peyote he didn't explain that you get violently ill before the tripping starts. I feel like there's an explosion taking place inside me, or maybe a hungry weasel gnawing his way through me doing the polka.

Grabbing my mouth and running out the back door, the alley lit by fluorescents putting everything into stark relief, exaggerated shadows from the trash bins, empty wine bottles, discarded pieces of industrial machinery. The smells of urine, puke, and rotting food complete the package. A little slice of Americana.

The puke comes out in Technicolor, not just multicolored but full of portents and omens just beyond my grasp. Projectile vomiting. No heaving. No gagging.

No pain at all; the relief almost orgasmic, my entire body breaking down into its individual cells, becoming part of the universe in a multi-level sexual awakening.

Knowing for the first time that I am one of God's creatures, flickering for a minute like a votive candle. Praying for eternity while fighting for minutes. Battling for supremacy, conquest, dominion. Control.

The ability to grab the reins and direct the way my fleeting moment of time is spent. Waiting to fade to black, determined to consume as much air as possible. To burn with eye-searing intensity until there's nothing left.

Back inside I spot Rosie immediately. She's standing with Mel and

Sydney. Mel's starting to get sloppy from the heroin and alcohol, still looking good but even with the strobe lights and psychedelics going on inside of me I know he's getting messy. Doing his W. C. Fields impersonation, Sydney coming right back with Mae West. You can tell, sloppy or not, these two really like each other, they're not just used to each other, not brand-new in love, they really like being together. I have a smile all over my face as soon as I see them, and Rosie's eyes are as big as record albums. . . . Tripping hard.

The strobe lights make them flash in and out like an old movie. Sydney's holding on to Mel's arm. They lean against each other looking like a couple of lost kids who've been trapped in aging bodies, and I wonder if that's what happens. If the years go by scarring and bruising us until there's nothing left but the reactions imprinted on us by learning how to survive.

What I feel is the need to protect them, knowing that as tough as they are they're as vulnerable as me and Rosie. Suddenly tears fill my eyes and rage wells up inside me for being weak. Feeling more than what I thought a man should feel. But shaking my head compounds the hallucinations and drives this awful feeling down to where I can deny it.

There's nothing I want to do except share this trip with my girl. Curl up into a ball with her and be safe. Banish the goblins. Not get old. Live happily ever after.

Psychedelics can expand your perceptions. Once you get past purging your body of all the poisons, reality changes. As I walk, moving like I'm under water, each step sends shock waves shimmering off the walls.

It's all part of a dream. A dream where I can't move fast enough and all that matters is making it across the vast distance that separates us. What seems like years later, I'm floating into the circle that is Mel, Syd, and Rosie. Feeling Rosie fitting herself next to me, my arm going around her shoulders, then . . . we're flying through the universe, watching the earth recede as we speed on our way to the Milky Way. Not having to talk, knowing what the other is thinking and feeling. Wordlessly sensing the passenger riding inside Rosie. Knowing that we are in the act of creation.

So heartbreakingly naive, *knowing* that everything is gonna work out just fine. Shooting heroin and meth instead of vitamins and minerals. Running till we drop. Pushing ourselves not to the edge but so far past it there is no way back. No parachute, no safety line, no net. Just us and gravity. Touring the universe as one.

Eating roast pork and drinking tequila, listening to rock and mariachi music, watching each rhinestone on the singer's suit turn into a star that explodes as soon as it takes form. Whether it's drug-induced insanity or a real psychic connection, for a few hours we are linked so closely that when she bites into a tortilla I can taste it.

. . . .

When we leave the party and make love it really is as if two people are becoming one. The way she tastes and feels is like coming home and everything she does is magic. Every time she licks me it is perfect. When I taste her the giving and taking turns us into one endless electric current. Entering her . . . turns the voltage into motherfucking lightning.

The drugs had started to kill our sex life and this is a rediscovery of each other, not just the dope, the cash, and the adrenaline, but her and me. Magic!

Jewels locates the douche bag that burnt us on the gold score.

The next few days will be busy—nonstop felonies. Taking one day to recuperate from the party, letting the hallucinations slow down, resting up. Me reading, Rosie watching TV, room service bringing up the food. But needing the adrenaline, as hooked on action as the drugs, and running low on cash. Have to go back to work and replenish our bankroll; and do it quick.

What slowed things down is that the guy changed the combination on his safe.

. . . .

Jewels has called for a strategy meeting at Dragos, possibly the best Italian restaurant in Denver.

We're sitting in this black-tie establishment, candlelight and chandeliers, uniformed waiters who are actually Italian. We have lobster and pasta all the way around, leaving broken shells all over the table.

Syd looks like she's gonna pass out. Rosie's got her head on my shoulder, starting to fade. Jewels is smoking a cigar and leaning forward. I'm playing with the lobster shells, following the conversation.

Mel's not whispering. Shit, he's not even talking low, the booze making him more careless by the day. "So I'm sure I got this right, Bobbie don't hit the pad by hisself. He and I go in, use a safe puller, rip the fuckin' thing to pieces, grab the swag, and vámonos.

"Roll down the road, hit the camera store. Yours truly cuts through the wall beneath the alarm, resets the motherfucker, and walks around back. Bobbie cuts through the roof, lets me in the back door. We load their delivery van. We're outta there, drop the van at your warehouse.

NINE

"Next order of business," Mel continues through his haze, "we go have a little talk with the fuckin' scumbag on the safe deal. Now, here's the question, are we gonna have to pull this mook's teeth out, chop his fingers off, or just politely ask him to hand over what he owes plus interest. Secondly, where are we gonna hit him? The office, at home, on the street? Maybe his kids' fucking nursery school? Walk in during milk and cookies, march the puke's kids out with shotguns to their heads, end up with a hostage situation or maybe multiple homicides?

"It's the fucking details. Details are what we need. Details, man. This has got to be perfect. Ba-ba bing, ba-ba bang. Like the fuckin' Mona Lisa. Got that weird smile. That's gotta be us. No one knowing that we pulled it off but us. Let's run through it one more time."

Jewels smiles, not showing any teeth it's more like a grimace on one side of his face, takes a hit off of his after-dinner brandy, and says, "One more time. *Quietly.* The combination has been changed. Guy got in a fight with boyfriend, took his car away, canceled his credit cards, took his house keys back, and changed the combination on the fuckin' box. It's the little bastard's own fault, got caught with someone else's dick in his mouth. This score is huge, bearer bonds, cash, rocks, loose and set."

I couldn't believe what I was hearing. All that paper in the safe. Jewels heard me sigh, smiled.

"It's all in a floor safe in the bathroom in the master bedroom. The safe is way too good to peel, and ya can't burn it 'cause of the paper. That means ya gotta use a safe puller on it." Jewels pauses, squints at Mel, and asks, "You know how to use one don'tcha?"

Mel lets his eyes cross and his whole face go slack like a mongoloid idiot. "Gee whillikers that's awfully complicated. . . . Punch the combination out, insert the hydraulic system, and jack it off till the door rips off the safe. I think we can handle it. Me and Bobbie both go in, lever the sliding glass door, punch the combination dial, run the puller inside, engage it, rip the whole fuckin' door off."

"Right on! It's still a piece of cake, you guys lever the back door, open the safe. Syd and Rosie keep circling the block until they see ya hit the sidewalk, they pull over, you two jump in the car, you're gone. Look like four lames out on a double date. I hate doing it but I'll drive the crash car. Can't have little pregnant Puerto Rican chicks getting into wrecks. Drop you guys at the camera store, just like we planned. Bobbie cuts through the roof. Mel, you cut a hole beneath the alarm, reset the sensitivity on the son of a bitch. Go in, load their van, drop it at my warehouse, my guys take care of it from there. Then the three of us go have a talk with our pal who sizzled us.

"As far as I can determine he's got two accounts in the same bank. One for his company, one personal. No alarm on the house. I lock-pick the front door and instead of an alarm clock . . . they get us. Think they'll be surprised? We duct-tape their mouths, wake him and wifey up, tell him, 'Top of the morning, ace.' We put some coffee on. Have him open the fuckin' safe."

Mel and I exchange looks; this is the part that hadn't been laid out, how to get to the guy that started this shit in the first place, Mr. Gold Plating himself.

I feel myself starting to rub my temples, my voice rising as I ask, "You mean you're going in on this one yourself? Something can always go wrong, never take a risk, king of the setup men, *you're* gonna go inside? You're gonna drive the crash car?"

I'm overwhelmed. Jewels don't have to do this at all. Rosie's been going nuts 'cause I don't want her to take any chances and I've been dying trying to do the right thing. I owe the motherfucker big-time on this one. But there's something missing.

Jewels stares at me for a minute, smiles from ear to ear, and says, "Kid, I'm the best lockpick in this business—I'll have this cocksucker's door open in seconds. Plus this is personal. This punk thinks he can burn me and get away with it, I got no choice but to set his thinking straight. You guys know about us macho Latinos. How can I not volunteer when there's a pregnant girl involved? Just name your first kid after me. As for business, I let one of the pendejos burn me and next thing ya know they gonna start thinking I don't care. *Wrong!*"

Syd suddenly comes to life. Leaning forward she takes a sip of brandy and, still grimacing, points at Jewels. "Listen bro," she says. "There's something you missed here. Look real hard and you'll notice me sitting across the table from ya. I don't take free rides, don't need 'em, Melvin and me are a team. Plus I'm getting real bored, so use that famous Mexican brain of yours to fit me into the equation.

"Matter of fact," Syd continues, "I'll *tell* ya what to do. You guys do the burgs just like ya laid out, but instead of having dickhead write checks or strong-arming him to the bank, me and his old lady go. You three stay with him and their kids. We make it clear to her that I'm gonna be calling my honey here every time we stop."

She leans forward and pinches Mel's cheek. He winks at her and says, "Right on, tell him baby, silly motherfucker must be starting to believe his own publicity."

Mel sits up straight and says, "Syd's right, Jewels, even if his wife hates the motherfucker she'll be leaving her kids hostage along with him. You can tune him up, break his legs, whatever, while they're emptying the bank accounts. We should pick up some toys and ice cream; me and Bobbie will entertain the kids while you get their dad's head straight."

I follow the logic of doing things this way, but I'm trying to learn the rules as well as the skills involved in this business, and this bit with the kids bothers me. Mel's the guy who taught me that residential burglaries were bad news, and anything that might end up with citizens getting hurt had always been out. Now he's planning on playing Tinkertoys with these kids while Jewels is breaking the dad's bones in the next room.

This feels wrong. Robbing dealers is OK but I got doubts about tuning a guy with his kids where they can hear his screams. I'm more than willing to do whatever it takes but I gotta get this cleared up in my head. I ask, "Mel, Jewels, if we're putting these kids at risk, and it sounds like we are, why not just hit this lame, clear out his safe, and fly kites at his bank? Why all this hostage shit? Blow his brains out if that's what's called for. Why change a winning hand?"

Mel and Jewels look at each other. Rosie squeezes my leg and kisses me on the neck; she's with me no matter what.

It's Sydney that does the talking. She laughs, laughs so loud that everyone in the place turns to see who's making this raucous noise, and says, "Shit, bubeleh, ya ain't careful ya gonna turn into a real mensch. All that philosophy ya been reading has had some effect, I see. Here's the deal, baby. . . . Number one, this has the potential to be a boss score, not as good as the one with the sliding glass door, but serious money. Number two, when those cretins tried to burn us back in Chicago we did what we had to and got out the back Jack, went down the ramp tramp. You know why? Why we aren't looking for whoever set us up? Why for us all that matters is getting in and out in one piece? Why for my little sweetheart Jewels the rules are different? No, ya don't, but I'm gonna tell ya since these two are tongue-tied. Pay attention.

"In showbiz any publicity is good news. For *us* any publicity is bad news. In our line of work the thing is to be invisible, get in, get out. We don't need reputations, don't want 'em; as soon as you start getting publicity your days are numbered. Sure we could go back. Bust heads and pay bribes till we found out who set us up, and whack 'em. Let people know that they don't want to fuck with us. But we came out twenty-five g's ahead and the Nazi fucks that tried to take us down got wasted. Doing anything more would be putting ourselves at risk for nothing except being able to tell ourselves what bad motherfuckers we are as they lock us up forever."

Syd flashes a grin around the table, raises one eyebrow, and asks me, "See what I mean, Bobbie? Ask Rosie, I think she'll agree this is a different situation. *This* dickhead still has our money. He owes us. He started the dance. Now we gotta finish it."

Something still doesn't feel right. Maybe it is the philosophy I'm reading until my eyes cross, but I want to feel like whatever I'm doing is right, at least by the twisted morality I'm starting to develop.

I take a hit off my old-fashioned, feel the whiskey burn its way down my throat, light a cigarette, and feel no different. Look at Mel and ask him, "So what makes this so different, killer? Why do a home invasion when we don't want that kinda heat?"

Mel studies his fingernails for a minute, obviously giving the answer some thought, and says, "Two things. For my own self-respect I can't let someone burn me and get away with it. He owes us, it's not like we don't know who this guy is. The other thing is Jewels."

At the mention of his name Jewels smiles and says, "Simone, ese, for a minute there I thought you gavachos were gonna forget all about me."

Rosie gives a snort and sneers at Jewels and says, "I don't know about my gringo friends but personally I wish we could forget about you." She looks at me for backup. I got nothing against Jewels. He's one hell of a thief and seems to be stand-up. Offering to drive the crash car was a class act any way you look at it. Plus I want to learn all I can about setup work; it's obvious that spotting and planning the scores is as important as having the balls and expertise to do them. I stroke Rosie's hair knowing that my confusion shows on my face. What the fuck am I supposed to do?

Mel breaks in before Jewels can respond, saving me from having to take sides, 'cause I know no matter whether it makes sense or not, if they start squabbling I'm on Rosie's side. Mel laughs and says, "Hey, no fighting at the dinner table, check it out. What makes it different is not only was what this guy did a personal insult, but our friend Jewels here has got a local operation and if he's gonna stay in business, he's *gotta* make an example of guys who burn him. If he don't, he's out of business. Right, Jewels?"

Jewels laughs, gets a crooked smile on his face, and still chuckling says, "Sheeit, pinche pendejo, that's why we work good together. We both know that the weak and meek shall inherit the earth . . . exactly enough to bury 'em in it."

He looks at Rosie, looks at me, says, "Me, I gotta maintain my reputation, not just with the guys I work with but for every barboso in Denver. It's enough to wear a Mexican out." He smiles, extends his hand across the table to Rosie, and asks, "Whatcha think, girlfriend, can we have a peace treaty? I'm not a bad guy, you just got that Latin thing against faggots, we really got a lot in common. Shake hands?"

Rosie grabs my hair and pulls. Points her finger at Jewels and says, "OK, as long as we don't have *too much* in common. Plus you got that Latin thing about women, want us to keep our mouths shut and hide in a corner. You drop that and I'll forget that you're a maricón."

Jewels looks at her sideways, no expression on his face, and finally starts laughing again. Says, "OK, mija. Friends, amigos. I'll treat you like my own hermana, my own sister. Shake."

Sydney takes up where Mel left off, points her dinner knife at me and says, "It's much more effective to do this than any of our other options. See what I mean, killer? We get our dough, Jewels maintains his rep, and we've demonstrated that fucking with us has repercussions. We don't have to worry about our enemies. As long as we always deal from a position of strength no one can fuck us, not business associates, not friends. That don't mean we don't got no friends 'cause we do. Shit, I love Jewels like my own sister. Until the reverend bought the farm he was the best friend any of us could ever hope for. The same thing applies to Ben. But before you can have a real friendship *it's gotta have the foundation based on respect.*"

. . . .

The grass is wet beneath my sneakers, each step making a tiny noise as my feet make contact. We vault the iron fence around the house running full out, get around to the back of the pad where, along with a tennis court, there's a full-size Olympic pool. Even in the starlight you can tell that the grass and shrubs are manicured. The place is beautiful. I just stand there for a minute wanting to have something like this someday.

The door only takes a few seconds. Shove a pry bar under the slide, lift the door out of its tracks and into Mel's hands, step through. Replace the door on its tracks, relock it, and we're in. No way to tell that entry had ever been made.

Stepping through is a rush, the inside of the house is outta sight. Everything spotless, a stairway with a curving banister, marble inlaid floor, paintings even a cultural wasteland like myself recognizes as classic, so perfectly done that I have to stop and just stare at them for a moment, trying to absorb every line, every shading of color.

Mel elbows me lightly in the side. "Fuckin' beautiful, huh? If they were the real thing each one of 'em would be worth millions. They're bunk but they still take your breath away don't they? Come on, ace, we got some work to do."

For the first time I can remember I feel out of place. I've never seen a house like this. . . .

Mel's already moving, following the floor plan we've memorized. Not creeping, walking like the place is ours. Directly to the bathroom in the master suite.

I click the lights on, open the closet, dump the towels in the bottom shelf onto the floor. Apply pressure to the right front corner and the floor to the closet rolls back into the wall, exposing the floor safe, stainless steel set into reinforced concrete.

Mel's looking in the mirror. Reaches into his back pocket, pulls out a comb, and gets his hair into a pompadour. Pulls down one strand so it's curling across his forehead and says, "OK, pal, let's get it done. You get the fun part. Get the dial off."

I look at him, think about telling him to pull the fucking dial himself, and then remember that this is how ya learn. Fuck it. Say, "Gimme the tools, ace, ya get to watch a master at work."

Out of one bag he pulls individually wrapped tools: sledgehammers, one large and one small; pry bars, different sizes and shapes; cold chisels; steel wedges; and a piston out of a small-block Chevy. Out of the other bag comes the safe puller, a piece of equipment that is about three feet long, has a stand on the bottom, and three arms clamped to the sides that release by pressing a button.

What we have to do is whack the combination dial off the safe, punch the locking mechanism all the way through the door, shove the safe puller through the hole we just made. Release the arms by applying pressure to the hydraulics and they literally rip the door off the safe from the inside.

Mel hands me a cold chisel and the small sledgehammer. "No sense in wasting time. Oh yeah. Make sure ya don't smash your fingers."

I've been going through this in my head for days, tips both Jewels and Mel gave me on the best way to whack the dial.

If you try to lay the chisel flat and just shear the dial off you risk crushing your hand; plus laying the chisel flat like that means you have no leverage. What you want to do is pry one side of the dial up a little bit so you can get an angled shot at it, work it till one side's pried up a half inch or so, then turn the dial and repeat it on the other side. The dial's still a motherfucker when the entire thing's pried loose, but by using wedges and different-size chisels it'll come off.

I'm into it. Shove the chisel under the dial at a slight angle and bring the hammer down as hard as I can. The action feels good. What happens is nothing. The dial looks the same, the box don't even have a scratch on it. I look up at Mel and the motherfucker is leaning against the wall smiling and it makes me crazy. Feel like I should be able to take this dial off with no problems. Not gonna ask for help. Grip the chisel tighter and put everything I got into smashing the hammer home.

The dial lifts maybe a tenth of an inch. I pull back again and get another fraction of an inch.

Once I get the dial so it's loose Mel grabs my arm and says, "Take a smoke break. You got the hard part, watch how I do this."

By this time I got sweat running down my face and two smashed fingers, blood seeping through my gloves. They're not broken but one of them is pancaked to this day, the end flatter and wider than my other fingers.

I sit on the edge of the bathtub and notice that it's not only big enough for three or four people but it's made out of what looks like solid marble. The faucets and knobs are gold for Christ's sake, and suddenly I start getting angry. Who has so much dough that they need gold bathroom fixtures?

Mel's got one of the steel wedges and is using the small sledge to hammer it as far under the dial as he can get it. Sets the hammer down, looks at the closet, and then kicks the lower shelving out. Smiles, says, "Gotta have room to swing." Grabs the big sledge and swings it like an Olympic hammer thrower into the wedge, smashing the dial most of the way off. The second swing sends the dial shooting into the back wall and ricocheting around the bathroom.

This is where the piston comes in; this particular small-block piston fits perfectly into the hole left by the dial. Mel hands it to me and says, "Punch it out, partner."

"What? Just hammer till it breaks through?"

"Yeah, that's how ya do it. Not much finesse to opening safes but, what the fuck, it's a living."

Mel's got sweat running down his forehead and I know I'm soaked. He reaches into the canvas carryall, pulls out a pint of Old Crow and downs half of it, shudders, and mumbles, "Guess I should stop drinking so much. Go ahead, punch it. I'll use the puller, that's the hard part." He starts laughing and sits on the toilet, takes another hit off the whiskey, and lights a cigarette.

The piston fits exactly. I grab the small sledge and punch it easily, back out of the closet and say, "OK, bubba, let's see the tough part, get your safe-pulling ass to work."

I light my cigarette and take a deep drag, getting more nervous watching as Mel shoves the safe puller through the hole and punches the release button. Hearing the muffled clack as the arms release. Forgetting to breathe as he uses the hand pump to pop the door.

Going through all the setup work I felt completely cool. Now the safe's open and we're looking down into a small treasure chest: a little felt bag holding diamonds, emeralds, rubies, opals; two Rolex Presidentials with different faces; banded hundreds and fifties and bonds that are as good as cash, the same as cash. Says it right on the bond, "Pay to bearer on demand." Pulling one of them out to see what it looks like takes my wind, a lot of fancy engraving and the sum of two thousand dollars; fifty of them, one hundred thousand dollars!

Without counting the cash and jewelry, this is a monster score and the adrenaline comes on like a tidal wave.

The shaking starts in my fingers, flowing like electric current up through my arms and shoulders, making 'em shake so bad that holding on to the bag is out of the question. Setting it down to catch my breath, thinking how much I want the life that the really rich live.

I was still a little kid. The shinier, the brighter, the louder things were, the better they had to be. Better, classier, nicer, and to be more coveted. I aspired to being a gentleman, having class, although I had no idea what either of those things meant.

Mel is still sitting on the toilet, watching me play with the swag, making piles of the stones, smelling the cash, shuffling the bearer bonds. Find myself singing, "Oh yeah, oh my. All this cash, now it's time to fly. Diamonds here, emeralds, too, sapphires burning midnight blue. Hundreds and fifties ultrathick, pick 'em up it's like holding a brick. Yeah baby all this cash, oh yeah baby too much to stash. Watch out world cause here's Kid Flash!" Stopping to catch my breath, feeling the lopsided grin lighting my face, shuffling the bearer bonds one last time. Marveling at the ridiculous amount of money these little scraps of paper represent, awed first by the beauty of the gems, the flawless fire dancing inside of them, and then by the knowledge that each of these little rocks is worth more than most people make in a month or two. Wanting to scream and do some sort of victory dance but knowing that I have to behave like this is an everyday occurrence. Determined to be cool, embarrassed by having acted like a kid. Think, Fuck it, this feeling's too good to hide.

Look at Mel, who's got his best poker face on, showing no emotion whatsoever, and I can feel my grin plastered across ear to ear. I ask him, "Whatcha think, man? Looks like it's damn near retirement time to me, got to be two large and change here," and start singing my little song again, grinning like a brain-damaged baboon. "Watch out world cause here's Kid Flash, balls like an elephant and loaded with cash. Kid's balls ain't just big, they're made out of brass. Yeah here I am world and after your ass!"

Mel's still staring at me, no emotion at all, read more feelings on a bowling ball. I'm staring back, why ain't this mook laughing or at least smiling, this is one monster score and he looks like an undertaker. I ask him, "Why the long face, pal? We got a fortune here and ya look like someone just killed your puppy."

He stretches and looks at me completely devoid of expression. "I don't know how to break this to ya kid," he says with a grim look on his face, "but ya better stick with your day job, 'cause if those noises you were making were supposed to be singing and ya didn't know how to steal you'd starve to death."

He starts laughing and jumps to his feet. For a guy that big he's too fucking fast. Rumples my hair and in a terrible falsetto imitates the last line of my song while holding an imaginary dance partner, bebopping around the room squeaking, "Oh yeah oh yeah that's right motherfucking world here I come and I'm after your ass." Does a pirouette and a bow so deep his forehead almost hits the floor and starts singing "The Wanderer." After the second verse says, "Come on, Elvis, let's pack this shit up and wander the fuck on out of here."

We do. Taking a minute to breathe, just to let our hearts slow down, then putting everything away, safe puller back in its case, other tools wrapped to stop clanking or rattling. Mel chain-smoking and overseeing the whole process.

"See, first ya put in a layer of towels, then the cash and the bonds." He pauses to inspect the placement of the paper. "Cool, now we start on the jewelry." He's got a roll of toilet paper and we start wrapping individual pieces; the loose rocks in the bag stay in the bag but get wrapped anyhow. Last of all are two books of old stamps. Mel stops and rifles through one of the books, each stamp in an individual holder, points at a stamp that's an obvious misprint, single engine planes merging together, superimposed double images. "Check it out, Bobbie, there's only twelve of these in existence. It's what they call priceless. Sad thing is because they're so rare it's almost impossible to sell this. What Jewels will do is ransom it back to the insurance company."

Sauntering out the front door, feeling the cool wind blowing on my face, strolling down the sidewalk, walking slowly, out for a midnight jaunt. Syd and Rosie pull up next to us in under a minute.

The trunk's already unlocked. We set the bags down carefully and slam the lid shut. Mel slides into the driver's seat and I jump into the back, shutting the doors as we get moving. Look over at Rosie and tell her, "You ain't gonna believe this one, mija. This has got to be the biggest score I ever heard of, let alone been in on."

Rosie runs her hand through my hair. "Oye, mijo. No more robbing tonight. Please. The cucaracha wasn't lying; Jewels was right about this score. But let's do the other one tomorrow. OK? He said it would be tasty, but the night ain't over yet. Let's just spend it together."

Driving slowly through the dark streets of the suburbs, streetlights casting soft shadows, the lawns and shrubbery looking even closer to perfect in the soft illumination provided by the quarter moon, stars, and the widely spaced streetlamps. The changing gradations of light softening and then highlighting the faces of my companions. The acrid smell coming from my own body; fear, adrenaline, and physical exertion mingling with the odor of perfume, soap, and lotions that gently surrounds Rosie.

Slowly we make our way back into the city, Mel and Syd in front, me and Rosie being chauffeured, feeling a moment of peace, knowing that even if the rest of the night goes bad this one score is big enough to kick back on for a while, smoking and feeling the smoke bite into my lungs. The smell and feel of the leather seats in the Lincoln Town Car that Jewels loaned us for the evening's work, rock and roll coming from the speakers. Life is *grand*.

Fifteen and rolling like a motherfucker. Invincible.

. . . .

Back at the hotel, swag piled on the bed, slamming to stay right. Get done. Jewels don't fix, he's watching the four of us. I tell him, "Yo come 'ere, man, I gotta talk to ya." Walk into the main room say, "Check it out, let's tie off on this other shit. I wanna kick it with Rosie tonight."

He raises one eyebrow, puts his hand on his hip, and in his most annoying lisp says, "Young love, how touching. You know Bobbie that I'd like nothing more than to take the night off so you and your rooka can roll and tumble and whisper words of love so soft and tender to each other all night long.

"Sadly there's other people involved in this little escapade: my guys at the warehouse; the courier waiting to fly some of this stuff, the stamps, and some of the rarer coins and jewelry to New York; the trucker waiting to transport the cameras into Canada.

"For all this to work we have to take both hits down tonight. It's part of doing biz. Make everything as cost-effective as possible; anything that is even mildly traceable—rare stuff like some of the stamps, coins, and jewelry, anything numbered like cameras for instance—has to be *all the way out of Dodge* to get a decent price.

"Ya try to dump any of that stuff here and we'll be lucky to get ten cents on the dollar. The longer it *does* stay in town the more chance of the heat finding it, getting a tip, surveying warehouses, grinding stamp and coin dealers, looking for us, catching up with us."

Over time I came to realize that information like this is priceless. It isn't enough to locate a profitable score. It's better to find a buyer and then set up the theft.

Now I walk back to Rosie and tell her, "Sorry, babe, we gotta go on this tonight, there's just no way around it. And you gotta stay here in case we need bail. That was the plan and if everyone else wants to roll tonight I'm in no matter how bad I want to take the rest of the night off and hang with you. I promise ya as soon as we clean out Denver we'll take a vacation. Maybe go to California and see Disneyland or something. How's that sound to ya?"

Get a wicked smile out of her with that one. Her eyes hold mine and she tries to punch me in the chest, hard, but I've gotten used to her inclination to punctuate her statements with left hooks and right crosses, grab her hand and swing her around so I have her locked up in a lightweight version of a bear hug. "How about California and Hawaii, whatcha think about that?"

"I think you loco, mijo. I think you better be careful. I think you let yourself get busted I'll break ya out just to shoot you myself. California and Hawaii sound great but having you around sounds better. Also you starting to get a little bit faster. That's a good thing. My baby with the blue eyes got to be on his toes all the time, gotta always be ready for that sucker punch. Now gimme a kiss and go make us some money."

. . . .

The camera store is boring, manual labor, stacking crates of film, cameras, lenses, tripods, and all the paraphernalia that go with that type of business. Filling the van, throwing the iron bars that hold the loading gate in place.

Mel's behind the wheel, makes a circular motion with his hand, meaning let's get rolling. I hit the button that raises the gate and, as soon as there's clearance, Mel's moving. The van rolls out, I slam the gate, and we're outta there. This is downtown, brightly lit, people still out and about closing the bars. This much light and activity has me wired for sound, feel like I'm gonna come out of my skin, I'm staring straight ahead and catch Mel wave at somebody out of the corner of my eye.

Looking over and in the lane next to us are two of Denver's finest, waiting for the light to change and looking at us. I'm on fire—do I jump out and run? give them a lightweight grin and ignore them? what the fuck do I do? Is Jewels gonna crash into 'em? It feels like I'm gonna explode, what I do is look at 'em and nod my head once, a friendly acknowledgment, and look back at the road.

Mel doesn't break stride, finishes waving at the cops, looks over at me, and says, "Just be completely cool. As far as they know we just headed out with a late delivery. People work around the clock, we're dressed right, the truck's right. Everything is cool. Beyond copacetic. Just hold your mud."

As the light changes to green they accelerate away, leaving us behind. I can feel the sweat running down my sides, hands shaking from adrenaline overload. One of the toughest things in the world is to do absolutely nothing when your whole body is in fight-or-flight mode, when ya know you're in danger and everything in you is screaming for you to take some kind of action.

Mel looks over, grins, makes a motion of jacking off, and says, "A smile and a wave do it every time! Fock 'em all in da neck."

. . . .

The house is in a tract of look-alike houses, three to four bedrooms, neat lawns, midrange cars. The chill in the air at 5 A.M. announces that summer is slipping away. The ghost of the moon is still hanging in the sky; opposite it the almost rising sun turns the horizon from star-studded black-blue velvet to burnished steel.

As we pull into the driveway I think again that this is a real circle jerk, no way this many people should be on one score.

Jewels is driving the yellow wagon, I'm shotgun, Mel and Syd in the backseat. Look at Jewels and know that he wants a piece of this dude's ass so bad he ain't thinking straight. Feel sick to my stomach, don't want nothing to do with this but see no way out.

Refuse to look like I'm scared as I watch Jewels-fucking-idiot pull a set of picks out of his pocket and select a rake and tension bar. Feel the car door handle in my hand and my feet hitting the driveway, know that my face betrays nothing, wonder why Mel hasn't called this off. We're standing on the front porch blocking any view of Jewels from the street.

Watching the way a lock is really picked, how the tension bar is fitted into the bottom of the lock and twisted as the rake is slowly drawn across the tumblers at the top. Fascinated, forgetting that I don't want to be here, and hearing the click as the bolt slides back into the door, starting to rush as the door swings open.

The entryway completely dark, crossing it and smelling lemon furniture polish and a hint of pipe smoke, letting our eyes adjust after closing the door, watching Jewels and Mel as they make for the master bedroom. Looking around the living room, staring at Syd for a second, and when she shakes her head back and forth, face showing a grimace, an upside-down smile that's barely visible in the dark hall, I realize she don't like this either.

Noticing that no one took the living-room phone off the hook. Even with no experience with home invasions I know that we can't have anyone calling out till it's secured.

Cross into the living room. Phone's on a coffee table, magazines scattered around it. I take it off the hook, hear the dial tone, hit 3. The line's now tied up so no one can call in or out, and I lay the phone on its side. Creep back to the entryway, look at Syd, who nods her head and whispers, "Good thinking, kid."

When the bedroom light comes on and I hear Jewels whispering so loudly it carries through the house, words punctuated by the sound of a fist striking flesh, muffled noises made by humans but not recognizable as words, I drift into the bedroom. . . .

Mel's holding the woman by her hair, her mouth duct-taped, hands twisted behind her back, she's naked, a little chubby from having babies. Jewels is sitting on her husband's chest. The guy's mouth is taped but in the few seconds that have passed Jewels has turned his face into hamburger. Both eyelids split open, nose flattened, blood gushing from it in so much volume that the pillow and bed all around him are drenched.

I look back at the woman and the terror she feels comes vibrating across the room like a sonic boom. I flash on the kids waking up to this and remember waking up to my mother screaming, face bloody, as my father beat her like she was a man. Punching her, uppercuts and hooks. All power shots—no slaps, no jabs. Full power behind every closed-fist blow and the terror and horror I felt and I'm five years old again watching as my feet move toward Jewels and my piece fills my hand and Jewels's face as he stares down the barrel. My voice echoes through my head as the words come out of my mouth. No thought, no planning, they form in the air, hang there and dissipate like yesterday's pain but as they bounce around in my head I know that I've never meant anything more: "Hit him again I'll kill ya, pal. This ain't business. Matter of fact this bullshit."

Fist caught in midair, face contorted, voice climbing like a broad's, starting to go into a shout he's saying, "Rat bastard punk pinche barboso I'll kill your Paddy gavacho ass." As his hand creeps toward the piece stuck in his belt, I hear myself, voice level, not screaming, calm even. "There's one in the chamber, tough guy, don't try it."

A Colt Mustang is a double action, that means you can cock it. That really don't make much difference in how it shoots but it makes a great sound when it's pointed at somebody.

When my thumb eases the hammer back the metallic click that seems as loud as a slamming door freezes Jewels like a rabbit caught in headlights and I tell him, "Get off the puke's chest. Ya wanna kill him take him somewhere. Ain't no more shit like this going down here."

Jewels is working on a smile, levering himself off the bed, and I know that he thinks he can make some kinda move; he's got one foot on the floor, both hands free, smile fully in place now. "Bobbie, what's the qué pasa, vato? Por qué, ese? You and me are tight, we're carnales, right, homeboy?"

"Yeah, Jewels, carnales. Gimme your fuckin' piece, don't make me kill ya." His eyes and face go slack as the knowledge that he's five pounds of pressure on the trigger away from dying sinks in.

I don't especially want to shoot him but at that moment in time five pounds of pressure is no big deal.

Mel's looking back and forth from me to Jewels. Syd's in the door behind me. I don't know if I heard her or somehow sensed her there but I know she is there and taking the whole thing in.

Looking into Mel's eyes, dull like tarnished blue mirrors flicking from me to Jewels to the iron in my hand, stuttering "Wh-wh-why ya doin' this pal?"

"You tell me, Mel. Tell me this kinda shit is cool, go ahead."

Syd is moving behind me, not fast, not creeping. I feel her footsteps as they hit the carpet, hear them as they come down as clearly as if she was a tap dancer and know there's no gun in her hand before my peripheral vision catches as she speaks softly to Mel and only to him. "The kid's right, this ain't our scene. Let their mom wake the kids. You play with them, make 'em breakfast. Bobbie can stay in here with Jewels and shithead, make sure nothing else happens."

She looks at the woman, who's shaking slightly, crying silently, and says, "Cut the crap, honey, let's wake your kids up and introduce 'em to Uncle Mel. Your old man got ya into this shit, let's try and limit the damage, OK?"

She's hiccuping, got snot running down her nose. Mel's released the hold on her hair, she's stumbling toward her husband, ripping the duct tape away from her face, she starts babbling, "Why? What do they want? Make them leave."

Her voice is starting to climb, going into a scream when Syd strides across the room, slaps her, and then brings the same hand around to backhand her saying, "Cool out honey, limit the damage. Pull some clothes on. I'll tell ya all about it." She points at the woman's husband and says, "Your other half fucked up big-time. Get it together."

"What do you mean?"

"I mean exactly what I said. You and me are going to your bank to get the cash your husband owes us. These guys are gonna watch your family. Work with me on this. Everything will be all right."

"No, no way. I'm not leaving my kids here with them."

"Yeah, you are honey, it's either that, or ya all die. Whatcha wanna do?"

. . . .

Jewels and the lame are on the floor, both sitting cross-legged, the walls and top half of the bed are splattered with blood. Looking into the mirror hanging over the dresser the person who looks back is alien to me, pale, eyes blank. Pivoting, looking at the two on the floor, wondering if I'm gonna have to kill Jewels, knowing that he won't forget me throwing down on him, suppressing the urge to shoot 'em both and realizing that inside me lives the potential to be either one of them, the abuser and abused, feeling like I'm suspended over a bottomless chasm, waiting to fall spinning through space till the inevitable impact comes, walk to the foot of the bed, sit on it, and lean back. I got the gun aimed between 'em and ask fuckhead, "What's your name?"

"Dick, Dick Saylor. Listen, youngster, I can tell you're a good kid, got mixed up with the wrong people. Hold this fucking spic here and let me go for the cops."

Looking at him and at Jewels, whose eyes look like black marbles, like a Doberman pinscher's eyes jammed into a human face. The only reason Dick isn't in the process of dying very painfully is the gun in my hand.

"Should be Dickhole, not Saylor. My friend ain't no spic. Spics are

Puerto Rican, like my old lady, she's a spic you fucking piece of shit. Homeboy is Mexican. Ya hurt his feelings, ya hurt mine. You patronize me again, say one more stupid thing, I shove this piece back in my pocket and walk out of here, leave ya to my partner. Got it, Dickhole?"

I know I'm capable of pistol-whipping this douche bag into a coma just to get away from my own feelings. That the rush will wipe out the sick feeling in my gut, like someone using sandpaper on my stomach lining, violence would remove the cotton candy that is encasing my brain, would kick everything into overdrive, and would ultimately hit my soul the way sulfuric acid hits a face.

I know nothing shows on my mug, don't say a word. The only thing that will remove the screening between me and the rest of the world is letting myself turn into an animal. Turn into my dad, into Jewels at his worst, turn into my own motherfuckin' nightmare.

Still numb, don't want to have conversation with either of these shitheads. Disappointed in Jewels, don't like Saylor at all, able to sense that this guy is no good, weak. Think maybe he *should* die, just not where his wife and kids will see it. Looking from my captives to my watch, thinking that Syd should be back soon.

The sounds of Mel being a choo-choo train coming through the closed door, the kids laughing like maniacs and their father don't care at all. Scared for his own miserable ass.

Jewels has slowed down, the mad-dog look that took over his persona is gone, now looking askance at me, he whistles and says, "Guess I lost it huh, mijo?"

"Yeah, Jewels, ya lost it."

"Fucked this vato up pretty good, huh?"

"Yeah, man."

Watching these two, tripping on the interplay. Jewels staring at me while watching Dick out of the side of his eye. Dick scared, but looking for angles. This cat should never play poker, his face, what's left of it, telegraphs what he's thinking. I observe his attempt at a smile and know he's gonna start as he says, "Jesus, man, I never been hit that hard in my life."

Jewels smoothes his mustache and gives Saylor his full attention. "You lucky you still alive punk."

"I know, man, believe me, I know."

"You about a stupid motherfucker, who'd ya think ya was burnin' . . . some fuckin' chump?"

"No man, no way. I fucked up. Woulda had the shit there. Your people went in on the wrong day. I'll do anything to make it up, just don't hurt me anymore." Saylor wipes at the tears and the blood covering his face, voice quivering, going falsetto. "Please man, no more. OK?"

Jewels is looking at this dude the way a starving dog looks at a pork chop, sitting up straighter grabs Saylor by the hair and pulls him right into his face, eyes inches apart. "Those are my favorite words. Say 'em again."

"What? Which words?"

"Ya said you'll do anything, say it again." Jewels eyes are burning like hot lava, his focus is entirely on this poor excuse for humanity. I can hear the increase in Jewels's breathing. Saylor is staring, mesmerized, a mouse looking at the snake that's going to eat it. "Yeah. Yes I'll do anything."

"Good, real good," he says, pulling Saylor's head into his lap, looking at me to see if I'm gonna go off again. I can't hang, don't know what to do. This score is completely fucked-up, no amount of cash is worth the discomfort I feel.

As far as I'm concerned this punk tried to burn us, put his wife and kids at risk, and is willing to suck a dick just to avoid getting hurt. I'd already cooled Jewels and the idiot created this new situation himself. Sensing my hesitation Jewels pulls his zipper down, undoes his belt, and looks to check my reaction. Saylor's not hesitating, he's helping Jewels get his pants down.

Enough. I can smell eggs and bacon frying; it sounds like Mel and the kids are having a ball, laughter and Mel's train and animal imitations coming through the closed door. I tell Jewels, "I'm outta here, no yellin', no screamin'. I got your piece, fuck this puke up any more and it'll be a bad scene."

"I ain't gonna fuck him up, ese. Matter of fact when I'm done he won't ever want to go back to women." I look from one to the other—it's like they reached an agreement without saying a word.

Shaking my head, realizing that I got a lot to learn about humanity, open the door, close it behind me, and step into a pillow fight. Mel's having a ball babbling away with these youngsters, got an apron on cooking. The kids stop throwing pillows and look at me, I tell 'em, "I'm his assistant, gotta help him hunt down the toast, wrestle it to the ground, butter it, and drown it in jelly. What you guys think of that?"

"Yeah, drown it. Cool."

It's late morning. Syd and Mrs. Saylor make it back in one piece, not exactly friends but getting along. Jewels and Dick come out of the bedroom just as they set the cash on the dining-room table. Saylor's wife's nostrils are pinched, face flushed as she tells him, "This is it, we're through."

Not missing a beat, he puts one hand over his heart and says through smashed and used lips, "Honey, baby, we can work this out. I love you."

. . . .

Time to go, got the cash, beyond copacetic. These people know better than to go to the cops on this. I want out of the whole scene. Going out the front door Jewels's voice says, "See ya soon." Dick Saylor's voice comes back, sounding tough now that we are leaving, putting a show on for his better half: "I hope so. We'll be able to do more business."

I want to gag, not because of the shit that's gone down, not because of this guy's hypocrisy or Jewels's actions, but because I don't know that sometimes there's no way to win. That not all situations can be resolved to my satisfaction. Not willing to look at the fact that I recognize parts of me in both Jewels and Saylor and that no matter how badly I'd tried to stay in control, the score took on a life of its own.

The wind is blowing gently, smelling of growing grass and wildflowers. Clouds like huge balls of fluffed cotton roll across an electric blue sky, the homes surrounding us are bright with pastel colors, well maintained and looking new. Even the street's a shiny black. The only thing in the entire neighborhood that looks thrashed is us. I can't wait to get back to Rosie, get a shower, clean my body if not my soul, and get the fuck out of Denver.

We ride back in complete silence. Jewels staring at the road. Mel and Syd immersed in their own thoughts. Me watching Jewels out of the corner of my eye. The only rule I know about guns is that if you pull your piece you've got to use it. Kill whoever it's aimed at. There's no way you can survive for long in the game by scaring people.

There's no doubt that no matter how friendly Jewels acts he'll never forget that I threw down on him, and that he's planning revenge; whether it's today or ten years from now he's gonna be planning payback.

I have two options: kill him, or make sure we never cross paths again. No matter how badly I want to see myself as a cold-blooded, rock-and-roll killer, I don't have what it takes to put this guy to sleep, not now, not in cold blood.

Leaning across the front seat, turning, staring at Mel. It seems that there's more gray in his hair, that somehow he is shrinking. Eyes puffy and tired he pulls on his earlobe and looks from me to Syd, reaches one hand over and gives her a halfhearted smile as she takes his hand in hers, raises it to her lips, and kisses it. I turn back to the road lost in thought, not sure how things can go almost as planned and still be so shitty.

. . . .

I'm ten years old, in juvie for what seems like the hundredth time, gladiator school. Just got done listening to a kid younger than me get gang-raped. His screams had been muffled by the socks jammed into his mouth.

He'd been put in there by his own parents. Not for criming like most of us but to teach him a lesson. He'd said his folks wanted him to learn about respect.

The crew that I hung with had respect, not the kind that this youngster's parents understood, the kind bought with blood. I'd learned that it didn't matter how you won, as long as anyone that crossed you went down for the count.

The toughest and smartest kid in our clique was called Pitbull; he'd been stabbed, had his front teeth piped out, and already had one murder conviction. Spent all day every day lifting weights and hitting the heavy bag, covered with tattoos, and would not hesitate to stab anyone that crossed him or our crew.

That kind of loyalty was the only thing that separated us from the endless supply of victims that pour into juvenile institutions.

We're grouped on our wall of the gym, metal clanging, the black kids playing basketball, Latinos handball, we own the weight pile and pass a Camel as we're training. Do a set of bench press, take a drag off the cigarette, and get ready for your next set.

Pitbull takes a hit, blows the smoke out through his nose, and says, "That punk's worse than dead, he pulled a shank and didn't use it, those niggers are gonna torture his ass twenty-four seven. He had two ways to go, pay protection or make his bones. Motherfucker had puddin' in his pants, fuck it, I told him those bugs were gonna take that booty. Now he'll understand why he's gotta pay."

For the next three weeks he paid, he gave us his smokes, candy, and food off his tray. When one of our crew wanted skull he gave it so we'd protect him. The fourth week he drank a full can of Drano. His death was anything but pretty.

This was one of the strongest lessons I'd ever learned. Never make a threat, never hesitate, act.

. . . .

I still couldn't drop the hammer on Jewels, even though I knew that if I gave him an opportunity my brains would be all over the floor.

Getting out of the car at the Grand, Mel puts his arm around my shoulders. Looking up at him, staring into eyes that appear to have been dry-cleaned, so burnt-out that nothing is left, hear him say, "Meet me at the Exodus in the morning. Gotta get this crap wrapped up."

Rosie's stomach is starting to show, I don't know if it's because she's actually eating three meals a day or if it's a growing baby.

Sunlight is filtering into our room, making the grains in the rich wood of the furniture stand out, slashing across the bed, hallowing Rosie's face, still deep asleep and looking like she's about twelve years old. I feel like my chest is gonna explode. So much feeling that I can't identify and don't think I can contain. Feels like I want to pull her inside me, protect her from life, and I know there's no way to do it. No matter what I do it's all a roll of the dice, sometimes ya win, other times . . .

Rising as silently as I can, choosing a T-shirt and a clean pair of jeans, pulling my combat boots on, checking the clip in my piece and putting it into my back pocket.

Look into the mirror and run my fingers through my hair, and know that my fear shows on my face.

Start my morning ablutions: spoon, eyedropper, needle, and medicine. The blood gushes into the outfit like salvation, as I squeeze the dropper it empties into my veins, liquid Jesus taking my fears and troubles, scattering them to the wind like dust in a typhoon.

Staring back into the mirror and looking good, calm, strong. Ready for whatever flavor of hell I might have to sample. Running a comb through my hair 'cause it is still sticking up, cleaning my rig, the mundane action, my daily ritual, is thoughtless, soothing.

Looking down at Rosie, feelings almost in control, grab my bankroll and walk over to the bed. Frozen staring down at her, the light breath barely indenting her pillow. She's more than perfect. I lean over, kiss

TEN

her stomach, lightly touch her face, and whisper, "See you two in a minute."

. . . .

Take a cab to the Exodus. Arriving in daylight is all different. The paint on the outside is trashed, the sign askew. Going through the door, the sunlight cutting through the darkness reigning within, pot and incense hitting me like a friendly invisible wall, the dim light and rock and roll enfolding me like a warm comforter.

Pausing to let my eyes adjust, finding the gorilla-like shape of Mel slouched in a sofa. Scanning the rest of the room for possible hostiles and then sauntering, almost a pimp stroll across the room, conscious of my every movement. Lowering myself into an easy chair and asking, "So whatcha gotta do to get a cup of coffee?"

"Tie off, waitress will be by."

"Cool. Check it out, stud, I don't know what to do about Jewels. Got any ideas?"

"Yeah. Nothin', don't do nothing. If he tries to move on you he's gotta hit all of us. That doesn't make sense for him. So he's gotta be pissed. So what? Fuck him in his faggot neck. You did the right thing, Bobbie. Did what I shoulda done. Homeboy went all the way off the wire."

"You said it, he went all the way off. That shit made no sense . . . What makes ya think he won't nut up again?"

Looking at Mel, slouched, not shaved, wearing a buckskin vest with no shirt, elephant bells, stomach coming over his belt. He reaches for his coffee with one ham-sized fist, drinks it, and sits up straight, making the muscles in his chest dance; flexing one tree trunk arm he says, "Don't write me off, kid, my act is kinda ragged right now but if anyone fucks with us I'll take their wind. Emis!"

"Yeah, mazel tov and all that shit. Mel, I don't trust the motherfucker anymore. I can park a slug in a motherfucker, you know that. I gotta tell ya this situation makes me hinky."

"I know pal, I don't like it either. Gonna meet my man Black Cloud in a minute or two and get new ID. Pick up our end of the dough tonight and head for Cleveland. End of story. Jewels can go all the way looney tunes. Who gives a shit? This time tomorrow we'll be driving matching Cads hundreds of miles from here."

"Matching Cadillacs?"

"Yeah, ace. One ivory, one black. You get your choice . . . anything ya want except the black one." The laughing nut that's resurfaced is unbeatable. Mel has the force that was there when we first met. The laughter that I feel starting in my belly is as much relief as anything else. Maybe I'll live to drive this ivory-colored, leather-seated piece of iron.

"Who's Black fuckin' Cloud?"

"A fixer, good for IDs, hot cars with paper, guns, whatever. Knows a couple jobs in Ohio that might be OK. Should be here soon. Not a bad guy for ya to know. He's good people, kill a motherfucker in a minute."

"Cool. How come the handle?"

"Dude's a righteous Indian, fuckin' Apache." Mel's leaning forward waving at the waitress, looks back at me. "Into it, too, weird ceremonies, taking scalps, the whole deal."

The waitress floats to our table, eyes dilated, tripping. Plain Midwestern farm girl in hippie garb inside and out. "Huh. I mean, yeah. What you guys want?"

A voice behind her booms, "Coffees, baby, gotta get that caffeine buzz. Ran out of crank. Ya got any? I'm coming down, sweetheart, been awake for a week, get us that mud and check on some speed for me OK, babycakes?"

Whatever she's on has got a roadblock erected between her and the rest of the world. There's no response as she drifts away in the direction of the counter.

The owner of the foghorn voice drops onto the sofa next to Mel and says, "Move over, fatty, either that or set your big butt in my lap and suck on my ear for an hour or two."

Mel does a slow take on this guy, tattoos all over circling his neck and running down both chest, up and down both arms, face pitted by hard living and hard time. Glasses magnifying eyes that are happily psychotic. No shirt, dirty jeans, and engineer boots. Got a knife hanging off his belt that must be two feet long and Mel smiles, first with his eyes, then his whole face. "Hot fucking shit in a champagne glass. Bring that ear over here, punk, then we'll see who sits on who's lap."

"So what's up, paleface? Whatcha need?"

"Regular shit, nothing special. This is Bobbie. Kid, this is Cloud."

"So this is the rookie I been hearing about." He looks dead into my eyes and starts chuckling. He says, "Nice piece of work in Chi, youngster, those motherfuckers needed killing, count beaucoup coup, get down with your bad self."

"Thanks. How'd ya hear about it."

"Guys know guys. It's a small world, ace, I try and keep up on who's who in da zoo." As he's talking he brings out a vial of speed, pulls a straw out of his pocket and sticks it directly into the vial, takes a huge snort, looks up with his eyes watering, and says, "Guess I lied, got some crank right here. Ya want some?"

"Nah, chief, heading downtown these days. Mel turned me out on smack. Go fast don't cut it anymore."

"Right, more for me. Word is that sissy ya been working with is not too fuckin' happy with your crew. What's up?"

The waitress comes to the table, distributes the coffee, and all conversation stops. The three of us regard her silently as she waits to get paid. Mel coughs and hands her a five-dollar bill. "Here's a nickel, see ya."

Black Cloud snorts to clear his nose, sounds like a buffalo, shakes his head, and says, "Speaking of Jewels, what's the difference between a faggot and a refrigerator?"

Mel sips his coffee, blows on it to make it cooler, and says, "The refrigerator don't fart when ya pull the meat out. So what's Jewels plannin'? What didja hear about that?"

"Heard he wanted to whack some kid, talking long shit. You tell me. Am I stepping into a shit storm working with you guys in his turf? 'Cause if I am my services are expensive."

"No, he was wrong, fuck him if he can't take a joke anyhow."

"He's a maniac but don't underestimate him, Mel."

This is unfolding like a bad dream. If Jewels's talking about hitting me it's for real. The only thing I can do is ice him first. I ask, "So what ya saying, Cloud, do I gotta kill him?"

Mel cuts in whispering, voice hoarse, "Jewels won't move on ya, Bobbie. We're out of here in a heartbeat, gone. Get our end tonight and we're history."

Black Cloud tugs on his lip. "You may be on the late freight, Mel. Jewels is a head case where his rep is concerned. Plus he owes ya a lot a dough. Run that one through your head . . . Fuck it. You guys ain't cherries. What can I do for ya?"

Mel lights a smoke. "Four IDs." Stops, digs in his shirt pocket, and hands Black Cloud a piece of paper. "Descriptions are on there. Want two Cads, clean, paper and number jobs, and a double-barrel twelve-gauge sawed off so it's about twelve inches from the handle to the end of the barrel. Tell us about Cleveland."

"Land of opportunity, especially for a crew of white pros like yours. You'll fit right in, niggers are going nuts. Black Panthers burning different parts of town every night, cops don't know whether to shit or go blind. Got a jewelry store and a dope connection. What do ya wanna do?"

This time I ask, "What's the setup? Creep 'em or are ya talking going in like John Wayne?"

Black Cloud looks from Mel to me, raises his eyebrows and says, "John Wayne. The jewelry store is airtight, ya gotta hit it when it opens. Armed robbery. Same thing with the connection, except your talking nigs that are armed to the teeth. They been taking connections down in NY, sellin' the shit in the Midwest. Already got multiple contracts on 'em. Shouldn't be a problem for guys like you. Check it out, didja hear the one about the Indian and the nigger that are waiting to get into heaven?"

"No, Cloud, haven't heard that one."

I look at Mel, who's just drinking his coffee, thoughts directed inward, and say, "No, man, not yet."

"Check it out, line of Indians as far as the eye can see. Got a short line of bugs. Nig in the front says to the Indian in the front, 'What happened? White man kill all you stupid motherfuckers?' Indian looks at him and says, 'Yeah.' Nigger says, 'Shit man, we be fuckin' their women, living on welfare, suckin' 'em dry. You Indians ain't about shit.' Indian laughs at the bug and tells him, 'Right, asshole, wait till they start playing cowboys and niggers.'"

Mel gives a small chuckle and Black Cloud starts busting up at his own joke, stops laughing, and says, "See? Should be a piece of cake.

The jewelry store guy will wet his pants as soon as ya throw down on him. With the connection just go in playing cowboys and niggers."

Mel comes back from whatever world he's been inhabiting and says, "You aren't talkin' about Kelvin and his guys are ya?"

The Indian laughs and says, "Give the man a cigar. Who else? Can ya think of a better group to play cowboys and nigs with? They burn their own people so they got no organized backup. I know your old lady hates those motherfuckers, and you probably don't got no love for 'em either. They burnt friends of yours, raped and sold a few chicks we both know. Fuck 'em."

"We aren't cowboys. We don't need the headaches."

Cloud stands up, says, "Think about it. Meet me here at around midnight. The paper and the cars will be here, have the dough."

Mel says, "Check it out, I want that gauge soonest. Attach a bungee cord at the handle. Solder a wire to the barrel so it's a sleeve hideout. Got it?"

Cloud laughs, slaps his hands together. "I recognize. You'll have it in a couple of hours, I'll drop it at your hotel. Catch ya later."

I stare into my coffee, the oil covering the top swirling like the emotions inside me. It doesn't matter how confident Mel is, we gotta meet Jewels to get our end of the cash and it feels like walking into an oven, the temperature climbing with every step. I say, "Yo Mel, fuck cowboys and niggers, maybe we should walk in on Jewels playing cowboys and queers."

"I hope that's not necessary."

"Right. What if it is?"

"Oh well."

. . . .

The bed is so soft it feels like lying on a cloud, rock and roll in the background and the smell of cigarettes, sex, and baby oil fill the room.

Rosie's as light as a firefly, her weight hardly making an impression as she sits perched on my butt rubbing my back, digging deep into the muscles, then raking lightly with her fingernails, working the knots out, doing her best to make me all better, and it almost works. She works her fingers into my traps and rolls them down my triceps saying,

"Fuck this cholo motherfucker, go in blazing, put his refried ass to sleep, mijo."

"Can't, mija, we gotta get the dough from the other scores from him. Mel doesn't think we're gonna have any problems. There ain't nothing to worry about."

"Gimme a break. Nothin' to worry about, that's why you got nothing but knots in your muscles. Maybe Mel's getting senile or something. Besides, they ain't having a baby. We are."

"Yeah." Her hands are taking the tension from my body as my brain dashes around my head like a turpentined cat. Round and round with dizzying speed.

Knowing that I fucked up, facing not just my fears but the fact that the courage I possessed was a fragile thing. Regretting stepping in, thinking of all the other things I could have done. Knowing that what I did was the right thing and still regretting it.

Scared of dying, not knowing if I'll be able to function if the shit hits home. Realizing that I would gladly trade Saylor's life for my own. Falling into the abyss with Rosie and our child perched on my back, terrified of crashing with them in tow and praying that I will have the heart to do whatever I have to.

Rosie works her way down my body, her hair now hitting my back, and starts to kiss and lick down my spine and sides, raking her fingernails before her tongue in patterns that move faster than the freak show in my head.

Tracing her tongue over and between my buttocks, reaching under me, gently taking my cock in her hand and running her thumb up and down the shaft until all that exists is this moment in time, saying to me, "Roll over, mijo, let me taste you." And I'm swinging around taking in the planes and shadows of her body, golden brown skin highlighted red by the last rays of the setting sun, the reflections dancing off her eyes. And I leverage myself so that as she takes my cock into her mouth I can bury my face between her legs.

Licking first the inside of her thighs slowly back and forth, edging always closer to her center, hearing her start to moan, sliding one finger inside her and knowing that she's dripping wet and hot, fastening my lips around her clit, chewing and sucking on it and as she starts to scream around my dick I'm coming with her, miniconvulsions racking our bodies simultaneously.

Slowing back to real time, twisting around and holding her as tightly as I can; knowing that she's crying. I don't care who I gotta kill or what I have to do, I'm not gonna lose this thing that's come to life between us.

Her head buried in my chest, voice small saying, "That maricón is loco, mijo. He's full of hate but he doesn't let it show. You took his pleasure away from him and made him look bad. I don't care what Mel or any-fuckin'-body says, he won't let this slide. He's gonna try and hit you."

"I'll leave his brains on the walls, mija. Jewels makes one wrong move, estuvo, no más vida."

She lifts her head, looks at me, tears still running down her cheeks but eyes blank, then shoots me that chipped-tooth, lopsided smile that this time doesn't reach her eyes. "Silly fucking gringo, my huero loco, I gotta make sure this baby is all right so I can't do it for you. Don't wait for him to bust a move, walk in and cap him. Don't listen to Mel, blow Jewels away as soon as you see him. Please?"

It feels like a roadblock inside me. The madness that comes when I'm hurt isn't there. The knowledge that hiding somewhere inside me is the capacity for an incredible level of violence does no good—it won't be summoned like an evil genie.

Trying to bring my level of intensity up isn't working. Doing violence to another human being isn't like getting your nerve up to commit a felony.

I realize I have to feel justified and Jewels hasn't fucked me over yet. Putting my most serious look on, faking a cold-bloodedness that's been part of my act for as long as I can remember, I tell her, "Don't worry, darlin', I'll walk in, give him my best smile, and empty my clip into his skull." Praying that it won't come down that way.

Pulling my clothes on, checking the clip in the 380, making sure there's one in the chamber, that the safety is *not* on. For the first time in what seems like forever mixing a hit of speed, sending it home and snapping into robot mode, on a mission, ready for whatever. Going so fast everything else is in slow motion, everything around me has the clarity of a black-and-white photograph and sounds, however small, are as distinct as individual notes of music.

Look at Rosie and for one flashing second feel words ready to come hurtling out of my mouth like Thoroughbreds from the starting gate. I hesitate, and all I can say is "See ya in a little bit."

. . . .

Syd closes the door to their suite behind me saying "Fuck, kid, your eyes are gonna come out of your head. You overamped?"

"Nah, ready though, real ready."

At the center table sit Mel and Black Cloud, smoke rising from their cigarettes, open beers in front of them. The Indian takes one look at me and starts laughing. "Shit, killer, for a guy that likes to go downtown you look like ya ready to break the sound barrier just standing there."

Mel's wearing a loose paisley top, jeans, and sneakers. Takes a hit off his beer and belches. "Whatever it takes. Got a backup piece for you, .22 Longrifle auto. And I got something just in case." Pulling up the sleeve to his shirt reveals the twin barrels to a sawed-off gauge. "Hope for the best, plan for the worst, huh, partner."

Syd's fixing her hair, bent forward and brushing it toward the floor, snaps upright, shakes it out of her face. She looks hard at me and giggles. "Take off your shirt, Bobbie, let's see that massive physique." Giggles again and holds up a tiny automatic and some duct tape. "Gonna tape this to your chest, a spot check won't find it. If this goes down wrong just rip it loose and start blazin'!"

The Indian booms out, "Start blazing shit, that ain't any more accurate than Mel's gauge. I'm gonna be as close to Jewels as I can get, one of you lames shoots me you'll wish you'd been born without fingers."

Mel cuts in. "Cloud is gonna be there to run interference. He'll get to Jewels before us. Things go wrong he's gonna be a surprise. . . . He's right about the .22. Ya gonna use it, ya gotta be real close, stick it right in the guy's chest. Know what I mean?"

"Yeah, Mel's famous class in marksmanship, already been there. Remember?"

. . . .

Driving slowly through the industrial section of Denver, warehouses, small factories, junkyards. The few streetlights not giving much illumination, our high beams cutting a tunnel through the night. The piece taped to my chest feels like it's as big as a cannon but every time I look down to see if it shows all I can see is T-shirt.

The adrenaline is starting to work with the meth, feeling is so acute the cigarette smoke in the car brushes against my skin like oily mist.

Pulling into a razor-wire-encircled parking lot. Security lamps surrounded by moths making it much brighter than day. Me and Mel exchange looks, he does an exaggerated wink, I touch the 380 ritualistically and check the .22 again. And then the rocks in the parking lot are crunching under my feet, the stench of chemicals and rust thick in the air.

The door is unlocked. Mel pauses for a second, looks at me, raises one eyebrow, says OK, opens the door and we glide inside.

The interior a dark maze, crates and boxes piled haphazardly. Radio playing oldies, the Big Bopper doing "Chantilly Lace," and Jewels walking across the oil-stained concrete to greet us, a different sharkskin suit shining green in the dim lighting, crystal goblet of wine in one hand, cigar in the other, saying, "Hola, amigos, qué pasa?"

"Not much, pal. Let's get this done." The words come out of my chest without revealing any anxiety, and that makes me feel better.

Jewels is smiling, not just with his mouth, his eyes are not guarded, and as he transfers the cigar to his mouth to shake hands I see Cloud and another guy coming out of the shadows behind him.

The new guy is a lanky clean-cut-looking Hispanic, saluting and starting to smile as he gets close. Cloud is still dressed in the same clothes, ambling slowly, taking it easy, and I realize that Mel was right, this is gonna go just fine, get our cash and get out of town. Black Cloud is standing next to the Latino yuppie and says, "Hey, do me a favor."

He hesitates, looks at Cloud, asks, "What ya need?"

Knowing that my relief shows as I reach out to shake Jewels's hand, feeling the smile touch my eyes as we clasp hands, and he kicks me in the nuts.

The shock that runs through my body is almost as strong as the outrage that floods my brain.

Aware that a guy wearing a cowboy hat has stepped out from the boxes with a pistol leveled at Mel screaming, "Freeze motherfucker," and that the one who'd been walking with Cloud is pulling a piece from the back of his pants just as Black Cloud says, "What I need is for you to bleed, punk," hitting him with a roundhouse to the chest, knife in his hand as if by magic.

Grabbing Jewels's wrist with my left, knowing that he's a boxer, that fistfighting him will be playing his game, leveraging with everything I got trying to break this motherfucker's arm at the elbow, feeling the ligaments tearing and the elbow giving way as I rush into him, wanting to snap his arm like a pencil, send the bones right through the skin.

He grabs my face, burying his hand in my cheek like it's a handle and rolling, slamming me into the floor, screaming, "Pinche fucking gavacho peckerwood piece of shit I'm gonna kill your Paddy ass, fist-fuck ya, and pull your heart out through your ass!"

Feeling the concrete cut into my back, pain going all the way from my groin to my shoulders, I grab his lapels and bury my head in his chest so that the punches he's throwing won't catch my face or temples.

Using my own pain as fuel, dragging myself forward far enough to get a handful of hair, feeling it tear out of his skull as I slam my forehead into his face, hearing the contact more than feeling it, sounds like a watermelon hitting the floor.

Seeing the blood running from his nose, I head-butt him again, pulling his face into my forehead, feeling his nose collapse and hearing the cartilage snap, the hair ripping out in my hand.

He grabs my throat, bouncing my head off the concrete, my vision doubling as I lock every muscle in my back and neck so he can't turn my brains into oatmeal.

Getting my thumb into his eye and twisting it all the way into his skull, feeling the eye rolling as it heads toward the brain, breaking his hold on my throat, letting me lunge forward and fasten my teeth into his cheek, grinding them, tasting the blood as his face is ripped open.

And as he screams the gunfire starts.

Mel's pulled the gauge from the sleeve hideout into his hand, leveling it inches away from the head of the guy aiming the pistol at him, and as the one in the cowboy hat parks one in Mel the sawed-off explodes, kicking the dude into the air.

I'm still on Jewels, trying to tear his eye out while biting into his face, but I can see every chunk of flesh, every drop of blood that surrounds the cowboy's body as it leaves the ground and drifts back to the concrete, bouncing as it makes contact; the hat landing at Mel's feet and Mel's doubling over, blood seeping through the fingers clasped over his chest.

I'm frozen for a portion of a second. Jewels whips his head away from me and rolls away. Getting to his feet, crouching, ripping the piece halfway out of his coat when Black Cloud, the better-late-than-never Indian, hits him in the side, steel gleaming from his fist. Freezes for one second, twisting his hand, and pulls back revealing two feet of bloody blade emerging from Jewels's side; grabs Jewels's hair and raising onto the balls of his feet swings the shank through the air and across and through Jewels's throat.

While the blood is still shooting from the gaping wound in Jewels's neck Cloud looks at me, smiles, and draws the blade across Jewels's forehead, plants his feet, grabs the hair, and with a sound like cloth ripping tears the skin and hair away from the bloody mess that was Jewels.

I'm stuck on adrenaline overload, looking for someone to kill. So enraged that I'm past anything resembling sanity and the only ones left standing are me and Cloud. The air is thick with the copper odor of blood, and the foul smell of shit.

Staring at the bodies of Jewels and his crew, glad they're dead. The one that walked out with Cloud looks like he's been run over by a sewing machine, too many stab wounds to count.

It seems like my feet are floating above the ground as I walk over to Mel—his eyes are crossed, the noise coming from his chest is one of wet paper ripping as I squat down next to him. "Yo, man, talk to me, you gonna be OK."

The Indian says, "He's finished, kid. We gotta get outta here."

"No, man, ain't happening. He won't die." Looking down at Mel, the bubbling ripping sound of his breathing slowing, getting wetter; blood bubbling from his lips and nose and then stopping permanently.

"That's it, kid, all over but the crying. Help me tear the office apart. Gotta find the dough."

I'm a cyclone of emotion. So many whirling so rapidly it feels like none at all. "Yeah, let's do it, get the fuck outta here."

Entering the office and smelling the sweet odor of patchouli mixed with cigar smoke. Modular furniture and a huge oak desk, the mirror covering the wall behind it shows two blood-covered specters walking toward it.

I stand inches away from the mirror not knowing what I'm looking for, searching my own eyes to determine what I'm feeling and seeing madness burning behind them like the pits of hell seen through blue glass, guilt and grief and bloodlust, my mouth a clown's smile, arterial red from biting through Jewels's cheek.

Spitting into my hand and rubbing at the blood till my face is relatively clean and seeing Black Cloud's reflection next to mine, turning to him, and saying, "What a fuckin' mess, shoulda listened to my old lady."

Wiping the gore covering his glasses on his bandanna, putting them back on, saying, "Shit, youngster, broads are always right, we just never listen to them. That's why it's always us dying and going to the pen. They got a lot more sense than we do."

"Wish I'd known that awhile ago."

"Wouldn'ta done no good."

"Fuck it. Let's get the dough and get gone. I gotta break this to Syd—think I'd rather trade places with Mel."

"Don't talk stupid, his ticket was up, happens to the best of us. No way out."

Forcing the feeling of loss that's clouding my eyes with mist and filling my chest with molten lead I say, "Yeah, sure ya right. No fuckin' way out." We grab the cash and jewelry. Gone.

. . . .

Syd's ready to go out, makeup on and dressed as we come through the door. The smile leaves her face like the setting sun. In its place is nothing.

She says, "Mel's dead."

I have no idea how she knows but she does. I just nod.

Suddenly the skin concealing her skull is sagging, her eyes lose focus and without anyone saying a word she lays a brick of the brown dope on the table, rips off a chunk the size of a cigarette butt, and starts the ritual of putting salvation into solution, drawing it up and shooting it into her veins like a nun would shoot prayers at heaven, not expecting an answer but hoping for absolution.

Black Cloud takes the pouch from his neck, dips into it, and places a small pile of dried leaves into an ashtray. Holding a lit cigarette to them, blowing and sending smoke billowing, deep voice rumbling, "Sweet grass and sage will clean us all, take the evil spirits and banish them." He looks up, sees the puzzled look on my face, and says, "Mel will go wherever Jews go when they die, the happy hunting ground, Valhalla, heaven, whatever. I don't know where, but this'll free his spirit."

Syd is looking into the spoon that held the dregs of heroin that seemed to have the answer to the pain she's feeling. Raising her head and scratching, more gowed than I've ever seen her, reaching for Mel's bottle of Jack Daniel's and chugging from it, shuddering, voice full of gravel from the smack and whiskey she says, "Heaven, Cloud, we go to heaven. Check it out, I don't know shit about spirits, is that faggot greaser dead already or is he still killable?"

I say, "Don't get much deader Syd." Voice coming out even and I'm glad that the pain inside me don't show.

Black Cloud reaches into his back pocket and pulls out the blood-encrusted piece of hair-covered skin that once sat on Jewels's head. "Not only dead, disfigured, shamed. Gonna wander through eternity looking for his scalp."

Syd holds her hands up and Cloud tosses the scalp to her. Catching it she turns it over in her hands and throws it back to the Indian. "Good, mazel tov, Black Cloud, shalom." I look at Syd, feeling lost—my faith in Mel was absolute. How could anyone that bad be dead, killed like an ordinary lame? Knowing that she needs solace more than I do but still asking, "What now, Syd, where are we gonna go? What are we gonna do?"

"If ya mean you and Rosie, that's up to you. If you're talking about me, count me out. I'm gonna see to it that my baby gets planted right. Then I'm going back to Jersey. To use one of Melvin's favorite lines, 'end of story.' I can't hang. You gotta blow town. You been kvetching about going to the coast, I'll give ya Billy Bones's number, shit, even call him and vouch for ya. It's nice out there, he's in Venice Beach, you guys take a vacation, ya need it."

. . . .

Rosie's looking at me from the bed, propped up on the pillows, has a paperback in her hand, cigarette burning in an ashtray next to her.

Sitting next to her, taking her hand, hating what is coming, feeling like Lenny the Lop, Mickey the Mope, Stupid fucking Steve in person saying, "Mel's dead, you were right, I shoulda gone in blazin'.'"

She sets the book down, pulls on her lower lip, and says, "I'm sorry baby," and reaches out to hold me.

I got my face pressed into her hair, girl and smoke fill my nostrils and I say, "Fuck, mija, it was a fuckin' nightmare. Goddamn Jewels was smiling, had backup. Went to shake my hand and kicked me in the balls. It was on. Cloud stuck one-a them, I'm wrestling with shithead, and Mel and the dude that had the drop on him wasted each other."

"Where's Jewels?"

"Dead, way fuckin' dead."

"Good, he needed killing."

"Yeah, he needed it when I first threw down on him. I fucked up."

"Naw, mijo, Mel fucked up. He was calling the shots, you went with it. Only one thing counts, you're here in bed with me and still breathing. Fuck everything else."

"Shit, man, I'm gonna miss that motherfucker."

"You got me, baby, you got me."

Pulling my face away from her so I can stare into her eyes. Seeing that she's telling the truth, the pain of losing Mel is countered by the feeling of belonging and I stutter, "Ya-a g-got me t-t-too," immediately looking away, lighting a smoke to hide my embarrassment.

Rosie whispering "I know I do, mijo, I know."

. . . .

Black Cloud has his feet propped up on the coffee table, looking into the distance. Syd's sipping a tall glass of whiskey rocks, wearing a terry-cloth bathrobe and standing in front of the window, staring outside. Rosie and me are sprawled on the couch. Syd turns from the window, eyes shell-shocked red and blue, says, "Talked to Billy. It's on; he's waitin' for us to call. Figure out how you gonna hook up with him. He's on vacation, running from the heat in Boston. He's Irish-mob affiliated, a certified fool. You'll get along good. Aren't you Irish, Bobbie?"

"Yeah, and Scot, half and half."

Rosie leans forward and asks, "Whatcha gonna do, Syd? Where ya gonna go? Ya sure you don't want to come out to the coast with us?"

"What you doing baby, writing a book? Need all my plans? Tell ya the truth I don't know. Going back to the lovely Garden State, Joisey itself. Maybe stay with my folks for a minute. I just know I can't take the game right now, I feel like someone cut my legs off, me and Mel were pretty tight. Know what I mean?"

Black Cloud clears his nose, shaking his hair out, says, "Listen up, how ya gonna plant him, gonna have a funeral or what?"

Syd pauses for a second and says, "Put him in a box and throw dirt on him." She's not making a sound but tears are running down her face, leaving black trails like war paint all the way to the corners of her mouth. Raising her hand to dab at the moisture, she continues still in a normal voice. "It's too bad he ain't Irish, he woulda loved a wake, but we're in the middle of goddam Colorado, most of the people we know here are affiliates of that fucking Jewels and would rather piss on Mel's grave than give him a send-off."

Looking at Syd, feeling the pain rising above her like a malevolent fog, I say, "Just us, don't need a whole crew, we're plenty. My people had wakes, just a bunch of drunken Scottish-Irish maniacs, talking about the old sod, crying, fighting, and once they got drunk enough, fucking. We'll stay till he gets buried. Then we'll split, OK?"

The Indian says, "Whoa, hoss, slow the fuck down. We ain't staying. You and me get linked to Mel's stiff and we also get linked to multiple homicides. No thanks, white man. If you got any plans for about the next twenty years you and your old lady want to get the fuck out of here. Better hook up with Billy on the coast."

"Yeah, but it seems like I should do something to show my respects."

The Indian looks at me and does a slow pan on everybody in the room. "We can show our respects. That's if Syd is up to it. When a warrior dies there's an Indian ritual called a pipe ceremony. We can do one and then get the fuck out of Dodge. I'm heading back to the rez. You two hit LA. Maybe we'll meet up down the road. Whatcha think Syd, want to smoke a pipe, send Mel on his way?"

Syd hasn't lost her blank look, she pauses for a minute and says, "Yeah. Why the fuck not?"

Pulling more herbs from his pouch, mumbling in Apache as he's doing it. Carefully loading the mixture into a hand-carved pipe and then saying in English, "We pass this to the left, always to the left." Walking over to the window, pulling it open, circling the room and opening the rest of the windows. "This is a wind ceremony, as the smoke is carried into the winds, it'll travel all over the world. Four winds, four corners, four directions, and right now four outlaws saying good-bye to the fifth."

As we pass the pipe the tears continue to seep from Syd's eyes, then Rosie's. As I feel mine filling I look at Black Cloud and he shakes his head with a nonverbal don't do it.

I take the pipe and draw in the sweet-tasting smoke, putting all my focus on the burning bowl, inhaling, and then my eyes are dry.

. . . .

The phone is pressed into my ear with my shoulder. The voice coming through the line's got a strong Boston Irish accent. "Yo. So you're Irish, huh, lad? Good, I like that. Here's what-up. Catch the next bird landing at LAX, call me before ya leave, I'll pick you up. You got green?"

"Yeah. Dough ain't no problem."

"Outta sight. I'm on vacation, if ya know what I mean. I could front ya some but I'm glad I don't got to."

"We're OK, don't sweat that, gonna see Mickey Rodent, hang ten, work on our tans, all that good shit."

"OK, Bobbie, see you when you get here. Let me talk to Syd."

I hand her the phone.

She gives me a weak smile, then says to the receiver, "Yeah. . . . I know. . . . Thanks. . . . Yeah, good fuckin' kids. . . . Uh-huh, he'll pop a cap if he's got to, he's a pro. . . . Thanks Billy, see ya." Hanging up, first hugging Rosie and then me, saying in the gravelly voice induced by heroin and whiskey, "Later, alligator."

. . . .

The Cadillac pours across the city streets like its on an oiled downhill slide. The smell of new leather like a drug, the seat's so soft that riding in it's almost sexual. I'm holding Rosie's hand and staring out the side window at the scenery floating by.

Black Cloud is driving and I look across Rosie, who's riding in the middle, take in the Indian's tattoos and long hair and say, "This was gonna be my fuckin' short. Mel was my fuckin' partner. Denver was cool. I even liked Jewels till he made us kill him. Now Syd's on her way to fuckin' Jersey, make that Joisey, and you're headed for the fuckin' reservation, and who the fuck is Billy Bones? Better than that, what kinda fuckin' name is Billy Bones?"

The Indian laughs and looks over at me, eyes still as merry as if the last twenty-four hours never happened. "Got your baby don'tcha, kid? Fuck a whole bunch of Denver. If you thought that fuckin' Jewels was OK you're as nuts as Mel was. The cocksucker wanted to rip you guys off from jump street. You just gave him an excuse.

"Billy is called Billy Bones for two reasons. One, he's about six-four, six-five and weighs about one-thirty, forty tops. Two, ya want to make somebody into bones . . . Billy's the guy to do it. That's why he's on the coast, dropped a hammer on one of those dagos in Boston and is letting his partners chill the situation. If the wops won't cool out Billy'll go back and the mortality rate will go up. Ya with me on all this?"

"Yeah man. So what's the deal, how do all you guys know each other?"

"Shit, paleface, we're the last of the independents. There's different crews all over the country, then ya got the I-talians and a couple of other mobs, Jewish and Irish who got their own style.

"Mob guys and guys like us are as different as my ancestors were from General sucking-a-dick-with-blond-hair Custer. Different animals. You a mob guy, they tell ya to whack your brother, ya do it or they whack you. All that loyalty shit they talk is just that. Shit.

"You an independent you don't answer to nobody except yourself. Me, I got my tribe. You, you got loyalty to you and your old lady, maybe one or two partners, fuck everybody else."

I look at Rosie, who shoots me that lopsided smile and squeezes my hand, check the road, and say, "My girl gotta come first, last, and always. Mel was my partner and he's dead. I'm an independent and I like that word. You're an Apache. If this Billy Bones is a mob guy how come he's helpin' us out?"

Black Cloud says, "The micks are different, they got more outlaw in 'em, not as structured as the dagos, and Billy don't give a fuck. He does what he wants. That's why he's in Cal right now. He hit a made guy, those cat's got no sense of humor."

Rosie cuts in. "Bobbie's a mick and I'm part Irish, does that give us any juice with his crew?"

"Not really, kid, the only juice ya ever have is your own power. What ya can do. That's it."

"Oh," and she squeezes my hand again.

I think about what Black Cloud said and know that as sad as I am, nothing is gonna stop us from making it.

If I coulda seen into the future I woulda got a job.

. . . .

We're sitting watching the planes take off and land. We're both wired, on our way to California, the land of opportunity, movie stars, Sunset Strip and Venice Beach.

As they call our flight's number and we line up with all the citizens I check the piece in my back pocket ritualistically and, holding Rosie's hand, board the flight for the Golden State, land of fruits and nuts. Walking down the chute into the plane Rosie asks, "Have you ever flown before, mijo?"

"Only on drugs, darlin', I don't got no wings."

"Are ya scared?"

"Abso-fucking-lutely."

She's got bonfires dancing behind her eyes, tough girl persona in place; leans toward me and lips brushing my ear whispers, "Me, too."

*L*os Angeles looks like the biggest Christmas tree in the universe, lights cutting through the night like a beacon home as the plane comes in for its landing.

I feel like it's all mine for the taking, like all I have to do is reach out and grab whatever catches my eye. Look at Rosie and see the same excitement I feel.

Take a hit off my drink, the plastic cup clicking against the ice and giving the whiskey a strange aftertaste like ashes have been mixed into it. Let it burn its way down my throat and say, "Here we are, baby, streets paved with gold, movie producers on every fucking street corner, dying to find raw talent like us."

Her face is flushed, eyes full of bad intent as she laughs. "Shit, mijo, discover us for what? Rob their fucking studios maybe. More likely, after a couple weeks, gonna have the motherfucking po-lice on every street corner dying to discover us."

"This is a vacation, darlin', we got enough dough to live good and not sweat nothin' for a minute or two. Heat out here don't know nothing about us."

"Yeah, we'll see. You think you can go that long without stealing?"

I hesitate for a second to see if I think that's possible and answer, "Piece-a cake, slice-a fuckin' pie."

The plane touches down and we both start laughing.

The terminal is full of people, squares, hippies, soldiers on their way to Nam or on their way back; all completely self-contained, focused on their own little missions.

Billy Bones is unmissable, six feet plus a few inches tall. Sandy hair greased back and curling over the collar of his black leather jacket.

ELEVEN

Under the jacket a black T-shirt. Levi's held up by a motorcycle chain belt, tucked into engineer boots as scuffed and marred as the face that tops all this off. Nose askew from being crushed at least once and cheeks acne-scarred. He's not moving at all as we approach but I can tell he's tracking us.

When we get within a few feet his head swivels. He looks directly at us, through shades even though it's the middle of the night, says, "Hey now, if it ain't the deadly duo. Welcome to LA. You got any baggage? Got me short parked in the red. This town's great, got parking places marked just for me, soon as I see the red I know it's my spot. I'm gonna let you guys use 'em while you're here. Least a guy can do, right? So ya got any baggage or can we just roll?"

Looking up into the black lenses of Billy Bones's shades thinking that this guy looks like an evil scarecrow. Raise the small bag we brought to carry the cash, drugs, and a few essential cosmetics for Rosie, and say, "This is it. We travel light. Call ya Bones or Billy?"

"Either one, lad, most people call me Bones." Gesturing at himself to call attention to his emaciated frame, continues, "It fits me pretty good, don'tcha think?"

"Guess so, pal."

"Let's not start this in a fucked-up way. Don't call me pal, or ace, and don't even think about buddy. I don't play that redneck shit."

I feel like laughing but don't bother, we're all tough guys and all play the same fucking games. I say, "So I guess Mary's outta the question, huh, Bones?"

"Mary? Who the fuck is Mary?"

"One more name you don't want to be called, kinda like ace and pal. Right, *slim?*"

He freezes for a second, slowly takes his shades off and mad-dogs me. I just stare back, gonna see where this cat's at. He loses the mad dog and his brown eyes actually warm up as he tells me, "Go ahead, badass, I like your style. I get tired of people being scared of me."

"Yeah, right."

"Stick to Bones or Billy. All right? Let's blow this Popsicle stand, come on."

Directly in front of the exit parked in the red is a '57 Chevy Belair, candy apple red with huge tires in the back. Bones opens the passenger door and says, "I went all the way native, lad, this state's got the baddest custom cars in the world. Ain't no backseat, we all gotta ride in front."

We slide in and Bones gets behind the wheel, slamming a tape into the eight-track. As Blue Cheer blasts out of the speakers, Bones blasts out of his parking place, tires screaming and smoking, smashing us back into the seat from the acceleration. Feeling the skin on my face pulling back and looking over at Rosie, seeing her laughing and realizing that I'm laughing also and that Bones is howling as he powers the Chevy out of the airport down Lincoln Boulevard and into Venice.

. . . .

The pad is right on the boardwalk, fog drifting sleepily across the beach, the sound of waves breaking on the sand drifts into the living room.

The furniture is early thrift store, maybe genuine Salvation Army. There's a new TV and a stereo taking up one wall, scattered all over are clothes and the remains of past meals—pizza boxes, burger wrappers, and buckets that once contained chicken.

Pointing at a doorway coming off the living room Bones says, "There ya go. I had this hippie crashing there till a couple hours ago. He ain't too happy, fuck him, it's yours now. I'm hitting Hollywood. Pandora's Box and probably the Whiskey. You wanna go?"

Rosie is taking in the surroundings, one lip slightly curled, and says, "Nah, not me. I wanna get settled in. Maybe rearrange some-a your decorations."

Bones laughs. "Go ahead, girl. See you two tomorrow."

. . . .

We've trudged the yellow brick road and ended up in Venice, California. Bloody rooms and dead friends are a long way away. The ocean's a cobalt blue; the sky turquoise fading into it; and the sand is covered with naked and scantily clad, loaded and blitzed humanity. It's like being in Oz.

As loaded as we are it seems like everyone on that strip paralleling the beach is even higher. Blazing on psychedelics, wobbling on reds, flying on speed, and all drinking wine or smoking pot. It feels good to be somewhere we fit in.

Rosie's got on a tie-dyed tank top and jeans. I'm wearing the same except my tank top is white, a classic wife beater. The breeze smells of salt, weed, and sewage.

I squint at Rosie. The sun is silhouetting her and under the shirt her belly is showing; the wind is blowing her hair toward me and I say, "Toldya, mija, California. Do one or two more scores and buy a pad out here, right on the fuckin' beach. Whatcha think?"

"It sure ain't Gary, Indiana, don't even see a smokestack. I thought we were on vacation, when you planning on doing these one or two more scores, Mister ain't-gonna-steal, piece-a-cake, slice-a-pie, Irish Blarney Stone motherfucker?"

"Easy, darlin', take it easy, this *is* a vacation. No bullshit. No robbin', no burgs, no nothing except havin' fun. For reals." And I pull her into my side, arm around her shoulders as we walk down the boardwalk.

Looking at the freaks juggling, singing, Hare Krishnas chanting, she says, "Buy me a Coke, gangster. . . . Do ya really like it out here?"

"Buy ya anything ya want, gangsterline. . . . Don't you?"

"Yeah, as a matter of fact, it's pretty fuckin' cool."

Sipping our Cokes, watching the passing parade, and hear, "Pssst, what's the qué pasa. Whatcha think. Fuck the resta the world, dis is what's happenin'."

Turning to stare into the center of a black T-shirt. Looking up to meet Bones's black shades, and say, "Sho-you right, this is bad to the bone. . . . What's up?"

"A couple whites to wake up, a few reds to stay mellow. Greeting a new day. Picked two chicks up at Pandora's last night. Fuckin' worn out, nut sack feels like a pillowcase with two raisins in it. Know what I mean, lad?"

"Yeah, man."

Rosie starts laughing. "You a class act, aren'tcha Billy Bones?"

"Missed charm school, lassie, you must pardon my lack of etiquette. The good sisters of St. Agnus usta wear their rulers out on my poor knuckles trying to teach me manners."

I take a hit off my Coke, check out a really pretty blonde walking by with no top, feel a twinge of guilt at my reaction and say, "Whatcha doin' right now Bones?"

"Lookin' for you. I'm like a vampire, sun goes down I get up. Knew you'd be strollin', thought I'd drag my ass outta me rack, leavin' those chicks brokenhearted no doubt, but I'm a man of my word. Told Syd I'd show you around and here I am. Billy Bones tour guide at your service. Whatcha wanna do?"

I'm happy cruising Venice Beach staring at the freaks, feeling a part of and getting loaded.

Rosie doesn't hesitate, she says, "Disneyland, I wanna go to motherfuckin' Mickey's house. OK?"

I look at her, look at Bones, and say, "Yeah, why not? Ya wanna go Bones? Where the fuck is it, anyhow?"

"We'll get directions, lad. Get a gang of acid, go down there tonight tripping. Gimme time to find a suitable companion."

Rosie's grinning from ear to ear, claps her hands and says, "All right."

. . . .

The broad comes through the door just as we get done fixing. I'm still wiping the blood offa my arm when she plops herself down on the sofa next to Rosie. Blond hair to the middle of her back, a headband holding it in place, a see-through lace top and blue jean bells, open-toed sandals showing red toenails.

Bones is a minute or two behind her, taking in the outfits and cookers. "That shit'll kill ya both," he says. "Make ya weak in the bargain. Me, I don't fuck with poison like that. Just what the good Lord intended." Taking out a Baggie full of reefer and rolling a joint, lights it and hands it to the chick, saying, "A natural herb. This is Susie. These are Bobbie and Rosie. I'm showin' 'em the sights. Got the sunshine, baby?"

Susie takes a hit off the joint and tries to pass it to Rosie, who says, "No thanks," extends it to me, and I just shake my head no. Pot stopped being fun when I was twelve and I have no urge to smoke it. It smells great but I got no use for the effects.

She hands it back to Bones, digs into the cloth bag she dropped at her feet, and comes out with a clear glass vial containing little oblong orange pills. "Here you are, Billy, orange sunshine."

"Bless ya, darlin'." Counting them out saying, "This is good acid. A lotta mutts take a half and think it's a trip. Me, I take four or five; got sixteen, four each." He hands them out. I look at Rosie, who is watching Susie chew hers up. Check out Bones, who winks and says, "Happy trails, Bobbie" as he pops his. I do the same.

Rosie sticks her tongue out at me. It's coated with orange dust. "Shit, mijo, hope it works better than it tastes."

. . . .

We're all piled into the front seat, flying down the highway, the suburbs going by in a blur. The acid making all four of us laugh hysterically as Bones shoots in and out of traffic like it's the Indy 500 instead of the 5 freeway at rush hour.

Rock and roll blasting from the speakers and the vibration of the engine working in harmony with the LSD to jack reality all the way up. Sound system, speedometer, and our brains all redlined.

As we get out of the car Bones says, "Good acid, huh lad?"

His voice bounces through the echo chambers that have been installed in my ears and the letters of the words flash behind my eyes. I'm still rushing from the flight down the freeway. The acid seems secondary to the adrenaline pumping through my system.

I take note of the manic grins on Rosie's and Susie's faces, look at Bones dressed in his mandatory black, shades still in place, and say, "Good acid, great driving. What a rush."

"Ain't nothin' folks, the Matterhorn awaits us."

Disneyland. Walking down Main Street as it flows like lava beneath my feet. Rosie melts into the pavement and reemerging says, "Man, it's all one fucking thing," and we go into hysterics.

On the submarine ride, knowing it'll never end, tripping on the squares as they trip on us.

Bones collapsing from laughter in Frontier Land after pretending to kill entire families. Aiming one of their toy rifles and with each shot doing dialogue: "Got mom in the crosshairs . . . right between the fuckin' eyes. See ya. Got junior . . . taking aim. Bam . . . blew his dick off. Here's little sis. Splat, splat . . . kneecaps gone. Let dad dig the situation, boom, through the throat. Let the motherfucker drown in his own blood."

Slamming down the Matterhorn. Rushing like it's really a toboggan flying down a mountain.

Coming down during the fireworks. The acid slowing, the hallucinations becoming gentle rather than overwhelming. Checking each other out to see if the journey was the same for all of us. Susie saying, "Shitfire, this is beyond cool." Bones actually taking off his shades to watch the display. Me watching the colored lines and shadows dance over my friends while running my fingers through Rosie's hair and thinking to myself, "Yeah, man . . . this is a good one" as Rosie looks at me and says, "Sí, mijo, muy bueno. Don't get much gooder."

Bones turns to us from the fireworks and I know he followed the whole thing, spoken and unspoken. "Glad I'm not nuts," he says as he puts his shades back on and they send another burst of stardust and liquid fire into the smoky velvet sky.

Dylan's playing on the way back. We're all silent, depleted, almost down. Bones is still driving fast but not like a bullet.

Rosie elbows me and says, "Mickey hugged me."

I grin and say, "That's it. He's one dead fucking rodent."

And Bones laughs, adding, "The only thing I ain't killed yet, lad, a cartoon. What a grand concept."

. . . .

Bacon and eggs filter into the dream, the decaying corpses of friends and loved ones recede and my own demise is postponed, the executioner banished by a Boston Irish accent crying out, "Awaken, it's a glorious fucking day for dying!"

Cracking one eye and wondering if the lingering dream is a preview of reality. Knowing Bones's fondness for homicide and finding his choice of morning greetings ominous.

Reaching under my pillow to have my piece in hand if that's the case when the brogue hits, "Bobbie, Bobbie, didn't you learn nothin' at your mother's knee? If you have to reach for your weapon it's too late. Sleep with it in your hand. Shoot 'em through the sheets. Me, I'm your friend, you don't get many. Susie's makin' breakfast, come eat."

I'm pissed when he turns Irish on me. "Learn to speak American, Bones. Whatcha doin' speakin' to a motherfucker in a foreign language first thing in the mornin'? Shoot 'em through the sheets my mother-fuckin' ass. Even you can't sleep with a piece in your hand."

"Learn to, lad, if ya want to grow old." Sticking his hands into his back pockets and saying without a trace of an accent, "Come on, tough guy, chow's ready. Pull your jeans on. Let's eat."

Shaking my head to try and dispel the last of the ghosts wandering through it, looking over to see if Rosie is covered and seeing her staring at Bones with a look of complete amazement and sleepy confusion, her hair sticking up at right angles, last night's lipstick smeared from making love before we crashed.

I roll back toward the doorway, looking into Bones's shades. He's got no shirt on and I really understand how he got his nickname. There's no meat on his emaciated frame, every rib shows, his arms look like strands of spaghetti but he's still intimidating. The revolver sticking out of his jeans might have something to do with that.

A voice in the back of my mind tells me the motherfucker was telling the truth. He would've killed ya before you filled your hand. I say, "From now on, Hercules, knock. Ya come walkin' in here unannounced again I'll be real upset. What time is it anyway, motherfucker?"

He shakes the hair out of his face, points his index finger at me, and makes a shooting motion. "Bang, you're dead. It's time to get out of your rack, you ungrateful sod."

Rosie groans and snuggles closer to me, saying, "You eat, I'm sick as a dog, part of being pregnant. Soon as I get done pukin' I'll be all right."

I tell Bones, "Gotta do my wake-up, Rosie's sick. Start in, we'll be there in a minute."

"That shit's gonna kill ya, Bobbie."

As he closes the door behind him, Rosie pulls on a shirt and dashes for the bathroom. I start my morning ritual, pick up my needle and spoon.

. . . .

Rosie comes out of the bedroom as I'm finishing breakfast. Still brushing her hair. Lipstick now in place, but she's got a yellow face. "Man, don't feel fuckin' good at all. This fuckin' sucks. Next time you carry the baby. I'll do the crimin'."

Susie's still eating, taking bird-sized bites. She says, "You two are nuts, I wouldn't have a baby. The world's a fuckin' mess."

Me and Rosie look at each other and shrug simultaneously. Rosie says, "Yeah, all the way fuckin' looney tunes."

I kick a chair out for her and as she sits she asks, "Whatcha think, mijo, are we nuts?"

"Yeah, baby, fuckin' bent. That's us."

Bones eats as fast as I do, a sure sign of being state raised. Inhaling your food before the guards are screaming at ya to get out of the chow hall.

He's got egg yolk all over his face, bread crumbs in his hair. Grabbing a dirty T-shirt off the floor and rubbing it across his face, saying, "Can't gain fuckin' weight, don't matter what I do. Check it out, ya ever hear of Whittier Boulevard?"

"No."

Susie raises her eyebrows as if only a yokel wouldn't be aware of whatever the fuck Whittier Boulevard is. "You will. Billy wants to be a lowrider when he grows up."

"Lowrider?" Rosie asks.

"Sheeit, darlin'," says Bones, "full-on cholo vato loco."

Susie has a small compact out and is putting eyeliner on, finishing one eye, the other untouched, looking like her face is lopsided. "Lowride tonight, I'll teach you how to surf tomorrow. Billy's scared of ruining his milky white complexion. It'll be nice to have company."

Bones says, "Milky white, eh, fuck the sun. Good only for mad dogs and Englishmen, the scurviest race of sodomites to ever curse the earth. I'll stick to nighttime activities. Such as riding the American auto slowly and lowly."

Rosie says, "I heard about it. Cruisin', right?"

Bones actually smiles, showing off yellowed teeth, chipped and cracked like weathered tombstones. "Rightcha are, Rosie, the finest autos in the world. Lowered, channeled so low sparks fly as they roll. Glass packs and cherry bomb mufflers. Fire coming out of 'em. Tuck-and-roll upholstery. Competing to see who can go the slowest. Oldies on the eight-tracks, cars and trucks so modified Henry fuckin' Ford would never recognize 'em."

I don't get it, don't have any idea what he's talking about. This is as alien to me as chickens and cows. I start to nod like I have some concept about what he's referring to and catch myself. Decide fuck it and ask him, "Tuck and roll, lowered, glass packs? What the fuck are ya talkin' about?"

"You'll see, lad, if it don't touch yer heart ya ain't got one."

Rosie is staring at Bones. "Ya don't gotta talk like that, why the accent?"

"Why, lassie, I like it. Can't be killin' people alla the time. Gotta keep myself amused. Besides, for me to talk without it is hard, I grew up in Belfast. . . . *You* got an accent. You keep yours, I'll keep mine."

Rosie has been slumped in her chair, now she sits up straight. "Accent? I don't got no focking accent, Meester Billy focking Bones. And fock a whole bunch of lowriding. I'm gonna be a surf bunny."

"Right ya are, lassie."

I laugh at both of 'em and ask, "So when are we leavin'?"

"Eight, nine o'clock tonight. Baby Al is gonna take us down there. He's from around here. Don't wanna go cruisin' in my race car. He's got one bad short."

. . . .

The fire's shooting out of the exhaust pipes like a dragon's breath, dual streams of flame accompanied by a noise like a string of small firecrackers going off.

The vehicle itself is a Hudson, big as a battleship and gleaming like a giant pearl in the light cast by the streetlamps, engine rumbling through its custom mufflers and so close to the ground a mouse would have trouble fitting under it.

As we pile in I understand what tuck and roll is. The upholstery goes halfway up the doors, black velvet sewn in diamond patterns. There's six of us and there's still space left. It's like being in a small room with upholstered walls.

As I sprawl into the backseat Bones says, "This is Baby Al."

The Chicano driving looks like a heavily muscled, tattooed Aztec. He's got a hook nose and oriental eyes, blue bandanna around his forehead. He turns around and says, "What's happening?" Pulling the girl next to him closer he says, "This is me heina, Valerie."

We do the hello routine and Susie asks, "Where's José and Elena?"

Valerie turns to her, beehive hairdo touching the roof of the car, bright red lipstick contrasting with her light brown skin. "They're picking up a bag of whites. Gonna meet 'em here."

As we sit drinking from a gallon jug of Red Mountain wine, smoking nonfilters, I wonder why we're hanging out in a car. Baby Al drinks from the bottle and passes it to Bones, saying, "My homeboy Payaso just got out of Soledad, did eight summers. We gonna head to the beach around midnight, party down. This José has a pass to be down here from up north. If a norteño can come sure as shit a couple a woods can. You gavachos wanna go?"

Bones takes a hit off the jug of wine, lights a cigarette, and asks, "Whatcha think, lad, shall we party with these lowriding vatos and their heinas or do we have other plans?"

I look at Rosie to see what she wants to do and realize that the whites are starting to hit, cutting through the heroin and mixing with the wine. My heart's hammering and my vision is blurring. Looking into Rosie's eyes I know she's coming on strong; they're as big as saucers. But even with the smack flowing through her system, her cheeks are pale as parchment. I wonder what's wrong. She smiles and nods yes. I say, "Yeah, man."

A customized VW Bug pulls up, two people get out and walk over to us. Valerie touches her beehive, making sure that no hair has escaped, and says, "All right, wake-up time."

José is a big chubby Chicano with tattoos showing under the three-quarter sleeves of his Sir Guy shirt. Elena is a really pretty Chicana; she's slim, has lots of makeup, and is wearing a short black skirt and a cashmere sweater.

As they reach the lowrider José tosses a bag of bennies through the window and says, "Wake up, carnales."

Baby Al catches the bag and grabs a handful of the crosstops saying, "Take six or seven, get all the way up," passing the bag around with the gallon of Red Mountain to chase the aspirin-sized pills.

José and Elena climb into the backseat with me and Rosie. Elena says, "Ándale, Al, let's ride."

As we start rolling, Bones leans toward Baby Al and says, "Where's the tunes, lad?" Wolfman Jack comes out of the speakers as we head for Whittier Boulevard.

*T*he Boulevard is a motorized two-way blacktop festival. Model Ts, lowered Chevys, chopped and channeled Studebakers, Day-Glo ambulances, VWs that would have given Hitler nightmares. The colors going from stock through flamingo pink with so much lacquer it's like looking into a pool of colored water. Metal flakes and starbursts that are so bright they have a light of their own. The cars are like nothing I'd ever seen, driving at five to a max of ten miles an hour.

I'm staring out the side window digging it all. My new associates are all babbling away, the whites have taken hold and the conversation's nonstop speed rap, too fragmented and disjointed to even attempt to record. Through it all Wolfman Jack and Original Rock and Roll.

· · · · · · ·

Pulling into Bob's Big Boy and watching the sparks fly out from under the Hudson as the body drags on the driveway. Baby Al saying, "Get a Big Boy, and ya gotta get a chocolate malt." Sliding into a slot and a female carhop takes our orders.

I got no desire to eat but ask for a special along with everybody else.

When she comes back to take the trays, each burger has only one or two bites missing, but all the malt glasses are empty. The only one able to get any food down is Bones. He downed his burger and fries and then finished Susie's. Looking back at me and saying, "America, lad, ain't it grand?"

I take a hit offa the Red Mountain and nod my head yes. We go to the end of the Boulevard, watching people pour out of cars, then drive back in. Baby Al laughing and saying, "Rotation stops."

Elena poking me in the arm and asking, "Having fun, white boy?"

TWELVE

Looking away from the window to say, "Yeah, tons of fun."

Rosie raises one eyebrow at me as José asks, "Tons of fun, huh, peckerwood?"

Rubbing Rosie's leg, saying, "Yeah, tons of fun." Holding his eyes. When he smiles letting him get away with the word that time, and turning my head to stare at the show going by on four wheels.

. . . .

Lowriding back. Feeling the sweat breaking out on my forehead and knowing that before we do anything else, me and Rosie are gonna have to get well.

Rosie nudges me and says, "I don't know about this party, I don't feel too good, mijo."

My nose is starting to run. As I wipe it on the back of my hand I say, "I know. We're gonna take care of it."

I lean forward and ask Baby Al, "You OK with us slamming while you moving?"

"What, homes, right in the backseat?"

"Yeah, man."

"Chiva?"

"Yeah, man."

"You malea, huh, homes?"

"Yeah, man."

"Got a taste for me?"

"Yeah, man."

"Go ahead, homes. Just be cool. The juras are all over the Boulevard."

I can feel the wine and the malt going to war in my stomach, the anxiety that I've managed to keep in check for so long is coming back with a vengeance, and Rosie's looking really bad.

Her eyes seem to be retreating into her head, her face is covered with sweat, and she's pale as skim milk. She gives me a weak smile and a halfhearted wink. I say, "Check it out, Al, pull into the next restaurant we come to. I'm gonna grab a spoon and some water."

"No problem, homes."

The lowrider scrapes its way into the parking lot of a diner and I'm flying out of the Hudson and through the swinging glass door.

Going through the restaurant as fast as I can without running, grabbing a spoon offa one of the tables. Entering the men's room, looking in the mirror and thinking that I don't look as sick as Rosie and wondering why. Disturbed by the paleness of her face and determined to get her well as quick as I can.

Dashing back to the counter and telling the cook, "Need a glass a water to go." He's dressed in white splattered with grease, has an old Marine Corps bulldog tattooed on his forearm, and his belly is coming over his belt. I'm looking into his eyes and the look on his face is anything but friendly. When he hesitates my anxiety starts to rip through my skin and I can feel my eyes starting to come out of my head. "Now. Fucking immediately."

Reaching into my pocket and peeling a five offa my roll, say, "Here's your tip. Now get . . . the . . . fucking . . . water."

His face goes slack and then he looks at me like I'm nuts and says, "Yeah, right away. Be cool," and pours, then hands me a paper cup of water.

Sliding into Baby Al's short, slamming the door and saying, "Don't drive too fast."

He snorts and looks back as we're pulling out saying, "You gotta be loco. I ain't *been* driving fast."

I pour some dope into the spoon, cook it, look at Elena and say, "Gimme one of your smokes." As she hands it to me she lets her fingernails drag across the back of my hand. Looking at her, her eyes half-lidded, and thanking her as she runs her tongue across her lips.

I don't know how to react, don't know if she's coming on or if I'm reading her wrong. I drop my eyes and rip the filter offa the cigarette, make a ball outta a piece of it, drop the ball in the spoon as a strainer, and draw the shit up.

Then do something that's unheard of in dope-fiend circles. Hand the rig to Rosie and say, "Go ahead. You slam first."

She ties at her wrist, hits the vein in the back of her hand, and I can see the stuff working as she cleans the rig before handing it to me. Slumping back into the tuck-and-roll seat she says, "Thank you, mijo."

I just shake my head to acknowledge her and start cooking my own fix. Look up as I'm drawing the murky brown fluid into the outfit and it registers that even though she has a light nod going, Rosie is still pale.

"You all right, mija?"

"Yeah, Bobbie, I just feel kinda weak. I'm all right. It's the malt, motherfucker was too sweet."

I think, *Wine, whites, and the fuckin' malt made her sick*? I say, "Go figure" as I pump a temporary lobotomy into my arm and go back to staring out my window.

. . . .

The ride to the beach is a California show.

Low as we can go.

Oldies on the radio.

Cruisin'. Going slow.

. . . .

Pulling right up to the sand, Baby Al says, "Party time, carnales."

Valerie kicks in, "Orale. Ain't seen Payaso since he capped that mayate from Sho-line."

Bones checks his eyes in the rearview mirror saying, "Does this mean we gonna hang ten?"

As the Chicanos start laughing Bones says, "Forgive me, folks, I forgot you weren't surfers."

Elena looks at me over Rosie's head, which is on my shoulder, and winks, saying, "I kinda like surfers."

José's opening their door, stops and without turning around says "Better be dead ones, mija. If you gonna be likin' 'em, they gonna get that way."

She blows me a kiss, once again over Rosie's nodding head, and says, "You my baby, José, don't be stupid."

Bones grabs me as I'm climbing out of the Hudson, got one hand on my shoulder and says to Rosie, "Excuse us, lassie. I must have a word with young Robert."

The sand is pulling at my combat boots, my balance is off from the wine, whites, and heroin. As the salt-laden wind comes off the ocean and the waves crash on the shore Bones leans down without breaking stride.

"Don't even think about it, laddie," he says. "She's a fine-looking piece of ass. You bone her, you're gonna have to kill José, or he'll kill you. It's a fact he ain't from LA, so if you gotta kill somebody while you're here he'd be a good candidate. Pussy would be a stupid fuckin' reason to do it though, Bobbie."

Keeping up with Bones's pipe-stem legs is taking all my attention. As his words register I pause to try and sort the thoughts that are echoing around my head. "I don't fuck around Bones. I got an old lady. Homegirl's just loaded. Why ya saying this, anyhow?"

"Stevie told me he saw a wreck coming."

"Stevie?"

"Stevie Wonder, ya fuckin' degenerate, and if he can see that bitch's eyes wanderin' so can José, and Rosie fer that matter."

"Don't sweat it, Bones." As the words come out of my mouth they're contradicted by the stirring in my gut and the guilty feeling that's forming even though nothing's happened.

He hitches his jeans up, spits into the sand, and says, "Listen to old Bones, boyo. We're all the same, every fucking one-a us. Don't do it."

As he turns to go back down the beach I tell his back, "Like I said, don't sweat it."

Standing still for a minute trying to clear the haze fogging my mind, then trudging back through the sand, looking from the moonlight gleaming off the oily black waves to the light from the moon reflecting off the Hudson's pearl finish.

Bones is disappearing toward the bonfire where the party is starting and Rosie is a tiny figure outlined against the glow from Baby Al's short.

My mind is its own Tower of Babble, one voice saying, "Go for it," the next saying, "The broad's just loaded, ain't nothin' happenin'." Then, "Ya love Rosie, are you fucking nuts? . . . But Elena's got great lips, just kiss her. . . . Shit, don't bust a grape, you're drunk. . . . Hike up her skirt, bone her on the sand, fuck José, he ain't your friend, kill the motherfucker. . . . You gonna hurt Rosie, asshole, don't do it."

As I approach the car I hold out my hand and pull Rosie into my chest saying, "Hey, mija, how ya feeling?" Her body feels like ice and my brain's still talking to itself saying, "Shut up . . . Shut up . . . Shut the fuck up."

"That ice cream fucked me up. I'm cold. Let's get next to the fire."

"Let's go."

As we approach the flickering flames voices carry across the sand with light Mexican accents and one loud Irish accent saying, "Hey, my own darlin' lovebirds. Join the party."

Rosie stands as close to the flames as she can, shivering, and I hold her from behind trying to warm her. Got my face buried in the back of her neck, the aroma of shampoo from her hair mixes with the smell of the ocean and the light odor of the burning wood.

I look into the flames that are dancing around the kindling and against the sand and night, feel the warmth touching my arms and face.

Looking through the fire see Elena's face floating in the dancing golden light as she stares at us. I stare back for a second and then retreat to the safety of Rosie's hair as my mind starts spinning. Whispering into Rosie's ear, "Are ya feelin' any better?"

"Let's blow this scene, mijo," she says. "I'm still cold and I don't feel good enough to beat that cunt's ass."

"Let's roll."

. . . .

The pad is in walking distance. We trudge through the sand, headed toward the blacktop.

I hold Rosie's hand as the boardwalk draws close and the noise of the city grows and the sound and smell of the ocean recedes.

I can feel her looking at me, turning and staring into her face. Rosie asks, "Well, what's up with that, Bobbie? You gonna fuck that puta? Is she finer than me? What's up?"

For a second I think about denying that I know what she's talking about, playing it off like I'm not aware of the trip that could've developed. Decide for once in my life to do what might be the right thing and hope that it doesn't blow up in my face.

"Shit, mija, ain't nobody finer than you. That broad is a fuckin' skank. The bitch is just stoned. I don't want none. Ain't gonna get none. You and me. Fuck all that dumb shit."

I drop her hand and pull her into my chest, standing there on the edge of the boardwalk, the wind blowing against my back, the street-lights casting weak illumination into the littered sand. Jazz is floating from one of the bars at the edge of the beach and I'm holding my girl.

She says, "You so full of shit, Bobbie. One thing that whore *ain't* is a skank. You *know* she's fine. But I'm glad you know you're mine. She'da made a move, I'd'a cut her face to ribbons."

I can feel her shivering in my arms and tell her, "Come on, gang-sterline, you can commence to cuttin' later. Just pretend your cutter's broken for now. Let's get under the covers. Snuggle. Fuck that broad. Don't trip."

"OK, mijo, only reason I ain't fifty-one-fifty is you been holdin' me all night. That pig starts eyeballin' your fine blue-eyed peckerwood ass again it's on."

"You loco, mija. Let's get outta the wind. Come on."

She grabs my hand and we hit the boardwalk and stroll in silence. Trash blowing past our feet, passing old winos, hippies, and cholos.

Walking from dark to dim light as we progress and the streetlights come and go. Jazz fades into blues and the noise of a party. Finally only the sound of the ocean and our own footsteps as we reach home.

. . . .

Under the covers, holding Rosie and her shivering won't stop, and I'm starting to feel scared. I ask her, "You sure it's just the ice cream?"

"Yeah, maybe something hot would help."

I tell her, "Tie off. Let's see what's in the kitchen." Rummaging through the cupboards and find soup and hot chocolate mix, yell out, "Ya want soup or hot chocolate?"

"Hot chocolate."

Cook the stuff, pour it into a mug, and bring it in. Smoke a Camel as I watch her drink it. She's blowing onto the steaming liquid and taking tiny sips, halfway through she looks up, eyes recessed and circled by black like a raccoon's, and says, "Those fuckin' whites are still workin'. Does Bones have any downs laying around?"

"Find out for ya."

Going into Bones's room and searching through the pile of laundry and shit on the top of his dresser, finding two stilettos, a .45 automatic and brass knuckles, acid, weed, rolling papers, change, and finally a bag of tuinol.

Count out six of the rainbows and throw the bag back on the dresser. Walk into our room and open my hand. Say, "Three each, sweet dreams tonight."

"Outta sight. Rainbow's my favorite sleeper." Rosie takes her three tuinol and chases them with hot chocolate and I do the same.

We fall asleep curled up like spoons, her back fitted into my chest. As the downs come on and the hammering of my heart slows, I feel complete, like life might actually be OK. While everything is shutting down, Rosie softly slurs the words, "Goin' surfin'. Wow. Good night, mijo."

The cool briny breeze is coming through the window and we're under the blankets in a pocket of warmth and safety. Tomorrow's gonna be a great day.

I've still never surfed. Sunny days depress me. I love the beach when it's foggy and kinda cold and there's no tourists. Just me and swirling fog muffling sight, sound, and smell. Allowing ghosts to come out of hiding and walk with those of us who love the thick mist.

But that was a beautiful day, a California classic, balmy weather, tangerine clouds drifting in a painfully clear blue sky. The palm trees bending slightly in the wind blowing in off the ocean. The waves cresting into explosions of white foam.

And all I wanted to do was to kill the sun, the trees, the waves. Kill everyone on the beach. It wasn't that they had no right to live. They were just crying out to be murdered. The pain I felt demanded that all laughter cease.

The tiny figure outlined against the beach and the cobalt blue waves lay on a stretcher and under a gray institutional blanket. Little feet poking up at one end, a blanket-covered orb at the other. What was Rosie in between.

. . . .

Bones following the ambulance in complete silence. No words. No radio. Just the whoosh of traffic and the sounds made by our breathing. No sirens, they're only for the living. A '57 Chevy and the absence of life, straight pipes and the sound of someone missing.

Bones trailing me into the hospital, the smell of disinfectant and floor wax. Patterned tiles on the floor, gray-green wallpaper and I feel nothing. None of this exists. The only real thing left in the universe is the emaciated figure dressed in black that silently mirrors my movements. Bones is real. The rest is a dream. A motherfuckin' nightmare.

THIRTEEN

. . . .

The doctor is almost as tall as Bones and looks at us through his expensive glasses like we're from Mars. His forehead wrinkles into a receding hairline as he makes a noise that sounds like "Tsk" and I know that if he starts speaking the dream will become real, black magic will win out, I have to stay deaf. His mouth opens. Words form, hang in the air like the smoke from burning tires, tangible and evil and deadly. Then it's too late.

He says, "What killed her was an infection. An infection and too many drugs."

His eyes are an off-green, magnified like a frog's behind his specs, and he's staring into mine. He wants to be sure I absorb every word. His voice gets a little bit more nasal and a little bit louder.

"An infection and too many drugs and too many venereal diseases as a child. Her insides were a mess."

But the words in my head are louder. Inside me I'm screaming, "Shut up. Shut up. Ya gotta shut up."

He takes off his glasses and polishes them with his tie, not taking his eyes off mine. More nasally and louder still he goes on. "Her insides were a mess and she must have been in terrible pain. Her insides were a mess and she must have been in terrible pain and it's a blessing that she's dead. . . . She had needle marks all over her body."

He adjusts his glasses and instead of "See ya" or "Have a nice day" he says, "What did she think she was doing carrying a child? Tsk. That's what one must expect if one lives like that."

His words are cutting through the roar in my head, which is now echoing, "Too late, Bobbie, it's too fucking late."

He shakes his head like he has been personally offended and says, "Promiscuity. Drug use." And one last "Tsk."

I'm watching these words etch their way through my flesh and into my soul.

Snakes are crawling under my skin as the smell of shorting circuits fills my nose and forces it way into my chest and I hear the sound of ripping silk echoing like thunder somewhere behind my eyes.

That's when my head starts vibrating so radically the whole world is strobing and I'm going for the doctor's throat and the only thing in the entire world is the need to quiet him.

The screaming around me recedes like insulation has been laid between me and everything except my fingers crushing his windpipe and the feeling, *not the sound*, of the life leaving him. And his eyes hemorrhaging from the pressure and the voice in my head calm and measured. It's saying slowly, "Shut his fucking mouth, as soon as there's no more noise everything will be all right. Keep squeezing . . . harder . . . harder," and then the orderlies rat-pack me.

The needle full of tranqs that they ram into the middle of my lower back doesn't hurt, doesn't even slow me down.

What saves that doctor's life is an attendant who looks like he eats steroids for breakfast, lunch, and dinner. This monster throws a choke hold on me and a white-coated gorilla that accompanies him kicks me hard enough to loosen my grip and what seems like a dozen orderlies are swarming on me. All in complete silence.

Then the noise that was there the whole time starts coming through the insulation that had been protecting me and I hear Bones saying, "You fucking faggots hurt this lad, yer mothers will be saying mass for your chickenshit souls."

That's when I know this *is* real and my own screaming fills the world.

. . . .

The Thorazine or Stelazine or whatever the fuck was in that syringe kicks in and I feel the howling die in my throat and all sense of identity, all the rage, all the hate disappear. The only thing remaining of me is pain and a void the size of the Grand Canyon.

Even though voluntary movement is out of the question one steroid-filled moron is attached to each of my arms.

The doctor is shaking and gasping. He tries to talk and only manages a hoarse rasp. Tries again and wheezes out, "He's insane."

Then, to me, "You're insane. You almost killed me you little bastard."

He's rubbing his throat and his eyes have streaks of blood running through the irises from me trying to pop his head like a pimple and he rasps, "Call the police. This animal belongs in jail. Call them immediately. Lock him up."

"That ain't necessary," says Bones as he runs his fingers through his hair. "My friend has had a bad day, as do we all on occasion. We'll be leavin' now. With your permission, a course."

Bones reaches for me with one of his pipe-cleaner arms and the doctor says, "Stick around and you can ride off in the paddy wagon with your little friend."

Adjusting his coat the doctor tells the orderlies, "Get this string bean out of here."

Bones smiles, the smile is all on one side of his face going from the edge of his mouth all the way to his shades. He raises his T-shirt to show the handle of the revolver sticking out of his jeans and says, "Paddy wagon, huh? String bean, huh? My friend's an animal now, is he? Lock us up, will you? You weight-liftin' punks let the lad go, be grateful I don't kill you, we already got enough heat."

Taking one step forward and pulling his piece as he's moving he says, "Self-righteous fucking scumbag," and brings the butt and then the barrel crashing into the doctor's face, smashing his glasses into his flesh and turning his lips into pulp.

Billy Bones continues in a regular tone like he's discussing tennis or how to hard-boil an egg. "Shouldn't hurt people's feelings. Know what I mean, Doc?" Grabbing the doctor by the back of the neck and heaving him face first toward the floor and as his head's rushing to the ground, kicks him in the face so hard that his body starts an upward arc before crashing into the tiled floor.

Bones is holding his revolver loosely on the orderlies, and standing over the doctor, breathing hard, the grin unchanged, he says, "Come on, lad, these fuckin' sodomites can kiss my Irish fuckin' ass. Paddy wagon indeed."

I can't move, whatever they hit me with has got me immobilized, trapped inside my own personal hell.

Bones grabs my arm and pulls me toward the exit, past the potted plants and the citizens imitating those plants, scared to move.

. . . .

I'm propped in the front seat, don't want to talk. Frozen and don't care at all. Bones is driving at the speed limit, hits Ocean Boulevard and stops at a traffic light, saying out of the side of his mouth, "Kinda lost it, Bob. Don't like the word 'paddy' don'tcha know."

I think about responding and know it's gonna be too much effort.

He continues just like I'd said something. "Rightcha are, killer. They been callin' us paddies and fuckin' us all around for centuries. Can't tolerate that kind of shit. They designed them fuckin' wagons to haul Irishmen, Paddies, micks, in other words, our ancestors. That shithead woulda been all right if he'd only kept his fuckin' trap shut."

The beach comes into view and as we approach the pad it's got heat all over it.

Black-and-whites and unmarked, cops for days.

A plainclothes is standing on the steps and points at us, yelling something at his underlings. Sirens and flashing lights fill the street behind us as Bones powers into a bootlegger turn and puts the pedal to the fuckin' metal.

Even through the Thorazine haze I know I should be scared. Bones looks at me and says, "This'll wake ya up, Bobbie . . . either that or kill ya." And we're flying through traffic, Bones slamming through the gears.

Driving into oncoming traffic and talking, either to me, himself, or the sorry motherfuckers who are in our way, screaming, "Look out, ya fucking sodomites. Fuck 'em all, Bobbie, they die or we die or we all fuckin' die. Who gives a shit, eh, lad?"

Slamming up on the sidewalk and my face smashes into the dash. Bones is howling like a wolf as people go flying into the air and the Chevy hits with the tires smokin'.

We're going down Lincoln like a magnum round and there's two black-and-whites blocking the street. Bones has a grin plastered on his face, shades knocked off by flying onto and off of the sidewalk, and there's blood running out of his nose and dripping offa his chin when he says almost conversationally, barely audible above the roaring engine, "Watch 'em fly, Bobbie."

We're going so fast everything is a blur and Bones yells, "Here comes the nitrous." Hits a switch under the dash and I'm crushed back into my seat. What seemed like flying was nothing, this is like getting shot out of a fucking cannon.

When we hit the cop cars there's an explosion, shit flying everywhere and then they're gone and we're headed inland on the freeway.

The '57 is smoking and clunking but still moving like a bat outta hell. Getting offa the freeway headed south and Bones says, "Gonna miss this piece a iron. Think Baby Al will be surprised?"

The adrenaline has cut through everything, this second I'm all right. I ask, "Surprised, why?"

" 'Cause he's the only one in this fuckin' state we can trust. He's gonna have ta stash us."

"Don't know Bones. Guess we're gonna find out."

. . . .

We're in a rundown neighborhood, graffiti all over, all the businesses have signs in both Spanish and English. The Chevy is dying, shaking and rattling. Bones pulls into a side street and parks saying, "Gotta walk a ways. Abandon the car. The locals will have her stripped or disappeared in a half hour. Let's go see Al."

I look at him and say, "Bones, wipe the blood offa your face, Bones."

He laughs. "Ya best be doin' the same. You're bleedin' like a stuck pig." I look in the rearview mirror and see he's tellin' the truth even though I feel no pain.

The people we pass look us over and then ignore us, even the gang-bangers hangin' on the corners don't bother fuckin' with us.

Two white dudes covered with blood and wearing torn clothes look like victims who've already been had. Not worth paying attention to.

Follow Bones into the wire-fenced yard of a small wooden house, weeds go halfway to the bar-covered windows. Bones knocks on the security door and the wooden door behind the barred one opens.

Baby Al looks us up and down, reaches forward, and flips the lock on the security door. He doesn't looked surprised. "Couple a sorry-lookin' peckerwoods. Better get inside."

The inside is a contradiction to the outside, polished hardwood floors, oak furniture, new paint, huge TV and stereo. Pictures of Mexican bandits and señoritas painted on black velvet hanging on the walls.

Bones folds himself into the couch and I follow. Baby Al turns the TV down so there's no sound, only the tube functioning, and asks, "So what's the qué pasa? What the fuck happened to you two?"

I light a cigarette and notice that my hands are still shaking, and grunt. Talking is gonna take too much effort and my brain has been novocained.

Bones looks at me, shakes the hair out of his eyes, and says, "Bobbie's girl passed on this morning. Had some kinda bad infection, whatever it was killed her. We called an ambulance, they musta called the rollers. Maybe they saw the firearms in my bedroom. Maybe the drugs. Whatever. When we got home there was enough pigs to supply the whole world with bacon. We left. My car is totaled. We need a hidey-hole. How about it, Al?"

"You a slob Billy fuckin' Bones. I seen your pad, fuckin' disgustin'. You gonna clean up after yourselves?"

Bones smiles. "Cook, too, if that's what it takes. You're a fuckin' saint, Baby Al."

Al scratches his head and looks at Bones sideways. "Fucking saint my ass, probably the stupidest Chicano in LA. I know you motherfuckers gotta be smokin' fuckin' hot. Let's see if ya made the six o'clock news."

We had.

I get even more depressed.

. . . .

The sun rising through the barred windows turns the smog into a light haze. The sounds of the city emerging from its temporary coma scrape their way into the living room.

The night and relative quiet have been almost soothing. I can pretend:

That Rosie is sitting next to me, just beyond my peripheral vision. Any minute she's gonna say something.

Anything.

. . . .

The light gets brighter and the day gets louder.

Baby Al stumbles through the living room and into the kitchen.

Bones groans from his spot on the couch and I'm staring out the window, eyes half closed trying to recapture the feeling that I am not alone, and not succeeding.

The aroma of coffee starts filling the room and Baby Al comes back into the living room and turns on the stereo. Oldies come on. Bones struggles into an upright position and Al sits on the couch. "Coffee be ready in a minute. Whatcha wanna do?"

Bones groans again and growls, "Wanna do? Wake up, ya fuckin' maroon. Whatcha think, go joggin' maybe? The cops got our money, our drugs, and most of our weapons. Young Bobbie's settin' with a broken heart. We gotta make some dough. I can't go back to Boston yet, but we gotta get outta LA." He looks at me. "Whatcha think, lad? Got any ideas?"

My nerves are coming out of my skin. Even though my brain has chosen to quit working, my habit is working overtime. "Only thing I know, Bones, is I need some motherfuckin' heroin. Quick. Maybe do a 211 or somethin'."

Bones gets up, walks into the kitchen, and comes out with three cups of coffee. Hands me and Al a cup, sits back down, lights a smoke, and finally says, "I'm not too big on robberies if I gotta go in cold. I know we got enough dough to score ya some medicine. Whatcha think, Al, lay low for a few days, get some smack for the kid and we'll put somethin together?"

"Shit, why the fuck not? Get some chiva for both of us though. Long as you got the cash, my homeboy's got balloons and he'll deliver. How many can we get?"

I'm emptying my pockets and Bones is doing the same. I say, "As many as possible, Al. All he's got if we got enough dough."

. . . .

The skinny Chicano that comes through the door is wearing Stacy Adams jeans and a long-sleeved Pendleton. Placing his feet into a T and slouching, he checks out us white guys and turns to Baby Al. "What's up? Who're these pinche gavachos?"

Al takes a hit offa his Camel, gives the guy a lightweight mad dog, and says, "Friends of mine. They in mi casa, right, ese? Cut the drag. Ya got the chiva?"

He smiles and then opens his teeth, revealing a mouthful of multi-colored balloons. Says, "Simone, ese. Quién tiene feria?"

Al grins and looks at me. "Bobbie, this is Flaco, give him the dough." I stare at Flaco for a minute not liking the bullshit about pinche gava-chos and decide, fuck it, as long as he has smack he can do no wrong.

I need some opiates so bad I'm ready to start screaming. I can smell the toxins in the sweat running down my face and sides, my insides are cramping like I got shot and, worst of all, the emotions that I've buried for the last week are invading my brain like demons from hell.

I count out three hundred bucks. "Trip c-notes. Let's count those balloons."

He spits the balloons into his hand. "Quarter T's, six for a hundred." Counts out eighteen and has three left and I say, "For three hundred throw in the other three. Make it seven for a hundred . . . carnal."

He looks at Al and says, "What's up with this vato?"

"He's my crimey, ese. Kick."

Flaco stares at me for a second, looks at the bills in my hand, adjusts his Pendleton, and says, "Fuck it. Early Christmas present, homes." Then spits the remaining balloons into his hand and gives them all to me.

"Thanks killer," I say. Rip the top offa three balloons and dump 'em in a kitchen spoon, tell Flaco, "See ya, pinche cholo."

Flaco laughs on his way out, yells, "Ándele, señor huero loco."

. . . .

That first hit takes all the aches and pains away, make me feel like I might live. But one of the things about stuff is once you're really good and hooked there is no more feeling euphoria. If you do enough you can have your head all the way in your chest, be fuckin' drool-ing on yourself and still be miserable if one shred of awareness remains.

I didn't know that this was inevitable. That my tolerance level had become toxic. Couple that with the kinda misery that inspires a good country-western song, shit, the kinda pain that invented the blues, and ya got a suicide run in the making.

I'm scratching, vision blurred, voice sounding gravelly even to myself, and I ask Baby Al, "Got any downs, homes? Reds, rainbows, yellows . . . whatever. This dope ain't strong enough."

"Ain't strong enough? You loco, wood, you're about one inch away from a coma."

"Bullshit, don't even feel this crap. Got some or not?"

"Yeah, man. But if you OD I'm throwin' ya in a Dumpster. Got it?"

"Don't sweat it, Al."

As Baby Al gets up Bones says, "Let me get a couple of them downs from ya, Alan. I financed halfa the heroin and don't even use the shit. Kick with some downs, Baby Al. Watchin' you junkies drool and nod is a drag. May as well get loaded with yez."

. . . .

Al's sniffling, I'm sick as a fucking dog. We're out of smack and out of money. It hurts. Muscles, bones, fingernails, fucking hair. Everything.

The hole in my chest has expanded to encompass the whole universe. With Rosie gone nothing in the world is gonna fill it, but enough heroin will take the jagged edges and smooth them. A handful of reds on top of the stuff will plunge me into unconsciousness. Right now oblivion is where it's at. I ask Baby Al, "You up for a 211?"

He hesitates for a second and replies, "Yeah, what ya thinkin?"

I look at Bones, who's slumped in his chair comatose from binging on barbiturates, and turn back to Al, who now seems smaller, leaner to me. The last week of shooting dope has thrashed him, too, and I say, "Don't know. Bank? Supermarket? I don't give a fuck as long as we get enough cash to get well. Let's go."

Al looks at his feet for a minute and then drags himself off the couch and heads into his room saying, "Gotta get my gauge, hang on."

Baby Al's got a trashed four-door Ford he uses for crimin'. Taking a fancy dress-white Hudson on a crime spree would not be a real good idea.

. . . .

The Ford's shocks are shot. Every pothole, every dip or bump in the road vibrates the car. Both of us are pulling our jackets off and putting 'em back on; hot and cold flashes are part of kicking. Oldies are on what passes for a radio and we're dying, both got the runs so bad that stopping at public rest rooms is taking up as much time as scoping possible targets.

It's lunch hour and I ask Al to stop at a well-known burger joint so I can use the head. I dash out of the car and into the restaurant and the smell of frying food hits me in the guts like a baseball bat.

Grabbing my mouth I run stiff-legged into the men's room. It feels like there's melted lead burning through my stomach. I make the toilet and feel a flash of gratitude when I don't puke or shit on myself.

I got poison coming out of my body from both ends.

Leaving the stall I stop to wash my hands and face. In the mirror is an old man with my face but so haggard and aged the guy reflected there is one step away from the grave.

I'm so weak that my legs are wobbling as I open the door and there . . . sent direct from God . . . is a uniformed cashier bringing her cash tray into the manager's office.

The door is flimsy wood painted white and as the cashier swings it open I see the answer to my prayers.

The office is a cubbyhole, the manager is sitting at a desk covered with cash, he's working on an adding machine counting it. In the corner there's a safe and the door's wide open. The clock on the wall says it's quarter to one, I check my watch to see if the times agree and walk out to the Ford and tell Baby Al, "It's on, carnal, hit this place in fifteen minutes."

"What, rush the cashiers? There's too fucking many citizens. Fuck that, homes."

"No, pal. Hit the manager's office and the safe. No fucking headaches. In and out. Piece-a fuckin' cake."

"Fuck a whole buncha fifteen minutes then. Let's do it. I'm malea like a motherfucker."

"Ten minutes now, Al. We go in at one o'clock and all the cash drawers should be in the office. Lunch hour's over then."

Sitting that ten minutes out takes forever. Each second drags like sandpaper against my eyeballs, like getting tattooed with a jackhammer.

The fear of something going wrong doesn't build. It erupts like a volcano.

Visions of Jimbo walking away from us strong and healthy and how we ran when the feds killed him. Of Mel going down for the count, his life bubbling out of his lungs. And, like broken glass slashing my flesh, Rosie lying still and lifeless, face a pale shade of blue, eyes open and filmed with dust.

All the pain that smack wipes away like an eraser for the soul is back, and my ghosts are having a committee meeting behind my eyes, calling me to join them.

The plastic seat is sticking to my sweat-soaked T-shirt, the cigarette I'm smoking tastes like shit, and my brain is flashing from Mel and Rosie and Jimbo to this second in time and how sick and scared I am.

Knowing that if the shit floods the fan I'm gonna go down right there. Hold court in the street. Realizing that I'm not especially brave, not ultra tough, just fucking desperate. That I really have no desire to keep breathing but that no matter what happens I've got to get well.

Needing the heroin so badly not only would I kill or die to get it, I would sell my own mother into slavery for a fix.

All the good times like mountains that recede behind you on the freeway.

Going, going . . . gone.

Baby Al has his cut-down shotgun under the seat. Pulls it out and pumps one into the chamber.

I take my 380 out of my back pocket, check to make sure there's a round under the hammer and the safety is off. Stick it in the front of my jeans under my T-shirt and watch as Baby Al jams the gauge down the leg of his pants.

I can see the fear and desperation in Al's face and wonder if my face shows what I'm feeling. All I say is, "Let's do it, brother."

Al grins and says, "Ándale, carnal, it's showtime."

Walking as casually as possible. Al has a pronounced limp from the shotgun running down his leg.

Entering the restaurant and hitting hyperspace. I'm a set of reactions with feet, moving through a dimension you can only understand if you've been there.

I reach for the handle of the office door with my left and hold my piece in my right. The door is locked. The knob won't turn.

Look down the hallway leading to the manager's office and there's a big black guy in a restaurant uniform staring at us as he comes out of the kitchen headed for the men's room. I mumble to Al, "Take him, Baby Al, keep this hallway clear."

The guy reaches us, stops, puts his hands on his hips and straightens up to his full height, puffs out his chest for maximum intimidation. He knows he's much bigger than either of us and feels pretty cocky. Probably thinks he's caught a couple of sneak thieves and says, "What the fuck you doing? Why ya fuckin' wid dat do? Huh, motherfucker?"

Al shrugs, raises his hands and has a confused look on his face. Says, "What are we doing?" and kicks the guy in the balls with the leg that has no shotgun stuck down it.

As the guy doubles over I yank the 380 out of my pants and smash the butt into the back of his head and kick him in the face as he's going down.

Al looks at me, pulls the gauge out, and smashes it into the dude's head. Then kicks the door. It buckles but doesn't open and we both kick it, smashing it open, revealing the manager getting up from the desk, mouth hanging open and hands already headed for the ceiling.

I got so much adrenaline running that not only has my illness disappeared, I'm all the way live. I look into the manager's eyes and know there's gonna be no John Wayne crap to deal with and say, "This is only a robbery, pal. Keep your hands up 'cause I don't want to turn it into a murder."

He's frozen, makes a noise like gargling and shakes his head up and down in assent. Baby Al is standing half in the room and half in the hallway, shotgun held at waist level in case we get rushed.

I empty the safe of cash and clear the desk into a "to go" bag. Look around the office and tell the manager, "Lay on the floor pal." As he stretches out by his desk I tell Al, "Let's roll, homes," and we're gone.

Time to get well.

*T*he days melted into weeks. Time turned into a blur of reds, heroin, and unplanned robberies.

Al's pristine little pad filling with junk-food wrappers and drug paraphernalia.

Bones and Al trying to talk me into doing less dope.

No chance.

Elena showing up, doing her best to interest me in something other than putting myself into a coma. That made everything worse.

Seeing her through the haze I lived in. Hair long and black, slim and pretty, lips that were designed for something more than talking.

Wanting to bone her and feeling Rosie watching and judging me.

Slurring the words I'm yelling at Elena. "Can't do it. Hit the road bitch." And feeling more guilt for hurting her feelings.

If I was conscious I was miserable.

The drugs would get me to the point that I was a drooling babbling idiot but didn't even begin to numb the wounds that festered inside me.

The arid deserts and toxic swamps of my own soul were killing me.

The only answer was more drugs.

. . . .

Bones kicks me awake yelling, "Wake up, ya fucking idiot. Look at me." He hands me a cup of coffee and says, "Drink this, ya fuckin' maroon. I been callin' all over the fuckin' U.S. of fuckin' A. Talked to Syd in Jersey. Some nig, another frienda yours name-a Ben, wants some work done. Said to call the Injun. I call Black Cloud. They got a score in Nap Town. Same toads Cloud wanted to hit in Cleveland. Now they fucked with some-a Ben's people and he's fifty-one-fifty. The job's in Indi-

FOURTEEN

◆◆◆◆◆◆◆◆◆◆◆◆◆◆◆◆◆◆◆◆◆◆◆◆◆◆◆◆◆◆◆◆◆

anapolis now. Get that java down. We gotta go to a pay phone and ring 'em back."

The coffee burns its way down my throat, bitter and strong, and I realize that I'm starving. So hungry that I feel it through all the shit pumping through my system. I ask, "Is there any food here, Billy Bones? I'm so hungry my stomach is eatin' my spine."

"Well, ya should be. You been out for most of a week. Look at you, look like a fuckin' wino. Take a shower. Finish the coffee first."

"Do we got any whites, Billy?"

"Fuck whites, drink the java and get clean. Shave for the love a Christ. Ya smell like a fuckin' goat. I'll order a pizza. Get some food in ya. Then we'll make the call."

Holding on to the shower wall so I won't fall, letting the steaming water beat on my body, easing the aches and pains that seem to have appeared all by themselves.

Getting my courage up, bracing my feet to be sure that I don't fall over, and going to work with the soap and shampoo.

Toweling off and realizing that some of my senses are still working. Suddenly it feels good to be clean, to feel the rough cloth drying my body.

Wiping the mirror and there's what's left of me. Skinny, patches of beard all over my face, and blue eyes that are as empty as a used syringe. Tell myself, "Ya look like shit, ace," and laugh as I pick up the razor.

. . . .

The streets trashed, potholed, and cracked. The stores that are open have security bars and gates. The smell of garbage coming from trash cans and crates.

The locals are watching us from the corners of their eyes. Are we undercover cops? Junkies down here to score? Idiots who don't know what time it is? What the fuck are we doing in their barrio?

Me and Bones look like what we are. Black leather jackets, T-shirts, jeans, and boots. Shades. Hair greased back. Two hoods. Bad news waitin' to happen.

Mel woulda gone outta his mind.

The phone booth has already had the glass knocked out and as Billy Bones hands me the scarred receiver I step into the booth. The words

ANNA AND CARMEN POR VIDA are carved into the aluminum shelf under the phone and Syd's voice comes crackling across the country, from Jersey to Southeast LA. "Yo, Sydney, that you?"

"Oh bubeleh, oy vey, Bobbie. First Melvin, now Rosie. I'm so sorry kid. Are ya OK?"

"Don't know what I'm feeling, Syd, but thanks for askin'. How 'bout you?"

"Better, gettin' better."

"So what's up, what's happenin', what's the hub-bub Bub? Billy says there's work in Indianapolis. Is that right?"

"Right as fuckin' rain, baby cakes. The crew that the Injun wanted to hit pulled two of the broads offa the compound in Illinois, sold 'em to a pimp in Detroit. Ben hit the pimp, got his people back. He wants to make an example of the schvarts that made the move. Whatcha think?"

"How the fuck did these cats pull two chicks offa that compound?"

"The girls went into the city. Did some partyin'. Usta be in the game. Got recognized and grabbed. Dig it?"

"So Ben wants payback but don't wanna use his own people?"

"That's about it, plus there's cash involved of course. Hit these woman-sellin', backstabbin' motherfuckers at the right time, and ya come up with a gang of smack and a couple, three bagfuls of cash. Ben just wants blood. Says it's Old Testament time."

"Hit 'em?"

"Hit 'em."

"What's it pay?"

"Ben covers expenses. I get a little bit a dough for gettin' ya guys wid him. Your crew gets the swag. Split it any way ya want."

"Cash and stuff?"

"Yeah."

"How many of 'em are goin' down?"

"All of 'em."

"So what now?"

"Billy says ya got some Mexican you're workin' with?"

"Yeah."

"Is he any good?"

"Balls like a Christmas tree."

"Bring him."

"When?"

"You're drivin' into Vegas, flying into Nap from there. Billy says ya got too much heat to fly outta LA."

"See ya there."

"No ya won't kid, I'm stayin' in Joisey. I ain't right yet, I'm just helpin' my friends."

"Bye, Syd."

"Shalom."

. . . .

Baby Al and Valerie are awake and starting their day when we get back.

I know that getting out of LA is a good thing.

For about ten seconds the thought of seeing Sydney cheered me up and then is scratched.

I don't care what the reason is. As long as there's oblivion at the end of it, it doesn't matter what the name of the road is.

I flop down on the easy chair. Baby Al and Valerie are on the couch watching the tube and drinking beer.

Bones is pacing and says, "Check it out, Baby Al. Talked to some people. Got a score in the Midwest. Need a ride to Vegas. Fly from there. Lotta cash and white heroin involved. Whatcha think, Al?"

Baby Al pops a couple of reds into his mouth, takes a hit from his beer, and gargles. Swallows and asks, "Why ya tellin' me? I'm just a poor Mexican. Don't know nothin' about Vegas and sure as fuck don't wanna know nothin' about the Mid-fuckin'-west. Cows and hillbillies. Fuck that noise. Sorry, carnal."

I cross my legs and light a Camel. I know that Al is rock steady when he's working and want him to be there. I don't want to depend on some guy I never met. If he's in, it'll be me, Bones, Cloud, and Baby Al.

"Check it out, crimey," I say. "This is more cash than we made in the last month. Probably five, six, ten times all the work we done put together. Plus enough good smack to stay well for a long time. Months even. Doing a good deed on top of it. Hitting bad guys. Piece-a fuckin' cake. I told 'em ya had big balls. Valerie can drive us into Vegas. Jump on a plane, get this shit done, fly back. You a motherfuckin' hero. Be a rich Mexican instead of a poor one. What's up? Still wanna pass, crimey?"

"What kinda bad guys?"

"Mayates. Kidnapped a couple a broads from this frienda mine who's a born-again nut."

"Chingao, homes, always wanted to be a hero."

Valerie grins and says, "I like the rich Mexican part."

Bones has stopped pacing and is staring at Al, says slowly, "Gonna blow 'em away, lad. Are you up to it?"

"Mayates? Simone, you Irish pendejo, I hate niggers. . . . I like the rich Mexican part even more than my heina does."

. . . .

The landing is terrible. The plane bounces so hard on hitting the runway that it blows my nod. The seat in front of me swims into view and the rest of the plane takes form. Whatever I was dreaming about has left me soaked in a cold sweat. Grab the whiskey rocks I started the flight with and down the warm, diluted mix.

Baby Al is staring out the window and I'm in the aisle seat. Bones is nowhere to be seen. I poke Al. "Welcome to the Midwest. Where's fuckin' Billy Bones?"

Baby Al turns from the window and in slurred voice says, "Chingao. Thought we were gonna die. He's with one-a the stews. They in the head. I think he's bonin' her."

I want to fix but settle for taking a couple a rainbows. Something has been gnawing at the back of my mind since my phone conversation with Syd. My mind is clearer than it's been in weeks and it hits me and I start laughing.

Baby Al is looking at me like I lost it and it probably seems like I have. He says, "Hey, carnal, what's up? What the fuck you laughing at?"

"I just figured it out. Syd set the whole thing up. She knows the toads we're hittin' and doesn't like 'em. She knows Ben and she knows me and Billy. I'll bet she set the broads up, then set the pimp up, and now is puttin' this one together and makin' dough on all of it."

"Shit, homes, sounds like a cold snake."

"Na, crimey, not cold. Smart as a motherfucker though. Like an Einstein of crime."

Bones comes out of the head combing his hair, got a smirk on his face and as he sits across from us the smell of marijuana comes with him. He takes his shades out of his T-shirt pocket and puts them back on. "Mile-high club, fellas. A little bit of pot and coke and a lot of blarney. The luck of the Irish boys."

I smile and say, "Let's roll."

While we get our carry-on bags down and let the citizens file past us, the stewardess that was with Billy Bones glides down the aisle. Red hair to her shoulders, tall with a pretty smile under bright green eyes. As she gets to his seat she says, "Call me, Billy," and she hands him her phone number.

"I certainly will, darlin'."

"Good."

As she's walkin' back to the rear of the plane Al twists around to check her walk and ass, then whistles between his teeth and says, "Go ahead, ese, that heina is fuckin' gorgeous."

"Kind of ya to notice, Alan. Let's make some-a that green."

. . . .

Black Cloud is wearing a turtleneck to cover the ink on his neck and a sport coat, slacks, and cowboy boots. Hair under a Stetson hat. Looks like a complete lame. I know it's him standing there waiting for us but he looks so different from the maniac I met that I hesitate.

Me and Al hang back while Billy walks ahead and they shake hands. The booming voice hasn't changed. "God-fuckin'-damn. I put this monkey suit on and you three look like ya should have your pictures in the fuckin' post office. If I was a cop I'd jack ya just for lookin' evil."

Bones laughs. "Seem to be doin' all right, even lookin' less than perfect."

Cloud looks me up and down and yells, "Com'ere kid. Look at ya. Mel taught ya better than that. This fuckin' mick is a bad influence. Who's the beaner?"

I grin at Cloud and tell him, "This is Baby Al. We been crimin' all over LA. He's down, he's gonna be with us, right?"

"Long as he's ready. Know what I mean?"

Al has an upside-down smile, the corners of his mouth turned all the way down, eyes slitted. Says, "I'm ready. Kill niggers. Indians. Whatever."

Black Cloud starts busting up laughing so loud that people across the terminal are looking. Claps Al on the back and says, "Don't plex, ace. These guys like ya, I'm sure you're OK."

"I'm more than OK, chief, I'm a walkin' fuckin' nightmare."

Cloud's still laughing as we head to the exit. "Sure ya are, Al, sure ya are. Gonna let ya kill the first one. Fair enough?"

"Simone, señor pendejo."

Black Cloud just grins and says, "Señor pendejo my motherfuckin' ass, Mister Baby fucking Al."

They slow down, grin, and keep walking. Being a tough guy is a job that goes on 24-7-365 and they've both established that they're working.

I'm worn-out. Don't give a fuck. Just want oblivion. Walk with 'em bringing up the rear. Thinking about the piece in my back pocket and the rainbows and heroin in the bag I'm carrying. Looking forward to the china white I'll have soon. Peace.

. . . .

We pile out of the Cadillac that was almost mine and march through the revolving door that leads into the lobby of the hotel.

I'm back in the world that was created for me by Syd and Mel. Uniformed bellhops, plush carpeting, the faint odor of good cigars.

We're standing and waiting for the elevator with the floor manager, who is wearing an ill-fitting suit, and an old woman wearing a lacy white dress and sporting blue hair. They are both openly staring at us. The manager asks, "Are you gentlemen registered here?"

Black Cloud sweeps his cowboy hat off, letting his hair tumble down to the middle of his back, and says, "We're a rock band, sir. I know these boys look kinda strange but it's part of the act. We all usta be Boy Scouts."

The citizen doesn't look convinced but walks away shaking his head.

Ben's wearing a short Afro, red sweater, slacks, and loafers. Comes across the room gold incisor gleaming. We shake hands and I do introductions. He waves at the wet bar and says, "Pick your poison."

Bones and Cloud go to mix themselves drinks. I nod my head toward the bedroom and make a gesture like I'm fixing and Ben says, "Go ahead, Bobbie, soon as ya get right I'll run this down to ya."

Baby Al and I head into the bedroom to slam. I got the needle stuck into the back of my hand sending the shit home when Baby Al says, "You didn't tell me that Ben's a mayate. What's up, homes? I don't work with niggers. We came here to down some. Not work with one of the motherfuckers."

"Musta slipped my mind, Al, sorry about that. The cat's OK. Don't trip. Ya gotta trust me on this, Baby Al. You don't gotta sleep with him, just do some work. Know what I mean, homes?"

"Shit, carnal, they yell, they smell, and they tell. I hope you right."

I think about trying to explain that Ben is solid, that Al shouldn't be down on him 'cause he's black, and realize it would be a waste of time and effort.

As the smack runs down my spine and through my limbs I know that there's nothing in the world that'll make me exert unnecessary effort. I look into Al's eyes and as he starts scratching say, "I *am* right. Don't sweat it, killer."

. . . .

Bones and Cloud are sprawled on the couch, I'm sitting backward on a kitchen chair, and Al's lying on the floor. Ben's leaning against the TV.

Ben says, "Here's the deal. These niggers are rippin' and runnin' all over the country. They burnin' the wrong people. Worst of all they burnt me. Took two of the women from our camp. Plied them with hard drugs, sold them to a gutter pimp. Coat-hanger-swingin', razor-totin' mo-fucker. He's where he belongs. Burnin' in hell."

He pauses to hit his drink and Bones says, "So they're not nice guys. Who gives a fuck? I gotta tell ya, friend, I'm here for the green. What's up with that?"

Ben puts his drink on top of the TV and starts pacing and talking.

"They be robbing connections. Not street-corner, nickel-dime-bag mo-fuckers. Heavyweights, righteous importers. Niggers and I-talians and Ricans. They be hittin' everybody. They don't care who they take off. They think they black asses bulletproof."

Baby Al sits up and asks, "So how do ya know where these vatos are located? How do ya know what they got? How many of 'em are there? What kinda firepower do they got? I don't got time for stories—save 'em. How do we take these punks? I guarantee you these pinche chongos aren't bulletproof. Let's get it done. Fuck all this dumb shit."

"There's nine of 'em. Got a little old house outside Talbot Village, that's the heroin center here in Nap Town. There's a nigger on the front porch. Has a gauge and a pistol. Another one in the back, same thing. Ice 'em and sledgehammer the doors open. Fast. Smash the doors open and start blastin'. We go in a van. Billy Bones does the drivin', stays behind the wheel. Bobbie, you hit the back of the pad with Black Cloud. Al, you go in the front with me. We kill everything breathing. If they got a dog, shee-it even a cat, don't matter, it dies. They robbed the guys they been sellin' to in Cleveland, robbed some big-time dagos outta NY. Got cash, boy and girl, it's yours. I jist want 'em dead."

I can't reconcile my memories of Ben with the killer who's doing the talking. I ask, "What happened to turning the other cheek and all that shit my man?"

Ben looks at me like he don't know me, like I've lost my mind even asking that question. "One of the girls they took was my old lady. They gotta pay. If your hand offends you cut it off, if your eye offends you pluck it out. These niggers have offended me and the good Lord. They gotta die."

The look on his face is completely serious. I realize that Ben is as nuts in his way as the rest of us and find no comfort in the thought. The whole world is breaking up around me. Nothing is solid, people dying, changing. There's nothing to hold on to and it feels like racing down a razor blade. Knowing that it's too sharp to feel it cutting. Waiting for it to slice you in two.

Baby Al is stroking his mustache. "Cash, heroin, and coke. How come I gotta go in with you? Me and Bobbie been workin' together. What's up?"

Ben grins and suddenly looks as evil as anyone I've ever met. He says, "'Cause me and the Indian both usta work for Uncle Sam. The guards gotta die quietly. I hit one, Cloud hits the other. That's how we gonna do it. After that it's a free-fire zone. You wid me or you wanna get on up out of here?"

There's a moment of silence and I'm praying that Al's gonna go with it, it's way too late to back out and keep breathing. Baby Al smirks and putting a thick accent into his voice says, "Yass*uh*, bossman. We be goin' in da front, suh."

As Al's agreeing I realize that there's a bad hole in this plan. I say, "Yo, Ben, if Bones is behind the wheel he's gonna look kinda weird in a black neighborhood. Only way I'm gonna feel all right about this is if you do the drivin'. Cops see Billy loiterin' they gonna roust him for sure. Neighbors see a Paddy waitin' around they'll remember. Its gotta be you behind the wheel."

Ben takes another hit off his drink and says, "Thought about that my ownself." Voice rising and face tightening he continues. "I want a piece of these sons-a bitches. But fuck me in the ass if you ain't right. Fuck it. OK. All right then. From what I hear Billy Bones ain't bad at killin', loud or silent. Him and Al can go in the front. You and Black Cloud hit the back. I'll stay behind the motherfuckin' wheel."

Billy's face is blank behind his shades and he says, "Driving, killing, it's all the same my black friend. I like 'em both."

"I'll be here at three-thirty tomorrow morning. We'll hit 'em around four." Ben starts walking to the door, puts his hand on the handle, and stops. Looks over his shoulder at me and it's the old Ben saying, "Hey, Bobbie, sorry about Rosie."

I got nothing to say, put my thumb up and nod my head. After the door closes behind him I open my bag, dig under the T-shirts and jeans, and pull out a Baggie full of rainbows. Reach in and grab a small handful, walk to the bar, get a bottle of whiskey to wash 'em down with, tell Al, Bones, and Cloud, "Back in a minute."

Cloud shakes his head, sending hair flying. "What the fuck are ya doin' Bobbie? Ya just took enough downs to kill five motherfuckers. Where do ya think you're going?"

Turning back and staring at the room and the fellas, it's like there's a sheet of plastic between me and everything around me. I can see, feel, smell, and hear what's going on but none of it seems real.

I know there's about twenty, thirty minutes before the tuinols knock me out, say, "Gotta make a call. Be right back."

Going down the hallway to the elevator and hear the air going past my head, the carpet rustling under my feet, snatches of conversation and music as I pass the doors of different rooms.

The elevator smells of metal polish and smoke. The gleaming copper walls showing reflections of me going deeper and deeper into the golden metal. A skinny kid in jeans and a T-shirt, hair growing out past his collar and falling across his forehead, and I wonder just who it is I'm looking at as the doors slide open to the lobby.

Walking across to the registration desk and ask the manager that was checking us out earlier for five bucks' worth of quarters.

Staring at him as he stares at me. Thick salt-and-pepper hair, myopic brown eyes, and pasty white skin, and as he starts to talk I smell cheap booze mixed with spearmint gum. "What's the name of your band . . . sir? Are you playing in town? Will you be with us long?"

I continue to stare at him, holding the five spot out for change. Don't want to talk. Finally say again, "Break this, please."

He counts out the quarters and repeats, "So what's the name of your band?"

Looking into his muddled eyes I say, "We're the American Dream. Thanks for the change."

. . . .

The phone booth is muffling the noise from the lobby, the ringing sounds far away, and then, "Hello."

"Hey, Sydney, how ya doin'?"

"OK. What's wrong, Bobbie? This is Bobbie ain't it?"

"Yeah, ya wanna call me back on a pay phone or is your line OK?"

"Cold as the North Pole baby. So what's wrong?"

"Shit, man . . . Nothing is wrong. Everything is wrong. . . . I gotta know, ya put the whole thing together. Am I right?"

"Ya learnin' how to think kid. Yeah, I put it all together."

"The broads from the compound?"

"Yeah, baby. Ya gotta break eggs to make a fuckin omelet. Know what I mean?"

"Ben's old lady, Syd?"

"Ya got a problem with it, Bobbie?"

"Yeah. But it's too late to change anything now. Fuck it."

"Mel's gone, Bobbie, I got nobody but me. The whole thing went off wire. The bitch that set it up for me fucked up. I tried to do it all over the phone and couldn't keep control. I didn't know it was Ben's girl till after it was too late. The contract is on this nigger Kelvin and his right-hand man Otis. Not their whole crew. Ben went nuts, all the way psychotic, wants to ice 'em all. I can't change it, the whole thing got fucked up. A girl's gotta do what a girl's gotta do. I'm gettin' too old for the game, I need a cushion. Are ya with me kid?"

"Yeah, I guess so. Can't be against ya."

"Thanks. I've been nuts since Melvin. . . . You know. With Rosie . . ."

"I know. . . . Been reading Machiavelli, Syd?"

"Shit, Bobbie, he coulda taken lessons from me."

"How much are the I-talians and the East Coast toads paying?"

"Plenty. So are the schvarts from Cleveland. You guys hit these motherfuckers it's fat city. I'll give ya a piece of the action. I didn't plan on you gettin' involved. I thought Ben would use his own people. I thought wrong. Come to Joisey and I'll take care a ya cashwise."

"Nah, I'll make plenty on this end. I may come to visit just to say hi. I don't need none of your end. I just wanted to know if I figured it right." The rainbows are coming on, my speech is starting to slur, and I know I gotta make it back to the room. I tell Syd, "I don't feel too good lately, Sydney, I'm scared all the time. Everything is all fucked up. I don't know what to do anymore."

She laughs and says, "I know, kid, ya just gotta keep swingin' till ya win. Don't let yourself get soft. Read Nietzsche again. . . . Shit, Bobbie, I don't know."

"Me either . . . See ya later, Sydney."

"See ya, kid."

I stumble out of the booth, make it into the elevator without tripping over my own feet. By the time it hits my floor I'm leaning on the wall so I don't fall over. Stagger down the hallway bouncing offa the walls, knock on our door and as it opens Billy Bones looks at me and says, "Jaysus fuckin' Christ. Lean on me, Bobbie, come on."

"Right."

He half carries me into the bedroom, where I collapse into a sleep as deep as the pits of hell.

One that is as filled with demons as the ocean is filled with fish. Circling, floating, drifting, and then lunging to rip chunks from my flesh.

Smiling at me through the blood-filled water as my entrails hang from their teeth. Cold fish eyes laughing as they come back for seconds.

. . . .

Struggling back to reality, Black Cloud booming, "Get with it, Bobbie. Get your ass up. It's time to rock and fuckin' roll. Come on."

Swinging my legs out of the bed and sitting up and feeling the combination of early heroin withdrawal and a barbiturate hangover. Say, "I'm up. Gimme a minute to get straight."

Drag myself to my bag, rummage through it and come out with my rig, smack, and a packet of Methedrine, mix the heroin and speed combination and hit the vein in my ankle. The shit works its way through my foot, feeling like it's on fire. Then hits my heart and my eyes open and the pain leaves my bones and muscles and my mind starts turning over. I'm ready.

*T*he van smells of paint and turpentine, everyone is wearing dark clothes, jeans and black sweaters or, in Al's case, a black-and-gray Pendleton. Black sneakers. Combat shotguns and throwaway pistols all the way around.

Everybody but Ben is crouched in the back. Al's staring at the floor, Cloud is humming some song, and Billy Bones is grinning, I guess in anticipation.

I'm smoking, watching the smoke spiral toward the roof, when Billy nudges my foot. "This is when I live, laddie. The Brits murdered my ma first. Tear gas canisters caught our home on fire. She burnt. My brothers they shot. I was like a ship with no rudder till the day I killed one-a dem motherfuckers. I came back to life. . . . I drift till times like this. It's a grand feelin', Bobbie. It's a lovely night for killin'. Or dyin' for that matter, it's all the same. Feed the maggots, now or later they're gonna get us all."

Baby Al looks up and whistles softly through his teeth, then says, "You fuckin' loco, Billy. Ain't no time good for dying. Especially not any time soon."

Cloud grins and keeps humming and I concentrate on my cigarette, watching the flame race down with every drag, not knowing if anything is ever gonna feel real again. The sheet of plastic between me and the world is still in place and I got no idea how to remove it. Wondering if this is what Billy Bones is talking about. Feeling like a ship adrift, going with the bloodred tide.

Cloud has his hair in a ponytail to keep it out of his eyes. We're creeping the side of the house. As we reach the corner he makes a hand motion for me to wait and gives me his shotgun and the sledge.

FIFTEEN

The quarter moon casts exactly enough light to make the blade of his knife gleam as it whispers from its scabbard into his hand.

Holding the blade in his teeth he hits his belly and in push-up position peeks around the corner, then slithers around the corner like a fucking snake, no noise, no wasted motion. Gone.

The adrenaline that would usually be carrying me isn't there. The drugs are allowing me to function but I know I'm clumsy, not on my game, still in slow motion. The veil between me and the world around me is thicker than ever. Even my old friend fear is absent. I'm numb from the neck up.

Staring at the sky and waiting as clouds drift across the moon and stars shine down on mankind's madness and my version of it, wondering if this is when I buy the farm, take the long nap, die.

If punishment for my sins and failings is at hand and if it means peace or burning in hell. Wishing that I could just take a handful of downs and go to sleep and wake up somebody else.

Black Cloud comes around the corner, walking not crawling, and whispers, "Done deal, pal." He takes the sledgehammer and continues, "You too light in the ass to take the door down. Both gauges got a shell in the chamber . . . right?"

I think for a second to make sure and the memory of working the pump, the feel and click of the shell going home and then checking to see if the safety is off runs through my mind, and I say, "Yeah, man."

Cloud holding the sledge over his shoulder, the black sweater he's wearing standing out against the lighter shade of the house, the moonlight reflecting off his glasses and the blood now spotting his face. He whispers, "Hold one gauge in each hand, finger on the trigger. I take the door down, come in behind me. Anything moves kill it. Soon as we're in, hand me one of the shotguns. Got it?"

It still feels like I'm in a fish tank full of gelatin, moving in slow motion, dragging. Each word takes forever to make it from his mouth to my ears. "Yeah," I say. "Got it."

As he saunters toward the back door the rear porch is illuminated by light coming through the cracks around the shade blocking the window in the door. To the side of the porch is a body lying in a pool of blood, arms and legs out at right angles, head turned backward.

Going across the porch Cloud goes into a full run, swinging the hammer around in an arc and smashing it into the door with the sound of ripping wood and breaking glass. The first swing doesn't take the door down, the second tears the lock out and sends the door smashing into the wall behind it.

As Cloud goes through the door a black guy is standing in the kitchen, sandwich coming away from his mouth, already whirling toward the counter behind him. Cloud's between me and him. I can't shoot. Just watch as he grabs a butcher knife off the counter and hits Black Cloud with it again and again. Cloud's going down and as I level both shotguns at the guy's chest I hear myself screaming over the roar of the gauges.

The recoil sends the guns toward the ceiling, knocking me backward, slamming into the doorframe as the double-ought buckshot rips the black dude's chest to hamburger, picking him up and hurling him onto the counter behind him.

Dropping the piece in my left hand, pumping a shell into the gauge in my right. No more slow motion, every mote of dust visible. Every sound from gunshots to creaking floorboards audible. I'm alive and suddenly intend to stay that way.

Dashing into the hallway leading into the front room and turn into the doorway on my left. A white guy with a huge belly and mongoloid eyes is shooting at me. I blow him back over the bed, pump another one into the chamber, and realize I'm not hit. Look to make sure he's not gonna do any more shooting and see a black chick huddled under the covers, I freeze for a second, then motion with the shotgun and say, "Split."

She's running toward the back door and I'm dashing into the next room, where Billy Bones has two black guys pinned with his gauge. I freeze as he says, "Would either of you lads be Kelvin or Otis? We get the drugs and cash ya live. Otherwise . . ."

The bigger guy, looks like a weight lifter, muscles on top of muscles, spits out, "Fuck you, Paddy. Suck my black fuckin' dick."

The roar of the shotgun drowns his friend's screams as blood and meat splatter him. He starts shouting, "I'm Kelvin. Don't shoot, mo-fucker. De dope, da money right here. Don't shoot ya fuckin' cracker."

Pulling a canvas bag out from under the bed and pushing it toward Bones, who says, "I lied, Kelvin." Slowly leveling his shotgun with Kelvin's head, Billy Bones smiles from ear to ear and then pulls the trigger.

. . . .

We're huddled in the back of the van, Cloud's body propped against the back doors, glasses gone along with the psychotic edge in the eyes behind them, his sweater and jeans soaked and caked with drying blood. Bones is staring into space, a million miles away. Baby Al has a tourniquet on his leg slowing the flow of blood from the bullet in it. He's swearing steadily in Spanish, "Chingao, pinche terrones pendejos, maricones mayates."

Ben cuts in from the front seat, "Cool it, ace, you coming with me. Have ya better than new."

I look up from the floorboard see the fright in Al's face and tell him, "Ben's a doctor, sorta. Worked on me before. Pulled bullets out of another partner of mine. It's cool."

Al manages a small chuckle. "Hurts like a motherfucker, homes. Feels like it's on fire. Can't feel my fuckin' toes. I can see 'em wiggle but don't feel nothin'." He checks the tourniquet and says, "He pulled slugs outta one a your crimeys?"

"Yeah man."

"Did he live?"

The barrier between me and everything else is returning. It seems like it takes forever to formulate an answer. I say, "That time."

Al doesn't look too reassured as he checks the tourniquet again. The van thuds over the streets of Indianapolis, streetlights throwing brief moments of illumination through the front window. The smell of paint and turpentine now overpowered by the smell of blood and adrenaline-loaded sweat.

Through my head like a song that keeps repeating whether you want it to or not the words *"No more, no more, no fucking more."*

We change, putting the blood-soaked clothes and shoes we were wearing into plastic bags, washing our hands with mechanic's soap and ammonia to remove the powder residue.

As we get out to switch cars Ben places a gas can with a cherry bomb taped to the top in the middle of the van. Lights a cigarette and implants the cherry bomb's stiff fuse in the end of the burning smoke saying, "Should give us about six, seven minutes. Let's get the fuck outta here."

Ben has me help him throw Black Cloud's body in the trunk of the car we switched to.

The blood drips from his body and bounces off the street like BBs, each drop echoing through the air and hitting my ears like thunder.

His body lands on the spare tire and takes up too much room. I lean forward and pull the tire out, feeling it scrape across him and think, "Sorry Cloud" as Ben slams the lid down.

I grab one of the smaller packets of heroin plus a bindle of coke and put them in my shirt pocket, then watch as Billy drops the bag of cash and drugs into the backseat of Ben's Lincoln. "Me and Bobbie will meet ya lads tomorrow." We climb into our switch car and head back to the hotel.

· · · · · · ·

Bones has his legs crossed watching the TV. I'm smoking and waiting, not sure for what but that's the feeling. Waiting for something. I'll know what it is when it comes.

Billy Bones looks from the TV to me and says, "Good night's work, laddie. Let's go to the bar, have a drop. Celebrate."

"Go ahead, I'm gonna kick back. Get some sleep."

"Ya sleep any more you'll be like fuckin' Rip van Winkle. Come down and have a drink or ten."

"Nah, man, I'm fuckin' tired."

"All right then. See ya."

When the door closes I realize what I'm waiting for and pull the smack and coke outta my shirt pocket. Get the rig out of its kit and put a normal-sized shot of stuff in the cooker, a dose that would put King Kong into dreamland, and add enough to kill him four times over. Cook it. Open the bindle of coke and dump that in, too. It's so thick it's like drawing honey into the outfit. Going for my pit. Want to get a sure hit. And the viscous fluid disappears into my arm and mixes with my blood, and the fumes from the coke fill my lungs, and the ringing in my ears fills the world as the floor rushes at my face and the words "fuck it" echo in stereo through my head.

I'm sitting over a pitcher of beer in an Irish pub in South Boston when Bones tells me what happened. Says he's sitting at the hotel bar. Downed his first shot and just ordered his second, eyeing a girl at the other end, when he decides it's his duty to make me do some partying. Raises his shot glass to toast himself in the mirror and heads back to the room. Opens the door and finds me on the floor, eyes rolled back, foaming at the mouth, the syringe still hanging from my arm. Calls an ambulance and starts doing mouth-to-mouth. Along with the paramedics come the cops. He makes his exit as they're keeping me alive.

Says he's glad to see me and what am I gonna do now? But that's a whole different tale.

· · · · · · ·

I come to in four-point restraints, wrists and ankles held to the sides of the hospital bed by leather straps, tubes running down my nose and into my arms. Round monitors glued to my chest going into electronic devices. A catheter stuck into my dick. Vision all fucked up, double and triple images of everything.

The doctor holding his fingers up asking me to count them, wanting to know what year it is, what my name is, where we are, and then a cop taking his place holding the packet of smack and my 380 asking if I admit that they are mine. Holding three IDs spread like a poker hand, all with my picture and different names, saying, "You're in deep shit, pal. What's your real name?"

I couldn't answer the doctor's questions. I know better than to answer the cop's.

· · · · · · ·

SIXTEEN

Ray Charles woulda seen that the cop slappin' me around doesn't like doing it. He's about six foot, probably two hundred pounds, gray hair combed to the side, and in good shape. If he wanted to this guy could cripple me, but every time he winds up he grimaces and pulls the shot. I'm handcuffed, starting to get dope sick, and he's not really hurting me, using roundhouse open-hand swings. He doesn't bother planting his feet to get his weight behind the blows and after ten or twenty shots he stops and says, "Check it out, asshole, we can keep doing this till I get worn out. Tell me your right name and where ya got the heroin, make this easy on both of us."

The blood dripping from my nose is all over the front of the jail jumpsuit I'm in and, even as fucked-up as my brain is, I know it looks like he hurt me a lot worse than he did. This guy is not a bully. I keep my head down and let my nose drip.

Eventually I raise my head and he's got a look of disgust on his face, can't tell if it's with me or himself for the job he's doing. Maybe the whole thing. The cop spits on the floor and says, "Listen, asshole, we got ya on possession of an ounce of heroin, which means possession for sale, plus trafficking, carrying a concealed and unregistered firearm, and you had enough different IDs that we can hold ya without bail till we get a positive. The charges ya got are good for twenty years plus. Give yourself a break. What's your name?"

Fear is cutting through the fog encasing my brain. Twenty years means I wouldn't get out till I was in my thirties. Life would be over.

This is compounded by the early stages of withdrawal and the possibility that I might get linked to the earlier bloodbath. I know I'm not gonna get bail and there's no way to bullshit my way outta this. I stare at him, my stomach plummeting in free fall, and say, "Get me a lawyer. I got nothin' to say."

He shakes his head, spits on the floor again, and says, "Fuck it. We'll find out who ya are. Come on."

The booking process begins. The mug shots with a booking number and the name John Doe over the numbers. Having my fingers rolled in ink and printed. Getting turned over to a rookie who's not a whole lot bigger than me, has a military-style buzz cut, bulging blue eyes, and acne all over his face. Takes one look at me and says, "Tough guy, huh? I'll fix that. Cut that fuckin' hair off you to start."

I'm thinking, "Tough guy? I'm so skinny and dope sick I couldn't bust a grape. I got my own blood all over me. Tough guy? I ain't giving nobody a hard time, just got done OD'ing and getting slapped around. I'm scared to death and this motherfucker is gonna cut my hair off. What's this tough guy shit?"

Look at him staring at me like he's crazy and before I can stop them the words "Fuck you, faggot" are out of my mouth and he's going insane.

Dragging me down the concrete corridor screaming and swearing, calling me every kind of motherfucker there is and shoving me into a room with barber chairs and a couple of trustee barbers.

Throwing me into one of the chairs and yelling at the trustee, "Buzz this motherfucker's head. I don't want to see anything but fucking nubs on this boy."

When he pulls me out of the chair the rookie makes sure his feet are planted as he rips an uppercut into my solar plexus. I'm still gasping for breath when he says, "Assault on an officer, huh, John Doe? Let's see how ya like the hole."

. . . .

The screen- and wire-protected lightbulb is burning into my dilated eyes, the steel bunk is cutting through the skin on my ass 'cause there's no mattress and no meat on my bones. The concrete floor is freezing and the odors of piss and fear that pervade this cellblock are being blocked by the toxic smell of my own sweat.

It feels like insects are running amok under my skin and the shaking that goes from my chattering teeth to my cramping toes is only a sideline to the fire burning in my stomach.

Can't lie down 'cause the steel bunk is freezing. Can't sit for long. Staggering back and forth across the cell till they come to take me to arraignment. Vision is starting to flicker like a badly timed strobe and bizarre smells are assaulting my nose.

Got my handcuffs attached to the chain circling my waist and leg irons on my ankles. Try to keep my balance while taking twelve-inch steps. Step too far the anklet cuts into your leg and trips you. Don't step far enough and the chain linking the cuffs gets caught under your feet.

Standing in the docket, so tired that my knees are buckling, and after the judge asks how I plead and gets my "Not guilty" he says quietly, "Defendant John Doe to be held in custody with no bail. Next case."

. . . .

There is no such thing as time. The day or night is broken up by feedings. A muffin, a dry bologna sandwich, a bowl of meatless stew. Trying to eat is absurd, the food is taken away untouched.

I didn't know about convulsions, didn't know about barbiturate withdrawal. To this day don't know if I went insane on my own or if acute withdrawal and lack of sleep sent me over the edge.

My arm goes shooting out all by itself. Before I can wonder what's happening my leg is twitching so hard that the vibrations rattle the steel bunk like a burglar alarm.

There is no transition.

Seconds, maybe hours later I come to on the floor. My face covered with drool and I'm bruised head to foot from my convulsing body banging into the concrete and steel that are my world.

Time is an artificial series of demarcations invented by man to create the illusion of continuity. That illusion disappeared.

Meals come and go, uneaten.

Sleep becomes a distant memory.

Coming to bruised and bloodied from grand mal seizures is almost a welcome diversion. The physical pain a distraction from what I feel inside.

Mel's sitting next to me, mouth moving, but I can't hear him. The closer I lean, the more he recedes. The more I focus, the more insubstantial he becomes. And then Rosie joins him, eyes sadder than ever, not trying to talk. Looking at me, head held slightly to one side. Looks like she's trying to figure something out. Then she's fading away.

Alone once more, searching for my friends, knowing that I've gone insane. The universe is composed solely of concrete, steel, and the tears running down my face. Wiping them away, they glisten against the skin on the back of my arm.

Looking around the solitary-confinement cell to be sure none of my ghosts see me crying. Can't be weak, not even in front of phantoms.

Letting my mind slip, leaving my eyes half closed to make it easier for my guests to appear until the cell is a distant backdrop to the world inhabited by people I have loved. Who are now solid enough to talk to.

The goal is to get close enough to touch them. Once I can do that everything will be all right.

Seconds, hours, days. The words are meaningless.

Eternity passes babbling to dead people, going in and out of convulsions, watching the meat melt from my body.

. . . .

I wake up in the fetal position, curled on the bunk, right arm asleep from lying on it. Vision blurred. Have no idea if it was two minutes or two hours but the knowledge that it had been sleep and not a convulsion registers.

When the sandwich on its paper plate comes through the slot in the door I manage to eat half of it. Stale, hard bread, rubbery greenish mystery meat. No mayo, no mustard, no anything except the absolute basics.

The watery stew comes next and it's delicious, hits my taste buds so hard it's like an electric current running through me. I lick the bowl clean like a fucking dog. This is great. Hunger.

Rosie comes back some time later. She's too far away to talk to and when she smiles and drifts away I realize I blew it. The food and sleep have trapped me and this time, when the tears come, I know I am alone. That no one will see my weakness.

I pray. For Rosie and Mel. For Jimbo and Cloud. For absolution. For freedom. For death. Then I start over.

There's a muffin on the way, hunger now defines me. "Where's the fuckin' muffin? It's got to be here soon. Where is the motherfucker?" These words chasing themselves in a circle. I want that muffin more than a fish wants water.

Eating it one crumb at a time, making it last forever. It's gone. Waiting for the sandwich.

Time is coming back and with time the awareness not only of hunger but the will to survive. Starting a push-up–sit-up routine.

The first set of ten leaves me on the floor gasping, feeling like my arms and shoulders are gonna fall off. I roll onto my back and get off ten sit-ups and collapse again. Into the third set my arms give out, leaving me on the floor until the sound of the sandwich arriving cuts into the daze I'm in.

Counting the bricks in the wall, studying the paint, looking for patterns or configurations and finding a small spiderweb with a live spider in the wire surrounding the lightbulb.

Push-ups and sit-ups. Watching the spider, sometimes he moves.

The day I get up to a hundred per set the door swings open and the light in the corridor is so much brighter than the light in the cell I'm blinded as the figure in the doorway says, "Sixty days is up, you're going to population. Get your smelly ass out here."

I try to reply and the process of forming words is beyond my reach. I don't know if it was damage from kicking or just not talking for so long, but as I walk into the corridor I'm unable to respond when the guard says, "So. How'd ya like the hole, tough guy?"

Looking up from the floor and recognizing the asshole that had thrown me in there. Wanting to go for his throat and knowing that as soon as I do not only will I go back in the hole but there's a good chance that the beating I'll get will kill me.

Maybe the inability to form words is a blessing. I manage a closed-lip grin and grunt. Thinking, "Fuck you and your whore mother, punk," as he turns me over to the two guards backing him up to escort me to my new home.

. . . .

Marion County Jail is primarily dorms, barred cages holding bunk beds run end to end. The outer door is solid steel, the inner door bars.

I walk into the dorm, find an empty bunk, and take up lodging. Lying dead, watching the eyes that are watching me.

The smell of tobacco burning reminds me that I smoke and there's a possibility that a cigarette might make me feel better.

Finding a white dude that's smoking and bum a Camel. That first cigarette gets me drunk, the nicotine making my head swim and my stomach flip.

The noise is constant, the smell of unwashed bodies only noticeable for a while. I keep my back to the wall and have few conversations. Everyone in this fuckin' trap is bigger than me and already clicked up. Hillbillies, scooter trash, and negroes.

I've never had any use for gangs, but being part of a car makes doing time a lot easier. In this trap the bikers or wanna-be bikers stay strictly to themselves, the hillbillies or rednecks have the most numbers but no use for a city kid with an accent different than theirs, the blacks are the loudest and perceive anyone white as the enemy.

I stay by myself, doing push-ups and sit-ups, eating as much as possible, getting ready for whatever's coming.

County time drags. When you're fighting a case there's no respite from your own mind. Regardless of the circumstances surrounding your bust, it keeps replaying.

Trying not to think about it is useless. Going back and forth between figuring angles, how to beat it in court, how it might be possible to escape, the things you did wrong and the things you should have done and always, at least for me, the feeling of loss that is there wherever I am.

The thing is that when you're locked down, the illusion that getting out will change the way you feel inside you is overwhelming. When awaiting sentencing the anxiety builds like a perfectly constructed monument, one stone at a time. It's almost a relief when you get your time. Then there's the daily routine and the possibility of escape. That's it.

Once you're doing a jolt, if you allow yourself to think about all the things you lost and threw away, it'll kill ya. The best thing you can do is concentrate on the second you're in and survival. That's what I do. Push-ups, sit-ups, and pull-ups off the bars.

Twelve days out of solitary and it's chow time. The trays of food are brought to the dorm and you line up, get your tray, and either eat on your bunk or try to fit in on one of the steel tables bolted to the floor.

I'm sitting on my bunk with my tray when three blacks roll on me. I've been waiting for a confrontation. There's no way to do time without having at least one. The hillbillies are watching to see how it goes down, the bikers are in their normal corner, and the other Negroes are getting louder, anticipating watching a white boy get beat down.

Two of the blacks facing me look like I might have a chance of beating them one on one, the third guy is huge. There's no way I can take this dude or the other two at one time. With three of 'em I know I got an ass beating on the way.

I stare at 'em and take a bite out of the sandwich as the smallest one says, "Gimme dat sanwich, cracker." I keep chewing and swallow, fear is kicking in, and I'm doing everything I can to control my face and actions.

The big one says, "You heard da man, boy, give 'im da sanwich."

Now there's no choice. I know that no matter what I do it's a losing situation.

The sound of blood rushing through my head like a flooding river fills my ears, then the tunnel vision starts and my body begins shaking and, like magic, I don't care if I get killed, crippled, or maimed. The only thing that exists is hurting these motherfuckers as bad as I can before they take me out.

I throw the sandwich on the floor and step on it. Spit into my tray and then drop it, saying, "You bad motherfuckers gonna take my food?" And kick the tray at them. "There it is, looks good, huh?"

The tray smashes into the big one's legs and it's on. I'm swinging as hard and fast as I can while getting beat back into the wall.

Going down but kicking and managing to head-butt one of 'em, trying to fight my way back up cause once you're down that's it, time for the boots to go to work. Terror slams enough adrenaline into my system to get my feet planted for a minute.

There's not enough room for them to really fuck me up, all three of 'em are trying to get in punches and blocking each other more than they're hitting me, and I'm still winging shots at 'em but not doing much good.

I can't breathe and don't know whether getting hit has got me dizzy or if it's from adrenaline overload when I'm so weak but I know I'm not gonna last much longer. I've got my back on the wall and on one knee when they back off, and I know I'm finished. Instead of trying to mob me they're gonna have the big cat finish me. That's the only thing that makes sense.

Nothing happens and I notice the yelling has stopped. Watching them back up and seeing every hillbilly in the tank surrounding my bunk area, not yelling, just standing and watching as the three black dudes thread their way through the wall of wood surrounding them. The threat of their presence as solid as the bars surrounding us.

In the front is the guy I bummed the smoke from. Pale as a dead man, balding, with shoulders that are as far across as the space between the bunks, spectacles over empty blue eyes sitting on a nose that has been broken more than once. Behind him a bearded giant, fat and sloppy, hair in a mat, breathing through his mouth. Next to him a guy with black hair, body covered with bad ink and weight-lifter muscles. Behind them every hillbilly and redneck in the dorm.

I wipe the blood off my face and stare at these guys, wondering what's coming next when the one in the front says, "Not bad, pal. When ya get commissary ya can kick with some smokes. Camels. Got it?"

It's the same old shit and while getting in a car is good, ya can't pay to join. If ya do you're fucked. If not literally, one way or another. I say, "No, man. If those niggers aren't gonna shake me down, you ain't either. You and me gonna sling 'em now?"

He mad-dogs me for a few seconds and then tires of it, smiles, says, "Badass, huh? Fuck it, you get any more beat up it'll probably kill ya, and there's a shortage of white boys with any heart. Stay down wood."

As they drift back to the card games and small groups he throws me one of his Camels. It tastes better than any advertise could express. Smoke it till it's burning into my fingertips, flick the ember into the aisle, and start back on my push-up routine.

Days go by and I identify a couple of white guys that keep to themselves and can talk about something other than jailhouse drag. One is the dude that led the group that stepped in when I got jumped. The other one was standing next to the giant. This guy looks like a fuckin' movie star. Sharp features, wavy black hair. If it wasn't for the bad tattoos all over his arms and chest he woulda looked more at home in Beverly Hills than locked down in Marion County, Indiana.

These two hang out and play cards. They even got a few books, which in a lockdown facility with no library is an accomplishment more impressive than smuggling drugs or weapons. Books are hard to conceal. No way to keister them.

I've gotten to the point where I can do handstand push-ups if I balance my feet against the wall. I've just finished a set and am sitting catching my breath and I sense someone staring. Look up and the one with the black hair is standing at the end of my bunk, arms crossed, and says, "Getting healthy, huh?"

"Trying. Got a long way to go."

He laughs and says, "Yeah, ya do. Look better than ya did though."

"Couldn't look much worse unless I was dead, right?"

"Yeah, man. Whatcha fightin'?"

"Possession for sales, trafficking, had a piece, bad IDs. Regular shit."

"Possession of?"

"Smack."

"Shit, boy, they gonna wash ya. Do they got a case?"

"Dead fuckin' bang, pal. Dead bang."

He looks at the pack of smokes sitting on my bunk and says, "Got a Lemac?"

I shake one outta the pack and hesitate. Then say, "Sure, man, loan me one of your books?"

Now it's his turn to hesitate. He walks to his bunk area, digs through his bag of possessions, and comes back with a dog-eared Ray Bradbury. Says, "I want this motherfucker back. You sure ya wanna borrow it?"

"Only way I lose it is if someone kills me. Yeah, I'm fuckin' sure."

He stares at me for a second, then tosses me the book, saying, "It's on you, pal."

I tell his back "Thanks" as he's walking away.

. . . .

This is as good as it gets. I got commissary so I have a few Snickers bars, choice of convicts everywhere, a carton of smokes, which is coin of the realm, and a book to read. Life is all right.

I light a Camel, take a bite out of the candy bar, and start the book.

Reading slowly is its own art form. When all you have to escape to is one book you learn to make it last. The same way you savor each bite of food or every hit off a smoke. You learn to read one word at a time, roll them through your mind, think about how they're put together and what they mean. Enjoy them 'cause they won't last forever.

The second time through I do fifty push-ups every ten pages. By the third pass I got it memorized. It's many years later and the title is still visible in my mind's eye. *Something Wicked This Way Comes.*

The fourth time I reach The End I know it's time to return it.

Walk over to the table where they're playing cards and set the book down and light a cigarette. Ask if they want one. The guy with the glasses says, "Nah, pal, pull up a chair. Teach us how to play poker. Ya look like a poker player if I ever saw one."

Sitting on the steel bench on the open side of the table I ask, "What's the ante?"

The movie-star-lookin' one says, "Got a live one, Steve."

Steve grins and says, "This is George. Like ya probably figured I'm Steve." He starts shuffling and says, "Seven-card stud, nothin' wild. No jokers. Ante is one Camel. Or any tailor-made. No rollies."

George rakes his fingers through his hair and bets on a king, saying, "Two on the cowboy," dropping two Camels in the pot.

I call and Steve is studying his cards. He says, "Dope fiend, huh, pal? Call two."

I study my cards and say, "Yeah. How can ya tell?"

They start laughing. George says, "We been shootin' dope for years. Takes one to know one. How else would a couple clean-cut fellas like us end up here?"

The game continues. After three, four more hands George says, "Gonna take a big bounce on this one. Three-time loser. Got out last year, made it a year on the streets, not too bad for me. Got caught in a commercial burglary. They're gonna do their best to wash me up, warehouse my ass. Can't stay away from the needle. Tried drinking . . . got violent, beat the shit outta my old lady, couple days later woke up in a holding cell still drunk. Caught a fresh burg and don't even remember it. Shit, man, wish I was a kid again. Steal with both hands. Get sent to Plainfield. Escape and start over."

I'm not really paying a lot of attention, nodding my head and making the appropriate comments. Watching the cards dealt and how these guys play, can't spot any signals or bottom dealing and I'm starting to get into the game. Got four to a club flush and three cards to go. These last two sentences grab my attention.

I say, "Raise two," put two smokes in the pot and ask, "Plainfield? What's that?"

George calls and Steve folds as George says, "Indiana State Reformatory for boys, send kids there. Good food, lots of fistfights but not like the pen where ya stab a guy over a cigarette. Get in a beef and usually nobody dies. Not like the joint, where somebody always dies no matter what the hassle is about."

George has a pair of threes showing, deals himself an eight and I catch a heart. I'm still betting on the come.

I drop two more smokes and ask, "Whatcha mean about escaping? How'd ya do it?"

George is holding his hole cards, sets 'em down and says, "Shit, man, just run like hell. They have caps, like baseball caps, red caps and green caps. If I remember right a red cap's got higher rank. Cap is like a trustee. They give 'em to the biggest, meanest, fastest kids there. You run, they chase ya. They catch ya, they beat the livin' shit outta ya. Then throw ya in the hole and the man whips the skin offa your ass."

The last card hits face down. I bet it blind and ask, "That's it?" Steve cuts in saying, "Yep. Don't take no genius, just big balls and good legs. That's how come I never got away, couldn't outrun those motherfuckers to save my life."

I check my last card and it's the ace of clubs. I know I got the boss hand unless George has a full boat or four of a kind. I bet three and say, "That's it, huh? Big balls and good legs?"

George calls and says, "That's what the man said. Why ya so interested?"

I take a moment to think this over and can't see any way that asking a general question about this can hurt me. If I understand what he's saying this is the only chance I have.

"So if they were holding a kid in here they'd transfer him to Plainfield?"

Steve is cleaning his glasses on his jumpsuit and says, "Yeah, except this is an adult jail, a kid wouldn't be here. You gonna play cards or gab all fuckin' day?"

George lays his cards face up saying, "Two pair, kings over threes. Whatcha got?"

"Club flush, ace high." I start to rake the pot and ask, "But what if they had a kid booked as an adult?"

These two look at each other, then both take a close look at me. George says, "Shit, pal. He'd be outta here on the next thing smokin'."

I'm making a stack of cigarettes. "Today, huh?"

Steve says, "Dense motherfucker, huh, George? Forthwith, fast like a hurry-up, gone like a chicken to corn. If I was in that position I'd catch the bull next time he circles this fuckin' cage and tell him my name and age. Get the fuck on."

I look at the floor to try and get my thoughts straight and when I look up Steve's looking at me with no expression and says, "I can hear the keys rattling, the motherfucker's comin'. Get outta here, kid."

I stroll to the bars protecting the bull from us and as he approaches say, "Yo, check it out. I gotta ask ya a question. What happens if you got a juvenile in here?"

"We'd be in deep shit. Is there one in here?"

"Yeah. Me. What happens now?"

"You're shittin' me."

"Nope, fifteen. Maybe fifteen and a half. Almost sixteen, I lose track."

"Motherfucker, you better not be lying," and he's headed back to the door out.

I walk to the table, mind racing. California and the Midwest have too many bad memories, too many ghosts. I never been to Boston and it can't be too hard to find a guy named Billy Bones. Gotta get my dough from Ben. Fixing sure would feel good. Ben probably knows how to get in touch with Billy. Syd's in Jersey, maybe see what's up with her.

I've no idea that it's possible to stay clean. As far as I know the only way to get clean is to get busted. The idea of living without drugs is as alien as Pluto. Beyond my comprehension. The years since then have been filled with getting clean and ending up loaded. In and out of the joint, watching my friends die and end up warehoused.

Right now I'm clean. *This* minute I'd rather die than get loaded again. But the thing is there's no vaccine, no guarantees except that if I don't get loaded today, I'll go to sleep clean tonight. It's been awhile since I dived into the cooker. But this is now and what we're talkin' about here is then.

The knowledge that I get another shot at fixing has my stomach rolling with the anticipated pleasure of turning my brain off, killing, at least for a moment, the feelings that have been bubbling inside me like boiling sewage.

As Steve and George look up from the game I lay my pack of smokes on the table and say, "Merry Christmas, fellas. I think I'm outta here."

Steve chuckles and says, "Told ya. Knew he wasn't eighteen. You owe a pack, George. Pay up."

"I will."

"Thanks, fellas," I say.

Steve just nods his head. George grins and says, "Cost me a pack, pal. Thought you were at least eighteen. Fuck it, good luck, kid."

The gray steel door at the end of the dorm swings open and two guards walk into the barred cage enclosing the gate into and out of the dorm. When they call my name I get up as casually as I can and walk toward the light shining into the cage.

Not sure how good my legs are, knowing that I'm not especially brave or ballsy. Aware of one thing only.

If it's possible I'm gonna escape.

Be on the road again.

Rolling.